BY THE
NECK

BY THE NECK

A STONEFACE FINNEGAN WESTERN

WILLIAM W. JOHNSTONE

AND J. A. JOHNSTONE

PINNACLE BOOKS
Kensington Publishing Corp.
www.kensingtonbooks.com

PINNACLE BOOKS are published by

Kensington Publishing Corp.
119 West 40th Street
New York, NY 10018

PUBLISHER'S NOTE

Following the death of William W. Johnstone, the Johnstone family is working with a carefully selected writer to organize and complete Mr. Johnstone's outlines and many unfinished manuscripts to create additional novels in all of his series like The Last Gunfighter, Mountain Man, and Eagles, among others. This novel was inspired by Mr. Johnstone's superb storytelling.

ISBN-13: 978-0-7860-4605-8
ISBN-10: 0-7860-4605-8

First Pinnacle paperback printing: March 2021

10 9 8 7 6 5 4 3 2 1

Printed in the United States of America

Electronic edition:

ISBN-13: 978-0-7860-4606-5 (e-book)
ISBN-10: 0-7860-4606-6 (e-book)

CHAPTER ONE

Rollie Finnegan, two-decade veteran of the Pinkerton Detective Agency, almost chuckled as he descended the broad stone steps of the county courthouse. Not an hour before, he'd taken no small pleasure in seeing the arched eyebrows of the jury men when he'd been called to the stand.

He suspected it would be a long time before the defendant's city-bred whelp of a lawyer would drag him up on the stand again. Finnegan had seen even more surprise on the pocked face of the inbred mess that was Chance Filbert, defendant and self-proclaimed "Lord of the Rails."

Trouble was, "Lord" Filbert was gifted with bravado and little else. He also liked to swill tanglefoot, and at Corkins' Bar he'd yammered about his impending robbery of the short-run mail train from Mason's Bluff to Randolph. It hadn't worked out that way.

Chance had managed to clamber aboard the train with the help of a fat cohort named Kahlil, who'd somehow mounted the rumbling car's fore platform first. Not receiving any response to their rapping on the door of the mail car—the train was by then cranking along on a flat, the grinding steel pounding for all it was worth and the men inside didn't hear the ruckus—Chance sent two shots at the door handle.

One bullet managed to free up the lock. The second found its way into the right temple of little Sue-Sue Campbell, who had been obeying her harried father, Arvin, one of the two workers sorting mail. He'd had no choice but to take her along on the run that morning, because her mother was deep in the agonies of pushing out a little brother for sweet Sue-Sue, who until then had been an only child. And so would her brother, Arvin Jr., be thanks to Chance Filbert and his eagerness to avoid a legal occupation.

Filbert's greasy, snaky head had entered the car before the rest of him, and though he didn't see the slumped girl to his left, he did see two men in the midst of sorting the mail. With hands full of letters, their jaws dropped, and they stared at the appearance of the homely man and the fat, long-haired one behind him, both with guns leveled.

In court, Rollie wore his twenty-dollar pinstriped, storm-gray boiled-wool suit, and capped it with a matching gray topper, what he referred to as his city hat. He recalled when the salesman had set it on his head while standing before the tall looking glass how much like his long-dead father he looked. He also had to admit that the salesman had been correct—the hat made the suit, and the entire affair looked damn good on him.

Though he'd rather tug on his old fawn Boss of the Plains, like he did most every day, Stoneface Finnegan did not ever miss a court date. He had vowed long ago to always see a case through, from top to bottom, front to back, and inside out. He knew, not unlike his old man once more, if he didn't do everything in his ability to nail shut the door on each and every lawbreaker and miscreant he nabbed, he'd be setting himself up for a month's worth of sleepless nights, all the while grinding down his molars and enduring his ticked-off-with-himself attitude. And at fifty-four, he didn't need that crap in his life anymore.

If wearing a fancy suit and shaving himself close and pink and oiling his hair and waxing his mustache (which he did each morning anyway) helped the prosecuting attorneys send the devils to the prison or the gallows, then he'd tug on the suit and do the job.

There had been ample and irrefutable damning evidence and painful, tearful testimony from the dead girl's parents. There had also been the precise recounting of events by Agent Rollie Finnegan. Despite this, in a last-minute courtroom effort, Moe Chesterton, attorney-at-law for Chance Filbert (and closet dice roller, much to the detriment of his anemic bank balance, had stood before the assemblage, red-faced and thumbing his lapels in an effort to draw attention to what he hoped were persuasive words.

He'd told the crowd stinking of sweat and the weary jury that Stoneface Finnegan had once more put his charge, in this instance Chance Filbert, in a most dire situation. Most dire, indeed. Yes, it was true, Chesterton nodded. And he could prove it. The lawyer's pink jowls quivered and drooped suitably. "Hold up your hands, Mr. Filbert . . . if you are able."

With much effort, the smirking killer had managed to raise his palsied hands aloft. Soon, they dropped to the mahogany tabletop before him and his head bowed, exhausted from the strain.

Rollie had rolled his eyes then, from his seat in the first aisle behind the prosecution. Not for the first time in the proceedings did he wish he had let his Schofield have its way with Chance when he'd finally caught up with him in that creekside cave in Dibney Flats. All that nonsense could have been avoided. Waste of time, waste of money.

But the law, was the law, and Rollie told himself if he had wanted to break it, he should have taken the owlhoot trail instead of tracking scofflaws after the war. Or gone into politicking, making laws to suit his base whims like those oily rascals in capitol towns everywhere.

Instead, on that thundering, wet morning in the cave two months before, after tracking the outlaws for a day and a night, the snout of Rollie's Schofield parted the desiccated viny roots draping the entrance. It was then he'd seen Chance Filbert seated inside on a low boulder. He'd watched the oily man a moment, uncertain of Kahlil's whereabouts in the dim hole. The close air, scented of warm muck, had forced thoughts of thick, slow snakes and crawling things.

Rollie had seen Chance and fat Kahlil ride there with intent, then dismount, tie their horses, and enter the cave. They'd lugged in what they made off with from the train, a small arch-top wooden trunk and a squat strongbox wrapped in riveted strap steel. They'd left their horses lashed to a low, jutting branch, saddled and without reach of water. The poor beasts swished and nipped and stamped at a plague of biting flies.

For minutes, Rollie had wondered if Chance was the only man alive in the cave. Of the two, Rollie had seen only Chance venture out with increasing frequency as the hours dragged by. He'd poked his malformed face between the mossy vines, then, satisfied he was not surrounded, would saunter out more loosely each time, limbered, no doubt, by drink. Of Kahlil, there had been no sight or sound.

Unless the man had a steel bladder or there was a back entrance to the cave, which from Rollie's reconnoiter of the region didn't seem likely, he bet himself a bottle of Kentucky's finest that Chance had knifed his slop-gutted partner.

Rollie had won the bet when he'd looked inside and saw a massive, unmoving dark form off to the left. Not even snoring. To his right and babbling in a whiskey stupor, Chance sat atop that boulder before the flop-topped trunk, torn papers all about the muck-rock floor— intimate letters unlikely to make it to their destinations, orders for goods long saved for by some lonely bachelor dirt farmer or farmwife helpmate, or perhaps awaited countersigned deeds to land and goods—all pillaged for cash by the stunted, drunken Chance Filbert.

The strongbox had fared better and appeared to be intact. Rollie hadn't heard shots, Chance's favored means of opening locked things. Maybe he had been afraid of a bullet whanging back at him, though Rollie had not credited the man with such forethought. Likely he was saving the strongbox for dessert and pilfering the easiest pickings first.

Subduing the killer had been a simple matter of pushing his way through the clingy green vines and thumbing back the Schofield's hammer. The hard, solid clicks would make a dead man rise. Except for Kahlil. Rollie had quickly inspected the dark shape enough to note it had indeed been slit open. He'd smelled the rank tang of blood mixed with the dank earth stink of the cave. He was glad he'd decided to keep his hat on his head, tugged low though it was, mashing his ears in an undignified manner. Beat having something with too many legs, or too few, squirming on his head and down the back of his shirt.

"Who you?" said Chance when his vision and his head had together in a wobble.

For a moment Rollie had considered replying, but he was not fond of excessive chatter. *Why speak when you could act?* The unspoken motto had served him well for years. He reckoned it was proven enough to keep on with. He stepped forward quick—one, two strides—while Chance made a sloppy grab for his own gun. His fingertips barely touched the nicked walnut grips as the butt of a Schofield mashed his hat into his head above the left ear.

Chance knew no more until he found himself lashed over the saddle of Kahlil's horse. The saddle and the horse under it smelled bad. Why was he on his dead pard's horse? He could see his own, perfectly good horse, walking along, tied, behind this one. But hold on there. Fat Kahlil was tied to it, dripping all manner of black-looking goo and cultivating a cloud of bluebottles that rose and dipped together as if they were training for a stage presentation.

But even that was the least of Chance Filbert's concerns.

He'd known for certain his head had somehow been cleaved in half and was leaking out what he was certain were the last of his precious brains onto the heat-puckered earth. Nothing less could account for the volleys of cannon fire thundering inside his skull.

The pain doubled as the day had ground on, one pounding hoof step after another. He'd tried several times to speak to the vicious brute who'd ambushed him, but his strangled pleas, which came out as little more than gasps and coughs, brought new washes of agony that ended in his throbbing hands lashed behind his back.

The man on the horse ahead showed him only his back, tree-trunk stiff and wide-shouldered. Who was he, and why did he think it was acceptable to bust in on a man when he'd been tucked away in a cave, tending his own business?

The farther they walked, the angrier Chance became. He'd regained more control of his throat, but the lack of water, a desperate need at that point, rendered his usually loud voice to little more than a hoary whisper.

Several yards ahead of Chance, Rollie had struck a match and set fire to the bowl of his briar pipe, packed full of his least favorite tobacco, a rank, black blend of what tasted like the leavings of an angry baby and a gut-sick drunkard. The thick clouds of smoke would drift back into Chance Filbert's face and gag him. With hours to go yet, Rollie had two pouches of this special blend. He had smiled then, for a brief moment.

In the courtroom two months later, Moe Chesterton had asked Rollie what he thought about the fact that Chance Filbert's hands had been rendered all but useless by the too-tight restraints Rollie favored—smooth fence wire.

"It's a shame," said Rollie.

"A shame," repeated the lawyer. "And, Mr. Finnegan, would you care to enlighten us as to why you feel this . . . this avoidable affront . . . is a shame?"

"A man without hands is near useless."

"Near useless, but not wholly useless? Hmm. I wonder what you could mean by that."

Rollie looked at Chance. "I assume he has his pecker. I guess he could be of use to somebody. Likely will in prison."

That had caused a stir and Rollie had nearly smiled, but not quite. He knew that Judge Wahpeton, indulgent though he may be, was not inclined to tolerate uproar in his court-room. His gavel rapped hard and his bushy eyebrows arched like the wings of some great, riled eagle. The court-room hushed.

"Any talk of prison will be of my own making, Agent Finnegan." The judge surprised everyone by stepping down from his dais and walking across the front of the room. Without warning, he pivoted and lobbed a palm-size brass ashtray toward the sneering defendant. The man snatched it from the air with ease.

Too late, Chance realized his mistake. He dropped the ashtray to the tabletop and fluttered his hands before him like two agitated sparrows.

"I think not, Mr. Filbert," said the judge as he mounted the steps to his dais and cleared his throat before proceed-ing to pass his commandments to the jury.

CHAPTER TWO

The jury took shy of five minutes to render its verdict.

And so, with Judge Wahpeton's final words, and then the mallet-strike echoing in his head and warming his heart, Rollie "Stoneface" Finnegan stood outside, waiting for a fringe topped surrey to pass by. It ferried a fetching woman wearing a long-feathered hat that looked to be more feather than hat, with a veil that didn't hide the pretty smile he imagined was meant for him. He was tempted to wave her down, strike up a conversation perhaps.

He crossed the street and recalled the reason he was walking west—yes, he could almost smell the heady aromas from Hazel's Hash House. The eatery was two streets over and one lane back behind the courthouse. His nostrils twitched in anticipation of hot coffee and the singular pleasures of Hazel's sticky, sweet pecan pie, a slice as wide as it was tall and deeper than the tines of a fork. He'd earned it, after all, helping cinch tight the legal noose on Chance Filbert's pimpled neck.

The bum's death wouldn't bring back the seven-year-old girl or even Kahlil, but it damn sure made Rollie's day a good one. Then came the pretty lady in the surrey, and he was about to indulge in a slice of heavenly pie and a couple cups of hot coffee before tucking into his next assignment. Yes, the day was turning out to be one of the best Rollie Finnegan had had in years.

He warbled a low, tuneless whistle as he angled down the alleyway that would cut off an extra block's worth of walking.

He never heard the quick figure catfoot up behind him, never felt the long, thin blade slide in. It pierced the new wool coat, the satin lining, the wool vest, the crisp white shirt, the undershirt, the pink skin. The blade was out, then in again for a second quick plunge into his back, high up, caroming off a rib and puncturing the left lung, before retreating for a third slide in.

Instinct drove Rollie to spin, to face the source of this sudden flowering of pain as his left hand shoved away the hanging coat, then grabbed at the holstered Schofield. But he was already addled enough that his gun never cleared the stiff leather sheath. He made it halfway around as the knife slipped free of his back a third time and plunged in a fourth, into the meat of his left thigh.

The spin lacked strength. Hot pain bloomed inside him with eye-blink speed. As Rollie's slow dervish spin gave way to collapse, he saw a dim specter—a thin, dark, wavering flame drawn upward. Red, not from rage but from spattering blood, washed before him, over him, becoming a choking black curtain.

Rollie "Stoneface" Finnegan would not get to taste his sweet pecan pie and hot coffee.

CHAPTER THREE

The room smelled of camphor and unwashed hair. But the worst stink was the base smell, the one that would not leave, no matter the washing, the cologne, or the window he insisted stay open, all day, all night, despite Nurse Cherborn's constant underminings.

It was that smell he could not disguise that haunted Rollie Finnegan the most. It reminded him of his father at the end. It was the stink of old man. Problem was, Rollie didn't think of himself as old. He was not a young man, but it'd be a damn long time before he was ancient. At least he'd felt that way before some gutless being knifed him in an alley two months before.

As long as he had the Schofield within reach, which he'd made certain of as soon as he regained his senses a week into this mess, Rollie would do his best to keep the window open and the nurse from treating him like a gimped old man. A stinking, gimped old man. That morning, he'd had to reinforce his intent where the window was concerned by cocking his pistol.

"Mr. Finnegan, you are impossible." The nurse rested her dimpled knuckles on her broad waist and tried to rile him with her sharp blue eyes, fierce specks in her doughy face. It didn't work.

"Not yet," he said. "But I'm getting there."

"The fresh air could well set you back a week or even two, if it doesn't kill you outright."

He stared at her. She stared back and after a full minute, he gave up, looked out the window at the blue April sky. The hard stare had always worked with his captives, why not with this dress-wearing devil?

"You have the best part of a month, I believe, before you will be fit enough to venture out-of-doors."

He didn't bother responding. She was almost done for the day anyway. What good would another argument with her do? Besides, he felt he owed her some sort of obedience, at least for a time. She'd nursed him the entire spell, from the day he'd been brought back to his rooms after a week in the doctor's office.

Without Nurse Cherborn, Rollie knew he'd have been dead months ago. He also thought she'd taken a shine to him. Otherwise why would a knowledgeable woman such as herself, all but a full-bore doctor, despite the fact she was a woman, tend him all this time for the paltry weekly sum he could pay?

Weeks in, Rollie saw how quickly his medical and nursing bills were gnawing through his modest wad of banked savings he'd managed to amass over the years of tracking criminals in and out of all manner of foul deed and nasty last-stand gun down.

It hardly seemed necessary, but he'd dictated a letter and had it sent to the boss requesting the agency cover his medical and nursing fees while he convalesced. He'd been surprised they hadn't stepped in to help him sooner. He explained that if he had good care he would be able to return to work sooner than with poor care. The boss had not agreed with him in saying he had been attacked because of his work. Instead, the skinflint had said it had happened while Rollie was off the clock, that it had doubtless been a random mugging.

How can a man be mugged when his wallet and six-gun are left behind, untouched? Rollie stewed over this for a couple of days, and was in the midst of a second letter to the boss when a messenger delivered a package. It contained a fancy-worded document that amounted to a brief and unconvincing "thank you for your service" note. The package also contained a small wooden box. Rollie opened it and saw a silver pocket watch nested in a bed of green silk. He lifted it free and clicked it open. Inside the cover was inscribed with his name, followed by the words *Indispensable, steadfast, and true.*

"Apparently not," said Rollie, not for the last time, and clicked shut the watch.

He would later credit his recuperation not wholly to the most-deserving Nurse Cherborn and her ample bosom that had threatened to suffocate him each time she fluffed his pillows and adjusted his sheets, but ultimately to Allan Pinkerton, whose miserly treatment of him left Rollie ticked off, near broke, and more determined to live than he'd been since he woke in the doctor's office, bandaged like an Egyptian mummy and too stiff and sore to move anything but his eyes.

And so it was in late April 1881 that Rollie "Stoneface" Finnegan, former top operative for Pinkerton Detective Agency, found himself pacing the largest of the three rooms he could afford for less than a week longer before resorting to asking favors, something he had never done and would never do. One, two, three and a half paces forward, turn in a wide arc on the board-stiff left leg, lean on the sturdy oak cane, one, two, three and a half paces back toward the door, for hours a day. His left lung whistling in time, and increasing in intensity and pitch, with his efforts.

While he paced he formed a plan, one step at a time, as methodical as he had ever been in dogging suspects and criminals. One clue at a time, one thought on another, then another, and by the end of the day, two days before his rent was due, Rollie had a solid plan. The newspapers had helped him as much as the nurse and Pinkerton had.

He hadn't let Nurse Cherborn shave his face as she had intended, each damn week. He'd let his beard grow rather than risk a stranger free rein with a razor blade over his face. Rollie had made a lot of enemies in his years as an agent, or as Pinkerton liked to call them, "his operatives." Rollie wasn't about to trust anyone any more than he had to. That was the ironic part of it all. He was beholden to strangers for saving him and nursing him back to life even as he plotted shrugging them off.

Before he'd been able to pace, he'd spent most of his time in bed and then seated, slumped, in his wingback chair, wheezing and coughing, with that eerie whistle leaking through his parted lips. He found he could vary the pitch of the sound with his throat and mouth. It was a game he played when he'd wearied himself of raking over again and again in his mind the savaging he'd endured in the alley. So many people over the years who swore harm to him should they ever again taste freedom. Who was it? Or had it been someone new? Then why not rob him?

The Denver City constabulary had come up with no clues, no answers. He'd read each edition of the *Denver City Bulletin* during his convalescence, and any mention of the attack had dried up after the first week.

A most odd slice of news that at first had incensed him, then had brought a grim smile to his mouth was his obituary, a short, tight paragraph with no flowered phrases, and only the barest mention of his occupation. Erroneous information from the doctor? A drunken mistake by a hack reporter? Did it really matter?

If Denver thought him dead, he could recover and reinvent himself somewhere else, anywhere else. As anyone else. And as much as the notion beckoned him, the one piece of such a plan he would not indulge in was giving himself a new name. He had been Rollie Finnegan since birth, and if the name was good enough for his sainted mother and red-faced father to bestow on him, by God, he'd carry it with pride . . . beyond the grave or come what may.

With a day left on the rent of his rooms, he rummaged through his meager belongings, packed two old canvas war bags, and cleaned and oiled his Schofield, a two-shot derringer, a Colt Dragoon, and a Winchester repeater.

If a stranger gazed on him they would see a medium-height-to-tall man, not overly muscled, but exuding confidence and solidity, despite the oak cane. He sported a full thatch of peppered hair, heavily silvered, and what was visible of his face beneath the pepper-and-silver beard was lined, weathered from years on the trail. A full handlebar mustache, his one indulgence in daily vanity, rode proud beneath a sharp nose, nostrils always flared, as if forever sniffing out the truth in a matter.

He had dressed once more in his favored work togs— black stovepipe boots, into which were tucked striped woolen trousers. He wore a short canvas work coat with a green corduroyed collar and ample pockets in and out, a tobacco-brown leather vest, and leather braces over a dark blue, low-collar work shirt. He topped it all with his sweat-stained fawn Boss of the Plains, tugged low. Inner pockets held various items including a Barlow folding knife, his two-shot hideout gun, an apple-bowl briar pipe, matches, and a leather tug-string sack of tobacco.

Given the limp and the peppery beard, stable owner Pete Buddrell, busy mucking out stalls, didn't recognize the man who shuffled in that day of April, working a cane, and followed by a stout lad lugging two war bags. The man paid the lad, who dropped the bags, took the coins, and bolted back out the big double doors.

"What can I do for ya?"

The stranger looked about him. He seemed to be sniffing in the rank smells of the stable then turned to Buddrell. "Rollie Finnegan's big gray."

Buddrell leaned on his fork, nudged his hat back. "Oh, nah. He's dead."

"The horse or the man?"

Buddrell looked at the stranger a long moment. "Both."

The stranger walked closer, into the stall and within an arm's reach. "Nope."

Buddrell couldn't see the face, but something about the

man was unnerving. He swallowed, ran a tongue tip over his dry lips. "Was told he'd died. Figured—"

"Nope." The man raised his eyes, looked into Buddrell's.

"But . . . you're dead!"

"Yep."

"You . . . you'll want a horse, then."

"Yep."

Within half an hour, Rollie rolled away from the stable on the seat of a rugged little one-horse work trap, his bags lashed in the back, the entire affair pulled by a fine gray, a close second for old Tip, who he'd come to learn had been long sold. That pained him. He and Tip had shared many adventures. He hoped the old lad had fared better than Rollie himself had.

Saddling up was not a possibility for him yet. Might never be again, but he reckoned the fairly new wagon was decent trade for his good saddle that Buddrell had also sold off. Rollie had been surprised to learn that the money he'd sent to the stable months before for upkeep of his horse and tack had gone to pay some mysterious bill for expenses accrued. By whom or for what, he never learned.

He could have pushed the matter more, but he'd come out of it pretty well, considering the situation, what with the horse and the wagon. It felt to him like one more sign that the past was truly a dead thing and the future was his only concern from here on.

Yes, this is fine with me, thought Rollie "Stoneface" Finnegan as he rolled down Denver City's Quigley Street. He threaded a northwesterly route toward another discovery he'd made while reading each and every word of the newspapers, day after day, while he healed and grew stronger in body, harder in mind, and lighter in wallet.

His destination . . . Idaho Territory's Sawtooth Range and a little raw knob of a place mentioned once as an afterthought. Boar Gulch. Said to have promise of gold, though with little proof as yet. It had been referred to as brand new, wide open, raw, and rank. And that sounded, to Rollie Finnegan the right spot for holing up, healing up, and rebuilding his savings with easy placer pickings.

CHAPTER FOUR

It had taken most of the first day moving northwest-ward from Denver City for Rollie to ease off on swiveling his head around every few seconds as if he were about to be set upon by road agents at every turn. Even on the flats, where turns were scarce, he had to resist the compulsion to scan the vista in all directions.

He'd always been a cautious sort while on the road, but the attack in the alley peeled away whatever skin of chance he might have possessed. He didn't mind. It would be one frozen-over day in the devil's stomping ground before he was caught unawares again.

This journey was different from any he'd been on in recent years. No one who'd done something they should not have done was ahead of him being dogged by him. There was no wrong to right, no one to chase, but there was a place to get to.

He made camp that first night not far off the roadway, but tucked behind a cluster of boulders as big as a full-size buckboard and stippled with pines. He settled back with a tin cup of hot coffee dosed with a modest splash of Kentucky's finest. Rollie wasn't the sort to second-guess himself, but as he ruminated on the day, adjusting himself from one leaning position to sitting to pacing and wincing each time he moved, he began to reconsider his plan.

What did he really know about Boar Gulch? And did he really think he was going to set to digging once he got there? He pondered as he sipped and, enjoying the warm trail the whiskey-tinged coffee left down his gullet, he added one more wee splash to the cup. He knew it wouldn't have mattered what the brief article had been about—hell, it could have illustrated the virtues of being a sea captain or a saloon dancer—well, maybe not a dancer. He didn't have the legs for that anymore. Rollie laughed, a slight, wheezing sound, nonetheless a laugh, surprising himself. Humor was something he hadn't indulged in in a coon's age. It felt good.

Yes sir, he had chosen an odd path to follow, but once he set his mind to a thing, he didn't like to give up on it until he'd dogged it to its end, killed it, or it killed him. Then why, he wondered, wasn't he more concerned with tracking down whatever vermin had nearly laid him low?

"Horse. You have an opinion?"

The gray beast did not respond. It stood hip-shot, fed, watered, and dozing a few yards away, no doubt enjoying the dancing, reflected heat off the boulders around them.

Rollie sighed. "I agree. I have made stronger decisions." But he knew if he gimped his way around Denver City as he was, he'd end up dead for certain. The same gut feeling he'd relied on so many times over the years in tracking miscreants had told him back in his rooms that it was time to shed that town like a snake sheds its skin. It had been a home base of sorts for years, though he'd never intended to reside in a city, and never really considered himself a resident of that place.

Heck, he was hardly ever there anyway. He'd made no time for the cultivation of friends, save for the acquaintances he'd made at the tobacco shop Dilbert and Dilbert on the corner. Twin brothers who bickered something fierce somehow managed their shop together. Same for Tully, the barkeep at his namesake pub.

And Hazel, of Hazel's Hash House, where he took a good portion of his meals when he was in town. Now that was a woman he could have loved, did love, in fact, for her heavenly cooking. And that pecan pie. If she hadn't been thirty years his senior . . .

Rollie smiled at the memory of the robust little Scotswoman, barking orders to her two kitchen staff, both equally as plump and red-faced as Hazel herself, and in no danger of losing their positions, though it was promised by ol' Hazel on an hourly basis. The old bird loved the girls as if they were her own, and was teaching them through example, no doubt, the skills of her culinary artistry.

He considered the thin meal he'd prepared for himself—a toothsome repast of elk jerky, two corn cakes that needed soaking in water to make palatable, and a short can of sliced pears in syrup. He promised himself he'd do better the next day. His first day on the trail had been a bone-jarring ramble, and he was relieved to climb down out of the wagon for the final time.

It had been an hour sooner than he wanted to stop, but the campsite looked ideal. Far enough off the road he'd hear anybody doing anything other than traveling on by.

He wasn't so sure they'd see him anyway, as the site was higher by several yards than the road.

The gray didn't appear to be bothered one way or the other by the day's travel. He was solid, Rollie would give the horse that. He intended to get to know him as he had his last. Only then would he work up a name for him. Seemed fair.

He rubbed a hand in his thick beard, scratching his chin. He'd never been much for beards, but this one suited him. At least for the time being. It did make him feel as if he were trying to hide from the world, trying to disguise himself.

"Bah," he said and indulged in a long yawn, stretching one arm out, then the other as far as his wounds would permit. He wondered if there would ever be a day when he'd not be reminded of them with each breath, each movement. He tipped back the last of the cupful, banked the fire, and inched off his boots. That took two minutes, stiff as he was and with his wounds tender. He laid his Winchester by his right side, his Schofield at his left, and pulled the brown wool blanket up under his chin, rested one hand on each gun, and bid that day good-bye.

CHAPTER FIVE

Two weeks after he began his trek from Denver City, Rollie Finnegan clucked his tongue and jostled the lines to let the gray gelding recently named Cap, short for Captain, know it was time for one last, albeit long, climb. They'd met a grubby man carrying a spade a few miles back. To Rollie's question about Boar Gulch, the grizzled fellow had nodded and pointed with a jerk of his chin back up the rutted narrow trail disappearing behind him into the trees. Not a talker.

Rollie had wanted to quiz him about the mine camp. He'd also like to have known why the man was walking away from the place with nothing more to his name than a near-useless shovel and clothes that were more hole than cloth.

The brief newspaper article had used the words *burgeoning* and *bustling*, but Rollie had seen enough such spots to know it was likely more a cluster of tents (one housing an enterprising woman or two) and crude log shacks housing overworked rock hounds whose hopefulness outweighed their good sense. A tent saloon with rotgut gargle and a plank laid across a couple of crates seemed probable, too. It was about as far from what he'd already begun to think of as his "old" life as Rollie had been in some time. And so help him, he was looking forward to it.

"Time to earn your keep, Cap." Rollie clucked and lightly snapped the lines again. Cap leaned forward and plodded up the grade as Rollie guided the rattling little work wagon around gullies carved by a recent rain. Between those and the gray jags of granite jutting at inconvenient spots throughout the ragged roadway, the horse had all the challenge he could handle. Maybe there really was little more to Boar Gulch than what he imagined. It was a sobering thought and he chastised himself for foolish thinking. "Keep in the sunlight," as ol' Benjamin Franklin had once said. To this, Rollie appended the words "until it rains."

The track wound through pretty country, much of it shaded by mammoth ponderosa pines and a scatter of aspen and oak clusters. The rises were lessened by repeated switchbacks that made the journey possible, if not entirely enjoyable. The jarring, thumping ride ached Rollie's wounds, and he found his breath coming harder than it had even a few thousand feet lower, his game lung whistling a stuttering rhythm with Cap's digging steps.

"Nearly there, boy," said Rollie, by way of encouragement to the sweating beast before him. No way could Rollie make the trek on foot. They were barely getting to it at that. Any steeper and Cap would have told him to go to hell and turn around.

At the perfect moment, the trail leveled and grassed out alongside a boisterous, roaring flowage Rollie guessed would be classified somewhere between a brook and a river. He guided the horse and wagon off the roadway and onto the grass, and admired the spot.

Could make a decent camp for the night, but he reasoned that the gold town, such as it was, couldn't be all that much farther. It felt like they were closing in on the peak. Then what? Downward? After all, it couldn't be called a gulch for nothing.

That word conjured images of a raw chasm of a place lost behind a scatter of rough-and-tumble mountains. With that sobering thought, he said, "We'd better call it quits for the day. What do you say, Cap? Rest up here?"

He eased himself to the ground and stood, stretching his back, then knelt on the grassy bank upstream of Cap and sipped. He looked up and saw an alert Cap, ears perked forward, water drizzling from his muzzle, staring across the river.

Instinct's insistent tingle guided Rollie's hand to drag free the Schofield even as he scanned the far bank for sign of whatever it was spooking the usually calm beast. He saw nothing but low-sweeping pine boughs hugging close to the edge. That bank was steep, but less than man height, before tapering back into shadowed forest. *Likely a deer,* he thought, keeping low and thumbing back the hammer.

The horse kept his ears perked and offered up a low whicker. Rollie was glad he hadn't unhooked the beast yet. He'd given in to a rare moment of laziness because the grassy span sloped down to the water, wide enough for him to drive Cap right to it.

The last thing he needed was a spooked horse, though from the terrain they'd scrambled through, and the road ahead, Rollie doubted Cap would get far. The horse resumed drinking, and so did Rollie. Then it was Rollie's turn to jerk his head up. He heard a snapped stick and a soft rustling, as of a footfall, followed by others. He squinted and was rewarded with a flash of honey-tone hair, then a broad, snouted face poked through low branches. A bear. Grizzly, it looked to be. The black nose twitched up, down, to and fro as if tugged by an unseen string.

"Oh, damn," muttered Rollie.

Cap took that as a signal to give in to his rarely seen flighty side and jerked back and forth in the traces. The wagon creaked.

Rollie was too far away from the horse to gentle him. At least too far away for someone who moved with a hitch and a wince. "Cap!" he growled.

Apparently the horse had forgotten his name. He kept on scuffling, not really getting anywhere or doing anything useful, but fidgeting and getting himself worked up.

The bear watched the commotion and sniffed and snorted, and then Rollie saw one, two, three small bear faces pop out beneath the lowest branches along the bank near the big bear. They made high-pitched, bawling sounds. The mother bear snorted, chuffed, and commenced to pop her teeth.

"Oh, damn again." Rollie dropped to his belly and pushed himself backward, not wasting any time in getting away from a mother bear and her cubs. If the bear had a mind to, she would be on him before he could gain the wagon seat. Better to stay low and make a slow retreat.

If he could get back to the wagon, he could slick his Winchester from its scabbard beneath the seat. He felt his shirt work its way upward from his trouser waistband, grimaced at the fresh, hot pains his damn slow-to-heal wounds offered, and then felt gravel scraping his belly. No matter, he'd whine later. He had to keep Cap from making an even bigger spectacle of himself. And he had to get that rifle. He didn't think the rifle would drop the bear before it dealt them damage, but a lucky shot in the eye might slow her. That had to be a last-gasp effort, though.

He didn't want to kill any bears today or any day. He had nothing against them. In fact he was inclined to liking them—from a distance. But this distance wasn't one he had in mind. He wanted distance.

He'd almost reached the wagon's front wheel, something he could use to help haul himself upright, when the mother bear let loose a great bawling roar. It stopped Rollie short, prickled the hair on his scalp, and he looked back across the water. Two of the three cubs were splashing into the river, making for a sandbar midway across, and looking intent on making the far shore—which was Rollie's near shore. The sow grizz saw this the same time as Rollie, and somehow, deep in her little bear brain, became convinced he was the cause of her cubs' misbehavior. She charged.

CHAPTER SIX

The ex-Pinkerton agent's fingers of his right hand grabbed for the rifle while he reached across his chest with the Schofield in a tight fist and rapped the horse on the rump to distract him. "Knock it off, Cap!" he growled. He should have known, all it did was rile the horse more. Rollie tugged free the rifle, but didn't take his eyes from the charging she-bruin.

Yep, she was on her way, surging through the river upstream from her cubs. She made such a commotion, raising explosions of spray as she thrashed on through, Rollie reasoned that if the water were a man, it would have been torn apart by now.

He swallowed back a dry lump like a clot of powdered clay lodged in his throat, and stepped away from the horse and wagon. He worked sideways to his right, missing the third leg the cane afforded him. *"Don't fall now, you fool,"* he told himself.

His intent was to draw the bear from Cap and give himself enough room that he might fire, crank, and repeat until the bear reached him. He had no doubt that bear would be on him in seconds.

And then the great geyser of spray subsided.

The beast, though in the river, had lessened the gap between them to a tight six yards when she paused, raised herself into a half-standing position, and swung her torso downstream. Rollie looked, too, and heard a high-pitched bawling. Then a second voice joined the first. He saw what the mother bear had seen—two of her cubs were being carried downstream. Little brown heads bobbed and spun in the swirl. She swiveled her head back toward Rollie and roared, and he saw pure, killing hate. She recognized him as a threat to her babies, but now there was a different, unexpected threat.

As quick as she looked at him, she was gone, shoving water before her, spraying it a dozen feet high in all directions as she grunted and surged downstream toward her struggling, wayward offspring.

Rollie didn't waste a second of the opportunity and dove into the little wagon, which the dancing Cap had conveniently half-turned in a churning pivot. Snatching up the slack lines, Rollie let off the brake, growled hard at Cap, and snapped the lines on the riled horse's back. The nimble gray didn't need any more urging and spewed gravel as they regained the rough road upward toward what Rollie hoped was Boar Gulch.

He glanced backward a good many times in the next few minutes, but of the enraged grizzly mama, he saw no sign. He hoped the unfortunate, but most welcome fuzzy little distractions would suffer little more than a thorough soaking, and maybe a tongue-lashing from their ticked-off mama.

It wasn't long before man and horse were back to their slow, struggling pace of the day before. That was fine.

While none of it was easy on Cap, at least they weren't getting their hair parted by claw and fang.

A couple of hours past the streamside ruckus, they crested what Rollie thought was the final rise. It was difficult to determine with all the pines clogging the view, but the air was thinner and any sweat he'd worked up had dried, replaced with a chill that made him wish he'd tugged his wool shirt from his war bag. Even Cap's glistening back was drying in the cooler mountain air.

They rounded a curve, and the roadway widened and kicked downward. To their left—the northwest—the thick ponderosas parted to reveal a long view of successive mountain peaks, one after the next. Clothed in green close up, they faded to black, then purple, before graying out in the afternoon sun. Rollie also saw why the trees had parted. Men had hacked down a number of them, leaving a ragged stump field, likely for cabins and firewood. "Getting close, Cap."

He was surprised to feel a nervous flutter in his gut. He couldn't recall the last time that had happened. *Out of the game too long*, he guessed. They rolled forward in no hurry and rounded another bend. And there it was—Boar Gulch. Had to be. To his surprise and relief, it looked better than he'd imagined.

From what he could see, the inhabitants appeared to have put effort into laying out the main and only road, spacing tents and log structures far enough away that two wagons could pass each other with room to spare. He saw five on one side of the street, four on the other.

That pleased him, given that most mine camps he'd seen were barely more than a scatter of crude shelters close by a miner's diggings. He hadn't read that any investments had been made in Boar Gulch, that it showed promise of becoming a *boomtown*. With luck, maybe he'd find himself on the early edge of that boom.

He'd seen plenty of diggings and was familiar with the rudiments of the enterprise, but his present lack of a robust body might present a problem. On the journey from Denver City, he kept telling himself he'd worry about that later. But later was almost on him.

He popped the lines. "Okay, Cap. Let's see what Boar Gulch has to offer."

CHAPTER SEVEN

From the logged knoll on down, the road was in decent condition, the best stretch of the entire trip into these rugged Sawtooth foothills. Rollie came into sight of the tents and cabins he'd seen from above. As he rounded the last dip and bend that led straight onto the main street, two things happened at once. Rollie saw a hand-painted sign, black letters on a fresh-cut plank that read BOAR GULCH, and he heard a gunshot, then another, then two more.

A woman screamed and a large man, not fat but tall and wide of shoulder, staggered backward out of a raised plank-and-canvas structure to his left. He looked to be wearing a grimy apron.

The big man held his gut with both hands and lurched backward across the narrow boardwalk, and kept going, right through a flimsy log railing. It snapped, and the man dropped and hit the dirt of the street, landing on his back. Dust puffed outward as his head and legs bounced, then he lay still, arms flopped to his sides.

Rollie had pulled up on the lines without thinking, and he and Cap watched the odd scene unfold before them. A handful of men pushed out of the same door the man had staggered out of. Some jumped down off the porch, a four- or five-foot drop, and bent low over the fallen man.

Through gaps in the small cluster of people, Rollie saw dark spots on the big man's apron. Blood, and a lot of it. Gut shot, a real bleeder, and given the size of the structure, not much distance could have been between the shooter and the recipient of the bullets.

From out of a tidy structure up the slight rise at the far end of the street, a thick man wearing a brown suit, white shirt, string tie, and a derby hat bustled his way toward the commotion. He puffed hard and fast on a thick cigar poking from the middle of a close-cropped dark beard, plumes of smoke trailing behind him as if from a hard-working train.

As he approached the others, he waved his hands as if swatting at flies and said something in a tight, sharp bark. Rollie couldn't quite hear what the man said, but the people parted and the man knelt, smoke boiling up.

He must have been asking questions, because a couple of the gathered men nodded and pointed back toward the wood-and-canvas structure from which the entire commotion had erupted. The woman, presumably the one Rollie had heard scream, began a high, false-sounding wail. No one paid her any heed, and she stepped back a few feet from the crowd, her wailing diminishing with the lack of attention.

So far no one had noticed Rollie. That suited him fine. That feeling lasted about ten seconds more, then the loud woman standing with her hands on her hips looked his way and said something. No one paid attention to her. She said it louder and kicked the boot of one of the kneeling men. He looked up at her, then to where she was pointing. At Rollie.

Within seconds all ten or so people were standing, staring at him. The suited, cigar-puffing fellow stepped over the gut-shot man and pushed past the rest of them, then thumbed his lapels and puffed on his cigar with renewed vigor. The rest seemed comfortable crowding behind him. The prone man notwithstanding, the scene reminded Rollie of a cluster of prairie schoolchildren he'd encountered gathered behind their teacher some years before.

He'd ridden up and relieved them of the fugitive he was seeking. Seems the man had been hiding in the schoolhouse, the only structure on the Kansas prairie for miles. How he got there, Rollie never learned, though he'd wanted to know, particularly as the man had made his way west after embezzling a tidy fortune from an ice-selling firm in Providence, Rhode Island. He'd been on his way to San Francisco, but his map had been inadequate.

Rollie hadn't dredged up that episode in years. *Funny,* he thought, *what will trigger a memory.*

The fat man in the suit beckoned toward Rollie with a wide gesture, then plucked the cigar from his mouth with the other hand and shouted, "Welcome! Welcome! Ride on in, sir!"

So Rollie did.

He wheeled up to within twenty-five feet of the group, then stopped. Everyone eyed him and he did the same to them.

"Well, well. Welcome to the business district of Boar Gulch!" The sentence was a loud proclamation accompanied with another grand wave of a thick hand, this time toward the sign Rollie had seen on his arrival.

He nodded and offered a slight smile, a touch of his hat brim toward the woman. He couldn't be certain, but it looked as if she blushed—a rare feeling for her, he bet.

The man stepped closer and held out a hand. They shook, Rollie offering a firm but not a crushing shake. His father had taught him long ago when he was a boy in knee pants that to squeeze a man's hand and prevent him from offering a fair shake in return was a sign of fear and weakness. It had taken Rollie years to figure out what his father meant, for it seemed the opposite. But Da had been right.

This man, however, gave him a soft, weak handshake, something Rollie couldn't imagine offering another man, even on his deathbed.

"I am Chauncey Wheeler, unofficial . . . ah . . . mayor, shall we say, of Boar Gulch!" The man said this again in the same way as before, as if the very words caused a frenzy within him. He reminded Rollie of a revival preacher, or a huckster with nostrums for sale, both pretty much the same thing, in his experience.

"I didn't hear your name, sir."

"That's right," said Rollie, meeting the man's gaze and waiting for him to break off.

He did in short order. "Yes, well, ah, you seem to have caught us good citizens at a most inopportune moment."

"Just him," said Rollie, nodding toward the shot man.

"Ah, yes, yes." The mayor turned toward the prone man. "Poor Dawber. We have lost our one and only saloon keeper." He turned back to Rollie, smiling, and poked the air toward him with that big cigar. "Unless you, sir, happen to be a member of that most noble, nay, vital, occupation?"

Rollie looked at the faces behind the man, a group of dark, unshaven, dingy faces on bodies clothed in trousers and shirts made of rough cloth, bookended with floppy-brimmed hats and well-worn boots. As if he needed reminding, mining looked to be hard work.

Rollie looked back to the well-rested, smiling mayor in his fancy togs and decent-smelling cigar. *Mining might well be hard work,* he thought, *but mining the miners?* That sounded like something he might be able to do.

"Not as yet." Then he smiled. Because he had an idea.

CHAPTER EIGHT

Rollie stepped down, aware he was stiff and moving like a much older man than he appeared. At least he hoped he wasn't regarded as that old by the staring miners. He got his feet under him and stretched, eyeing them back until they looked away. It always worked.

He slid his cane out from beneath the seat and ran a hand across his backside. Even though he'd managed to make the plank seat more comfortable by sitting on his draped winter coat—a sheepskin-lined affair that had kept him from freezing on many a winter day—it had been a bone-snapping journey up the savage pass. He was only too glad his wounds hadn't somehow worked themselves open again and leaked out his life juices. And poor Cap. He was a trouper who deserved a feed and a rest. But first things first. Rollie sensed that the town blowhard had something to tell him that might be of importance.

As if reading Rollie's mind, the self-proclaimed mayor said, "Let's take a short stroll up our grand promenade and chat, shall we?"

Rollie and the mayor walked side by side slowly. They

moved toward the far end of the street, a few hundred yards north.

"You see, my new friend," said Chauncey Wheeler, trying to drape an arm around Rollie's shoulders. Finnegan shrugged it off without looking at him, but it didn't slow the man's patter. "As of quite recently, the good citizens of Boar Gulch find themselves in a pickle. As I mentioned, Dawber was our saloon keeper. And while he called himself the owner of said establishment, he was that only in theory."

"Let's cut to it, Mayor." Rollie looked down at the fleshy fellow. He'd added *Mayor* to stroke the man's obvious formidable ego.

"Excellent. I see you are a man of action. Good, good. I like that."

Rollie sighed.

"Yes, well, I take it from your arrival here in Boar Gulch that you intend to stake a claim and strike it rich, eh?"

"Something like that."

The mayor chuckled.

"Is that funny to you?"

"No, no, but you'll excuse me if I say you don't exactly seem suited to the . . . rigors of the mining life." Wheeler stepped backward and held up his hands in mock defense. His eyebrows followed suit. "I apologize if I have offended you, but if I am correct, well then, I have a deal for your consideration."

Rollie regarded the man. He had to admit that his cane, the limp, and the fact he was no young cockerel might have given that impression. But he wasn't ready for the stewpot yet. Still, none of it added up to him appearing as though he were as spry as he imagined himself. And he did roll into town riding in a wagon, not on horseback.

He was disinclined to like the mayor. He had seen too many of his ilk in the past, and to a man they were annoying ticks feeding off the labors of others. But nonetheless, there was something interesting about Mayor Chauncey Wheeler. Not much, but something. *Maybe I'm going soft,* Rollie thought. "Go on."

The mayor smiled, resumed walking and puffing his cigar. "The saloon, such as it is, while in Dawber's name was, or rather *is*, my property. You may have noticed on your arrival that the town of Boar Gulch, for it is a town or at least it will be if I have a say in the matter, has already taken on the look of a burg much larger." He smiled at Rollie, puffed.

When Rollie didn't answer, the mayor continued. "That is because I platted this town out before another soul arrived."

"You were here first?" Rollie's surprise showed.

The mayor chuckled. "Yes, it's true. Two, no, three years since. Well, there were two of us at the start. Me and my partner, Pete Winklestaff, who has since departed this place."

Rollie wasn't certain if that meant the man had died or pulled up stakes and left for richer ground.

The mayor anticipated the question. "All a matter of timing. He did not want to wait. I was willing to. I bought him out, then acquired more claims, eventually amassing most of the land you see hereabouts." He swept a pudgy hand around them. "Ah, but you're wondering why? How did I know it was going to prove up?"

Rollie shrugged.

"Because, my good man, I . . . well, I didn't. But sometimes a hunch is enough in life, eh? Besides, you have to be somewhere. And I like it here. At least for now." He winked and puffed.

Again, Rollie responded with little more than a nod.

"Let me ask you, sir, how did you happen to hear about Boar Gulch? Nobody shows up here accidentally."

"It was mentioned in a newspaper."

"Ah, yes. That would place you in Denver City."

Rollie looked at the man, not affirming or denying the guess.

"It pays to have a friend who is a journalist in a bright and shiny city such as Denver."

Rollie was beginning to not like the sound of this. Was it all a smoke game?

"I know what you're thinking, sir, but the fun of it is . . . there really is gold in these hills! Why else would that saloon fill up each night and folks have to stand outside drinking? Why, these hills are dotted with hardworking miners each on their individual claims, many of which I either sold or leased to them." The mayor winked again. "And most nights, they make the trip into town not because they don't have their own libation in their own cabins. Nay, but because they are lonely and in need of conversation with their fellows. They commiserate with each other, you see."

"Are there women?"

"Ah, a prime question. And one for which I have an answer, as you may have guessed. They are on their way. Of that I have little doubt. You see, it takes time for a mine camp's reputation to reach the larger world. Already I have had word, by way of our supply wagon's weekly runs, that a wagonload of divine creatures of the fairer gender may yet be on their way from east of here, from Montana Territory."

"If this town holds so much promise, why don't you want the bar?"

"Ah, but I do. I just don't want to spend my time as a saloon keeper."

"I see. So you want an employee."

The man shrugged. "In a manner of speaking."

"Why not get one of them?" Rollie nodded toward the cluster of townsfolk watching them, though they were slowly trailing off, mostly toward the unguarded saloon.

"Ha!" said the mayor. "They have all been bitten by the gold bug. Besides, there isn't a one of them I could trust. In fact," he stopped walking and turned to look at the saloon as the last of them walked inside. "I'd say they are thieving from me as we speak."

"Why me?"

"Because you are new here. You are fresh, as they say. And you are, as we have determined, I believe by mutual consent, not ideally suited to digging a hole in the ground. You, sir, look to me to be a man of action and education. A man of the world, a—"

Rollie held up a hand. "All right, all right. Enough of the grease. I'm flattered, but not interested. I won't work for another man." It was something he had decided against and promised himself he'd not ever do again. Especially after dogging for the Pinkerton Agency all those years, only to be handed a pocket watch—which had been useful, he had to admit—and shown the door.

"Ah, but don't we all work for someone, in some form or another?"

"Nope."

"Is there nothing I can do to change your mind?"

Rollie stopped walking, half-turned, and looked at the bar. It wasn't much to look at. A straight structure, if something half canvas could be called a structure. It wore planking halfway up, and was topped with a canvas wall and peak. It would be simple enough to touch brim, nod, and roll on out of this odd mountain community. And yet . . . it was the type of place that tended to attract the sort of people he'd spent the last twenty years of his life tracking down and hauling in. Now he was here, attracted to it, the same as them. What did that say about him? Was he really nothing more than a snob, someone deluding himself into thinking he was better than folks who were actually his equals?

Rollie looked harder at the place. Despite the broken railing and the fact that the previous owner had been shot by someone apparently still in the place, presumably drinking away the memory of the killing, there was an undeniable appeal in mining the miners. Especially if a boom really was about to begin.

Besides, what the hell else did he have to do? And where could he go? He needed to rest up, finish healing up, and recoup his lost savings. No better place than a potential boomtown. It was a gamble, but it seemed more fun than living in a city and living in fear—same thing, as far as Rollie was concerned.

He looked at the pudgy little mayor. "Sell it to me."

Judging by the droop in the man's cigar, that was not the answer the mayor had expected.

"But . . . well, it's a moneymaker, no doubt, but—"

"But what?"

Wheeler didn't reply, so Rollie turned and began walking back toward his wagon. He'd taken two steps when the man touched his sleeve. "Hold on there, friend. You caught me unawares, that's all. Perhaps we could come to some amicable terms."

And that is what they did, over the course of the next ten minutes, right there in the middle of the main street of Boar Gulch. The only other souls in sight were Cap, the tuckered-out gray gelding, and Dawber, former proprietor of the town's only saloon and former living man. By the end of the conversation, during which Rollie barely had to speak, they had haggled, then settled on a price that took most of the remainder of Rollie's meager savings. He learned about the weekly supply runs to Bella Springs, some miles down the mountains to the northeast, and that the saloon offered him modest living quarters at the rear. The rest of it he figured he'd learn soon enough.

"Let us retire to my mercantile yonder," Wheeler nodded, "and we can draw up a contract. Two copies, so we each are happy. I'll also show you the contract I had with the previous keeper, poor Dawber over there."

Rollie glanced at the dead man in the street. He hoped someone buried him before the flies brought their friends. Inside the store, he said, "I'd like to see the papers proving your ownership of the property in question."

"Naturally."

"And before I sign, I'll need a couple of clauses inserted into the contract."

"What sort of clauses?"

"One, that you don't open a rival establishment in Boar Gulch for a period of one year."

The mayor's face actually began to drain of its pink color. Rollie was enjoying himself.

"And the second clause?" said the mayor, his tone colder than before.

"That you don't back someone in such a venture in Boar Gulch within the next twelve months."

"Preposterous! Why, I . . . I don't know a soul who would agree to such terms. I won't do it."

"Fine," said Rollie, stuffing his thick wallet back into his inner coat pocket. "I hope you won't object to selling me a few supplies for my journey."

"Now, now, hold on a moment. I only meant that, well, a year's a long time, especially up here in the mountains."

"Yep."

"Six months. Take it or leave it."

"I'll leave it," said Rollie, suppressing a grin. He had the mayor backed into an uncomfortable corner.

"Eight months."

Rollie pooched out his lip, scrunched his eyes as if in deep thought. He hadn't thought the man would go for either clause, to be honest, so eight months was all bonus time. "Fine," he said, extending his hand.

The mayor looked at the big hand and gulped, then shook.

The two men fell silent, the mayor jotting down a simple, half-page document while Rollie took in the limited but decent selection of comestibles and hard goods—sacks of cornmeal and beans, shovels, picks, coils of rope, wire, fuse, kegs of nails, canned goods, tobacco, tin dishes, leather boots, canvas trousers, rough-spun cloth shirts, and one woman's straw hat hanging from a nail overhead. Its blue and yellow false flowers dusty from lack of attention.

"I'm curious, Mayor," said Rollie. "Your willingness to sell some of this so-called priceless land makes me wonder if you aren't as confident in the longevity of Boar Gulch as a mining concern as you let on."

"Not at all, not at all. In fact, I am so confident in its future I feel it incumbent on myself to share in this great, good fortune of which I find myself keeper."

"Magnanimous of you," said Rollie.

"To a fault, sir." The mayor sighed. "It will bite me in the backside one fine day. But that day, God willing, resides in the far distance."

Once they had each read and signed the contract, they clinked glasses of whiskey from a bottle behind the mercantile counter and sipped.

Decent bourbon, thought Rollie, hoping he'd have some of the same at his own new establishment, which he was eager to actually see. Never had he been so foolhardy in such a large decision. And he had to admit he liked the feeling.

They finished their drinks, shook hands once more— Rollie detected a strengthening in the mayor's shake, and he wondered if he'd jumped into a small hole with a big snake. In for a penny, as his mother used to say.

As he reached the door, the mayor's voice stopped him. "I'll be along shortly, Mr. Finnegan, to make introductions and welcome you to Boar Gulch." He grinned.

"Fine, thanks."

"Oh, by the way, Mr. Finnegan. You should have come

to town by the northeast road. It's a longer trip, but it's a maintained stretch—and decidedly more comfortable."

"Hmm. Good to know." With that, Rollie folded his copy of the contract in thirds, tucked it into an inner pocket, and with a nod, turned and heeled it back down the lane toward his new saloon.

CHAPTER NINE

Not wanting to appear insensitive to the death of the previous barkeep, even though the man lay faceup dead in the street out front, Rollie tried to slip in without attracting attention. He lugged his two bulging war bags up the steps and across the narrow front walk, his Winchester lashed across the top of one and used as a handle. Booze-fueled chatter laced through with jags of laughter jerked short when he nudged open the door.

The room's light was dim, enhanced by two oil lamps turned low. The air was thick with tobacco smoke and the stale funk of dried sweat and old beer. It reminded him of the seedier of such establishments he'd been in all over the West, from dugouts with dirt walls where the stink of stacks of green animal skins warred with the grime of men too long alone to the cloying perfume of bawdy women aping for dim-eyed gamblers in Dodge City gaming halls.

Once more he surveyed the assemblage . . . and they him.

His long-held inclination in such situations was to stare them down, one at a time if need be, almost shaming them to turn away as if they had violated his privacy by looking at him. *Worked well in the past,* he told himself. He directed his thoughts to the now. *Now, Rollie Finnegan, you are a publican, a figure who is expected to dole out advice and smiles if you want to make sales. And more to the point, especially if you want to make a home here, however long* here *might last.*

He cleared his throat, smiled, and tipped his head forward. "Howdy."

A few low mutters of the same drifted back to him. Then, once more, silence. Thankfully, a squat, bearded man with no hair atop his head and bright apple-red cheeks strode forward, a glass of beer in one hand. Even in the poorly lit room Rollie saw the man had vivid blue eyes. The man smiled and in a voice far too deep and large for his demure height, said, "Well, and who might you be?"

Rollie opened his mouth and from behind him the mayor's voice boomed, "That, Mr. Ogilvie, is your new saloon keeper. Lady . . . and gentlemen of Boar Gulch, meet Mr. Finnegan."

A ripple of lighter noises of surprise rose into the stale air, then Rollie said, "A round on the house." They all cheered and then stared at him once again.

The mayor leaned close. "I believe they are waiting on you."

Rollie's eyes widened and he understood. He moved behind the bar to his left and set his bags down on a somewhat dry patch of floor. Once more they cheered and lined up, ready for their free libation, which, judging from the wet floor and the tumble of empty bottles, would not be their first of the waning afternoon.

The mayor had sent a man and his son, whom the mayor

said he trusted—at that Rollie tamped down the urge to flinch—to unhitch Cap and feed, water, and stable him out back with his own horses behind the mercantile. Rollie knew he had to trust the mayor at least until he knew him better.

The same men would then lug the dead saloon keeper to the back room of the mayor's mercantile, where he would be laid out properly, boxed up, and buried. For a fee, naturally. Rollie wondered aloud how he would get money from a dead man. The mayor had winked. Was there nothing the man would not do for a dollar?

With the mayor's help, Rollie discovered where everything was kept, learned how to unbung a beer keg, and served up round after round, taking in money that he hoped was the correct amount. No doubt he lost more than he gained, but he reasoned he had plenty of time to learn the game and make his own rules. Eventually, he would make it all back, and then some.

That first night began with a nervous Rollie, and ended only slightly better. He'd stood everyone to a second free round before it occurred to him that getting booze up to the town could not be a simple endeavor. He also kept a sharp eye on each new face as folks came in to give him the once-over. He wanted to acquaint himself with his new townsmen, and there was the slim chance he might recognize one of them from some past pursuit. If he knew them, they would no doubt recall him. Likely not favorably.

Never had he offered so much unfelt cheer in his life. Well past midnight, he nodded, smiled his last smile, and finally ushered the last drunk patron out the door, making certain he didn't tumble off the edge of the porch. He'd have to fix that railing in the morning.

The saloon, much like he'd found the town on his arrival, was not as coarse inside as he'd expected. This was due, no doubt, to his lifelong habit of expecting the worst and ending up surprised that a given situation wasn't as bad as it might have been. The floor was planked with rough-sawn boards worn smooth where a couple of years' worth of boot traffic had slid and stomped.

Up to waist height the walls were of the same planking. Thick canvas rose from there and sported a half-dozen unrepaired three-corner tears a few inches in length. He made a note to sew them tight, and to finish the full construction in wood when he had time—and money—to do it.

The bar itself lined much of the left side of the twenty-five-foot room. It was half that in width. A door in the back wall led to his new home, a space the full width of the bar but ten feet in depth. A sag-rope bed in a wooden frame sat tucked into the back left corner. A thin, hand-made mattress sack leaked pine duff and tufts of ticking. On top were a couple of balled blankets.

At the foot of the bed, something topped with filthy sheeting filled an entire corner four feet square and man height. He lifted an edge and peered beneath. Stacked wooden crates bearing the words *Finest Whiskey* gladdened him. He slid the sheeting free and coughed at the puffs of dust as he dropped it to the floor. He lifted down the crates and checked—all full of full bottles. That was something, anyway.

He slid a bottle from its spot in a case and worked the cork free. He'd not had a drink since signing the contract in Wheeler's mercantile, how many hours before? Too many, he decided, and took a long pull. It burned and stung and scorched and then smoothed its way down his gullet to his belly, where it sat a moment like a bright coal in a campfire before releasing its heat to the rest of him. Bottle in one hand and the bail of an oil lantern in the other, Rollie set about inspecting the rest of his new home.

Crude shelves, chest high, stood in one corner. A couple of shirts, a pair of trousers, and a few other scraps of garment trailed off the shelves. A red and black checked wool coat hung on a nail on the wall. A crooked back door took up the rear right corner.

The room smelled stale and felt to Rollie dreary and depressing, as if Dawber had not enjoyed good sleep in it. He would have to spiff up the place. No need to live like an animal in a cave.

The saloon had been built against a slope, as had the rest of the few buildings along that side of the road, most of them log cabins for miners. Out the back door, a pair of planks made a short ramp down to a short, worn path, at the end of which he found an outhouse. He'd visit that later. Another smelly spot, no doubt.

He noted he'd have to make certain the front and back doors, as well as the door from the bar to his quarters, could be secured within and without. Cravings for drink could make people behave in foolish ways, especially people who may be losing their shirts, meager savings, and their souls to the elusive allure of gold yet to be found.

CHAPTER TEN

By the end of his first week in Boar Gulch, Rollie had met thirty or forty people, about the limit he was told by the mayor that the town held. "So far!" the chubby man had told him with a smile and a raised finger as if he could smell the coming hordes.

Rollie had lost count after two dozen, but he didn't forget their faces. He'd met the majority of them at the end of the workday, when they'd wandered, ragged and exhausted, into town on foot, on horseback, on mules, and a few on donkeys. All the critters of burden would be lined up out front, expected to wait for their masters until they would wobble out again hours later, drunk and braying louder than the mules. They'd ride the beasts through the dark, down and up mountain trails, back to their own diggings.

Rollie had no idea how they managed to find their way home each night. And in fact, he learned that some of them didn't, and ended up sleeping it off on the roadside, the beast dozing nearby. *All well and good,* he thought, *but what about when winter comes?* He felt some sort of odd obligation to keep those fools alive.

Of all of them, there was one woman, the one who'd screamed during the killing of the previous keeper of the bar. She was known as Camp Sal, a woman who, while she didn't appear to be much older than thirty, had, from her own accounts as well as those whispered by others, been a camp follower for years. She routinely took up with various men, drifting from one cabin to another as the whim grabbed her.

She was willing to keep house, to launder and mend torn clothes, and do whatever else the man she was with at the time required of her. Though it sounded to Rollie like a recipe for a dozen jealousy-fueled gunfights, no one seemed inclined to fight over her. To a man they spoke kindly of her and perhaps with sympathy, as one might talk about a relation who'd failed to live up to early promise.

All that was little more than a curiosity to Rollie as he had no intention of availing himself of her services. He could mend and clean and cook for himself, and loneliness was something he'd never been much tormented by. From its ravages on the lives of other men he'd known, he counted himself fortunate.

On his first night he'd been told about the killing of Dawber, the previous saloon keeper. It seems he had been an unpleasant sort who'd grown too fond of his own product, and who had been in the habit of wearing a long knife on a belt strapped above his apron. On the afternoon Rollie had arrived, Dawber had been in his cups, having started well before his midday opening time, and hadn't slowed as the day lengthened. Everyone in the Gulch knew his bristly demeanor did not improve as his drinking progressed. It grew worse, darker and meaner.

Ogilvie had asked him for another beer, but didn't think Dawber had heard him. He'd asked again, and the surly publican lurched around the end of the bar and set on Ogilvie with both hands about the little man's throat. They tussled, thrashing around and around the room, knocking over chairs and tables, sending a friendly game of euchre to the floor and upending drinks in the process.

Two other men finally intervened. They had almost pinned the big barkeep to the floor. He kicked one of them in the crotch and slammed their heads together. He was up and searching the wrecked room for Ogilvie once more—with his long knife drawn. Dawber slashed at the smaller man as if he were a lion raking the air before him in a fog of raw rage. He advanced, growling threats, and finally lunged once more at Ogilvie.

The smaller man remembered he wore a clunky but serviceable revolver and clawed it free in time. Its presence, aimed as it was at Dawber's gut, seemed to enrage the big drunk even more.

He'd growled and howled, "I'll kill you!" and indeed, was an eye-blink from plunging the great knife into Ogilvie's chest when the smaller man sidestepped and fired.

The first bullet caught Dawber high in the gut. It stopped his momentum and he wobbled in place. He focused once more on Ogilvie, and the surprised look on his face slid back into a mask of rage. The barkeep advanced once more. Ogilvie shot again, stopping Dawber a second time.

Ogilvie advanced and squeezed another bullet out, backing Dawber to the door. Another, and the big man dropped his knife and crashed backward through the door. The momentum carried him across the short porch and through the railing. He hit the packed earth out front, flattening a fresh dumping of donkey dung, and expired right there, with a host of townsfolk staring at him and one newcomer in a small work wagon reined up and watching from the south end of the street.

Back inside, Ogilvie poured himself that beer, then finding himself alone in the den of his now-dead nemesis, followed it with a couple of quick shots of whiskey, learning that the "good stuff" Dawber had charged more for was the same swill they all paid too much for every day. So he had two more.

"Well," said Rollie when Ogilvie had told him the story. "I can't promise I'll never come after you with a knife, but I can promise I'll gladly sell you a beer when you ask." He thought it was funny, but the rest of them all looked at him as if he'd threatened them.

In that first week he made a number of changes, keeping the former owner's schedule of opening at noon only as long as it took him to instigate a few others. He intended to open in the mornings as well, to serve coffee to whoever required it. First, he had to spruce up the place. It was dark and dank inside, and if he was going to spend so many hours a day and night there, it had to be a more welcoming place.

He began by making a quick leather strap cradle for his

rifle, easy to grab should the need arise. He vowed to purchase a sawed-off shotgun as soon as he was in the chips enough to afford it. They were brute tools but effective for close-in work such as keeping the peace in a roughneck saloon.

For all doors, he built crude but effective locks, simple wooden bars to slide in place that would serve to keep out the nosey and ill-intentioned, and hopefully keep his goods and gear safe. That completed, he turned his attention to the scant living quarters. He rearranged the cramped space and found his solution gave him more elbow room and made him feel as if he were finally sleeping in his own home and not that of the dead former barkeep.

For his personal possessions, he cobbled together a wooden locker secreted between his bunk and the stacked crates of libation. He fixed it with a padlock atop, and in it he stashed his valuables—a few small items he'd kept that had belonged to his parents, a small stack of important papers, and his daily takings from the bar.

He had intended to stuff the silver pocket watch inside, too, but he'd worn it too long now, and had come to rely on the convenience of having a timepiece close at hand. That it was solid silver didn't hurt. He liked the look and feel of it. Besides, he reasoned, what was the use of owning something decent if you kept it locked away? He had never been one to wait on a rainy day, and if his near death in the Denver City alley told him anything, it was that life was a fickle wraith, here and gone with finger snap speed. No time for saving something away—except money. He had time now for doing that.

Rollie swept, scrubbed, and spit shined every surface he could reach, in and out. He repaired the snapped railing out front, and replaced the weakest rails with stout, skinned lengths of spruce. He framed up two windows and made shutters for them, barred from the inside during closed hours. And then he borrowed a paintbrush and paint from the mayor at the mercantile and hung a new, sizeable plank sign above the front door.

"The Last Drop, huh?" A kindly old regular everyone called Wolfbait shuffled in right at noon that Friday. "That's a good one." He winked, then looked at Rollie in mock horror. "Well, you didn't think I was illiterate, did you? Just because I ended up here in the mountains, clawing away at a dirt pile doesn't mean I've always looked and behaved like this." He climbed aboard his usual stool at the end of the bar.

"Never thought about it," said Rollie.

"Was a time I taught school at a private academy in Connecticut. That's a state in New England, in case you didn't know." Wolfbait winked again and sipped the foam off his first beer of the day. "Ayuh, I instructed a genera-tion or more of young minds in the fanciful and fickle ways of the classics." He sipped again. "Good God, what a waste. I could have been out here, drinking in the beauty of the mountains and the mule piss that is this beer. No offense intended."

"None received," said Rollie, smiling as he draped a towel over his shoulder. He had turned around to take stock of the levels in the bottles behind the bar when he heard footsteps. *Another customer,* he thought, as he turned and grabbed a beer mug to dry.

He saw a trim, handsome man in his early thirties stroll on in through the propped-open front door. The stranger wore a brown derby hat with a noticeable bullet-size hole in it, and wandered in without looking up from the note-book he was scratching away in with a pencil. The man didn't look much like a miner, but then again if Rollie had learned anything in his years as a Pinkerton man it was that people were nothing if not full of surprises. The stranger mumbled to himself as if in conversation with someone, walked behind the bar to where Rollie was drying glasses, and continued right on behind him.

The stranger slipped his notebook in a trouser pocket, slid his pencil over his right ear, and hung his jacket on a hook. Then he lifted down an apron and tied it on. When he'd finished, he looked up at Rollie.

"Who are you?" he said, his eyebrows scrunching.

Rollie shook his head. "That's my question."

"I am Eustace Parker. What are you doing behind the bar?"

Again, Rollie shook his head. "That's my second question."

The stranger walked over to Rollie and stared up at him, the new barkeep being half a head taller.

"You know, with your face, you'd be better off without that beard." The stranger pointed to old Wolfbait. "On him, a full beard is unfortunate, however. I have made a study of such things. Do I know you? You look familiar. Have we met?"

Rollie felt his face heat up, his ears redden. It had been a long stretch since he wanted to punch someone in the mouth for being annoying, but this whelp came close. He decided instead to boot the fool out of the bar before he said anything else.

He heard Wolfbait wheezing. It sounded like he was having a seizure, but looking close, Rollie saw the old buck's shoulders working up and down and tears sliding down his wrinkled cheeks. Finally he cut loose with a "Har har har!" and slapped his leg.

"Don't you mind him, Finny. That's ol' Nosey Parker, on account he can't keep himself from doling out advice and pesterin' everybody with questions until they're about ready to choke the life out of him!"

Rollie fixed Parker with a hard stare. "That doesn't explain why he's behind my bar."

"I work here when I'm not at my claim."

"You work here? I haven't seen you, and I've been here a week."

"I told you I work my claim."

"Ha!" said Wolfbait. "I seen plenty of worked claims in my time, boy, including a few of my own, boom and bust, and I tell you, yours ain't hardly been touched."

"I admit to being distracted of late," said Nosey. "I am working on an opus. A grand-scale piece of work that requires time I can't spare on digging in the earth for a fantasy." He turned back to Rollie. "And who are you?"

Rollie sighed and set the mug down hard on the slab bar top. "I am Finnegan. I own the place."

"Where's Dawber?"

At the same time, Rollie and Wolfbait said, "He's dead."

"Oh." Nosey pooched out a bottom lip in thought, then said, "Not surprising. But why? How did it happen? Was there gunplay? Knowing that cantankerous drunkard, I would place bets on it. Oh, did he employ the use of that brutal knife of his? More of a scimitar, I should think. What a madman . . ." He muttered to himself like that for another few minutes, edging in front of Rollie and taking over the drying of glasses, sweeping the floor, and tidying.

All Rollie could do was watch in what was a mixture of anger, surprise, and disbelief. Finally he snatched a damp rag from Nosey's hand. "How much was Dawber paying you?"

"Oh, I don't know," said Parker.

"What do you mean?"

The younger man shrugged. "I never counted it."

No sooner had he said that than a couple of early-afternoon regulars, Tyson Jack and Swede, walked in. "Nosey! Good to see you. Any luck at your claim yet, boy?"

This was met with laughter from everyone but Rollie and Nosey, who didn't seem to notice the dig at his poor mining skills. He drew two beers and set them on the counter before the men.

As the afternoon wore on, Rollie began to see another side of Nosey. Despite the young man's odd, detached demeanor, he'd pop into a conversation with a series of pointed questions. It appeared Nosey heard everything being said. The ex-Pinkerton man in Rollie half-admired the trait.

The kid also seemed to know how to make change and, most important, the customers knew him. And though he was odd, they liked him. Rollie decided he could do with a bit of help. Only a week into his ownership, the long hours were wearing on him. If he wanted to go to the store or visit Cap to take him out for a walk or a ride, his time was limited. But with Nosey around, he might be able to relax a little. Trouble was, the man seemed to come and go at his whim. He'd only be useful if he could be counted on.

No sooner did he think this than Nosey turned to him and said, "So what's your story? You weren't born suited to tend bar, that's obvious. How did you end up here? What are your plans for the future? I don't think this camp has much promise as a gold town, but I'd welcome your opinion if you have experience in such matters."

Rollie was set to chuck out the window any charitable thoughts he might have entertained about the kid. He was about to tell him to get the hell out when another miner walked in.

"Nosey Parker! Where you been, boy?"

As the place filled and Rollie saw that Nosey did indeed have a knack for tending bar and that instead of taking offense at the man's annoying—nosey—questions, the miners found him amusing and seemed to like talking with him.

Another admirable trait, Rollie had to admit. He had found keeping up conversation to be the single most challenging task he'd faced since arriving in the Gulch. He was by nature not a talker. Hence the unfortunate nickname *Stoneface* he'd earned years before from a smartass prisoner.

Later, as the place quieted and Rollie was cleaning up, he leveled questions of his own at Nosey.

"I am a displaced journalist from back East," said Parker as he righted chairs and shoved them under tables.

As an old hand at sniffing out lies and peeking into shadows, Rollie knew from the vagueness of the reply that there was more to Nosey's story. But unlike Nosey, he didn't want to know more about his fellow Boar Gulchers. At least not until they offered their stories, unbidden.

"I am out here to seek my fortune in the vastness of this fabled place."

Rollie knew what he meant, but looked around the bar. "Here?"

Nosey either didn't understand the stab at wry humor or chose to ignore it. Before locking up, he held up two glasses and a bottle of whiskey. "You drink?"

Nosey smacked his hands together. "Does a priest marry?"

Rollie didn't know what to make of that. As far as he knew priests weren't allowed to marry, so that was a no. At least not in the Catholic church. Of course, they did perform weddings for others, so maybe yes. But Nosey had slid himself into a seat at a table as if waiting for the drink. Rollie poured them each a dose and sat down himself with a groan and a sigh.

"Some injuries you have there, Finn," said Nosey.

Rollie nodded and sipped. "How often did you work here in the past? And don't tell me whenever you felt like it, because that won't work."

"Oh no. I was going to say three or four days a week."

"And the times?"

"Oh, when I walk in until I leave, usually about now." Nosey looked around as if a clock was going to appear on a wall.

"The thing is, Eustace, I would consider keeping you on, but I need to know that you're going to show up when I need you to."

"Understood," said Nosey, downing the last of his drink.

Rollie waited for the remainder of the reply he wanted to hear.

Nosey stood, tugged on his coat, plopped his bowler on his head, and whistling, walked out the door, leaving Rollie as confused as he'd been hours earlier when he first met Nosey Parker.

CHAPTER ELEVEN

Much to Rollie's satisfaction, within two weeks after his arrival in Boar Gulch, the mine camp showed signs of becoming a genuine town. More people arrived daily, one or two at a time, but by the end of the second week the population of the camp had doubled.

As he suspected would also happen as the town's population rose and with no law in sight, men who appeared to have little interest in digging for gold themselves also showed up. These fellows were little more than skeevy thieves in the guise of gamblers, confidence men looking for a quick dollar before vanishing in the dark.

As The Last Drop was, at present, the only gambling den in town, Rollie saw most of the grubbing newcomers as they plied their trade. One good thing about them was that since they were in his establishment, he could keep them in sight. Another benefit, they all seemed to be thirsty.

He'd had a run-in with one of their ilk. Enjoyed it, too. Dressed in dusty black togs with a gray silk ascot and pocket kerchief that had been new a long time before, the man had sauntered in before everyone else. He'd glanced at Rollie then dragged a gloved fingertip across the nearest poker table, and selected a seat facing the door. He sat with his back to the side wall.

Rollie took his time lining up the washed mugs and kept his gaze pinned on the man. Within a couple of minutes, the newcomer responded as he thought he might.

"You appear to be interested in me, bartender. Should I be alarmed?"

"Not alarmed, no. But now you mention it, there is something I can't figure out."

"What's that?" said the man, a slow smile spreading across his shiny face.

"I can't figure out if you're a pimp or a low-class gambler, or both."

The smarmy look on the man's face slipped. "A lesser man might be offended by what you've said. But I am no lesser man. I am not a man to take offense to the words of a mudslinger. No, sir. No, I say. I am a businessman seeking opportunities, no more, no less."

"Then you should fit right in here in Boar Gulch."

"Who are you to speak so boldly to a newly arrived, well-meaning stranger in your midst?"

Rollie snorted, taking no pains to hide the humor he found in the man's words. "Me? I'm the owner of this establishment. As to you being newly arrived, I'll grant you that. But well-meaning? Nah. You're a card sharp, nothing more. I've seen your ilk in a hundred grimy little towns and big burgs and never have I seen one worth the effort I'm wasting on you with words."

The man's face became a mask of supreme indignation. He made to move, but Rollie shook his head. "I'm not through yet. Now, you are welcome to stay and play—

provided you conduct yourself in a legal fashion and, of course, that you drink your share. I'm going to make certain everyone knows what you are. Then you can do what you feel you need to do. That way the good folks of Boar Gulch who are inclined to wager with you will go into the game knowing they might lose."

The man shoved back his chair and stood, the fingertips of one hand splayed on the baize tabletop before him. With his other hand he swept back the dusty tails of his frock coat and rested his hand on his waist, above a small, holstered nickel-plate derringer.

Rollie beat him to it. The serious end of his Schofield wagged back and forth. "Not in my establishment, mister. Hand that thing over and await your prey or leave my bar. Choose. Now."

The bar was quiet for long moments while the gambler considered all angles of play he might make. Rollie was tempted to sigh. He'd seen this behavior far too many times and it rarely ended well should the fool decide action of the sudden sort was the way to proceed. This man was smarter, albeit slightly, than he looked. He reached slowly for his derringer.

Rollie nodded. "Slower. Pinch it out and lay it on the table. Then sit down."

The man did so and Rollie smiled as he palmed the little gun. "You'll get it back when you decide to leave town. Now," he holstered his revolver. "What'll it be?"

The man was doing his best to kill Rollie with a viper-like look. It wasn't working, and he finally realized it. He sighed. "I'd like a half bottle of decent whiskey and a glass."

Rollie smiled a smile that offered no promise of mirth

and backed behind the bar. He knew better than to show the man his back. The seedy gambler was likely packing a hideout gun and had about him the rank tinge of a back-shooter.

Over the next few hours, the man had surprised him in staying with it, shuffling and reshuffling his deck of cards, smiling as regulars dropped in. He sipped his whiskey, which Rollie insisted he pay for when he'd set it on the table. He also kept a thin smile in place as Rollie announced to each new patron that the man was a professional gambler who'd come to Boar Gulch seeking to mine the miners.

That, Rollie was certain, dissuaded a few of the weaker and poorer among his regulars from sitting down to a game with the man. Well into the evening, the man rose from what had been a weak game between himself and Bone and his slow-to-think son, Young Bone, and walked to the bar. "You win, bartender. I will pull up stakes first thing in the morning and seek my fortune elsewhere. For the night, I will camp outside of town."

"That's fine," said Rollie. "Good night."

"My gun, if you please."

"Oh, drop in before you leave in the morning. I'll have the coffee on. You can have your derringer then." He smiled and let his right arm hang down by his side, a bit of a show, he knew, but he'd gotten a rise out of it.

The gambler gave him another snakelike gaze and stormed out. Stray chuckles from the other patrons followed him.

When he'd returned the next morning, Rollie had given him a cup of coffee.

"Why do you object to gambling in your saloon, sir?"

said the man, sipping the hot brew and eyeing Rollie over the cup's rim.

"I don't object to gambling, but I do not like dishonesty and treachery, and while you didn't display either of those two rank traits, you carry the whiff of them."

"How on earth can you make that assumption?"

Rollie shrugged in response and sipped his coffee.

"Oh, I see. You are a lawman. Or you were. Do I know you?" The man narrowed his eyes and looked at Rollie hard.

"I doubt it." Rollie set the man's derringer on the bar, but kept his hand on it. "So, are you going to try your luck here again today or move on?"

"No, I'll stick with my plan and move on."

Rollie handed him the gun.

"And my bullets?"

Rollie shook his head. "Those I keep. You best get a start if you're leaving the Gulch today. It's not a quick trip to anywhere from here."

The man made it to the door, then stopped and pointed a wagging finger at Rollie. "I swear you look familiar. It'll come to me."

"Feel free to write, if it comes to you." Rollie wiped the bar, and when the man finally left, riding a sag-bellied brown horse northward down main street and out of sight, he felt relief. He suspected he'd been too rigid, but he took cold comfort in the fact that in the past he'd seen too much of what liquor and money and anger and guns and men could do when they got tangled up together.

The thought didn't make him feel any better, only tired. And the day had barely begun.

Rollie kept a tight count on his bottles and casks, and

worked out how many days he would be able to serve before running out of stock. He didn't know how long he'd be able to keep a lock on being the only place of business to serve booze to the burgeoning populace, but he'd ride it as long as he was able.

Fortunately, Chauncey Wheeler was experiencing the same situation with beans, flour, coffee, and other staples of mining life. The two men worked out agreeable terms and Rollie agreed to drive the mayor's big work wagon to the valley town of Bella Springs to fetch the vital supplies early the next morning. Wolfbait agreed to ride shotgun. As a bonus, the old buck had his own weapon, though he didn't seem hale enough to Rollie to heft a double scatter-gun. But, two beat one.

All he had to do was pin Nosey down to committing to tend the bar. If not, he would shut the doors for the day. Chauncey had assured him if they left at first light they could return with the laden supply wagon by dark. A long day, but a vital trip for them all.

The northeast road, he'd been told once more, was in far smoother condition than the one he'd taken to get there. Rollie limped back to the bar and asked Wolfbait where Nosey's claim was located. "Up yonder of a hill and down again. Odd spot. But then again he's an odd fellow, is Nosey Parker."

"Okay, but how would I get there?"

"Bah, I'll go fetch him. Easier than yammering all day about it." He slid off his polished stool and ambled to the door.

"Thanks, Wolfbait."

In reply, Rollie received a grunt and the sound of the

old man blowing his nose into the big, grimy red hanky that always trailed from his back pocket like a tail.

Rollie nipped out back for a quick visit to the outhouse. When he walked back inside, he was faced with two large men, half again as tall as Rollie and twice as wide, identical in appearance save for the various tears in their mammoth bib overalls. They stood inside the front door of the bar, grinning and pointing twin converted cap-and-ball pistols at him.

Rollie grabbed for his Schofield, which rode on his hips from waking until he retired to his bed. Both the grinning twins thumbed back their hammers. The one on Rollie's left shook his head. The other said in a high, thin voice that surprised Rollie, "No, no, mister-man."

Rollie stayed his hand, a claw in the air an inch from his holster.

"You be Finnegan."

It wasn't a question, so he didn't answer. Not that he would have anyway.

They advanced on Rollie, the other brother spoke in that same high voice. "Toss that away." He wagged the snout of the pistol, indicating Rollie's gun.

"Like hell," said Rollie.

They kept grinning and moving forward. They split, one angled behind Rollie, the other stopped in front of him. Closer, the stink wafting off the two grimy beasts was awful, like they'd rolled in a week-old skunk carcass. Rollie's eyes teared and he fought to keep from grabbing his nose. He wasn't certain he could prevent retching, though.

Their dirt-caked hair hung in slick, waxy clumps like yarn dragged through the mud. Their fleshy faces were accented with creases packed with grime. Tobacco juice stained their lips and mouth corners, trailing down in runnels where they'd drooled as they chewed. Painful-looking green-and-blackened stumps jutted where their teeth should be.

Rollie backed up, trying to keep both men in view, but he was too far from the door to his room. The man behind him was quick, quicker than Rollie thought a large, fat brute had a right to be. The stranger snaked a thick hand out and snatched Rollie's Schofield, shucked it clean out of his holster. Rollie felt only vanishing steel as it whisked by his own grabbing fingertips.

The man before him stepped closer, the gagging reek clouding off him in waves. High on the man's chest, Rollie saw clusters of pimples on the skin flecked with dirt. Breasts larger than those of many women sagged out from behind the man's coveralls and jiggled as he moved.

A quick movement behind him caused Rollie to shuffle sideways—what they wanted. The one he couldn't see brought a hand down and Rollie pulled away. His reflexes were good, not what they once were, but thanks to the long days of labor, they were better than they'd been in months. He ducked low as the unseen blow glanced off his head. He felt hot pain above his ear, but knew it could have been worse. It was all they needed.

The one before him had holstered his pistol and wrapped a filthy arm around him, locking Rollie's head in flesh and suffocating him with soft, stinking fat. Rollie clawed, tore at the tightening arm, pinched, tried to pull out handfuls of meat, anything. Nothing seemed to slow the viselike squeezing. He would black out soon.

He grabbed the arm with both hands and, suspending

himself from it, kicked hard backward with his boot heels. Once, twice, connecting each time with what had to be the fat giant's legs. The squeezing lessened and the man dropped Rollie, who fell to the floor, holding his head, one leg bent beneath him. He gasped from the pain in his gamy leg and from the squeezing he'd received.

Wheezing laughter came from two high-pitched voices, and he saw the man who'd been behind him. The savage muscled onto Rollie's shoulder and lifted him like a child's doll off the floor, then shook him. The laughter continued. Rollie lashed out with hands and feet, his wounds aching him as if hot pokers were held to each spot. But he used them to keep his mind clear and intent on somehow defeating these two brutes. He'd worry about who they were and why they were attacking him later. If there was a later.

One flailing fist landed a lucky blind punch, and he felt the fleshy grip loosen, and thought he heard an "Oof!" as air left the pig's body. Rollie repeated the move over and over and thought he might have made a success of it. But as quick as the brute tossed him down, the other scooped him up.

And so it went for what felt like hours to Rollie, but he knew was mere seconds. One of the massive twins shook and squeezed him only to have Rollie flail in some lucky sequence, landing blow enough to gain a momentary reprieve while the other fat savage scooped him up to exert yet another round of pummeling.

He heard a voice, a familiar one, and saw from between two rolls of fat, Nosey Parker standing in the saloon doorway, staring at them all.

"What are you three doing? This is no place for a

wrestling match. You want to do that, take it out of doors. You should know better, Mr. Finnegan!"

"Aha!" shouted one of the twins.

"It is him!" shouted the other.

"Of course it's him, you moron," said Nosey, walking behind the bar and hanging his hat and coat on a hook. He turned, walked back out from behind the bar, straightened his vest, and shrieked, assuming a low defensive pose, moving his hands slowly before him, which he held in curved, bladelike shapes.

He advanced on the three men, chopping the air and howling louder than ever in a lingo Rollie had never heard. He wasn't sure it was a language. He didn't really care, but at that moment he sure wished Nosey carried a gun. The man was weird, but at least he was game.

The twin Rollie had been floundering with, trying to pull free of, whipped him around in a circle, avoiding the advancing Nosey. This seemed to suit the odd man fine, for he focused his shrieking, hand-chopping efforts on the other twin. He'd advanced within three feet of the grinning big man when Nosey launched himself at him.

Rollie wasted no time in renewing his thrashing, kicking, pummeling efforts, reigniting the stalled, sweaty dance. He winced as he heard wood crack and splinter as they flailed around the barroom, knocking into the spindly furniture. If he could get the man down on the floor he could drive his thumbs into the fat man's eyes, distract him enough somehow to steal the man's pistol and end this foolishness.

He caught quick glimpses of Nosey grappling with the other fat man and heard one of the little man's hair-raising shrieks pinch off in a gag as the fat man muffled him by stuffing Nosey's face under his armpit. *Poor kid,* thought Rollie as he landed a decent kick at his twin's crotch. The sloppy beast never lost his grin and kept coming. Rollie gave him another kick, and a third. That did the trick. The fat man slowed his progress, his demented smile slipped a little bit, and his fat lips parted. He let loose with a squeal such as a giant pig might make.

Meanwhile, a crowd of regulars clustered on the street outside. They stared at the tent and plank structure, wincing and clamping hands over their mouths as another round of crashes and howls rose from within.

"Somebody should do something," one of them said, but none made a move.

More people joined them.

Among them was a solidly built, bone and muscle black man with short salt-and-pepper hair partially covered by an aged brown bowler. He wore patched denim overalls, toted a ratty satchel over one shoulder, and smoked a corncob pipe. If the commotion inside the bar hadn't been in play, he would have received that afternoon's full attention, but he was given little more than sideways glances. He regarded the vibrating saloon with the rest of the crowd.

He pointed with his pipe stem. "Any of you seen two huge, lookalike white boys, dumb as stumps and smelling worse than goats?"

A high-pitched squeal rose up from inside.

"Never mind. I found 'em." He walked up the steps as if he'd been there before, opened the door, walked on in, then closed the door behind him. "Well now," he said, assessing the scene before him.

A young man was laid out on the floor, either dead or

knocked cold. His nose appeared to have been broken. With gun drawn, the fat man he'd been wrassling was advancing on a trim, north of middle age, bearded man with a fancy mustache, who was otherwise engaged in playing slap and tickle with the other fat twin.

"Damn you Dickey boys," muttered the black man, shaking his head as he unclasped his satchel.

The fat man thumbed back the hammer on his pistol and was about to squeeze the trigger and blow a hole in Rollie's back when the newcomer reached into his satchel and with a deft move in the bag's depths, cocked and triggered a sawed-off Greener.

It blasted a ragged, smoking hole through the end of his satchel and made an even bigger mess of the back-shooting twin's massive belly. The shot punched the big, slop-bellied beast backward, squealing like a knife-stuck hog on slaughter day. He slid, then skidded to a stop in a greasy smear of blood, his arms and legs raking feebly in the air.

"Stings, don't it?" said the black man, his lips tight to his teeth in a grimace. He swung the satchel around on the second twin, but the bearded man was in the way. He sidestepped this way, then that for a cleaner view, but found no clear trail to the second twin.

Rollie used the distraction of the shotgun blast to snatch the pistol from his adversary's low-hanging holster. He cranked back on the pistol's hammer and jammed it into the sagging gut before him. As soon as it sunk in good and deep, he pulled the trigger.

The mountain of flesh seized, stiffening—as much as was possible for such a pile of fat—and a high-pitched squeal leaked from the man's mouth, much like the last sound wheezing out from the lips of his brother. Blood and tobacco spittle drooled from his maw and he began to lean.

Rollie stepped away. The man lunged at him as he pitched forward, his squeal rising, growing louder. Rollie thumbed back and touched off another round and the fat man slopped forward, his belly slapping, then his face slamming the wood floor.

For the second time in moments, everything in the room bounced. The fat man sagged against the floor, blood leaching from beneath him as he twitched and gurgled. Seconds later he lay still. Rollie stepped backward once and the movement seemed to trigger a final act from his bloated foe, for the newly dead man released a quivering fart and the room filled with an ungodly stench.

CHAPTER TWELVE

A wheezing cough rose up from behind the first dead twin.

"Gaah! That stink . . ." Nosey sat up, bleary-eyed, holding his head with one hand.

"Surprised you can smell anything with that busted sniffer of yours." The black man threw wide the door and pushed open the shutters of one window.

Rollie did the same with the opposite window, crossed the floor, and extended a hand. "I appreciate your help."

The men shook and moved to the front door for fresh air.

The newcomer said, "Glad I could." He patted the Greener, which he'd tugged free of the shredded satchel. "Me and Lil' Miss Mess Maker, that is. We been tracking these boys a while."

"Are you a bounty man?" said Nosey, shuffling over to the two men by the front door.

"Naw, I'm me. I pick up wanted dodgers now and again. Figure I'm out on the road flipping over rocks anyway, might as well make money when I can while I'm at it."

"And by *me*, who might you be?" said Nosey.

The black man looked at Rollie. "He always like this?"

Rollie nodded. "Unfortunately." He walked back behind the bar, set up three shot glasses, and filled them with whiskey. They each downed a silent shot, then Rollie filled the glasses once more and raised his. "My thanks to you both."

They sipped that round.

The newcomer said, "My name is Jubal Tennyson. Most everybody calls me Pops." He looked over at the two dead men. "Like I say, I been trailing these two for a spell now. Been trying to figure a way to get them to a lawman alive."

"Nothing for them if they're dead, then," said Rollie.

Pops nodded and chuckled. "Useless when they were alive, same now that they're dead."

"Sorry about that."

"Naw, saved you and this one, didn't we? That's enough. Except now I got a big ol' hole in my bag and I believe I have ruined my clean shirt, too."

Rollie nodded. "I'll gladly pay you for them. I'm . . . Finnegan, by the way."

"Uh-huh. Good to meet you."

"You don't seem surprised," said Rollie. "Have we met?"

In response, Pops bent low, pipe clamped between his teeth, and rummaged in the pockets of the twin Rollie shot. He found nothing, and repeated the same on the one he shot. He reached under the fat man's backside and tugged something from the dead man's back pocket. It was a few pages of a folded-up newspaper. He chuckled as he unfolded them, walked over to the bar, smoothed them out on the bar top, and tapped on a crudely circled quarter-page notice.

Rollie and Nosey, wincing as he pulled on his wire-rimmed spectacles, leaned in to read the paper. The top of the page showed it was from Denver City.

Nosey read the first few lines. "Former Pinkerton Agent Rollie 'Stoneface' Finnegan is alive and well and living in the Boar Gulch Mine Camp, Sawtooth Range, Idaho Territory. He welcomes old friends to stop in at his bar for a drink and a chat about old times."

Rollie sighed.

"Ha!" said Nosey, looking at Rollie. "That's you! I knew there was something about you! You're . . . well, you're famous!"

"We all got something about us boy," said Pops. "Don't mean we deserve to be run aground by pigs."

"Yes, but . . . he's Stoneface Finnegan! What a life he's . . ." He turned to Rollie. "I mean what a life you've led. Think of all those folks in your past, now seeking vengeance."

Rollie sighed again.

"Could be worse," said Pops. "Could be a price on your head."

"From the looks of this ad, there might as well be," said Rollie.

Nosey nodded. "Especially given the number of corrupt politicians and tycoons who lost face and money over the years because of you, Stoneface, I mean, Mr. Finnegan."

"Thanks for reminding me, Nosey."

"Not at all," said the young man, retrieving his notebook. He licked the end of his pencil and began jotting in earnest.

"How did you know," said Rollie to Pops.

"I can read. And I heard those two fools yammering about you by their campfire not long ago. Should have dealt with them then. Wasn't sure I could have, though. So I followed them to here. I take it you didn't have dealings with them in your . . . past life?"

Rollie shook his head, regarded the ad, then the dead men.

"If two such as these can make it up here," said Pops, "makes a fella wonder who else might be coming. And why."

"What do you mean?" said Rollie.

"I bet good money someone's offering bad money . . . for your head, Mr. Rollie 'Stoneface' Finnegan."

Rollie grunted and sighed. "I have to get these two out of here. I can't take the stink much longer." He bent to grab up the nearest Dickey twin's fat wrist, and Pops grabbed the other.

"You don't have to do that."

"I know," said Pops, tugging on the arm. "But neither of us can do it alone." He chuckled, and together they dragged the dead man toward the front door.

Nosey wadded bits of torn rag up his swelling nostrils and set to work sopping up the blood with rags and a bucket of water. The crowd in the road out front had migrated toward the door and they peeked in, though none offered to lend a hand in cleaning up.

"You gonna open today or what?" said the hawk-faced, bald man Rollie only knew as "Bone."

Rollie looked him up and down. "If I can get these two hauled up to the hill and buried, yeah."

The gaunt man jerked a thumb toward his equally gaunt son. "Me and him'll do that for . . . a dollar apiece."

Rollie nodded. "Okay. But bury them together. They were brothers, after all. And deep. We don't need to see them again. When you're done, come on back for a couple of beers on the house."

"Okay," said the thin man, rubbing his big-knuckled hands together as if he'd struck a prime deal. "Come on, boy."

Rollie shooed everyone off the porch and shut the saloon door. For the next half hour, Rollie, Pops, and Nosey scrubbed the inside of the bar, straightened up-ended tables, cobbled snapped chairs, and listened to Pops whistle. When they were done, Rollie drew three beers and passed them around. "Once again, I thank you men."

He received nods in reply from Pops and Nosey as they all sipped after the thirsty work. Rollie smacked his lips and said, "Normally I don't trust a man in a bowler."

Pops' eyebrows rose for the first time that day. "That's a foolish generalization. That's like me saying people who wear fancy sculpted mustaches should be put on an island somewhere where they can't hurt anybody."

"Ha," said Rollie, hiding a grin behind his beer glass.

"Ha what?" said Pops.

"You said people."

"That's right I did. You would've, too, if you'd seen some of the women I've seen in my travels. You'd swear they were men, the hairy faces they were sporting."

"Where have you traveled?" said Rollie.

"Why?"

"Because," said Rollie. "I don't want to ever go there."

Pops offered up a full-bellied chuckle.

"That's quite a weapon you carry."

"Oh, you mean the Greener? I told you, I call her Lil' Miss Mess Maker, for obvious reasons. I took her off a dead man who wasn't looking. Found the barrels to be adequate for my style of fracas—that is to say, up close and personal. Anything long distance and you are crawling into coward territory."

Rollie nodded and squinted, deep in thought. Finally he said, "Look, I am not a man to take it lightly when another man steps in to help me at his own peril. I can't offer either of you much, yet. But I could use help with this place."

"You offering a job?" said Pops, already shaking his head. "I appreciate it, but I got places to get to, things to find out."

"And I already work here," said Nosey, adjusting the bloody rags trailing from his nose.

"No, not jobs exactly. I'm offering shares in this business. As I said, I can't offer much in the way of money for what you both did today, nor would I want to insult you, but how about becoming partners in the saloon. Not equal, of course, but junior partners, I think it's called."

Pops set his beer down on the bar top. "In case you hadn't noticed, I am not a white man. Fact is, I was born a slave. And now here you are, a white man who wants me to be a partner in his business?"

Rollie nodded. "I could use the help, and you'd be building up a stake for yourself."

"All I did was what any man would have done."

Rollie jerked his chin toward the front door. "None of them did."

"Okay, then," said Pops, nodding. He stuck out his hand and the men shook for the second time that day.

Rollie said, "We can work out the details later. The only thing I ask is if you want to move on, I buy you out. This isn't a transferable stake."

Pops nodded. "That works for me."

Rollie looked at Nosey. "Same goes for you, Nosey."

"Oh, I thank you kindly, Mr. Finnegan. But I will decline, though not without regret. I am not someone you could rely on, as I don't know how much longer I'll be with you, to be honest."

Pops and Rollie both looked at him. "No, no, I don't mean I'm dying or anything as morbid as that." He sighed. "Okay, then. I'll tell you why. Though, as with Mr. Finnegan, I ask your discretion in sharing it in the future."

Both men nodded.

"Good," said Nosey. "I am a journalist by trade and training. From that mighty East Coast bastion of bold living, Boston, Massachusetts. I am, as you say, on the run from a certain tycoon, a powerful political man whose name is not important right now. I'd exposed his true nature a number of times. Pilloried him in print, in fact." Nosey smiled at the memory. His nasally voice sounded to the others as if he were on the verge of a sneeze.

"I have also accrued a substantial amount of gambling debts in the form of markers that filled my pocket on my way west. It is my intention to return to Boston one day. In the meantime, I plan to track down the big names of the day—Hickok, Cody, Earp, Masterson, and yes"—he nodded at Rollie—"the infamous Stoneface Finnegan."

"Why?" said Rollie, his curiosity overriding his annoyance at that pet name he'd been given long ago and had never been able to shed.

"Why? Why, to write about them—and you—of course! The public wants to know more about such men who are, as we speak, carving a wide path throughout the untamed wildlands of the boundless West!"

"You mean them dime novels," said Pops, lighting his pipe. He shook out the kitchen match and stuffed it into the front pocket of his bib overalls.

"Precisely," said Nosey, nodding.

"No, absolutely not," said Rollie. "I do not want to be written about at all. *Ever.* By you or anyone."

Nosey frowned. "But—"

"No. While I am not cowardly enough to have changed my name before I moved here, I don't go out of my way to talk about myself with folks I meet. Somehow"—he pulled out the folded-up newspaper clipping he'd stuffed into his shirt pocket—"someone has figured out where I am and he's invited every unsavory character from my past here to brace me. My plate is full enough, Nosey, without having a pack of foolish lies in the form of a dime novel heaped on top. Have I made myself clear?"

Nosey nodded. "As water. Oh, Pops?"

"Yeah?"

Nosey nodded toward his new acquaintance and patted himself on the chest. "You appear to be on fire."

Pops looked down. Smoke curled up from his front pocket. "Oh." He repeated Nosey's move, vigorously patting himself on the chest.

"I take it from the burn holes and scorch marks that setting yourself on fire is a habit?"

"Yep," said Pops, looking uninterested in the affair.

A hard knock rattled the door. "It's Mayor Wheeler, Rollie. You opening up today? We have a town brimming with thirsty folks out here."

Rollie nodded and Nosey opened the door. Pops busied himself with repairing a table leg with splints and twine wrapping. The place filled, and Rollie and Nosey kept busy filling glasses and taking coins. Neither said much about the attack, and Pops said even less. Yet an amusing, skewed version of the truth took shape in the blathering conversations going on in the saloon.

The mayor planted himself at the end of the bar, between Pops, busy with the table leg, and Rollie, washing glasses. "What about the supply run tomorrow?" said the mayor.

"What about it?" said Rollie.

"Well, will you be able to make it? I see Nosey, but who knows if he'll show up tomorrow."

"As it happens, Chauncey, I won't be making that run. But I'd like to introduce you to my new partner, Jubal Tennyson."

"Call me Pops." He stuck out his hand.

The mayor did not shake. "You trust this man?" he said to Rollie, looking Pops up and down, nostrils flaring as if he detected an odor.

"With my life," said Rollie.

The fat little mayor turned from Pops. "You can't be thinking of sending him to make the run with . . . with our goods. With my goods!"

"Can you drive a team?" said Rollie to Pops.

Pops puffed his pipe and rocked on his heels, eyes half-lidded as if in deep thought. "I can drive a nail, I can drive a hard bargain, I can drive the Rebs out of my business, and the devil out of a self-righteous sinner. I expect I can drive a team."

"I don't know," said Chauncey. "This isn't what I had in mind when you and I came to our agreement. Not what I had in mind at all."

Rollie shrugged. "Not a problem. Pops can make the run with my wagon."

"But that's not big enough."

"Big enough for my booze."

The mayor brooded for a few moments more, nibbling his fleshy lips. "Oh, all right. But I keep a close eye on my inventory, do you understand me?" He directed this at Pops, who chuckled.

"Better than you think I do, I expect."

Wolfbait walked in and up to the bar. He looked Nosey up and down. "You mean you been here the whole time? I been all over and back again searching for you. Least you can do is tell a man where you're not at so he don't have to waste his time looking there. Am I right?" He looked at Rollie. "Well, ain't I?"

Rollie nodded. "Makes sense to me, Wolfbait."

"You bet it does," he said. "I am wore out and thirstier than a madman walking in the desert."

Rollie poured the man a glass of beer. "Wolfbait, I'd like you to meet your new freighting partner for tomorrow."

Pops held out his hand and smiled. "Pops."

"Well," said Wolfbait, shaking the outstretched hand. "I am pleased to know you. Now I don't have to spend the day riding with him," he gestured with his head toward

Rollie, then leaned toward Pops. "Man talks less than a rock, I swear it. No respect for the fine art of conversation. Now, I hope you ain't that way, because we got a whole lot of ground to cover, so we might as well fill the air with words, don't you think?"

Pops nodded. With narrowed eyes he looked over Wolfbait's grimy hat toward Rollie, with narrowed eyes. "Nothing I like better than a good chinwag, as the man calls it."

CHAPTER THIRTEEN

Early the next morning, Pops and Wolfbait rigged up the team. True to his word, the old bearded man began chattering as soon as they rolled away from the stable behind the mercantile. Rollie walked back to the saloon and cooked up his own breakfast on the little woodstove on the south wall. He'd already made a feed for Pops, who'd spent the night out on the floor behind the bar.

Rollie figured he'd spend time that morning rigging up a bed for Pops in the back room along the north wall. Plenty of room for the two of them back there, especially considering Pops had even less luggage than Rollie. Somehow he had complete faith in this mysterious newcomer. It was something about the way the man carried himself, assured and calm, and cracking wise even in the middle of a skirmish.

The one he was surprised with had been Nosey. The young man didn't appear to have all that much. And if his story was true, why lay low for these several months in Boar Gulch, of all places? As quickly as he presented himself with that thought, Rollie knew he'd answered it. *To lay low.* Had to be. Isn't that why he was there?

His thoughts turned back over and over to the newspaper clipping. He'd already memorized the brief notice. How could someone have known where he was? He didn't have enough of the paper to know the date, but he'd told no one where he was headed. In fact, the only thing he hadn't done was go by a different name. He'd been cautious to only use his name when he needed to. Most folks in Boar Gulch knew him as "Finn." The only one he'd used his full name with had been . . . Chauncey Wheeler, the mayor. When he'd signed the paperwork transferring ownership of the bar.

From his first day in town, Rollie had had his suspicions about the self-titled mayor. Though he regarded the man as oily, he hadn't thought Wheeler would divulge his name to others. Besides, who else was there to tell? Recalling that Chauncey had been down to Bella Springs in the valley at least twice since selling the saloon, it was possible he'd divulged too much about recent doings in Boar Gulch.

The man needed questioning. But first, if Rollie's location was known and if he was going to deal with more folks such as the Dickey twins, trying to cash in on a bounty on his head, he'd feel a whole lot better if he looked the part of the man they would all come to town looking for.

He pulled out his razor, his strop, a small, clouded hand mirror, and his shaving soap and brush.

By God, he'd give them the Stoneface Finnegan they all expected to find.

CHAPTER FOURTEEN

The coolness of fresh air on his newly shaved cheeks and chin was a daylong surprise to Rollie, so much so that he occasionally rubbed a hand over them as if to remind himself the beard was indeed gone. He thought he'd looked all right in it, but now that he was back to his lightly waxed and curled mustache, it seemed he'd finally gotten over the attack in the alley. No longer did he feel, as he had throughout the months since the attack, that he'd been riding a riled mustang he couldn't break.

It had thrown him a few times, piled him into the rails more than once, but odd as trekking to and then settling in Boar Gulch had been, for the first time since he'd arrived, Rollie felt like it was the best decision he'd made in many years. Maybe it had been the only real choice.

He didn't mind giving over to trailing threads that led deeper into thoughts, but today he was content to enjoy the notion that he was well and truly back. As close as he was likely to be, anyway.

He ran his fingers over the repair job Pops had done on the table leg—impressive given the lack of materials at hand—and felt pretty good about his offer to the man to make him a junior partner. If not jumping up and down with excitement, he could tell Pops had been surprised by the offer. Even better because it had been heartfelt.

Rollie needed help, and without money he had little to offer a man with Pop's estimable talents. That notice in the newspaper told Rollie he was going to need more than help with running the bar.

At that moment, a shadow emerged, angled in through the doorway and followed by the person who made it. Rollie's hand sliced down to palm the grip of his revolver. Even backlit by the sun, Rollie could see it was a woman. Lugging a carpetbag and squinting a little at the darker interior, she stepped into the bar.

Rollie walked from behind the bar. "Here," he said, "let me help you with that bag. Come on in."

From behind her in the doorway, Big Swede's voice rumbled. "Don't mind if I do." He chuckled and followed the woman inside. Two more men, smaller than Swede but no less offensive in smell and sight and demeanor, trailed in behind him like hopeful ducklings after their mama.

"Gents," said Rollie, turning his attention back to the woman. "Don't crowd the lady."

They paid him no mind.

"It's all right," she said, unwrapping a scarf she had draped over her hair and tied beneath her chin. Her hair was long, pinned loose atop her head in thick swirls. "They kindly gave me a ride up the last bit of road to here." She regarded Rollie from three or four feet away. Her brow furrowed as if trying to place him, or as if making a decision about him.

For a brief moment, Rollie felt fixed to the spot like a butterfly pinned to a board. Then he broke the spell and smiled. "Can I get you something to drink? I don't have much in the way of food, but I do have some bread and decent cheese. Coffee, how about coffee?"

"That sounds fine. Thank you."

She arranged her hair and smoothed her coat. Rollie could tell she wasn't wealthy, but it appeared she'd preserved what she had. The coat was older and mended, but by someone who took care to match the cloth and sew patches on with tiny, precise stitches.

"Ain't you gonna ask us what we want, Finny?"

Rollie looked at the three men. "Seems like you ought to be working those claims of yours, it being daylight. Unless I'm wrong and they've proved up beyond your wildest dreams."

"Don't you go mocking me, barkeep. And don't go telling me what I should be doing, you hear?"

Rollie eyed the man in silence until Swede dropped his eyes. Rollie poured three beers. While he was doing that, Swede and his two cohorts surrounded the standing woman.

"Come on, woman. We give you a ride and all. I'm about to offer you another one." He grinned at his friends, who made low, grunting animal noises. "You know you need what I got."

The woman looked up at him. "The crotch itch? Nope, got that already. About the only thing with any worth my husband left me. Worth more than the claim, I reckon."

Big Swede shrugged. "That don't matter to me none, lady." He stepped in close, brushing his ample belly against her breasts. "I got that already. And the drip, too.

Plus I got this sore that won't heal. I even have a lousy claim, too!" He thought this was worth braying over.

She was staring up at the man crowding her, and didn't seem intimidated by the big idiot in the least.

"That's enough, Swede. Looks to me like the lady's not interested in your proposal." Rollie watched the big man's cheek muscles bunch like a flexed arm. Something changed and Big Swede's leer melted. A grunt rose up from his throat and he shoved his two pals aside to get to the beer.

Rollie took over the woman's coffee and set it down on the table top beside her. "Bread and cheese coming up," he said.

And that's when Swede's big meaty fist drove into the side of Rollie's head. The blow dropped the barkeep to one knee, and his head whipped to the side. He saw stars and felt hot pain, as if fireworks were going off inside his skull.

Rollie kept low and drove upward with both fists clenched tight together. The battering ram caught Swede under his big, bony, hard chin. It would be too much to hope the man would tuck tail and scamper home to his run-down log shanty a half mile away along the northeast road. His two dumb friends stared at the unfolding fight and backed away.

So much for friends, he thought.

Rollie stood fast, pushing up from the floor and using his momentum to land another solid blow angled inward at Swede's temple. It worked. The big man grunted, and a thin, whining sound whistled through his nose as he dropped to his knees, then flopped to his side.

"You two," said Rollie to the underlings. "Drag him out of here. I don't want to see any of you for at least a week."

The woman didn't look at Rollie. He wasn't looking for thanks, but it seemed odd that she didn't thank him for getting rid of Big Swede.

He walked back to the bar and she said, "I'm Delia. Delia Fitzsimmons." She extended her hand.

He took it and shook. "Folks call me Finn."

"Nice to make your acquaintance."

"So, you have a claim."

She nodded.

"Well, that's good. Talk is that the hills hereabouts are promising." He chuckled as he dried an already dry mug. "In fact, to hear the miners tell it, we're all standing on a mountain of pure gold. The soil's the only thing between us and a vast fortune."

"That doesn't sound so bad," she said.

Rollie looked up to find her once again studying him as if she knew him somehow. He was certain he'd never met her before. But that didn't mean he wouldn't welcome getting to know her. She was the prettiest woman he'd seen in a long time. Certainly since leaving Denver City, which, he knew, didn't mean all that much. Camp Sal was about the only woman he'd seen in all that time.

He was about to do yet another thing on this fine day that was out of character for him. He had a sudden idea and told himself he was going to act on it. *A picnic.* He'd ask her to accompany him on a picnic.

As soon as he opened his mouth to suggest it, she stood and said, "How much do I owe you for the refreshments? And for your chivalry?"

"Oh, no, that's nothing. Welcome to Boar Gulch." *I'm an idiot,* Rollie told himself.

"Well, thank you once again, Mr. Finn. I must get going. I'm renting a room from a Chauncey Wheeler. Could I trouble you for directions?"

"Oh, right, Yes, that'd be Wheeler's Mercantile. He has a shack out back he lets out to miners until they get their cabins built." Out on the porch, he pointed to the store. "Can't miss the mercantile. It's the only one in Boar Gulch."

She turned to face him, giving him that same odd stare. Maybe he thought he saw something of eagerness, hopefulness, admiration in her eyes. *Ask her,* he told himself. *Ask her to go on a picnic . . .*

"Good-bye for now, Mr. Finn. I appreciate your hospitality."

Rollie watched her walk down the main street of Boar Gulch, then sighed and tidied the bar for the second time that day. *Idiot,* he thought. *I am a top-grade idiot.*

Hours later, Pops and Wolfbait clanked, squawked, and rumbled into town with the week's shipment of supplies. At the mercantile they unloaded everything that Chauncey had ordered then proceeded on down to the saloon. Pops grabbed a wooden crate of full bottles and caught Rollie spiffing his mustache in the mirror behind the bar.

"Pardon me, young man," said Pops, setting the crate down on the bar. "You seen a cranky old guy with a beard, oh, about your height?"

Rollie couldn't help offering a quick grin. He shrugged and headed for the door to help unload. "Now that I'm in the news, might as well give up any pretense of laying low."

Wolfbait appeared in the doorway. "You two want to give me a hand unloading these crates, or are you going to yammer the day away up there like a couple of old hens? Don't know how I got roped into this anyway. I'm too old and mean to go bouncing around the mountains on the plank seat of a buckboard. I've sat on rocks softer than this!"

"Not my wagon," said Rollie. "Bring it up with the mayor."

"The mayor," said Wolfbait as if he'd tasted something foul and couldn't get the flavor off his tongue. "In his own head, anyway." He swung a crate over the edge of the wagon for Rollie to grab. "Say, Nosey was right. You look better without the beard. Course, he was wrong about me." Wolfbait fluffed his own long, food-speckled beard. "The ladies like what I have growing here."

"What? Mushrooms?" Pops winked at Rollie, and they both rolled their eyes as Wolfbait launched into a fresh tirade of choice words directed at the two of them.

"I can't recall ever being called a *young whelp*. You?" said Pops.

"Nah. The trip okay? No troubles?"

"No," said Pops. "Nothing odd. Only folks we saw were two, three down at the depot. Course, they all looked at me like I was about to rob them blind. Wolfbait had to reassure them I was a good boy."

"I'm sorry to hear that."

"Not a worry. I'm used to it," said Pops.

"I mean that you had to be defended by Wolfbait." It was Rollie's turn to wink at Pops.

Nosey walked in, carrying only his notebook and writing in it as if daylight were about to pinch out any second. Half-moon smudges of rosy-gray and purple were lined beneath his eyes, and his broken nose was swollen worse than the day before. Rollie suspected the man had set it himself. That took some doing.

Rollie had been down that particular path a few years back after a boisterous apprehension of a drunk embezzler who'd landed a lucky punch to Rollie's face. He'd rapped the man on his bald bean a few extra times for good measure.

An hour or so later, with the addition of a couple of quiet, early-afternoon drinkers staring moodily at their emptying glasses, the near silence was broken by Wolfbait. "Shh! Shush, I tell ya. Everybody hush!"

The other patrons and the three barmen quieted down and stared at the old man.

Wolfbait looked around. "You hear that?"

After a few moments, Pops said, "I don't hear anything."

Then silence again.

"There!" Wolfbait said, pointing toward the bar. "It's coming from over there." As if he were an old bloodhound following a thin scent, he got up and sniffed his way around behind the bar and right over to Rollie. He put an ear to Rollie's chest. "It's inside you, mister!"

They all crowded around. Rollie backed away from the old man. "All right, all right. That's enough. Who needs a refill?"

Nosey regarded Rollie a moment with narrowed eyes, then said, "You should get that looked at."

"Why? Then I'd sound like everybody else."

"Man has a point," said Pops, chuckling. "Good thing his hat covers it."

Though red-faced, even Rollie joined in the laughter.

CHAPTER FIFTEEN

Rollie didn't see the buxom blond woman again for a full day. By that time he had chided himself a couple of times for using up any pretenses he could think of to look up and down the road for sign of her. He'd seen her once out front of the mercantile, laughing at something Chauncey had said to her.

Before that, the mayor had not given Rollie many reasons to trust him, let alone like him, but it rankled to see the mayor charming her. Even though Rollie had received little from her in the way of encouragement, amorous or otherwise, there was something about her that intrigued him.

The analytical part of him wanted to know why he felt this way. What was it about her, apart from her obvious charms—that long hair the color of turning aspen leaves, the full bosom and slender hips beneath her tidy, obviously older but maintained dress. He'd caught her eyeing him, not in a lusty sort of way, but as if assessing him. That part intrigued him.

"Mop water."

Rollie turned to see Pops, aproned and squinting at

him, holding a tall tin bucket brimming with brown water. "The mop bucket. Where you want it dumped?"

"Oh, I . . . ah, out back."

"Uh-huh. Why don't you go talk to the woman? Then maybe you'll be worth something."

Rollie gave Pops his best Stoneface stare and walked in the opposite direction. He hadn't gone far before wishing he had his cane. He needed it now and again, but he'd be damned if he was going to gimp around town in front of that woman.

Later that day, Rollie and Pops were alone in the bar, except for Wolfbait, who had become even more of a fixture seated at the bar than usual. Rollie didn't mind, and kept him in beer or coffee, depending on Wolfbait's preferences. The old man had proved useful in accompanying Pops on the weekly supply run. Pops said the old-timer was a dab hand at driving the team, so they'd switched off now and again, with Pops covering them with Lil' Miss Mess Maker.

Delia Fitzsimmons appeared in the open doorway. "Knock knock."

"Come on in," said Rollie. "Care for a cup of coffee?"

"Sounds good."

He poured one for her and one for himself. Pops found yet another chair that looked to be on the edge of falling apart, retired to a far corner of the room, and set to work fixing it. Wolfbait wandered over with his own cup of coffee to lend a hand.

"So, Miss Fitzsimmons," said Rollie, leaning on the bar. "How do you like Boar Gulch so far?"

She looked right in his eyes and her smile slid away. With it went any vestige of warmth in her blue eyes. "I hate this foul little lice-infested rat hole. I'm here for one reason, but it's a good one. And that alone makes it worth enduring this place." She made no attempt to keep her words quiet. If anything, she spoke them loud enough for Pops and Wolfbait to hear.

Rollie stood up. "Oh, well, I'm sorry to hear that, Miss Fitzsimmons."

"Aren't you curious to know why I'm here?"

"You mentioned a claim your husband left you."

"Ha!" she smacked the bar top with a palm. "There's no claim and there's no husband. Might have been at one time. But not now. Not ever. Here's a clue. My name is not Delia Fitzsimmons, you idiot. It's Delia Holsapple." She stared hard at Rollie, urging him to recall that name.

He did, and stepped back a pace, hands by his sides.

"What? Going to kill me, too?" she said. "Glad to see you remember the name, though. You recall my father, don't you?"

"Roger Holsapple," said Rollie, returning her hard stare.

"Yep, the one and only. My dear daddy, the man you killed."

"He was an embezzler." Rollie remembered the case as well as he did any of them. Maybe more so. But this girl, she couldn't have been more than . . .

She was nodding. "You remember me now, don't you, you randy old goat?" Again she swatted the bar top. "I was a teenage girl, sure, but not too young to lose everything, eh, Stoneface?"

Rollie remembered the trial. It hadn't been anything too extraordinary. The man was father to a large brood, and as unlikely seeming as anyone to commit a crime. But Rollie had learned years before that there was no particular look of innocence or guilt, just as there was no black or white in the world. Everything in life was a shade of gray. Good and evil; dark, light; right, wrong. Didn't matter. Nothing was all one or all the other.

Holsapple had been a trusted clerk, and he had a large family. Too large to feed and clothe properly on his modest weekly takings, apparently. So he'd begun to supplement the paycheck with a little bit of cash here and there from his employers' books. No one need ever know, no one need ever find out. But someone did know. Someone did find out.

The harpy of a wife of one of the partners for years had quietly double-checked the company books on a monthly basis. She trusted no one. Rollie always felt a bit bad for her husband. Slope-shouldered, he walked about the firm from waking to sleep as though he wore a weighted ox yoke.

It was she who'd suspected Holsapple, but could not prove it. Pinkerton had been contacted and had sent Rollie in as an undercover clerk. That had been a stretch, as such positions usually went to younger men. But he'd been taken in and had, over the course of a month, discovered firsthand the crimes and the techniques Holsapple had used to commit them. He was a creative numbers worker, Rollie had given him that much.

The entire thing was expected to be open and shut, and was. Rollie's testimony had once more nailed the lid closed on the prosecution's case. Holsapple was given a five-year prison sentence. He'd wept like a shivering babe in the courtroom, and Rollie had silently wished the man would be more of a man, take the punishment society deemed suitable for his crimes. But it didn't work out that way.

Within days, Rollie had gotten word that the meek clerk and father of six had sliced open his wrists and bled out in his holding cell rather than endure his lengthy prison sentence. Sad and spineless, Rollie had thought then and still felt that way, leaving his large family to carry on without him.

And the oldest of the children, Delia, was in Boar Gulch, telling him . . . what? "Why are you here, Delia?" Rollie's eyes narrowed and he felt his heartbeat speed up.

"For a man who is regarded as being what the old-timers call *some smart,* you really are a dullard, aren't you? Why, I'm here for you, Stoneface Finnegan!" She reached out and playfully touched the bar near his coffee cup.

Rollie stared at her, an unbidden sneer pulling his mustache downward.

"Let me catch you up on what's happened to my family. Or as I like to call us, your victims. Let's start with me, okay? We all know that my father held a respectable position."

"He was an embezzler who got caught, Delia. Case closed."

"Oh shut up! Now where was I? Oh yes, you see," she shifted on her bar stool and smiled over at Pops and Wolfbait.

The old man had dropped any pretense of helping Pops and was watching the girl as if he were in the front row at a stage play. Pops, on the other hand, was working on the chair leg, quietly puffing on his corncob pipe, but Rollie knew the man was hearing every word. He also knew from the way Pops had seated himself that he could be counted on in the speed of a finger snap to break out the little hideout gun he wore under the bib of his coveralls.

"My life was about perfect, and it was set to become even more perfect a week before Daddy's trial. But of course, there was Percy, my disgustingly wealthy fiancé, did I mention I was engaged to marry Percy Tibbs, of the Tibbs Brewery family? Yes, it was all set to happen. We were to be wed at the family estate in Bentonville. There was going to be an orchestra and hundreds and hundreds of white doves and a children's choir and . . ."

As she waxed on about the wonders of the wedding that never took place, something clicked in Rollie's mind and he somehow knew for certain what he'd only guessed at moments before. She was the one who had placed the notice in the newspaper.

"Are you listening to me, Stoneface? Good, because I am far from through. So you see, dear, sweet, charming, wealthy Percy Tibbs dropped me from his life when he found out my father was branded a criminal. I bet it was his mother, Martha-Louise Tibbs, a more spiteful prude you'll never find." She sighed. "Then my mother, poor, desperate, weak Grace Holsapple.

"She never was much in the way of strength. Father liked to say she had the core of an oak, but I think he only said that because it made her smile at him with her bedroom look. They spent far too much time in that room, I can tell you. Before the trial she was a wreck, during it, she was a weepy mess, and then Father killed himself in desperation and she took to laudanum like a duck to water, and in short order became a true drugged fiend, useless for anything save drooling on herself and glugging more laudanum."

Delia glared at Rollie, her cheek muscles bunching. "I did my best to tend the little ones, as I always had, but I also had to earn money. Let me tell you something, Stoneface Finnegan, if you are a young woman with five mouths to feed, clawing and dragging at you all hours a day, the whimpers and sobs from the poor little wretches asking for food, for warmth, why, you will do the only thing you can do to earn money."

She raised an eyebrow. "And no, it's not sewing hems at a dress shop. I tried that and all it did was give me bloody fingertips and bad eyesight and precious little pay. It was piecework. No, you do the one thing pretty young women the world over have done since time began. To earn money you sell yourself all night long. And during the day, you tend to your laudanum fiend of a mother and her whimpering brood."

Only then did her features falter. Her bottom lip quivered. "Still, it wasn't enough, and soon my mother's habit got the better of her. We buried her at the poor farm, not with my father, because that wasn't allowed. The state took his body away, and I don't know where he lies for all eternity. Despite my efforts, my waifish siblings became scattered/ Taken away, they drifted from me like chaff from the stalk in a hard breeze."

Rollie wanted to say something, even though her weepy story didn't bother him at all, but she plowed on ahead.

"The one bright spot in all this was learning I was good at something besides being a money earner for children. Without my mother and the children to tend to, I was able to sleep during the days and get food to eat. I worked for a woman who made certain I made money. She took her cut, to be sure, but I made enough to do the one thing I needed to do. And do you know what that is, Mr. Stoneface Finnegan?"

He shook his head, certain she was going to tell him. He was also not inclined to think this conversation was going to end well.

"No? I'll tell you then. I made enough money to do lots of things, things I felt needed doing. One of them, I will admit now, was a premature mistake. Like hiring a man to . . . well, almost a mistake. Oh, but you see, I am talking in riddles aren't I? I kept a close eye on you, sir. And I was so disheartened to hear you were laid low in Denver City. And then I was so happy to hear you had not died from that sad episode in that alleyway. So relieved. Not as much as you, ha, but I was pretty happy, mister. Yes, I was."

She said this in a singsong way, and it annoyed Rollie almost as much as seeing her sitting in his saloon. Almost.

"But I kept abreast of your situation while you were healing. I had friends, if you can call people you pay for information friends. Maybe they are ticks, leeches, but I had them report to me with progress of your convalescence. Do you remember Nurse Cherborn? The one you called *the major* because she was so strict? I don't blame you, really. Between you and me, I wouldn't have wanted her for a nurse. She was frightening to look at. She even had a mustache. Nothing to rival yours, but on a woman it was something to see. She told me something curious. She told me how you had begun asking for the newspapers, how you would circle with a pencil every single mention of a new gold camp called Boar Gulch. Coincidence? I think not. My father may or may not have embezzled money, Mr. Stoneface Finnegan—and yes I see now how you earned that name, staring at me, not saying a thing, but oh, if your eyes were weapons, mister, I'd be dead right now."

Yes, thought Rollie. *You bet.*

"Where was I?" she said.

"You was telling about that ugly nurse and Boar Gulch and all," said Wolfbait, who was apparently enjoying what he was hearing.

Rollie thought maybe the man was smiling. Pops nudged the older man with a boot. Wolfbait caught his eye and looked down as if he'd been caught peeking into a window. Rollie hated to admit it to himself, but he wanted to know how she found out where he was.

Delia Holsapple laughed. "That's right. I put my mind to work and got to thinking, and while I was doing that I also learned that you, Mr. Stoneface Finnegan, had been let go by the only employer stupid enough to hire you, the Pinkerton Detective Agency. Yes, I did learn that much. And then do you know what I did? I came up with an idea. I figured if you were now a free man, though nearly dead, and with no job, you might want to make some money and quick, or else you'd end up as a swamper in a runty little saloon somewhere.

"Oh, pardon. I see you have aspired to that very position. But where, oh where would you go? And then it came to me. Why the very place you'd been so interested in finding out more about in the newspapers. Boar Gulch, of course. What does all this have to do with anything? Well, you see, I saved all the money I'd made working at night, Mr. Stoneface Finnegan."

If she thought such talk would shame him, she was mistaken. Pity wasn't even in his mind.

"And do you know what I did with it? Well, back in Denver City I hired somebody to kill you, for one thing, but when that didn't work, and you lived, I said to myself, 'Delia,' because I always call myself Delia. 'Delia, you need to look on his survival as a gift! You have the chance to savor his long, slow comeuppance for a long, long, long time to come.'" She giggled and it almost sounded genuine to Rollie. Almost.

"And do you know how I plan on doing that? Why, a few months back, with all that money I saved, I took out notices, advertisements of all size and shape in every major newspaper in the West. And I explained how you were relocating yourself to Boar Gulch and how you would simply love to have the company of all those people whose lives you ruined for all those long years you worked as a Pinkerton Detective. Why, after such a long, illustrious career, I expect you'll be ass-deep in outlaws for years to come! Unless one of them holds a grudge, that is. Then all bets are off, as they say. I don't gamble much, by the way. But when I do, I go for the sure thing."

She slid off the stool and walked to the door. "Oh, Mr. Stoneface Finnegan, thanks for listening. It's been a long time and I am glad to finally get all that off my chest. And thanks for the coffee. It's been nice catching up with you. I'll be around, though. You see, you ruined my life, Mr. Stoneface Finnegan, and I must do no less to you. Oh, all this excitement is going to be so much fun to watch."

Rollie listened to her boots clunk the boardwalk out front, then down the steps, and the softer sound of her footfalls as she walked up the street. Something inside him that he used to have—a rod of iron that kept him stern, straight, and lean but had been missing since the alley attack—was back. He felt its presence as surely as if someone had driven it into him with a hammer through his head.

He needed to think.

He didn't doubt anything she'd told him. She may have exaggerated here and there, about the glories of her wedding that never was, for instance. Because it made sense for it to be so, he knew that she had been behind the attack in the alley.

She had hired someone to kill him. That alone made her a criminal. But he had no proof. She hadn't really said that's what she did, had she? Even if she had, what good were the testimonies of Pops and Wolfbait? In a court of law, neither would be considered a qualified witness.

He could not touch her. And she knew it. He couldn't touch her legally, anyway. But then again, he knew he wouldn't do anything to her that was illegal. No matter how much he hated her. And he didn't think that hatred would do anything but grow. She knew that, too. She was a clever one, was Miss Delia Holsapple.

But then again, so was he.

CHAPTER SIXTEEN

Boar Gulch was doing exactly what Rollie hoped it would—attracting more people each day. Squawks and squeals harkened their arrivals, their wagons' axles screeching for grease as they rolled into town from each end, the rough route he'd taken months before could only have become a more rutted, nearly impassable mess with each gully washer of a storm that passed through. They seemed to have had more than their share of rainstorms this season. Considering he didn't have much to compare it with, Rollie shrugged and lived with it.

Yes sir, it all seemed to be working in his favor. But if all those newcomers meant money, then why wasn't he happier? Why was Rollie Finnegan annoyed with himself? He knew the answer, even before the question rattled itself into being in his skull. That foul, whining woman, Delia Holsapple. The notion of blaming others for one's problems in life had never set right with Rollie. He'd had plenty of setbacks and thumpings over the years, but he knew he was to blame for them. Or at least to blame for not getting a leg up and over them in due course. But that

Holsapple woman nurtured her self-pity and revenge as if it were a precious child.

The way he looked at it, he could tuck tail and run, which he wasn't about to do, or he could stick to his vague plan of staying put in Boar Gulch, making what money he could by mining the miners. And handle each situation as it arose.

Trouble was, the Gulch didn't have so much as the whiff of a lawman to tame the terrors Rollie knew were only beginning to bubble to the surface of this place fertile with ore, some of which he was responsible for, just by being there. It was up to him to lay low the coming swarm of rats seeking cold revenge for bringing them to justice through the years. *Retirement,* he thought. *Could anyone ever really retire from enforcing the law?* It did not matter if he had worked for a private agency or held a public office, the law was the law.

Then again, he reasoned, he wasn't strictly in the law business any more. He was in the stay alive and make a dollar business.

Rollie sighed. Had to be the mountains. Sometimes when sleep kept itself hidden from him, he would drag a chair out onto the meager front porch of The Last Drop. With his feet up on the railing, he would watch the night sky. Purple over the distant peaks, it would become lacerated with great jags of lightning like the ghostly white of old scars.

Most of the time those storms never drew any closer. Heck, most of the time they amounted to mammoth displays of heat lightning with little more to offer than a passing rainstorm. Bold and slashing and silent, it became a far-off skirmish that would whisk Rollie back to the battlefields of the war, when men and horses screamed together in their private agonies, only to be drowned out by the piercing whistle of cannon fire and explosions that erupted like angry volcanic rents in the earth.

He would sit, sipping whiskey and smoking his briar pipe, lost in the past, watching but not watching the storm, farther away in his mind than the past that never died. Sometimes a purple dawn would find him still there, asleep and twitching in the last of a dream's dredged agonies.

Sometimes he heard the sounds of miners coughing up gouts of phlegm as they stretched and yawned like skinny, hairless cousins of grizzlies, scratching their way into another day. Hopefulness bloomed anew with each sunrise. That very day may well be the day they, among all the other rock grubbers and dirt hounds, would sink their pick and tug it free, dislodging a clot of soil and gravel. The simple act might reveal true sign of that most precious thing they wanted above all else, the thing that drove them to uproot whatever lives they had known, often lives of safety, of comfort, of predictability.

After all wasn't that why they were there? For the promise of untold wealth even though the wealth itself may never come. And the allure of the search. Few of them, Rollie knew, ever thought that deeply about it. Or if they did, they hid such thoughts in a bottle. For that's what he heard each night—the promise of ore.

"I'm guessing from the dew dripping off your hat you been out here all night again, huh?"

Rollie looked up to see Pops emerge from the bar with two steaming cups of coffee. He handed one to him.

"Thanks." Rollie sipped and made the gratified sound men the world over make every morning after their first sip of the day. "Something about coffee," he said.

"Yep," said Pops.

They sipped a few minutes longer, watching the sun squeeze its way skyward, carving everchanging rivers of slow-moving light. The colors of fire shifted from black to purple to blue-gray and cut through with red flares of matches blooming to orange that finally became the mild disappointment of full daylight once more.

"You ever wonder if it's nothing more than greed that brought us all here, Pops?" Rollie didn't look up, but he knew his friend had heard him and was, in his usual way, considering the notion before giving voice to his thoughts on the matter.

"Way I see it"—Pops paused to set fire to his first pipe of the day and get it going like a train steaming up an incline—"greed's the mask over it all. Take you for example—you didn't come here to be rich."

Rollie chuckled. "News to me."

"Naw, naw, now listen. You opened this can of peaches. We're going to eat every damn one. I'm thinking you came here to figure out some things for yourself. You ended up here because you need to be here. At least right now, for this time. If you make money, that's all well and good, a bonus if you like, gravy dripped over the steak and taters."

"What happens when I figure out whatever it is I need to figure out? Will the gravy dry up?"

Pops shrugged. "How do I know? I look like a fortune-teller to you?" He laughed his deep, raspy chuckle.

"How about the rest of them?" said Rollie, gesturing outward, toward the surrounding hills where their customers were greeting the day.

"Oh, all as different from each other as they can be, I reckon. Some want adventure, some running fast from whatever they thought they hated back wherever it is they come from—Ohio or Kentucky or England or Ireland."

Rollie nodded. "And you?" Again, he was met with the silence that meant Pops was chewing over his thoughts.

"I tell you what. You never asked much about what I am, where I come from. I appreciate that, Rollie."

"You don't ever have to tell me anything, Pops. I wasn't prying open the lid on anything."

"I know, and I appreciate that. I do things in life because I want to do them, because I need to do them. If I tell you something, it's because I choose to." Pops drew on his pipe again in silence. A lengthy silence.

Rollie wondered if he'd stepped over some line with his partner that he hadn't known was scratched into the ground in the first place. He was about to change the subject when Pops spoke up.

"Some time ago, I had a wife and a daughter. That was back before the war. We were slaves, which I believe I have mentioned and which I am certain does not surprise you anyway. Near as I can tell my wife is dead. Things got tight for the colonel who owned the farm where we lived. That's because he was an idiot, couldn't gamble to save his ass. He began selling off his moneymakers, the slaves. I reasoned that my wife was safe, safe as any of us could be anyway.

"She had skills, knew three languages and could read them all, too. I figured that would put her in good with the big house. Turns out she was the first of us to get dragged off. I needed to go after her, but she'd made me promise to look after our daughter. Our little girl needed me worse. I heard the caravan my wife was in was set upon, and whoever did it killed all the slaves. Every single one of them."

He paused and Rollie, as was his custom, said nothing. He'd always found that perfuming the air with words of sorrow was useless. He waited for Pops to continue, and in a few moments, he did.

"I was out tending to the sorghum like I did every day with the rest. My little girl was too young to work, so she was kept by an old woman too old to work the fields. Ma Grunt, we called her. I don't know why. She always had that name. One night, we got back from the field, and all the babies was gone. Ma Grunt was bruised up, stoved in like she'd taken a mighty kicking, which I am certain she had.

"We come to learn that the master shipped off all our babies to the slave market, and when Ma Grunt tried to stop his men, she took a beating, a hard beating. Died later that night, on a pallet on a dirt floor, all alone and blaming herself for those babies being taken off like that."

Rollie nodded, not looking at his friend, and sipped his cooling coffee.

"The rest of them, they talked big and cried and carried on. Me, I left. That night. Had to find my baby. I had nothing but my own two feet, pair of old trousers more hole than cloth, and a shirt with no sleeves. Then the war got in my way. I did my part, figured I should. But that left me as poor as ever, and with a couple of scars, and a cold trail. I been chasing clues and notions since. Never did find those babies. But then again, I ain't dead yet, neither."

There was another long pause as they watched Chauncey part the curtains in his store windows and prop open the front door.

"So," said Rollie.

"So what brought me to Boar Gulch? It isn't the conversation." Pops chuckled. "Talking with you is like talking with a stick of firewood. Except that will eventually crackle and tell you what it's thinking."

"Yep," said Rollie, knowing Pops was right, and also knowing he wasn't about to change.

"You know I was trailing those nasty Dickey twins. I guess you could say they led me here. But I was only after them so I could make money to keep going. Only reason I'm here is to make money to keep going."

"To find your daughter," said Rollie.

"You bet." Pops nodded.

"That's fair. Anything I can do to help?"

"You've done enough already."

"Not really. It's been mutual. I used to track people. I might be able to help."

"I know, and I appreciate it. Truth is, I have come to the end of the rope I was following some time ago. I've been guessing for a couple of years now."

"Pardon me for saying so, but that usually doesn't end well."

Pops nodded. "I know that, too."

"Well," Rollie stood, stretching his back and massaging his game thigh. He clapped a hand on Pops' shoulder. "You let me know if I can help. Might be two old heads are smarter than one." He walked to the door.

Pops nodded. "Unless they're our heads."

Rollie glanced up and down the street. He'd only been in Boar Gulch a few months, but he guessed the town had tripled in population since his arrival. And all manner of businesses had emerged to help satisfy the needs of the coming hordes. The most notable to Rollie had been the appearance of another saloon that doubled as a gambling den, the Lucky Strike.

When the owners, a husband and wife, first arrived, they'd visited Rollie and Pops and made their intention known. He'd appreciated their candor, but what could he do? Competition is a healthy thing, Pops had said. Rollie didn't say much, but decided he could live without competition.

The structure they'd set up was no more or less than The Last Drop. He figured they didn't have much of a stake to begin their venture with, so he'd wished them well and did his best to keep the miners coming to his place. He and Pops built more tables, had Chauncey order more poker chips and cards, and they were considering a faro setup.

The clincher was when Nosey said he had experience bucking the tiger. And more important, he knew how to deal.

"I can't argue that a faro table would bring in money," said Pops. "House usually wins. But as a junior partner in this venture, I am obligated to remind you that Nosey's out West because he's on the run from powerful folks back East, folks he owes a whole lot of money to. Money that he lost while gambling. I don't know about you, but that doesn't sound like the sort of fellow who should be running a gaming table. Of course, maybe I'm wrong and he's what you call a reformed gambler. Maybe he's gotten very good at bucking the tiger."

Rollie had grunted and turned back to fighting with the bung on the new keg. He wondered how hard it would be to learn to deal faro.

Aside from his direct competitors, there was also the tent filled with all manner of hardware that set up at the far end of the street, bookending Wheeler's Mercantile and Emporium. In contrast, it was run by a moody little man, Horkins, from New York City, who wore a full black suit even in the hottest weather—he was consequently ripe much of the time. He squinted through his thick spectacles at each item a person wanted to purchase as if he were reluctant to let it go. In the end he did let go, but not without making each file bought and each pick purchased a painful process.

His younger brother, Horkins the Younger, a smaller version of the hardware merchant, set up an assay office next door. He seemed to have the proper credentials and more important, the equipment to make his professional assessments with validity.

In this instance, competition was something Rollie highly recommended.

The other big topic of chatter in Boar Gulch proper was the construction of a hotel backed by the mayor himself. The underpinnings were built of overly robust logs so that it would last for a long time, so said Chauncey.

Pops figured Wheeler's cash flow was pinching out, otherwise he wouldn't have sold off the various lots around town so easily, which would no doubt have earned him more money if he'd waited for the town to prove up, as he had predicted it would.

A blacksmith came to town—a welcome addition to the community as nearly everyone had need of tool repairs, shoes for their horses, wagon parts, nails, and more. Pieder Tomsen, a slender fellow with a full, black beard and deep-set blue eyes that glittered like shards of river ice, set up shop on a ridge a five-minute walk from the main street. He was close to trees, which soon fell to his axe blows, at first for a meager cabin, and then for fuel for his forge.

He spoke not a lick of English but seemed to understand everybody fine, if his nodding head were to be believed. He turned out good-quality work in a timely manner, and everybody was impressed with his industry. Smoke chugged upward around the clock from the chimney in his open-air shop, and from first light through dusk, sparks flew from his hammer blows, and the sharp stinging smack of steel on steel rang in the air throughout Boar Gulch.

At the south end of Main Street, an eatery was erected overnight by a strapping man who looked more like a blacksmith should than their blacksmith did. Geoff the Scot hung the sign FOOD above the always-open flaps of his tent, though most folks sat around outside on stump ends of logs, balancing their tin plates heaped with solidly made—if unimaginative—fare such as fried potatoes, fried venison steaks, biscuits, beans, and coffee. He was savvy, though, and told Rollie he was going to hire a woman to cook as soon as he could find one.

That became a joke in camp because despite the mayor's arguments that a wagonload of prostitutes was set to arrive any day from over in Montana Territory, the only available woman around, other than Camp Sal, was Delia

Holsapple. And cooking wasn't something she seemed interested in. Rollie had heard she was a popular attraction among the miners, and it became apparent that she'd been talking about him to her customers. While he sold more booze than ever, he noticed a drop in the number of folks who'd sit at the bar and tell him all about their lives.

He didn't much care if everybody in town knew he'd been a Pinkerton agent. He was proud of the work he'd done. What he was bothered by were the rogues who were sure to descend on the town because of the notices Delia had placed in the newspapers.

It bothered him more than he let on. So much so that Pops and Nosey had asked him if something was eating him.

"Truth is," Rollie told Pops and Nosey one afternoon, "I am a tiny bit worried. I can handle myself, or at least there was a time when I could have."

"What happened to change that?" said Nosey, actually looking up. It was a rare moment when he wasn't half-listening, his eyes stuck to the pages of his journal, his left hand scribbling words fast, or with his nose sunk in a copy of a Dickens novel or a ratty copy of *Deadeye Davis, Demon Gunhand of Death Valley*!

Rollie looked to the door, then back to the two men, and told them about that day in the alley in Denver City, and about his subsequent convalescence. He told how Delia Holsapple had as much as admitted she had hired the man to kill him that day. Pops had overheard but it was news to Nosey.

"So that's what she was on about. I thought she was off in the head and talkin' in riddles." Pops tapped his temple.

"Well, it doesn't mean she isn't deranged," said Rollie, offering a rare half smile.

"That would also explain why that lung of yours whistles!" Nosey picked up his pencil, licked the end, then said, "Are you certain you don't want me to usher your life story into print? You are a national treasure! Why, we could make a mint. Naturally I'd split the earnings with you."

"Oh, that's big of you," said Rollie. "But no. And never. But you can do me a favor and keep an eye on the door, on newcomers in town. It's getting to where I'm starting to see faces I think I recognize on every greenhorn in the Gulch."

"Any idea what we're looking for?" said Pops, drawing on his pipe.

"That's the trouble. I helped put a pile of people behind bars over the years, and another pile ended up at the end of a rope."

"That narrows it down," said Pops, chuckling.

Wolfbait strolled in then, and the day began.

A few hours later, Nosey and Pops were playing blackjack at the end of the bar. For the third time in ten minutes, Nosey shouted, "No! It can't be!"

Pops stepped back, hands wide and eyebrows high. "You think I'm cheating?"

"Well, no, but . . . I'm broke, Pops."

Pops jutted his chin and tapped it with a long finger. "You know, I expect you and I are about the same size. And I could use a new shirt . . ." The statement hung in the air like smoke.

"Oh, no. Not the shirt off my back!"

Pops shrugged, said nothing.

Rollie glanced up from drawing a beer and tamped down a smile. Nosey sighed and began unbuttoning his shirt. When he finished, he peeled it off and held it out toward Pops, not looking. He held it that way for a few long moments, and only turned around when he heard a wheezing sound.

Pops was laughing so hard silently that tears squeezed out of his eyes. The rest of the bar had fallen silent during the exchange, but burst out with laughter. Nosey, for the first time that any of them could recall, turned red. But he held out the shirt to Pops, who shook his head.

"Keep the shirt, Nosey. But the next time you are tempted to do anything with cards, you run, okay? Next fella you lose to might want the whole suit!"

"I don't understand. I've studied treatises on gaming. I've pored over books devoted to poker, let alone blackjack. I have memorized the intricacies of every game devised by man."

"Books are for stories. You got to play cards by instinct, son. I play because it's fun. I don't play because I have to win money. I did that, like as not, I'd lose."

As soon as he said it, he knew he was wasting words. Nosey was already sorting through the deck of cards, shuffling and analyzing them, his brows tight in concentration. Chuckling and shaking his head, Pops walked out back to visit the outhouse.

"Stoneface Finnegan! Where you at?" The bellowing shout ripped through the low hum of conversation in the bar.

All the men huddled over drinks, cards, checkers, and dominoes swung their heads up like a herd of cattle on hearing a coyote too close. The clink of poker chips ceased and glasses were set down.

CHAPTER SEVENTEEN

As usual, the door was propped wide open, letting in bluebottles, cool breezes, and sunlight, which backlit the man in the doorway.

"You and me, Stoneface! Outside! Now!"

"You bet," said Rollie in a tight, grim growl. He ripped off his grimy apron and let the fingers of his left hand brush his Schofield to make certain it was there, riding right where he needed it, midpoint on his hip, belted tight, hammer thong slipped free. He needn't have checked. He'd oiled the gun, loaded it, and double-checked it before he strapped it on at the start of the day, as was his custom.

"You and me!" the man in the doorway shouted even louder.

Wood cracked and splintered as the door to the back room burst inward. "Naw," shouted Pops. "Just you!" The door slammed into the plank wall and spasmed in place on it's hinges. Pops bolted through, closing the gap between him and the man in the doorway, with Lil' Miss Mess Maker leading the way.

Within ten feet of the far end of the bar, he triggered both barrels of the sawed-off Greener, and the room filled with cannon fire. Smoke and flame bloomed outward, following buckshot that drove straight into the man silhouetted in the doorway.

The man whipped backward as if jerked by ropes. He smashed through the new railing, his arms and legs trailing and flailing, a spray of fresh blood blossomed skyward as he flew into the street. He slammed to earth inches in front of a loaded, ox-drawn ore wagon grinding its way down the slight decline.

The oxen, barely flustered, dragged forward. The wagon rolled on—and over—the twitching stranger, creaming him into the roadway, damp from the previous night's downpour, making a gruesome paste. Two onlookers gagged and one revisited the meal he'd just eaten at Geoff the Scot's Food Tent.

"Pops!" shouted Rollie, aiming his pistol out the side window.

The man with the Greener dropped low out of instinct, joining the bar's patrons hugging the floorboards. He dug out two smoking shells and thumbed in a second fresh pair. He didn't need an explanation from an old trail-hound like Rollie.

All was still within the bar. The ex-Pinkerton man's intentions were telegraphed to every tense soul in the smoky, metal-stench air of the barroom.

In the next instant, they saw why. A tall, black, slope-crown hat rose up in a corner of the open side window. It kept rising to reveal a forehead, then two dark eyes followed by a long bent nose topping a drooping dragoon mustache. A wide mouth fronting a scatter of horsey teeth sneered. A long-barrel Colt rose up with the face and leveled off inward toward the room.

The black eyes widened as they saw Rollie. "You!" the mouth spat.

"Yep," said the barman, and cored the Peeping Tom's forehead with a dead-center shot. The man dropped from sight, back onto the narrow catwalk running along the outside of the bar.

At the same time, Nosey gripped a thick beer glass by the handle and swung it out the opposite window. A thin groan rose up. He knew it grazed something, pulled his arm back, and swung the blood-smeared mug out the window and downward once more. Whoever was out there grabbed his arm by the wrist.

Nosey dropped the glass and shouted, "It's got a hold of me!"

A quiet little Pennsylvania miner in a floppy straw hat grabbed onto Nosey's other arm and tugged, which only made the former journalist wail even louder. A bald head appeared at the bottom of the window—and stared straight into the double-barrel snout of a smoking Greener, with a narrow-eyed Pops holding the shotgun and shaking his head at the bald man.

Behind them, they heard Rollie bolt for the shattered back door, his game leg making an off-rhythm sound on the puncheons. Keeping low, he poked his head through the back door, saw no one to either side, and scampered down the boards to the dirt and sparse clumps of grass to the corner of the building.

Scanning around the corner, he saw the man in the black hat he'd shot in the head. Minus the hat, the man was flopped half off the narrow walkway on the side of the bar. Rollie heard rising voices inside the bar. *Good.* That meant everything was getting back to normal. His job was to find any other attackers. If there were three, there might be four. Or more. He didn't hear any more shots and assumed Nosey and Pops subdued, but kept alive the third man Nosey had wailed with the beer glass.

Rollie made it to the road out front, saw the crowd gathering around the dead man in the road behind a stalled, loaded ore wagon hooked to a pair of oxen dozing in the roadway. He kept one eye on the crowd as he made his way around the raised front of the bar.

Around the north side of the bar, he saw no one at the window and figured Pops and Nosey had yanked the third man through. He backed up and climbed the steps. At the top he eyed the snapped railing. Maybe Pops could fix it for good. Or maybe they should leave it broken, save them from having to deal with it the next time killers came knocking.

The patrons saw him and filed out past him, eyes wide. He noted that three of them were carrying their drinks. He'd remind them later. Glassware wasn't cheap.

Pops saw him and through a cloud of pipe smoke—he always puffed up an extra hard after a fight—he dragged a small bald man to his feet. He held him by the collar. "You recognize this one?"

Rollie walked over to the man, his Schofield cocked, poised, and ready. He looked him up and down, spent extra time eyeing the man's face. He saw a pocked, stubbled face of a man who looked prematurely old because he had no teeth, only a puckered hole of a mouth.

"Who are you?" When the man didn't answer, Rollie whipped a savage backhand across that pocky little puckered face.

The man's head snapped sideways and he grunted out a quick, high-pitched squeal.

"Why are you here?" Rollie didn't wait for a reply. He smacked the man again, snapping his head to the other side.

"Stop hitting me."

"Don't like that, huh?" said Pops. He cinched the man's shirt collar tighter in his big hand. "Too bad." He smacked the man on the side of the head. "I ought to knock your teeth out, but it looks like somebody beat me to it."

"Now that ain't right."

"What isn't right?"

"Funning on another man's infirmities."

"Hmm, never thought of it like that. You may be right. But it's true."

"I know it," the man said.

Rollie noted the man's head was bleeding. "I see Nosey's beer mug landed a blow."

Nosey ambled over, nursing his strained arm. "Hit him again. He nearly broke my arm." He gritted his teeth tight and leaned close to the little man's face. "If I can't write, I'm going to . . . well, I'll think of something. And it will be unpleasant."

"He means it," said Rollie. "Now talk. Or I'm going to shoot you in the gut. Once."

The man swallowed, his eyebrows rose higher.

"Ever seen a gut-shot man?" said Pops. "You will. Takes forever and a day to die. Got to work through all that poison first."

Again, the man swallowed. "It was Joe. He's dead."

"Both of your friends are dead. Which one was Joe?"

"You killed Bonny Bob? Oh, he wouldn't have hurt you."

"His pistol pointed at me led me to think differently."

The man lolled his head and it looked like he was about to sob.

Rollie raised his Schofield, opened the cylinder, and emptied it of five bullets. "Tell you what. I'll leave one in and spin it. See what happens. Okay?" He held the pistol to the man's head, spun the cylinder, and triggered. It clicked.

The little man howled. "What do you want to know? Oh God, oh God . . ."

"God?" Rollie looked around the room. "In Boar Gulch? I think not."

"Oh God, oh God. Look in Joe's pocket somewheres. He's got a page he tore out of a newspaper. In Denver, I think it was. He said he owed you one. Me and Bonny Bob, we rode along with him. We was hoping he had another job in mind. We been broke since we took that bank—"

Rollie nodded. "I'm guessing you were about to tell me about a bank you all robbed, huh?"

The man stared at Rollie, eyes wide. Rollie jammed the snout of the Schofield's barrel under the man's chin and jerked it upward. "Which bank?"

"I don't know." The man tried to shake his head but the barrel prevented it. "Brick, in Virginia City. All I know."

"Okay, I believe you." Rollie lowered the pistol.

The ratty man relaxed, shaking as if a fever gripped him. "You could let me go. I didn't know any of this was going to happen."

"Oh, we'll let you go. In a manner of speaking."

"What's that mean?"

Rollie turned to Nosey. "When you're through nursing that wounded wing of yours, go fetch a rope from the corral out back, would you?"

Nosey paused in rubbing his elbow. He looked from the man to Rollie and back, then to Pops, who nodded. As if agreeing with himself, Pops nodded once more.

"Wait now," said the man in his grasp, struggling and squirming. "You . . . you said you was going to let me go!"

"Oh, we'll let you go, of course, but you'll be going in one or two directions, depending on the life you've led."

"I-I don't understand." The man's voice came out choppy, sounding dry and small.

Rollie had turned away and was peering out the door at a big ponderosa pine with a branch twenty feet up, thick around as a man's thigh. Toward the south end of the street it appeared stout enough for the job.

"Why you need rope? Why you need rope? It ain't right!"

Rollie pulled in a deep breath through his nose and bent close to the little man's face. His voice came out as a low, even growl. "Mister, by your own mouth you admit you have robbed a bank and ridden with outlaws who tried to kill me and my friends. You are men who rode here with vengeance in mind. And you put the lives of all these hardworking people of Boar Gulch in danger. No sir. That cannot stand."

"It ain't lawful!"

Pops chuckled. "That's good, because there's no law in Boar Gulch, mister."

"But there will be justice." Rollie said this low, almost

muttering to himself, but Pops and the simpering man heard him.

"That ain't right! You . . . you'll be no better than murderers yourselves! It ain't lawful, I tell you!"

"Law can go to hell. I've had my fill of it. It's justice we deal in." Rollie echoed his own sentiments.

The man's knees gave out and he sagged against Pops.

Pops pulled the back of the man's collar high. "Get up, fool." He jerked the man upward.

The man stood, trembling and mumbling, "Ain't right, ain't right . . ."

Rollie stepped in close. "You have any kin, anybody who'll miss you?"

"No," the man shook his head. "I don't know nobody." He looked up at Rollie, thin hope on his puckered, trembling features. "I am an orphan, alone in the world."

Rollie nodded. "That makes two of us."

"But it ain't right. I didn't shoot at any of you."

"You would have," said Rollie.

"Now, don't disagree with the man who has all the cards when your hands are empty." Pops turned his gaze on Rollie. "I will see to it you have a marker."

Rollie looked away. "The others, tell me their names as you knew them."

"Oh God. I-I'm Pippin Salazar."

"Pippin? Like the apple?" said Pops.

The man shrugged. "Don't know nothing about apples. Only name I ever had. I expect it's true."

"The others," said Rollie again. He nodded toward the street. "Your man out there. You called him Joe. Got a surname?"

"Joe. That's all I know."

Rollie nodded and stared at the floor, eyes sharp and jaw muscles bunching, nostrils flexing.

"You're him, ain't you?"

Rollie looked up. "What?"

"Stoneface Finnegan. That's you."

Rollie said nothing.

"Joe, he talked about you. Was crazy-like ever since he found that newspaper at the bar in Denver. God, I wish he didn't know how to read."

"Your bad luck," said Pops, guiding the man over to a chair.

Rollie poured three shots of whiskey, passed one to Pops, one to the man, and downed one himself. "The other man, black hat—what was his name."

"Oh him, he was Bonny Bob. He was okay. But that Joe, he was mean as a two-headed snake. Foulest sort. Always picking at something, calling me names."

"Like what?" said Pops.

"Huh?"

"Names. You said he called you names. What did he call you?"

"Oh, I don't know."

"Man called hurtful names by another ought to recall what it was that set him off."

Pippin shrugged.

Pops ignored him. "Could be he was tainted in the head from birth."

Rollie looked at both men and rubbed his temples. Nosey walked in the front door, a coil of thick rope wrapped like a bandolier around his chest.

The toothless man's eyes widened. "Oh, we won't be needing that, mister. We come to an agreement."

"Like hell," said Rollie.

"But . . . we was talking. Hell, we had whiskey together!"

"Hang him high."

"I can't participate in this, Rollie, Pops. It's—"

"It's what?" said Rollie, taking the rope from Nosey. "Barbaric? Yep. Unlawful? Maybe, if we were anywhere but a place without law. Is it justifiable? That depends on your perspective. That man would have killed you if given the chance."

"How do you know that?"

"Because I know him. I know who he is, I know what he is. What he's done."

"I don't understand."

"That's right you don't. And so far he doesn't think I remember him. That's why he's calling himself *Pippin*."

Nosey softened. "Well, what's this man who isn't who he says he is supposed to have done?"

"No supposing about it. He is one Tea Leaf Jackson, isn't that right, Tea Leaf?"

"I don't know what you're talking about." The toothless man sniffed and looked away.

"Yeah, about what I remember, too. Denying everything right to the bitter end. Well this time, there's no jury to watch you whimper and whine and pull a sad face. How about those children you sold as slaves to that old harpy of a witch woman who took them to Canada?"

"They never proved that!" said the toothless man before pinching his toothless mouth shut.

"Uh-huh. And those sheep you let starve to death because you were too lazy or too mean to haul water to them? Or the prostitute you gutted with a dull pocketknife so you wouldn't have to pay her from the money you robbed from the missionaries in Wyamont's Point?"

"I don't know what you're talking about!"

"I do. It's been, what? Twelve years since I last saw you in that courtroom, Tea Leaf? Because you lost all your teeth and most of your hair and shriveled up like an old apple-head doll doesn't mean I don't recognize you. Those other two, I don't seem to recall. But you, I know who you are. And I know you deserved to die all those years ago and you deserve it even more now."

"He's crazy, I tell you! Look at him! He's got some sort of problem with his thinker." The little bald man looked at Pops. "You have to believe me. I don't know what he's talking about." He began to sob again, the sound louder. A wailing, keening moan.

Pops looked at Rollie. "He's good, I'll give him that. I heard professional mourners who weren't half as convincing."

"You mean—" said Nosey.

"Yep," said Pops. "Rollie is right. And even if he wasn't, everybody in town knows who Rollie is by now. Who he was, what he was. They know, too, there's likely to be a price on his head paid out by somebody he put away or somebody who was left behind after he brought in their kin who got his neck stretched."

"But this man, what if he didn't shoot anybody here. I-I subdued him with a beer glass! It's up to me, then, to deal with him. I'll deal with him myself. I'll borrow a wagon. Until then, we should imprison him, take him to the authorities."

Pops smiled. "I admire your thinking, Eustace. I do. But in life, we all make choices, see? Some of them don't work out so well. Each one leads to another and another and so on until we draw our last breath. But each choice helps decide when that last breath will be. You see? This fool made some poor choices. Same as those weasels he rode with. And now those choices are biting him in the ass.

"Besides, if we don't do this, only thing saved this fool from a double dose of lovin' from Lil' Miss Mess Maker was your fool arm. Elsewise she would have cut him into bits. The rest is gravy on the potatoes."

"Stand up," said Rollie to the toothless man,

He begun to blubber again. His mouth was a quivering, pink, drooling mess.

"Stop that and hold still. This is going to happen, mister," said Pops. "So do yourself a favor and make peace with whatever it is you believe in. You trotted out the word *God* an awful lot, so might be you want to start there."

"Oh God, oh God!"

"Yeah, like that. Only quieter."

The toothless man began sobbing and sagging again as Rollie tied his hands behind his back. He jammed a bar rag into a trouser pocket and they marched him out the door, down the steps. At the bottom, Rollie saw three horses tied together down the lane. "Which one is yours?"

The man didn't answer, but sobbed. Rollie jerked him hard by the wrists. "I said which one is yours?"

"The buckskin."

"Okay." He prodded the man again. Over his shoulder, he said, "Nosey, bring that buckskin along."

"Which one is that?"

Rollie sighed, looked at Pops. "How did he ever make it out here?"

"That brown one on this end," said Pops. "Yep, that one."

By then the townsfolk saw what was coming and turned en masse to watch the small group of men walk toward the south end of the street.

"See here, Finnegan." The mayor hustled to stand in front of Rollie, and held out a pudgy hand. "You can't hang a man!"

"No?"

"No! You above all others should understand that."

"I do." Rollie pushed his way past the mayor,

Wheeler hustled around him again. "See here!"

Rollie sighed and stopped once more.

"What's he supposed to have done?"

"Let's see, it's been a dozen years since I've been acquainted with Mr. Tea Leaf Jackson here, but when I knew him he was a murderer, a thief, and a coward. And as he was supposed to have spent twenty-five years in Silburg Prison, I'd say he's also a jailbreaker."

Chauncey Wheeler put a hand over his mouth and backed up.

"It ain't true. None of it, " wailed the toothless man. "I'm innocent. I ain't killed nobody in a coon's age, ain't stolen nothing since the bank job. Oh, I can't go back to prison!"

"There you have it," said Rollie. "Unless of course you'd rather I turn him loose here in Boar Gulch. Maybe you could take him on as a stock boy? Give him a room in your fine new hotel. As soon as it's built, of course. Meantime, you could let him sleep in your store, in the back room."

"Oh, no, that's quite all right Mr. Finnegan. I-I apologize for second-guessing you."

"Uh-huh." Rollie nudged his prisoner in the back. "Let's go."

Pops had gone ahead and had tossed an end of the rope up over the branch. He made it on his second try.

"Easier if you make the noose first," said Rollie.

"Easier if I watch you do the whole thing." Pops turned his back on Rollie and fussed with the rope.

"Okay, okay." He waited, listening to Tea Leaf's protestations and lamentations. "You do know how to tie a noose?"

"One more crack and I'll be tying two," said Pops, turning around to reveal a perfect noose. The sight of it elicited a fresh round of wails from the toothless man.

"Shut up, Tea Leaf. Or I'll shoot you instead."

"It'd be a whole lot kinder," said the whimpering man.

"In the gut," said Rollie.

"Nah, the knees," said Pops. "Then we can set him out in the woods for the bears to play with."

"Now that's not a bad idea, Pops. Not bad at all. And here I was thinking you had no heart."

"I have my moments."

"Oh, for heaven's sake," said Nosey. "Hang the man and put him out of his misery. If he's done as much as you said, surely he deserves to meet his Maker with a quick jerk."

"Changed your tune, eh?" said Pops.

"No," said Nosey. "But I don't think it necessary to make fun of a man when you are about to kill him. That's what beasts do. They torture, play with their kill. Are we not men?"

Rollie looked at him with narrowed eyes. "Bring the horse over."

Nosey led the buckskin beneath the swinging noose. The horse nudged him in the arm, then stood and flicked an ear.

"He likes you," said Pops.

Rollie slipped the noose over the man's head and tightened it behind his right ear.

"Climb up there, Tea Leaf."

The man growled and kicked at them. They wrestled him up into the saddle and he fought them, thrashing the entire time. Rollie had to thumb back the hammer on the Schofield to settle him down.

Pops took the other end of the rope and looped it around the trunk of the tree twice, lashing the latter wrappings over the first, then tied it to itself to secure it. The rope was rigid from the limb down to the man's neck. It was rigid, too, from the limb down at an angle to where it wrapped around the red, craggy trunk of the ponderosa.

The man cried and dripped snot all down his shirtfront, blubbering and moaning.

"Be a man about it. Be a man." Pops said this in a low voice, squeezing the condemned's boot above the ankle. Tea Leaf settled down to a hiccupping sob.

"I'd like to say I hold no ill will toward you," said Rollie, "but I'd be lying. You have anything to say, you best do it now."

"I'll . . . I'll . . ."

"Yes?" said Rollie.

" . . . see you in hell!"

"You bet." Rollie smacked the horse hard on its rump and it lurched and bolted, whinnying.

Tea Leaf Jackson was dragged backward over the cantle and out of the saddle. The branch tremored, the rope creaked, and Tea Leaf danced a jig in the air, one leg, then the other, stomping unseen floorboards. His head bent too far to the left, as if he were trying to watch his trembling boots.

His tongue bulged from his vacuous mouth. His eyes popped wide and white, showing their amazement at the greatest shock of all. He swung in a slow arc and spun as he swung, his dying eyes taking in the view. He first saw the forest, the hills, and the far-off peaks. The long, grimy main street and the clot of townsfolk gathered halfway to the tree were next. They stared at him, no words spoken as he sagged and leaked out his fluids. The foul reek of him drew the first of a cloud of bluebottles.

No one spoke as the three men walked back toward the saloon, passing the people of Boar Gulch. Rollie saw no anger on their faces, only fear, likely of him. *Good*, he thought. *Keep it that way.* His grim mouth and hard eyes bore into each that dared look on him. Except the mayor.

Rollie sighed. "What is it now, Chauncey?"

"If ever we possessed the fine line of law in this town, you stomped all over it."

"Yep," said Pops, smiling and rocking back on his heels. "I'd say Rollie and me and Nosey are the closest thing to law this town has ever seen."

Rollie looked at him from under his bristly, eyebrows. "Don't say that."

"Okay, then I will," said the mayor.

"You know, Wheeler, you have an annoying habit of being annoying."

"That's my job," said the man.

From Chauncey's drawn brows, Rollie could tell the mayor wasn't sure how to take his comment. *Good.*

"Now, as the duly appointed representative of Boar Gulch—"

"Appointed by who, Chauncey?" said Pops, his Adam's apple bobbing like a bouncing ball as he laughed.

This spurred the rest of the crowd to do the same, despite the grisly mess in the tree before them, the dead man in the street and the other hanging off the porch of the bar.

"Ahem, yes, well, as to what I was saying before I was rudely interrupted. Rollie Finnegan, as we now all know your former occupation, thanks to the edifyingly delightful Miss Holsapple, I say it is your right, nay, your duty to Boar Gulch to become our official lawman. You owe us that much, sir." The mayor puffed up his already puffy chest and thumbed his lapels, his red jowls and ears growing more crimson by the moment. He tried and failed to keep his eyes locked on Rollie's.

"Owe you?" Rollie stalked as close as he could to the priggish little man, his boot tips jammed against the other's, his nostrils flared and he stared down at the shrinking mayor. "Owe you? How in the hell do you figure that, Chauncey?"

"The . . . those men, the others. There will be more!" Wheeler grew emboldened by his train of thought. "Yes." He backed up, puffed again, and continued. "And who will protect us?"

"You don't need law. You need a backbone," Rollie growled and walked back to the bar. Over his shoulder, he said, "All of you!"

Pops and Nosey followed along, not saying anything, though Pops kept a smirk tamped down.

Half an hour later, back in The Last Drop, a long silence settled on the three men.

Finally, Nosey spoke, his voice sounding quiet and old, somehow. "What about their horses?"

"Well, you need one and the buckskin likes you, so there you have it," said Rollie.

"But I could never. It . . . it belonged to a dead man. It's not right."

"No right or wrong to it, Nosey," said Pops. "Horse doesn't know the difference, and he needs somebody to take care of him."

Rollie rubbed his clean-shaven chin. "Pops, you choose a horse for yourself from the other two. We can sell the third. As to their gear, we'll divvy it up. Keep the weapons and ammunition, and sell the rest. Boots should bring something. Maybe enough to pay for their pine boxes."

"That is savage." Nosey turned away and folded his arms like a petulant child.

Rollie's thick right hand snatched at the reporter's shirtfront. He filled his hand and pulled the younger man close, so that their faces were inches apart. "Now you listen to me, you little whelp. You're welcome to your opinion, but that dangling criminal was a stone-hard killer—and worse. The world's rid of a menace. Besides, I am in the gun sights of more such malcontents and I will do what I need to so I can save my own skin and keep decent folks from misery. That's all there is to be said on the matter." He let go of Nosey's wadded shirt, and the men exchanged a long glance. Nosey nodded slowly then walked to the door.

Pops and Rollie watched him leave.

Finally Pops broke the silence. "He'll come around once he thinks on it, realizes there was no other way."

They looked at the mess in the bar—overturned chairs, spilled beers, poker chips and playing cards everywhere. Rollie poured two cups of coffee and they each sat on a stool and sipped.

Pops spoke. "I been wondering on something."

"Hmm?" said Rollie.

"Why don't you go deal a rough hand to Miss Delia Holsapple?"

"No," said Rollie, shaking his head. "She's suffered enough."

"Suffered enough? She made her own misery. We are all dealt hands in life we didn't ask for. Some worse than others." After a poignant look passed between the two men. Pops continued. "That woman has made her own miseries in life. And she's passing them on to you. That's not right. Don't care what you say."

"I can't disagree with you. But she'll get what she deserves. Might not be from me, but I've seen this happen before. I'd as soon let it play out."

"Well I think you're loco, but it's not my decision. Until she does something to me, that is."

"Understood."

Another few moments of silence settled on the room.

"Well," said Rollie, scratching his chin. "We best get this mess cleaned up, then see if our clientele will return."

"There's whiskey," said Pops. "They'll be here."

CHAPTER EIGHTEEN

The air was cooler in the stand of timber, and a soft breeze rummaged high in the ponderosa needles before drifting down to play in Cap's mane. The horse perked his ears and Rollie watched toward where the horse looked. The incident months before with the mother grizz and her triplets wasn't far from his mind. Cap relaxed and jerked aspen leaves from a close branch.

"You're a snacker, eh, boy?" Rollie patted the gelding's neck. He'd forgotten how good it was to get out into the hills and ride. The day was fine, the sky a blue he could not begin to describe, and his lung and leg pained him so little he could finally climb aboard a horse once again. He'd not ridden Cap and had been unsure if the horse would take to the saddle, but Pops had let it slip he'd been giving Cap saddle time now and again, knowing Rollie would want to ride when he was ready.

That day had come, though Rollie didn't need any excuse beyond the riding itself or getting out away from the dreary little confines of downtown Boar Gulch. It had been too long, and he was glad to be out and away from the squabbling and small-mindedness he'd forgotten about that infects any place where the residents are packed in cheek by jowl with their neighbors.

This day brought extra incentive to get out and away from town. Nearly a week before he and Pops had assumed full ownership of a claim they'd taken in trade for a bar bill. Jed Neeland had looked beaten down beyond measure by the pummeling lot in life he'd dragged himself into.

Rollie had seen the grief for his family back home written across the man's face. He'd also noticed that the man had developed a taste for whiskey. Rollie had told himself when he bought the bar that he would not interfere with any man's private affairs, but with Neeland, he'd been sorely tempted a number of times to cut him off, and instead serve him as much free coffee as he could stomach. Neeland had run up that bar tab lately, so Rollie's soft touch would only go so far.

Though he'd tried over the past few months, with such comments as, "You sure?" and "Don't know how you do it," he'd served him the booze, telling himself it was none of his business. Rollie knew he'd have bristled were the tables turned, so he had let Neeland be until the previous week when he wearied himself on into the bar as always and plunked down.

The place was quiet in the afternoons, and on that day even Pops was off tending to his own affairs. Wolfbait was there, dozing in a chair in the corner, slowly dribbling chaw juice into his beard with each quiet, exhaled snore.

"Hello, Jed," Rollie had said as the man settled himself onto a stool. "What'll it be?"

Jed's eyes were redder than usual and his hands shook. He didn't look at Rollie when he answered, but lowered his head into his hands, his grimy fingers raking through his long, unwashed hair. "I made a hellacious mistake, Rollie. I . . . I need to get out of here. I'm done, beat." He looked up, leaned forward. "You wouldn't want to buy a claim, would you?"

Rollie wasn't expecting that. He ran his rag over the already clean bar top and said nothing for a few moments. "I don't know, Jed. I expect your claim's worth more than what you owe me for whiskey."

"Maybe. But . . . but what if you stake me some cash to get me back East. I travel cheap, could walk much of it until I make it to the trains southeast of here. I could sign that claim over to you."

"You've put some thought into this, I think."

"No, honest. It came to me."

Rollie drew them both beers. No whiskey for Jed yet. Rollie wanted him thinking clear, in case there was something to this. "What makes you think I'd want a claim that you can't make a go of?"

"Aw, it's not the claim so much as it's me, Rollie. I'm not suited to this. All I ever wanted to do was have my own shop back home in Pennsylvania. I'm a furniture maker by trade. There'll always be a call for tables, chairs, and such. As long as people need to sit, that is." Jed smiled weakly and looked out the window.

Movement past the sullen man caught Rollie's eye. It was Wolfbait back in his corner. He was wide-eyed and nodding big nods to Rollie, as if to say yes, this is a good thing. The barman didn't dismiss it—Wolfbait might be a lot of things, but he also knew these hills and had been around long enough to know a claim of promise.

"I'd have to talk with Pops, since it'd be part his, too."

Jed had looked back at Rollie, more hopeful than Rollie had seen him in weeks. "That's fine, Rollie. Fine. But . . . if you could let me know soon, I'd be appreciative of it. It's Estelle's birthday two months from yesterday. She's my girl. She's been waiting for me to come home. I'd like to be able to show up there, surprise her."

"Sure, Jed. I'll talk with him this afternoon. Come by tonight, okay?"

Jed slid from his stool and shook Rollie's hand. "Okay, that sounds fine. I'll be back." He hustled to the door and turned. "Thanks, Rollie. I'll be back."

Rollie watched the man go, then looked at Wolfbait, who'd ambled on over. "It must mean a lot to him, he didn't even touch his beer," said Rollie.

"No sense in letting it go to waste, now, is there?" Wolfbait settled himself on Jed's vacated stool and quaffed the brew, winking. "Solid claim he's got. You and Pops could do a lot worse."

And they fell to chatting about the value of the claim. Pops came in after a spell, and Wolfbait waved as he headed out. "You two need to talk. See you later." He winked and Rollie caught Pops up on Jed's offer. The two men agreed that, depending on Jed's expectations, they could pull together enough cash to see him home, and with something extra for his time and effort, too. After all, if Wolfbait's assessment was to be believed, Jed was leaving a decent little cabin and a claim with promise.

That's what led Rollie to ride out that morning, nearly a week later, enjoying the day and the ride. Since Wolfbait vouched for Jed, and since Rollie and Pops had been busy, neither man felt the need to see their investment before then.

Jed had lit out the next day, smiling and walking with a spring in his step, carrying little more than a packboard laden with few personal items, a hat on his head, and a sidearm to deter two-legged varmints, and maybe plug a critter for food along the way. Rollie and Pops had given him a bottle of whiskey, a sack of coffee, and good wishes for him and Estelle. Jed promised to write.

Rollie used a crude, hand-drawn map to locate the claim, and it took him far longer than it needed to for him to ride there, given that he'd taken all manner of detours and stops for fun. For the first time in weeks, he didn't feel as if he had a rifle aimed at him. His left hand drifted down now and again, making certain his coat was tucked behind the time-polished handle of the Schofield.

His Winchester rode in its scabbard at his knee, ready to be plucked and levered at the slightest prickling of danger he relied on from long years in the saddle tracking foul men bent on dark deeds. It always began as a tickle, as if a lovely woman was running a light fingernail slowly up his spine, tickling more the higher it inched until it reached his neck. The hair at his collar would bristle and a chill would creep up over his scalp.

By then he'd be down, out of the saddle, and taking cover behind the nearest tree, boulder, gulley, or if need be, his horse. But it hadn't happened and he didn't expect it to happen.

But it did happen on that fine and pretty day, and he wasn't ready.

He was leaning back against the cantle, eyes closed, pulling in a deep breath of fresh mountain air while Cap played at nibbling leaves. Rollie cracked open his eyes and thought he could see the roof of Jed's cabin downslope through the trees.

A bullet whipped his hat off, pitching it forward as if a prankster had poked it from behind. Rollie bent low, tried to shake his right boot out of the stirrup but it fouled, he cursed it, and Cap danced, hopping like a crow and whinnying in the little clearing. Pretty soon another bullet whistled in, sending up a spray of red bark chips from a big ponderosa that Cap seemed determined to scrape Rollie against.

Rollie grabbed for his Schofield, but it had shaken loose and dropped to the ground. He gritted his teeth and jerked his leg hard. His socked foot slid free of his boot, which stayed in the stirrup.

He wrenched backward, flailing as if he were breaking a green mustang, and slammed once more against that cursed big, hard tree. His growls and limbs thrashing against Cap nerved the dancing, sweating horse into a more robust frenzy. Finally Rollie freed his left boot and spun away from the horse, who jerked away from him, then danced in place, eyes wide and white.

"I'm no grizz," muttered Rollie, "but I could be if you keep this up, damn your hide." He kept low, inching toward the horse, whose right side was nearly facing him. He scanned the east, where the shots had come from. He saw nothing but trees.

As he moved, he glanced at the ground for his Schofield. Couldn't have tumbled too far. That'd teach him to ride with the hammer loop off.

He reached Cap and snagged the reins, keeping low and nudging the horse between himself and the east, hoping the shooter was alone and hadn't moved. He was reaching for his boot, which was snagged in the stirrup, when he heard a voice behind him.

"Nah, I don't think so, Finnegan. Anybody don't deserve to die with his boots on it's you."

Rollie looked up, one hand on the horse. He inched his left hand toward the rifle scabbard and for his efforts heard a hammer click back into the deadly position.

"Again, I will repeat myself. You will die sooner than I wish if you keep up this stupidity. Now both hands up high, lest I be tempted to shoot you in the back now and be done with it. Wouldn't be the first time I did that to one such as yourself."

Rollie knew who it was. The voice, a thin, flat sound, gave it away. "Woburn." He turned slowly to face the man who was about to kill him.

CHAPTER NINETEEN

"Yeah, been a long time, Finnegan." The man who had the drop on Rollie was one of the most troublesome hauls he'd ever made. Chester Woburn. Not only had the human eel led him on a chase across two states and one territory, but he'd continued his filching ways along the route, leaving a trail of gutted, burned-out businesses and beat-up women, weeping and pregnant.

Yes sir, Chester Woburn was one fertile menace. The Pinkerton Agency had initially been called in by the Iowa state government regarding him because it had not had a whole lot of luck in capturing the miscreant. In short order, other states followed.

That was about the time that Rollie's status as a Pinkerton Agent had been quietly upgraded to one of a handful of men who were sent on more covert, dangerous assignments, or as the boss called them, "missions." Rollie suspected that was to make him and his fellows feel special. He'd never liked such feather stroking and ignored it when he could.

He'd also said no to the boss's offer of sending a partner to track down Woburn. At the time it didn't make any sense to Rollie to think he'd need a helper to bring in a bad seed. But Woburn turned out to be far more than a mere bad seed. He was a full-grown nightmare.

As the chase progressed, Woburn had taken to leaving him notes that he had been certain Rollie would find. Infuriated, Rollie vowed he'd capture the devil. Somehow. And he had. That had been eight or so years ago.

"Why am I hunting you now, Finnegan? I should think that would be obvious. You took six years of my life and fed them to the hogs. Now, prison might not have been so bad, but Dayton Valley Prison, now that was a hellish place I will simply not return to. So let's get that notion straight in our heads. That place was brimming with killers, rapists, flat-out murderers. I tell you, I have never been so frightened in all my days. So I did the one thing I knew I had to do. I got out of there early."

He chuckled and Rollie scanned the trees. No sign yet of the babbling fool.

"Not because I was on my best behavior, mind you, but because I was deserving. Even if I am the only one who thought so. Took me longer than I anticipated, though. I decided to get out of there pretty much within my first week. And though I kept my eyes wide open, it took me two years before my first opportunity came up. I stowed away in a garbage wagon. It stunk so bad. My God. And do you know, that's what gave me away in the end. Mm-hmm. I started gagging in that gut pile. Things were crawling around on those old carcass bones from the kitchens. Things I have never seen in all my days on the trail."

"All this chatter is nice," said Rollie. "But you're assuming I care. I don't. I'm also going to put down my arms."

"Do that at your own peril, Finnegan."

Rollie did it with a smirk.

Woburn let him. "But do me a favor and step away from that fidgety horse of yours."

Rollie did that as well, glancing at the ground. No sign of the Schofield.

"Now, where was I? Oh yes, my first attempt at liberation. That ended poorly. The fools who drove the wagon found me gagging and retching. Apparently they were not used to hearing sounds coming from a pile of garbage. They dragged me back to Dayton Valley. The warden chained me in what they called the pit, a natural cavern of sorts gouged in the rock in the bowels of the place. I waited out that stint and eventually after forgetting and then remembering me a good two, three times, they dragged me on out of there and put me right back in the cell I'd been in I don't know how many months before."

Rollie sighed and shifted from one foot to the other.

"I'm sorry. Am I boring you? Too bad." Woburn continued. "I'd developed a taste for raw rat meat while in the pit, but it didn't take me long to fatten up again—on undercooked, wormy beans and biscuits garnished with weevils."

He let that hang in the air for a few silent moments. "That was a joke, by the way, Finnegan. Good eating all, if you don't know any better. Problem is, Finnegan I knew better. I know you know where I'm from. It came out in my criminal trial. Yes, I was from a wealthy family back East. A shipping magnate who built a mansion in Portland, Maine. I had one sibling, a sister, who I assume is still an invalid. We had the best of everything, you see. Best food, best tutors, horses. All of it."

"And you wanted none of it, if I recall," said Rollie,

ticked off that the man wouldn't show himself. *At least, if I keep him talking, I keep him from shooting me and leaving me to die out here.* "Why did you take to a life of thievery and cruelty, Chester?"

"Cruelty? Ha, that's a rich thought, Finnegan, from a man who sent me to hell for six years. As I remember it, you were smiling when they led me out of that courtroom. I tried to spit on you, but I think my snot landed in a woman's feathery hat. You remember that hat? It was god-awful. Even in the deepest tropics, birds don't exist with plumage in such colors."

"Are you going to talk me to death, Chester, or are you going to do something to liven up the afternoon?" While he said it, Rollie shifted his weight to his right foot and scanned more of the ground close up, hoping for a glimpse of his revolver.

Chester Woburn kept on talking as if he hadn't heard Rollie. "People deserve so little from each other and yet expect so much. But enough of that, where was I? Oh yes, I escaped a second time. It was a couple of years after the first, but I did it. And do you know what? It was simple. In the end, I waited for the perfect moment, then I clubbed a guard in the back of the head, dragged him into the shadows of a half-closed door, stripped off his clothes, took his gun, and, well, here I am."

He raised both hands up and Rollie finally saw where the man was hidden. It looked for a second as if Woburn might actually turn slowly as if to show off. No luck.

"I recall you were a talker. See that hasn't changed. Some of the women you left behind said the same. Right in the middle of things, they said you'd be blabbering away about yourself."

That got him. Woburn's bottom jaw stuck out and he poked the air with the pistol. "You'll be laughing as I kill you slow. You'll wish you'd kept me talking longer."

"Spare me from that fate, please."

"With pleasure." Chester Woburn raised his pistol to head height and sighted along it.

Rollie lurched to his right, toward Cap's backside, and jammed a hand under his coat. He knew it was risky, knew he'd get shot at best, and might get Cap shot as well, but he had to try. Standing and waiting to die wasn't Rollie's ideal way of shuffling off from the world of the living.

Woburn's gun barked and Cap did what Rollie hoped he would. He spooked. Rollie shoved into him, pushing the big, dancing beast with his shoulder. He kept himself behind the horse. It wouldn't be but a second before Woburn shot measured or blindly at the two of them, man and horse, gouging holes in their legs and crippling them.

In the ruckus, Rollie had retrieved his hideout gun from within his coat. It was a two-shot derringer for such occasions. He used the momentum of the horse's wide, wild pivot to crouch low, ignoring the hot pains in his old wounds unaccustomed to the odd commotion of jerking and stretching and bending. He knew the horse would only tolerate so much, but Rollie did his best to keep Cap's length between Woburn and himself. He smacked the beast on the backside, hoping to direct him straight at Woburn.

Cap would never go for that, but Rollie wanted every inch he could get. It turned out to be a couple of feet, for Chester sidestepped and cranked off another round, then another. How many was that since he'd begun firing? Three, if he had counted right. And that was a six-shot revolver Woburn was using, though the man had two, worn cross-draw style, a new look for him. Maybe he'd picked up skills on his killing trail northward from Dayton Valley Prison.

Rollie dropped, dove for safety behind a long, low jag of ledge no more than a foot and a half high, but long enough for him to lay out straight. He had two shots before reloading. Had to make each earn its keep.

His knee ground down on something hard, a spine of rock likely. Rollie eyed Chester, felt a fast breath of air part his hair, heard the stinging whistle of a bullet, and knew he had to keep his head lower. That was as close to dying as he wanted to come today.

"Finnegan! You are trapped and done for, old man! This dandy is about to kill you for keeps. I will leave you with one thought, though. And it's that I can't disagree with you. I do talk too much. You're right. It's a lifelong habit I can't shake. Not so sure I want to, though. As soon as I finish with you, I aim to ride on down out of this place, visit Boar Gulch again."

He let that statement linger but a moment. "Oh yes, I was there yesterday, availed myself of a cooling drink at your rival's establishment, and then I inspected yours. Now doesn't that make you feel odd? I watched you for a time, Finnegan. Then I heard your slave talking about how he rode the rough off your horse so you can go on your little ride into the hills all by yourself the very next day, which we both know is today. And that, my friend, brings us to right now."

While he said all this, Chester Woburn had walked slowly, one careful step at a time, toward Rollie.

"What's it going to be, old-timer? You going to stand

up and take a bullet to the face like a real man, or should I shoot you in the belly while you're cringing in the dirt?"

As soon as Woburn hove into view, Rollie pulled the trigger on the derringer. His shot went low and caught Chester in the grapes, right between his legs.

A long, high squealing sound whistled up from Chester Woburn's wide mouth, almost as wide as his eyes. The sound was so odd that Cap stopped crashing through the trees fifty feet away and stood still to listen.

Chester's gun hand clawed like a gnarled branch off a long-dead, stunted alpine juniper. It looked as if he were trying to peel something apart with his fingertips. The pistol dangled for a moment upside down from his pointer finger, then it dropped and fired into the thick root of a ponderosa pine. His other hand, equally clawed, cupped around his bleeding crotch.

"Sorry about that, Chester," said Rollie, rising with a grunt, keeping the two-shot aimed at Woburn's midsection. "I was aiming for your gut. No call to shoot a man in his seedpod."

In response, the would-be killer released a scream that sounded like a cross between a woman giving birth and a calf being savaged by a coyote. It was not a pleasant sound.

"I do not blame you, Chester. Though you can't say you didn't beg for a hurting." Rollie stepped forward, nudged something with his boot, glanced down, and saw his Schofield at his feet. He looked back up, but Woburn was holding himself, blood leaching out between his fingers.

The gun was the hard thing he'd jammed his knee on when he'd lunged down behind the ridge of ledge. Turns out it had traveled quite a distance when he'd made his spinning lunge out of the saddle. Rollie bent low, kept the derringer aimed at his visitor, and crabbed with his hand in the pine duff, sticks, and gravel until he felt the comforting walnut grip of his revolver.

He raised its reassuring heft, felt relief at the memory of reliability it gave him. He also felt something different on his palm, and knew it was a nick in the wood of the grip. He hoped the working parts of the gun itself weren't damaged. He'd have to risk it.

"Not much I can do for you, Chester. I was heading for that cabin yonder. You don't try anything stupid, I'll do what I can for you. But I am going to hang you."

The man groaned and started to walk, the first real movement he'd made since getting shot.

"Hold up there, Chester. You're wearing your gun belt and a gun. Might be you have some other weapon about you, too. Hands up. High."

"But . . . my . . ."

"I know. Your huevos are fried. I don't much care. Raise your hands."

"I . . . can't . . . can't do it." The words from Woburn came out thin, almost hissed instead of spoken.

"Raise them. Now." Rollie advanced from the left toward the wounded man.

Woburn snatched the second gun from his belt and, though he was shaking, raised it faster than Rollie expected. Rollie thumbed back the hammer on the Schofield and triggered. The gun spat smoke and death, close up.

The bullet caught Chester Woburn in the left temple, parting the curved bone of the man's head, then ripped through the dark place inside that skull and took away the far side as it escaped, spraying blood and bone and brain against the broad trunk of a ponderosa.

"Damn," said Rollie as he watched Woburn wobble from his blasted pate downward, his entire body quivering as if gripped by a brief fever, before folding at the knees and collapsing in a tangle of limbs impossible to achieve by anything living.

Part of the ex-Pinkerton agent felt rotten inside about having to kill Woburn. Yes, the man was a foul beast craven enough to pursue his base pleasures above all else. Yes, he was annoying, particularly when he spoke. But he was amusing, in his way, and unlike anyone Rollie had ever met—or suspected he would ever meet.

He sighed, moved to holster the Schofield, and looked at it. There was indeed a fresh nick in the right grip, a pale, tiny canyon where a rock had gouged it in its tumble. "Damn again," muttered Rollie. He slid the pistol into its holster and looked up, taking in the dead form of Woburn. Scanning right, he saw Cap, who had crashed through the undergrowth ringing the stand of sparse timber.

"Okay, boy. Okay." He made his way slowly to the silly, stamping horse. The beast neighed and worked his head up and down like a pump handle. "I said take it easy." Rollie grabbed one drooping rein, thinking it was easier than he expected, considering the horse had been dragged through a lot of strange behavior by humans in the past few minutes. And then he saw the other rein had snagged on a gnarled juniper limb.

He led Cap over to a nearby tree and tied him tight. "Don't go anywhere." He scanned the thin forest all around. Somewhere out there, hopefully not too far away, was a horse laden with Chester Woburn's gear. Likely a stolen horse, but he'd need it to drag the fool's body back to the fresh-mounded soil of Boar Gulch's Boot Hill.

Rollie stood, listened, and watched Cap for indications that the horse heard something he didn't. Nothing. Rollie sighed and looked around for sign left by Woburn. He knew the man had come from back there somewhere, east of where Rollie had been daydreaming the day away. That dumb man had had him dead to rights in his sight. He could have lowered that first shot a pinch and Rollie would have been dead before he dropped.

As he searched, he wondered, not for the first time, if dying might not be a bad thing. Did he really have anything in his life that was worth tugging on his boots for every morning? His folks were dead, he had no idea if he had any relations back East or in Ireland, the place of his father's birth, or in Scotland, that of his mother.

He woke each day to throbbing pain deep in his chest, somewhere south of his shoulder, and a numb leg that felt like it was going to give him a whole lot more trouble before it was through. And Delia Holsapple was that she-devil from his past who was bent on grinding her axe all over him. If redressing her own complaints wasn't satisfying enough for her, she invited the rest of the known world to his house for tea and bullets. Only because he'd done his job for all those years.

"Some job, ha." He scanned the granite-studded earth for brass bullet casings. All those years, and what did he get out of it? No support from the headquarters. Nothing but a watch and a kick in the backside.

A low-swooping hawk passed over, close to the tree-tops. The broad reach of its wings beat a sound like tight, rapid breaths. The bird's shadow, then the wind sounds, pulled his gaze upward. The sky was beautiful, a creamy blueness he had lost touch with these past months holed up in Boar Gulch.

He thought back to when he'd enjoyed himself the most in recent memory. His mind flickered to the trip in to the Gulch, alone with Cap on the trail, his confidence growing with each mile under his wheels that he wasn't being tracked, wasn't making the worst decision he'd ever made.

He wanted to feel that happiness again, every day. Why shouldn't he? It wasn't like he'd spent his career abusing those he rousted. He treated them no better or worse than they deserved.

"Oh, knock it off, Finnegan," he said aloud. No sense feeling sorry for himself. That got nobody anywhere. Except maybe Delia Holsapple. It got her into a sad, stunted life of revenge and anger. He didn't want that for himself. But neither did he want to drag Pops and Nosey and the others in town into a mire of his own making. Maybe it would be better if he moved on. At least then the diseased, warped creatures bent on revenge would leave Boar Gulch and its denizens alone and follow him instead.

Rollie pictured himself holed up deep in a box canyon. Somewhere windswept and forbidding, backed to a wall of ragged, raw, gray rock. Armed with more well-oiled weapons than he'd ever need, fresh ammunition mounded about him, he'd face down every single one who ever sought vengeance on him. They would not stand a chance. He would drop them all in a vicious, thunderous sweep. Then what? Wait for the blue smoke to part and climb over the ramparts of bodies?

Rollie shook his head at his foolishness. If all those idiots who called him Stoneface ever knew what he was thinking when his mind wandered, they'd rush to attack him a whole lot sooner than they were.

He smiled and toed a mound of pine needles behind a boulder large enough for a man to crouch behind. Nothing in the needles or in the crevice beneath the curve of the rock, but something was there, to his left, in the same wave of duff. He resisted the urge to reach for it. Sticking your fingers anyplace you couldn't see was a quick way to get snakebit.

He eyed the thing in the needles from a different angle, and it glinted a dull sheen up at him. A nudge with the toe of his boot showed him a casing. He picked it up, and it matched what Chester Woburn was shooting.

Now that he knew where Woburn had stood, firing at him, maybe even toeing the needles beneath the boulder himself—Rollie shook his head and spoke out loud. "Okay then, Rollie. Which way?"

Town. Chester had said he'd come from town. It was doubtful he knew the route to Jed's cabin. Heck, Rollie hadn't been too certain of it himself, plus he'd taken plenty of odd turns and meanderings for the sake of prolonging his enjoyment of the day. That meant Woburn had followed him the entire way from Boar Gulch.

The notion zinged up Rollie's spine like a cold finger. *Why had he waited to ambush me?*

Didn't matter. He'd survived. That was all that counted. He gave up on scouting a second shell, and looked wide for the horse. He stood on the boulder and turned around on it twice. Hand low over his eyes, he saw nothing. He squinted southeastward once more and something dark moved, something he had before taken as the bark of a large ponderosa. Trees don't move, except when persuaded by an axe or a stiff wind or a big boar grizzly.

Had to be a horse. Or a bear. Rollie stepped back to Cap and shucked the Winchester from its scabbard, cocked it, and checking to ensure the pistol was nested once more where it should be, he ambled his way, slow and low, through the trees. He paused to make certain whatever it was hadn't drifted out of his sight. If it was a bear, and there was a good chance of it, he didn't want to emerge from behind a tree and trip over the thing. He could afford to spend a few more minutes of caution stalking it.

Then he saw it for what it was, a gleaming black horse, well-groomed and wearing a handsome brown saddle. He advanced, offering what he hoped were soothing sounds, clucking and whispering to the horse. Unlike Cap, it stood unmoving, watching Rollie walk toward it. Rollie reached it and ran his hand up its neck, slow and tentative. The horse leaned into it.

"Now where did Woburn find such a gentle beast, eh?" He laughed a quick snort, hooked his fingers through the ground-tied reins, and led the horse back toward Cap. "More to the point, where did he steal you from?

"Now you two best get along. We have a damn lot of effort ahead of us and I don't want headache from back-biting, nipping horses. Remember, I'm the one with the guns." His speech didn't seem to have much affect on the horses. Neither did they seem inclined toward bothering each other, apart from communicating through whickers, head tosses, and snorts.

The trio threaded back toward the timbered copse and Chester's crumpled body. He tied Cap well back from the dead man, who'd already begun to attract flies. When he led the black over to Woburn, the horse balked, but not as much as Rollie expected. Hoisting the bloody dead man up onto the horse was going to be a pain.

He planned to roll him in Woburn's own blankets, but when pulling apart the man's gear, he found a rain duster as well. He thought to wrap him in that first, then roll him in the blankets. He tugged the dead man's legs straight and arranged his arms by his sides.

The oilcloth duster looked to be in good repair, near new, in fact, and Rollie thought it might fit Pops. Rollie had one he'd worn for years and it would serve him well, he expected, for as long as he might need it. In the end, he pulled Chester's coat up over his blasted, broken head, and cinched it in a wad to prevent leaking.

He laid out the man's blankets close beside him, and flopped Woburn on, rolled him in it, then rolled the second blanket around the first, in the opposite direction. Next he lashed the bundle head to toe and cinched that at both ends.

The entire time he nibbled on a notion that dogged him. Why should he rush back to Boar Gulch because this jackass decided to kill him and ended up with his nuggets blasted for his efforts? Nah, Rollie decided. He'd be damned if he was going to let this fool ruin his day. He'd planned on inspecting Jed's cabin and claim—now his and Pop's—and he was going to follow through with the plan.

He pooched out his bottom lip in anger and lifted Woburn up onto the black's back. The horse sidestepped, held, and Rollie steadied the dead load, noted blood had soaked into the coat and seeped through into the blankets.

One more length of rope lashed around the load and tied around the saddle horn secured the dead man.

Rollie glanced back at Cap, who stood with ears perked looking toward Rollie and the black. "Don't worry, Cap. I'll be back. You're not being replaced." He led the horse through the trees and rocks toward the cabin. He lost sight of the roof a few times, then all of a sudden it was there before him, a tidy, four-square structure.

From first glance Rollie could tell Jed knew what he was doing with wood. The cabin was trim, well built, no sloppy, jutting log ends. All were squared and the chinking showed no gaps. He'd even taken care to give himself a bit of a view by thinning out the trees before the cabin, the slope gradual and falling away suddenly for a long, deep, precipitous drop a good hundred feet before the site.

The cabin was as solid but plain inside as out. Jed had even crafted a chair and a table, and though a packrat had taken up residence in the corner of the room in the few days since Jed had vacated the place, the single-room cabin was fresh and welcoming.

Rollie lashed the horse's reins to the nearest tree at the edge of the clearing before the cabin. He untied the dead man and let him slide and flop to the ground. The body made a hard, smacking sound. Rollie winced. He grabbed Woburn by the shoulders and leaned him up against a ten-foot log bordering the clearing, as if ol' Chester were relaxing.

"Okay then, chum. You hold on and I'll go fetch our other party guest. Don't go anywhere."

Later, as he sat on a stump seat before Jed's well-built fire ring, Rollie was amused that he was there at all. He wondered if it was odd that he didn't feel horrible about sitting before a fire in the wilderness with a dead man not twenty feet away. He'd killed the man. Shot him to death, in the seeds and then in the head, but a few hours before. In self-defense, yes, but did that matter? The man was as dead as he'd ever get.

Pops would tell him he was thinking too much. *Brooding,* as Nosey called it. "To hell with them," said Rollie, swigging once more from the bottle of the good stuff he'd brought with him. "Even if they are my friends."

He chuckled, then stopped, knowing how very drunk he sounded. It had been a long while before he let himself dissolve into a puddle of drunkenness. *Why now?* He thought maybe it had something to do with the dead man sitting not far away. He stared into the dark and wondered if maybe he should haul Chester over by the fire. He was close to rising, staggering over, and dragging the dead man closer, when he recalled Chester's head exploding, spattering against the pretty tree.

"Damn," he said, and let the bottle slide to the ground, upright beside his boot. He wasn't so drunk that he'd waste the rest of it.

"Maybe it's time to go to bed, eh, Cap?" He half-expected his horse to respond, but he heard only night noises—a cricket, some small critter high up in a tree scratching at bark, the yip of a coyote on another ridge, hunting for his belly, for his family's bellies.

Family, thought Rollie. Something he'd never had, never would, it seemed. Unbidden, Delia Holsapple's pretty face danced into his mind as a spirit, not fiendish at all.

Stoneface Finnegan stared at the dying coals in the fire pit as the night darkened and closed in around him.

CHAPTER TWENTY

Chauncey Wheeler tugged shut the slab plank door of the back room of Wheeler's Mercantile. He slipped the chain and padlock through the steel loop he had had Pieder Tomsen forge for the door. Let them break in now, he thought, giving the chain a last tug. But he knew the store was as secure as it was going to get for Boar Gulch.

It mattered little, as he was always about the place. Where could a fellow go in the Gulch, anyway? The Last Drop, yes, and now the other businesses in town, too. Or heaven forbid, a walk in the forest. The thought shuddered him. All those dirty woodland animals . . .

Chauncey had wanted a reason to interrupt the predictable routine of his days, and Delia Holsapple provided him with such an excuse. Ever since she came to town seeking her odd revenge on Rollie Finnegan, men such as Wheeler had wondered how she was going to make a living, a go of it in Boar Gulch. Turns out, they didn't have a long wait to find out.

Within a week, word among the camp's single men, which meant nearly the entirety of the population, was that they had been invited, or thought they'd been, to

Delia's little rented cabin, a fair jaunt on down the lane off the north end of the main street.

Miss Holsapple was not hosting card games, but what she was doing was earning money as she used to. And though it was tiring work, she was good at it and took gold dust from some of the men who spent time in the various streams about the local peaks. She called it *mining the miners* and would not have been surprised at all to learn that's exactly what Rollie Finnegan called what he did, via The Last Drop.

She was feeling tuckered out from having entertained three men since waking. She had to haul water from a stream that snaked down not far from her cabin, when she heard that annoying little man, Chauncey Wheeler. Her landlord, no doubt dropping by to "check on his investment." As if the little cabin were worth anything more than what she did in it.

"My word, Chauncey. You were here last week." She rested the pail on a stump and dragged her wrist across her forehead. "You back to check on the ballroom of your investment, or perhaps the servant's quarters? I tell you, it must be taxing for a fellow such as yourself to always be running here and there keeping an eye on his properties. Why, renting out an estate such as this to someone such as myself must be downright worrisome."

She tried to force a smile to show him she was funning him. He could be a sensitive little man, as she found most men were, particularly about their bodies. If she let slip one little word that didn't sound as if it were mighty praise regarding their animal nature or their stunning muscles, why, they were apt to snap her mouth with a set of hard knuckles. Others might act moody and revert to grunts and single words. That's when she had to work extra hard for her money, cooing and pretending they were something none of them were—real men.

So far she hadn't found one, not in Boar Gulch, not in Denver City, nor anywhere else she'd worked herself sore. She reckoned she had a wrongheaded notion of what men were. She damn sure knew what they weren't. They weren't tough. Inside, they were all like wilted flowers. Tender and whiny. But they did have money and that was one thing she wanted.

After she'd tired of toying with Stoneface Finnegan, she was going to lay a price on his head and pay whoever laid the old Pinkerton agent low. Then she was going to bed that hired killer and kill him, then take back her money and leave the flea-ridden rat hole of Boar Gulch. But it was early days yet. Her notices in the newspapers were only beginning to pay off. She expected she'd see a whole lot more folks from Stoneface's past make their way to the Gulch.

In the meantime, she would mine the miners. Or in the case of Chauncey Wheeler, she'd mine the merchant. There was no doubt he was a rich little pig, if his boasts were to be believed. He owned a number of choice lots in the town proper, and a handful of claims in the hills surrounding town.

In fact, he was someone she'd been trying to mine for a while. And she believed she was finally making headway. She knew he fancied her, maybe enough to do that thing so many men before him had tried to do—pay her to give up her occupation if she'd be true to them and them only.

The thought made her snort back a laugh. Especially

watching Chauncey panting and gasping his way up the path toward her.

"Good day, Delia," he said, smiling, even as he gasped and trembled for a breath, his red cheeks puffing.

The sight of his gasping face reminded her of how he'd look in another ten minutes. She decided she'd better go easy on him. He looked pretty rough. She waited for him to catch his breath, then played a little game with him. She looked at him, then down at the full bucket sitting on the tree stump between them. Then she looked back at him. Then back to the bucket. He knew what she was doing, but he pulled out his hanky, dabbed his forehead, and proceeded up the trail toward her cabin, talking as he walked.

She sighed, grabbed the bail on the bucket, and did her best to keep it from spilling. "So how's your friend, Stoneface Finnegan? He strung up anybody else lately?"

That got to him. Chauncey stopped in the trail and didn't look back at her. Delia stopped, the water sloshing on her begrimed work dress. Maybe Wheeler had limits. Maybe under all that bluster and baby fat, some part of a man was hidden. Doubtful, she thought, but possible.

"He is not my friend, Delia. In fact, I'm not overly fond of him." Chauncey turned to face her. "But that doesn't mean I approve of what you've done to him."

"What I've done to him?" She slammed the bucket to the ground, advanced on the plump mayor, and poked a long, thin finger in the air, an inch before his nose. "You seem to think you know something you don't know a damn thing about, is that it?"

Wheeler blinked rapidly and shook his head. "I . . . yes, I mean, I . . . I don't know what that means."

"You're damn right, Mayor. Stoneface has caused me

and mine no end of grief, and don't go telling me what you think is the truth, 'cause it ain't. I've heard it all and none of it makes a whit of difference to me. He was doing his job, my father broke the law, blah blah blah."

Chauncey bit the inside of his cheeks and had to keep his eyes from drifting down to her chest. My word, but she was something when she was testy.

She caught him looking at her and said, "Get on up there to my cabin. I perform best when I'm worked up! Go on. Git!"

He thought for a second she was going to spank him and send him packing, as if he was a shameful pup who'd filched pie off a windowsill. Oh, but this was far better. Chauncey scampered up the trail, trying his best not to look like he felt—chunky and awkward.

From behind him he heard Delia's voice urging him with shouts of "You best be ready! Git!"

Not long after, Chauncey woke, moving only his eyelids, and saw an empty space next to him in the bed. And it wasn't his bed. That's right, he'd had a bit of a time with Delia Holsapple. Where was she? Usually when he awoke she was staring at him, shaking her head and wearing a look like she was sucking a lemon.

He half-rolled over and saw her standing naked at the foot of the bed, his trousers in her left hand, his wallet in her right. For the first time since he'd met her, Delia looked surprised, maybe even shocked and ashamed. That emboldened him. "You afraid I wasn't going to pay, Delia?" He smiled. "Or are you taking up the family line of work?"

Her shocked look ended as soon as it began, and her eyes narrowed. "What's that mean, Chauncey?"

"Oh, you know." He pulled the thin blanket up under his chin.

"No, I don't," she said, staring at him. "Tell me."

He swallowed. "Oh, I was joking. I . . . I was going to say embezzlement, heh, heh, but that would be in poor taste, I see that now. Forget it, Delia." He sat up.

She dropped the trousers in a heap. The wallet, too, and moved toward him. "But that's the thing, Mayor. I cannot forget it. Ever. Not until he's dead and gone." She lunged at him. "You too!" Her long fingers raked at his face, his bare chest.

"Hey!" he shouted and shoved her away.

She tripped up on something on the floor, and her hands flailed as she fell backward, offering up a surprised, "Ohhh!" as she dropped from his sight. Something smacked something else hard and she thudded on the floor.

Chauncey knelt on the sagged bed and stared down at her. "Delia?" His voice was a quiet thing. Outside he heard a crow's cry as it winged over the cabin. "Delia?" he said in more of a whisper. She didn't move, and the way she was laying wasn't the way anybody with a choice would arrange themselves.

The cabin's one window, an open-air hole with wooden shutters, was half-closed, forcing shadows across much of that far end of the room where Delia's head lay. In the dimness, Chauncey saw a black shape beneath her head grow wider. She'd hit her head on the stove he saw behind her. On the edge of the rust-pocked woodstove.

Oh no. What to do? Chauncey began breathing hard and fast, too much so, and he lost his breath. He'd never been useful in situations where most folks somehow knuckled down and did what needed doing. Not him, no sir. Alone, he was near useless in a bad situation. He needed to check on her, to see if he could do something for her.

Somehow he found the strength to climb off the bed and placed his foot with care between her parted legs. Unable to help himself, he took a look at her, then, cursed himself for doing so. She was hurt, for pete's sake. What's wrong with him?

"Delia, girl, look. You need to be okay. Come on now, you can have everything in the wallet. I didn't mean a thing by my comment. It was in poor taste, yes, poor taste." Chauncey nodded, agreeing with himself. He bent low over her, and saw the black thing that was moving, growing, saw that it was shiny. Even in the dim light, he knew it for what it was, though he'd hoped he was wrong. It was blood, spreading fast.

It touched his big toe and he jumped and stumbled back onto the bed, which cracked under the sudden weight, and he sagged into it once more. "Delia!" he said louder, struggling to right himself.

Standing again, he grabbed her leg and shook it, but she gave no response. He groped and found her right arm and felt along it until his fingers reached her neck. He thought that was the spot where pressing somehow, you could tell if a person was breathing. There was no movement. He cupped a hand close over her mouth, but felt no breaths.

A thin sound filled the air of the little cabin. It took him a few moments to realize he was making the annoying noise. He was whining like a mosquito in the ear.

"Delia Delia Delia . . ." He repeated her name like a prayer, and looked about the room.

Wasn't much there, a wooden crate along the back wall, atop which was heaped a jumble of clothes, none folded. Beside that, was a small table and a chair with one broken leg. A small looking glass hung on the wall behind the table. It held a silver-handled hairbrush, a bottle of toilet water, and a small jar of something, more lady things. He didn't care what they were. He had to figure out what to do.

Chauncey looked around the room again, took in the bed, the woodstove—that vile tool. Atop it sat a coffeepot, and in the back corner, another small table with a fry pan, an open flour sack, a plate and a bowl, and a few pieces of cutlery looking as if they'd been tossed from across the room.

"Think, Chauncey, think." He rapped himself in the forehead with white knuckles. He had to get dressed. That was the first order. He tugged on his shirt. *Then what? Then get the hell out of here. Leave her? Let someone else deal with her.*

"No no no. That's not right," he said.

It was sort of his fault she'd fallen. If he had only stayed asleep for a while longer, he knew she'd be alive. Why did he have to shove her? Sure, she was angry with him, but she wouldn't have hurt him too badly. He recalled the fiery look in her eyes, felt anew the raw scratches she'd given him. He touched a finger to his face, patted the shirt where underneath she'd clawed his chest.

As he pulled on the rest of his clothes, he made the whining sound again, and didn't stop.

The blood ooze had reached his trousers, bunched where she'd dropped them, and left a sopping spot on the left leg. He almost didn't pull them on, but he had to walk back to town. He gently moved her legs to one side to get at his brogans. They slipped on easy enough, then he patted his pants, his pocket, out of long habit. The wallet! He fingered his pants, his coat again, but remembered she'd had it. It was down there on the floor somewhere.

The room was beginning to smell of the warm stickiness peculiar to fresh blood, and Chauncey's finicky gut was beginning to rebel.

He had to find that wallet. *Then what?* He had to tell somebody. He couldn't leave her there. It was his cabin, after all. He'd been letting her stay for free. That thought came to him as his hand folded over the wallet. He felt it quickly and was relieved to find it was blood free.

The cabin was his, and she had stayed there for free. Where would she keep her own money? The thought dogged him as he escaped outdoors. He breathed the fresh afternoon air, pulling in deep draughts of it over and over until he was dizzy.

The thought of her money crawled back into his mind. Surely she had made a fair bundle while plying her trade in the cabin. Surely it was there somewhere. Likely buried, hidden away. He would have to find it.

When? Now or wait until after he had gotten help? His first thought was Rollie Finnegan. No, the man and the woman hated each other. That would be a bad mistake. But Pops was a man who didn't have a problem making money. Did he?

Chauncey didn't usually willingly associate with people like Pops, former slaves and all, but he had to admit that Pops seemed different, maybe even trustworthy. He might be able to help, might know what to do with her.

No, he had to find that money. Chauncey reentered the

cabin. A quick look at poor dead Delia showed she hadn't moved. Somehow he had hoped she would have, surprising him, telling him she had a headache but felt like she would be okay. Maybe he could get her up on the bed.

He turned and lifted the thick ticking of the mattress. It was a homemade layer, poorly done, and separated in his hand. Maybe she had hid her money in the midst of it. No, that would be uncomfortable to sleep on—or do other things on. He raised it and looked as best as he was able. Nothing. Once more he took in the room.

Perhaps the flour bag, the other few cans on the shelf. He stepped over her and rummaged, spilling beans and flour and coffee beans, but turned up no money. He saw the crate again. Surely she would not hide her valuables in so obvious a spot. But might be something in there. An address to let her kin know she had gone to meet her Maker.

That was a phrase Chauncey had not heard nor thought of in some years. It was one his old Gran used when somebody died, or was about to. A fading memory of her wrinkled face gave him a quick smile as he shoved Delia's pile of jumbled clothes from atop the crate. It was a crude trunk, much battered from use, but solid. He thumbed the latches and lifted the lid.

Inside were few items—an oblong envelope of creamy paper with inky fingerprints along one edge. The end had been sliced open, and he peeked inside. It was filled with papers. He tucked that inside his coat and continued the search. In one corner of the bottom of the trunk was a small hat, one of those impractical hats women liked to wear, with a fan of colored flowers. In the dim light it was difficult to make out what the hat's color was. Maybe green? A veil was rolled up along the top. He lifted the hat and beneath it saw a bulging buckskin pouch.

He grunted, picked it up, and felt the familiar hefty, dead weight of a thing heavy with coins and perhaps more. He didn't bother looking inside, but double knotted the drawstrings and slipped the pouch into his coat pocket. It pulled his coat down on the right side. He picked up her clothes—they smelled of sweat and faintly of perfume—and jammed them in a wad back on the closed lid of the crate.

Once more at the door, he looked in on her and noticed he'd stepped in her blood and left boot prints all over the room—by the little kitchen area, over by the crate, and back to the door. He groaned and closed the door. There was no way such stains would clean up. Anyone he took there would see those stains and wonder what he'd been doing there. He would tell them something. He had the entire trip back to town to think of an excuse.

CHAPTER TWENTY-ONE

It was nearly five o'clock by the time Chauncey made it back to Boar Gulch proper. It had been years since he'd done that much walking in one day. His legs felt like they were filled with water, and his feet sore, and his best brogans were soiled and scuffed. He tried not to think of the blood on their soles.

It didn't help that he was lugging Delia's sack of money hidden in his coat. He didn't dare carry the sack in his hands, which would have been far more comfortable. He could have been seen. People were nosey, had to know other people's business all the time. He'd stop at his house first. He had to change out of his trousers. Then he'd go to the bar.

With each step toward his house, he could feel Delia's blood touching his leg through his trouser leg. The money and the envelope were things he could investigate later. He must hide them. It wasn't like he was stealing. She was his tenant and she had not yet paid him a dime of money toward rent. Other ways had been arranged, yes, but no one else knew what they were. It had been a business arrangement, pure and simple.

He couldn't help wondering how much money she had in the sack. And what if she had hidden even more somewhere? Maybe under a floorboard? Outside, buried under a rock? Those thoughts made him excited, and he wondered if that meant he was a heartless person.

No, he told himself, *this was nothing more than the death of a business acquaintance.*

In clean clothes, he stood outside The Last Drop. He summoned Rollie and Pops outside while Nosey tended bar. The mayor did his best to avoid the stares of the rest of the people in the place. He found them all suddenly irritating. Didn't they have anything better to do with their time than spend every evening in the saloon?

Not that it mattered. He'd thought of a good story on his long walk back to town. Something that might shed him in a favorable light, or at least keep folks from guessing that he'd been at Delia's cabin. He didn't think anybody saw him with her. If anybody said anything, he would say he merely went for an afternoon walk, to look at his various investment lands. He was entitled to do that, after all. He was the founder of the damn place.

"What can we do for you, Mayor?" Rollie leaned down, closer to Chauncey's face. "You okay?"

Chauncey backed away. "Yes, why, why wouldn't I look okay? Well no, if you must know, I'm . . . flustered. That's it. *Flustered.*"

Rollie and Pops exchanged looks of surprise. "Okay, then Chauncey. Maybe you better tell us why you're flustered."

"Yes, yes I intend to do that." He licked his lips.

"I'm waiting. In case you hadn't noticed, we have a full house tonight."

"Yes, yes, Finnegan, don't rush me. Okay, here's what I found. I . . . I found Delia Holsapple."

Rollie nodded.

Pops pulled his pipe from his mouth. "From what I hear, lots of folks are finding her these days."

"No, no. I mean I found her dead."

"What?" Rollie looked shocked

That's good, thought Chauncey. "Yes, you see, I . . . as you know, she lives in a cabin I rent to her for a nominal fee."

"Yeah, I have heard about your nominal fee, Mayor."

"Balderdash! It's a business arrangement, pure and simple. Now where was I?"

"You found her dead."

"Yes, she's in a pitiful state, I'm afraid. Naked, blood everywhere. As I say, I . . . ah, I found her that way. I doubt it was an accident."

"What makes you say that, Chauncey?" Rollie stared at him right in the eye.

The mayor looked away and shrugged. "Stands to reason, doesn't it? She was naked, still is, I mean, and well, the place looks to have been rummaged through, as if someone were . . . were looking for something, yes, that's it." He looked Rollie in the eye, did his best to not look away. "You wouldn't have any idea of what may have happened to her, would you, Mr. Finnegan?"

Rollie folded his arms and looked down at the chubby man. "What is it you're driving at, Mayor?"

"Oh, no, I'm not accusing you of anything,"

"That's good, because I'd hate to think what that might mean, Mayor."

Chauncey held his smile, but neither of the three men

spoke. He wasn't certain what Rollie had meant by that, but it might have been a threat. "What I meant was that you and Miss Holsapple have a history, more so than she did with anyone else in this town. And as we all know, it wasn't a savory history, now was it, Mr. Finnegan?"

"Am I on trial here, Mayor?"

"No, no. I am merely stating the facts of the situation. Potentially crucial facts, I might add, in determining how she died, and at whose hands."

"Why are you here, Chauncey?"

"Well, I should think that's obvious. As the town's appointed lawman, I think it's your obligation to—"

"Hold right there, Mayor. I never accepted any official or unofficial appointment. Did you, Pops?"

Pops tapped his chin and looked up at the evening sky. "No, no can't say I have."

"Oh fine, then as unofficial whatever it is you call yourself—"

"A saloon owner, Mayor. Nothing more, nothing less."

"Fine." Chauncey sighed. "Look, I need help, gentlemen. I need someone to bring her back to the town cemetery. This . . . this situation can't remain as it is. I have an investment to protect. And we have to protect the town. If it should get out that something bad has happened to the town's one . . ."

"Prostitute, Mayor. The word you're looking for is *prostitute*."

"Yes, well, I wouldn't have put it in such an uncouth manner, but then again, I am not you."

"That's a blessing, Mayor."

"You should go fetch her before others find out."

"Only way either of us is going out there is accompanied by you. For obvious reasons."

Chauncey thought of what those reasons might be. Maybe he meant that without him he could accuse them of doing something untoward. The notion was a good one. After all, with Finnegan and Pops out of the way, Chauncey felt certain he could figure out a way to once more resume control of the bar. That was an especially promising thought, as Rollie had done a fine job with the place, and made it into a spot people liked to visit for more than liquor.

He didn't know how much money the man made, but he'd added more gaming tables, and he'd been told that Rollie and Pops were looking to expand, which was promising. If he could own that, oh the money would flow.

But he could think of no way to pin the woman's death on Finnegan or his partner, though the notion of implicating Pops was a good one. Who would believe a former slave in the death of a pretty white woman? Chauncey had to make a decision right then and there, and he couldn't for the life of him figure out how to do that.

"Fine," he finally said with a long sigh. "I'll go with you. But we'd better leave now."

"What's the rush, Mayor? You said so yourself she's dead. If you're certain of that, then she's not going anywhere."

"Please, we need to go fetch her."

Rollie turned to Pops. "You mind going? We're swamped in there and . . . well I don't think it would be wise for me to go there, you know."

Pops nodded. "Good thinking. I'll go." He looked at

the mayor. "We'll need a horse. Trail out that way's too narrow for a wagon, not like the road out to the diggings."

"Take Cap," said Rollie. "He's calm enough."

"Okay, let's go, Mayor," said Pops, lighting his pipe and walking toward the little stable they'd built out back of the saloon.

CHAPTER TWENTY-TWO

The walk out to the cabin was a quiet one. Pops led Cap and Chauncey lugged an unlit lantern. Pops had tried to converse with the mayor, and asked him all manner of questions about the girl and how he found her, but Chauncey kept his mouth closed.

Halfway there, the mayor said, "Are you planning on staying in Boar Gulch, Mister . . ."

Pops didn't reply at once, but puffed his pipe for a few more steps. Then he said, "Way I look at it, Mister Mayor, a man has to be somewhere in life, doing something useful each and every day. I am in Boar Gulch right at this time and I believe I am being of use, at least to Rollie. That's enough for now. We none of us knows what waking up tomorrow will bring us, now do we?"

It was Chauncey's turn to be silent. He'd be damned if he was going to respond to an impertinent former slave. Some whites he knew would do that, but not him. They continued threading their way through the trees and reached the cabin ten minutes later.

Pops tied Cap to a close tree and saw the pail set by the cabin. "Did she have to haul her water far, living here?"

"No farther than most," said Chauncey, as if defending the practice.

Pops thumbed the crude wooden lift latch and pushed open the door. He peeked in, then opened it wider and peered into the darkened little cabin. "Bring that lantern over here, will you, Mayor?"

Chauncey hesitated. He didn't like the idea of this man telling him what to do. But this situation was different, so he decided he'd let it slide this one time. He puffed up his chest, jutted his bottom jaw, and held up the lantern out of reach.

Pops looked at him, then at the lantern, and made the extra step toward it. "Obliged, Mayor." He lit it, then looked at Chauncey. "Let's get something straight betwixt us, Mayor. You called on me. I didn't stumble on this little mess you made."

Chauncey began to speak, but Pops held up a hand. "No, I ain't through. I'd much rather be back at The Last Drop playing poker. I had a hand going that you wouldn't believe. Expect I could have won Nosey's trousers this time"—he smiled and shook his head—"but I'm here instead. So a little more help and a little less baby play would be much appreciated."

Chauncey felt his face redden. He gritted his teeth but didn't speak. Pops was right, of course. He had gone to the bar looking for help. But that didn't mean he had to like the situation. It would go quicker if he made the best of it.

Pops lit the lantern and nudged the door open as wide as it would go. He took a breath and walked in. "Come on, Mayor," he said, waiting inside.

Chauncey followed. He looked over Pops' shoulder and

there was Delia as he'd left her—sprawled on her back, her head bent at that bad angle as if she were trying to bite her own shoulder. Her eyes were half-open, her naked body exposed.

"You didn't have the decency in your head to put her up on the bed? Or at least cover her? What is wrong with you, Mayor?" Pops shook his head and gritted his teeth as he looked the scene over. He touched the back of his hand to her near arm. It was cold. "Yeah, she's dead all right. Seen enough death in my time to know."

He looked closer at her, closed her eyes, then used both hands to pull her head up off the floor. "Looks to have hit her head on the stove there." He nodded at the low woodstove within arm's reach. There was a spot on the front edge that looked like it could be bloody.

"Straighten that bed, spread out blankets wide so we can lay her on there and cover her up for her last ride." Pops set the lantern on the little table, caught sight of the mayor in the mirror, staring down at the dead woman. "Mayor!"

The man jerked his gaze upward as if he'd been awakened. "Yes, the blankets, yes, okay."

Pops held her under her armpits, Chauncey held her ankles, and they lifted the woman onto the bed, her body stiffening but soft enough that they had to grip her tight. Pops had no choice but to step in the blood, though he tried to cover much of the thickening puddle with extra bedding. They laid her on the sagged, broken bed and Pops covered her with the rest of the quilt. Then he wrapped her with a coil of rope he'd brought.

They lugged her outside, and Pops hefted her up, then laid her on Cap's back and secured her. The horse flinched, then stood still as Pops spoke in low, soothing tones to him.

Chauncey cleared his throat. "I'll pay for the coffin. And I can speak words over her grave. It's the least I can do."

"I'll say." Pops looked at Chauncey until the man looked away. "We both need to go back in there, make certain we each see what the other's doing. You understand?"

The mayor nodded, his face drawn tight as if he might throw up, but didn't make a move toward the door.

Pops sighed and swung the lantern. "Let's go, Mayor. The night's not getting any younger."

Pops waited for the mayor to enter before him, then he entered the cabin. The yellow light cast their shadows long on the close walls and low ceiling. "We should bring some of her frocks. Maybe we can get Mrs. Pulaski at the Lucky Strike to clean her up, dress her for burying." He held the lantern down low to the floor. "Hoo boy. What a mess. Someone walked all over this place after stomping in the blood."

"Oh, oh, I'm afraid that was me. I . . . I wanted to make sure no one was hiding in the shadows, you see." The man did not look at Pops, but concentrated on studying the bed, the wall, the doorway.

"Uh-huh," said Pops eyeing the mayor. He found a cloth rucksack, vaguely recalled it as the one Miss Holsapple had lugged with her when she arrived in town, and stuffed in what clothes he could find. Beneath the clothes stood a wooden crate, like a traveling trunk of sorts. "You happen to know if there's anything in here?"

The mayor looked about to answer, then shrugged and looked away again. Pops lifted the lid and held the lantern low. He saw an odd little flowery hat. He pulled it out and looked it over. "Might be she liked this hat." He laid it on top in the rucksack. "I can't say I like it, but then again, I'm not the best judge of a lady's finery. Hope she liked it enough to spend eternity wearing it."

He squinted about the place but saw nothing else that might be of use in laying Delia Holsapple to rest. "Okay then, Mayor, I'd say we're done here. I'll tie this bag on the horse, you lock up the cabin so no critters get in. And as you're the owner, I recommend you clean it out soon. Even at that, the blood might be too soaked in to come up. You never know."

The mayor put a hand over his mouth. "Oh, I never thought of that." He peeked in once more, though he could see little beyond dark shapes. Shapes that seemed to beckon and leer. He slammed the door tight and tugged the latch, though he knew the crude lever was as set as it could be.

They began walking back to town, Pops leading the horse, Chauncey walking behind, carrying the lantern.

"'Course," said Pops, "you could always set fire to the cabin. Quickest way of getting rid of anything you don't want others to see."

The mayor heard him, then stopped walking. He looked up the trail at the man's back, less visible with each step in the gloom.

Say what he will, thought Chauncey, *it was not a bad idea.*

CHAPTER TWENTY-THREE

Delia Holsapple's funeral drew everybody in town. She was carried up to Boot Hill by four men from the downstairs back room of the partially built hotel where Mrs. Pulaski and Camp Sal had tended to her, in what the men regarded as that mysterious way women had among their kind.

Rollie doubted that Delia in life was well-regarded among the few other women in town, in part for her profession, in part because she was a fiery sort who kept to herself when not entertaining her customers.

Though he admitted not knowing much about women, at times he'd seen that given a shared cause women could be more than kind and generous with each other, to the point of squint-eyed suspicion of any men at their fringes. *What a difference from men,* he mused. Men in a group were generally more apt to get drunk and shoot each other.

There were a few quivering lips and red eyes in the assemblage, most among the men. From the number of brute miners holding back their tears, it appeared Delia was one popular gal. Hell, until he'd learned who she was, he was all worked up about her, too. But not after. No, thank you.

He felt bad about the way her life had turned out. While he didn't feel responsible for much of it, a spark of guilt flickered in him for his role in the rotten mess her family had become.

Rollie paid attention when Chauncey Wheeler cleared his throat and held up a worn leather Bible. A red silk ribbon swung from atop the spine and danced in a light breeze. The mayor's wet eyes and quavering voice added weight to the passage he read. "Yea, though I walk through the valley of the shadow of death . . ."

Not original, thought Rollie, *but fitting.* Rollie knew a crowd would soon be at his bar and it would be expected of him to splash out the first round of drinks for free, in honor of the departed. Especially so since it seemed everybody in town knew of his relationship to her. Or thought they did. He'd overheard enough of their blather to know the townsfolk were largely off the mark.

They alternately thought Rollie had been a relative of hers once, or had been her estranged husband she'd finally tracked down, or that he was her father—that one stung when he'd heard it, and he'd almost said something. The closest to the truth the rumors came was that he was a disgraced lawman who'd had something to do with the downfall of her family.

As he looked around at the faces of the people in the town, he realized he knew many of them enough to smile and greet them by name each day, others to nod to, some trying to avoid his gaze because they owed him money or because they were drunk the night before and may well have told him things they regretted sharing.

Chauncey Wheeler's voice clipped off with, "Now let us pray." The fat little man closed his Bible and bowed his head, and everyone else did, too. Rollie was the last to do so, and once more he took in the assemblage and mused on the notion that Delia Holsapple was more responsible than he for him being there. The arrest of her father, then the alley attack, all led him in a clear, if crooked line to Boar Gulch.

"You looked suitably bothered by the ceremony," said Nosey some minutes later as they ascended the steps to The Last Drop.

Rollie realized the journalist had been talking to him. He shrugged. "My heart's not made of stone."

"Nope, only your face," said Pops and winked.

Because it came from Pops, Rollie decided he could let a crack like that slide. But nobody else. Now why was that? He'd only known the man a few short months but in that time Pops had become perhaps a closer friend than anybody he'd ever known. Not that he'd ever had close friends.

Even as a kid in Providence he had been a lone wolf, roving the stacks of the Brown University library, keeping busy while his father arrived home and drank himself to sleep each night. His mother always held out warmed stew, dumplings, or biscuits for him. His father was not a mean drunkard, but he was dedicated to the task. It was something Rollie was thankful he'd not become.

When Rollie was fifteen, his mother, a slight but formidable woman, and midwife to the neighborhood, had taken ill with what she called "chesty croup." It grew worse and finally, two weeks before Christmas, she had taken to the bed far later than she should have. "The good neighbors needed me," she'd argued. Within the week she was gone.

Rollie tried to keep his father in good health, tried to replicate all the ministrations and quiet, dogged kindnesses his mother had bestowed on them both. He'd cooked and washed, and none of it mattered. By the last days of February, his father, too, had wasted away.

He'd seen them both buried. His father's service took place on a dank, wet afternoon in the churchyard with four people in attendance—himself, the priest, and two of his father's pub chums Rollie had seen in the past. The priest droned his way through the requisite words, glancing at Rollie throughout. At the end, Rollie tossed wet soil down into the long, slump-edged trench onto his father's coffin.

As he walked away, the priest had touched his sleeve and suggested he come back to the rectory for tea. It had been a wet day, and the thought of a cup of hot tea before a warming fire sounded good to Rollie.

He nodded yes and they trudged through the burial ground and up to the stone house beside the church. A plump woman Rollie did not recognize brought them tea and scones and the priest talked of the eternal nature of the human soul as the mantel clock's gears ground away. The fire was warm and the day had been so long, Rollie was soon asleep in the chair.

He woke some time later to see the priest seated across from him. A small oil lamp did its best to light the rest of the dark-paneled room that the open fire couldn't reach. Someone had draped a quilt over his knees.

The priest spoke again, his voice cracking the silence of the room. "Master Finnegan, it was your mother's wish, and yes, your father's as well, that you be taken in by the church. You are far too young to spend your time alone. You must have a family. You must dedicate yourself to something greater.

"Therefore, I have, at no small cost to myself, undertaken to have you placed in care of the young men's dormitories at St. Damian's Monastery as an acolyte. There you will receive such training as suitable for a young man pursuing a life dedicated to his God. Perhaps, in time, you will become a priest. That is not for me to say, but for your Lord to determine. I have taken the liberty of having your things sent for. You will need little, save for good shoes, a willingness to work, and a heart open to the glories of God. You leave tonight."

Rollie stared at the priest for some long moments. The man's words echoed, one on another, over and over in his head, as if shouted into a stone cavern, only to bounce back and wash over themselves, again and again. Finally he licked his lips and stood, grabbing the little blanket before it slipped to the floor. He laid it on the chair's arm. "I am grateful to you for that, Father. If I may . . . I would like to visit my parents' graves one last time before I leave."

The priest smiled.

Like a cat, thought Rollie. *He looks like a cat who has cornered a mouse and knows it will soon feed.*

"Of course, my son." The priest plucked out a shiny gold pocket watch and clicked it open. "You have twenty minutes before the driver arrives. Don't be late."

"Yes, Father." Rollie bowed and shook the man's hand and found his way outside, into the dark, rainy night. He did visit the graves of his mother and father long enough to pat the shared stone. "Thank you and good-bye." Then he walked out of that city and never ventured back.

He worked his way north, south, and west, never east, and after a year and a half of drifting from job to job, he joined the US Army. He wasn't yet eighteen, but he suspected he had learned more on his own than he ever could have learned shut away in a forbidding rock pile of St. Damian's as a slave to others, in the service of a God he had yet to discover for himself.

CHAPTER TWENTY-FOUR

"Rollie?"

He heard his name, or at least the name he'd gone by most of his life, *Rollie,* short for Roland The voice sounded far off, as if spoken through water.

"Hey!"

The voice sounded like it was shouted right into his ear. Because it was. It also didn't hurt that somebody poked him in the arm.

"You okay, Rollie?" It was Pops.

"Why?"

"Why?" Pops shrugged, and went back to sweeping the floor. "Because you've been acting odd since the funeral yesterday. Why don't you take a walk and I can tidy up the place."

"Nah, I'm fine. Thinking, that's all." Rollie resumed wiping down the bar top and saw Chauncey Wheeler walk in. The mayor greeted the two men with a weak smile and a nod.

"A little early for you, eh, Mayor?" said Rollie.

"Yes, well"—he looked about the room as if there

might be a dozen men hiding behind chairs—"there's been an accident."

"Another one?" said Pops, glancing first the mayor, then at Rollie.

"No, no, nothing like that." The mayor sneered at Pops. "That is to say, poor Delia's cabin, which as you know I owned, has burned to the ground. Bone and his son found it nearly gone. There was nothing they could do." He shrugged and made certain each man saw his hound-dog eyes all but welling with tears.

"Well now," said Pops. "That is a shame. Yes, a convenient shame, but still a shame."

"Convenient?" said the mayor as if he'd been hit across the face with a ripe trout.

Rollie nodded. "Now we'll never know the cause of her demise. I expect any clues have been lost for good."

"Ah yes, well, that can happen in life, eh, gentlemen?" Chauncey tugged his vest down once more. "Which brings me to the real reason I am here." From out of his coat he tugged a cream-colored envelope and set it on the bar top before him. "Some of Delia's personal papers."

"How did you get those?" said Rollie, eyeing the man.

"She . . . entrusted them to me some time ago." He nodded as if agreeing with himself might lessen the feeling that what he said sounded like a lie.

"Uh-huh," said Pops.

Chauncey frowned at him and looked back to Rollie.

"Why tell us?"

"Because there's something here you may find of interest. I know I did."

Rollie leaned on the bar, resisting the urge to punch Wheeler in the face. Sometimes the man's very presence was like having a sliver jammed beneath a fingernail. "What is it, Mayor? We're busy here."

"You know," said Chauncey, straightening. "I am bringing this to your attention out of the kindness of my heart. I don't have to do this."

"You don't do anything out of kindness, Chauncey. You always have an angle. That much I know about you. Now out with it and I'll see if it's worth paying you or not."

"Well! If that's how you feel," the pudgy man turned and made to put the papers back in his coat.

"Bye," said Rollie, resuming to wipe the bar top.

"Oh, all right." Chauncey slapped the envelope on the bar. "There are at least a dozen receipts in here, perhaps more, from newspapers. Big-city papers."

Rollie stopped once more. Receipts from newspapers in Delia Holsapple's things. He didn't like the direction this conversation was taking.

Wheeler fanned them on the bar, angled so Rollie could read them. Pops leaned over and gave them a once-over. Among them was a copy of the initial large notice the Dickey twins had had with them. So that was her game.

"If these dates are true, most of these haven't run yet," said Pops.

Rollie sucked air through tight teeth.

"And they're spread out from now until next year." Pops looked at his business partner.

"All marked PAID IN FULL, too," said Rollie, reading the receipts.

"You could always write to them, ask them to cease and desist running the advertisements. Perhaps under threat of legal action."

Pops said, "That's not a bad idea, Mr. Mayor."

"Nope," said Rollie, looking at the ceiling. "I think I'll let them come. Settle this foolishness one idiot at a time."

"But that's . . . that's suicide."

"Thank you for your vote of confidence, Mayor."

"I won't permit it. You can't allow society's dregs to continue to descend on innocent Boar Gulch! I . . . as mayor won't stand for it." He crossed his arms and tried to maintain a gaze with Rollie. It didn't work.

As much as Rollie hated to admit it, the mayor had a point. It was selfish of him to ignore the rest of the Gulch's citizens.

"Yeah," said Pops reading the receipts. "From these dates, some of these have already been published. She bought a whole lot of newspaper space."

"Which means we can expect fresh rounds of law-breakers to wander on up to the Gulch." Rollie sighed. "Okay, I'll write to the papers. But I doubt they'll do anything to change it."

The mayor sniffed and smoothed his lapels. "Good. And in the meantime, I suggest you . . . both"—he looked from one man to the other—"decide your pecking order."

"What's that mean?" said Pops.

"Why, who's going to be town sheriff and who's going to be deputy, of course."

Rollie disagreed. "We don't need law up here, Mayor. What we need is justice. We've been doing a solid job of doling that out for some time now. At least I haven't heard any complaints from the good citizens of Boar Gulch."

The mayor responded as if he hadn't heard them. "And we'll need a jail, too."

"Nope," said Pops. "Haven't yet."

"That's because your tactics are thuggish and heavy-handed, the same as those of your visiting friends."

Rollie walked out from behind the bar, hands on his hips.

The mayor backed up a step and gulped as he took in the Schofield in the polished leather holster. "I expect you both have things to discuss . . . a course of action. We can talk later at length about this." He left the receipts on the bar top and all but ran for the open door.

"That does leave me sort of trapped here," said Rollie, almost smiling.

"Nah," said Pops, pulling his Greener out from under the bar. "*We're* trapped . . . partner. Now, isn't it your turn to wash the glasses?"

Rollie stroked his chin. "Speaking of unwanted questions, you seen Nosey?"

Pops shrugged. "He'll turn up. We're supposed to play a few hands." He smiled. "Kid thinks he can win his trousers back."

CHAPTER TWENTY-FIVE

"Who you?"

Nosey turned to see a large, block-headed man, thick with muscles stressing the seams of a black wool suitcoat. He wore a full, trimmed beard, once brown but gone gray throughout. His bristled eyebrows looked like ravens taking flight.

"I beg your pardon. May I help you?"

"Only if you're Finnegan."

The man's voice reminded Nosey of stream gravel grinding between stones. He wished the man would clear his throat.

"Me?" Nosey smiled and shook his head. "Not hardly. He and Pops are gone to—" He recalled too late the one thing above all others he really shouldn't do. That was to let anyone know anything about Rollie. Not so easy these days, what with all the newcomers to town.

"I know you ain't him."

"How do you know that?"

"Because I know ol' Stoneface."

"Ah," said Nosey, unsure what to do next. Likely the man was in Boar Gulch because of Delia's newspaper advertisements. It stood to reason that Nosey had to do whatever it would take to keep the man from attacking Rollie on his return.

"Let's go," said the man, wagging a huge plate-nickel revolver. The gun had appeared in his hand unbidden, as if by magic.

"What do you mean *go*? Go where?"

The big man sighed. "Stands to reason that since you ain't him, and you said he's not here, that he truly is here. And it stands to more reason that you work for him or you know him, both or one, makes no never mind. Either way, you are of some value to him. Knowing what I do of Finnegan, he wouldn't want anything bad to happen to anybody, let alone a person who works for him. You must be friends with Stoneface. I don't know who Pops is, but if he's chummy with Finn, I aim to include him in all this, too."

"What do you mean, *all this*?"

"Exactly that. Want to see how much you're worth to ol' Stoneface. You ask too many questions."

Nosey stood straighter. "Surely you don't intend to abscond with me. If the answer is yes, then I have the right to ask all manner of questions."

For the first time since he walked into The Last Drop, the big man smiled. His mouth was filled with gold teeth. "I like your spunk, boy. And yes, that's exactly what I intend to do. Use you as bait."

"Oh." Nosey ducked down behind the bar. "Not if I have a say in the matter." He rose with the bar's twelve-gauge shotgun and pointed the single-barrel at the stranger's big face. The man leaned forward and stuck a sausage-shaped finger into the snout of Nosey's shotgun and laughed his gravelly, wet laugh. "Now as I said, let's go. I don't like repeating myself."

Nosey considered his options. One, he could pull the trigger and blow this man's hand apart. But he didn't like shooting guns, and didn't particularly like hurting people. After all, what if the man was somehow a friend of Rollie's and this was a joke?

He could also shove the gun at the man and run for the door. He was slimmer and smaller than the stranger. Yes, Nosey thought maybe he could make the door well ahead of the man. Then what? He'd be outside, running away from the brute. With his back exposed. The man would shoot him deader than dead, as Wolfbait might say.

And yelling wouldn't do a thing to save him. Might only attract other folks who'd get themselves hurt in the process. Besides, people in Boar Gulch yelled all the time, and for little reason, it seemed. Sometimes just to yell. It was an odd place that he hadn't much gotten used to.

Nosey didn't know the man in the least, but he suspected he was a hardcase. Otherwise how could he have known Rollie? Especially as he called him *Stoneface*. Not many options. "Why should I go with you?" Nosey couldn't help himself. Asking questions was for him as natural as talking was to Wolfbait, silence was to Rollie, and cracking bad jokes was for Pops.

"Because if you don't, I'll kill you where you stand. Got it?"

Nosey gulped and nodded. He lowered the shotgun and set it on the bar top. "Okay, then. Where are we going? You don't think you'll get away with whatever it is you're mulling over, do you? Where are you from, anyway? Rudeness is obviously something you're accustomed to, so I am going to guess you're from New York City. Am I correct?"

"Wrong all the way. Now move." He rammed his gun barrel hard into Nosey's spine.

"Hey! Enough of that rough play, mister. I am a student of the martial arts. At first opportunity I am contemplating rendering you incapacitated. The only question is with a spinning kick or with a series of deadly chopping blows about your neck and face."

"One more word from you and I will shoot you now and be done with it. I'd prefer not to as yet. I want Rollie to squirm. But not that bad."

Nosey pulled in a breath as if to speak.

The man cranked back on the hammer. "One word."

Nosey kept his mouth shut and the man said, "Back door."

They walked through to the storage room with the bunks set up on either side of the far back door. The stranger said nothing but grunted, "Hmm."

Nosey didn't think the man knew much about the layout of the town, because out behind the bar the trees had been cut down, save for a few scraggly, hopeful pines. That meant that other than outhouses and shanties for storage, and a few poorly built corrals, the place was wide open. Anybody who happened to be behind their own tent or cabin or shack, the various structures that made up the main street buildings, would see him being pushed out and away by a big, surly, dark stranger.

Nosey poked his head out the door and looked quickly left, then right—and saw nobody. He tamped down the urge to shout, remembering the man's threat, and walked down the wooden ramp that served as entry to and exit from the back door.

"Walk straight back and up the hill."

Nosey did as he said, and scanned below as they crested the rise overlooking the usually busy main street. Nobody.

"Seems like you won't be all that missed," The man chuckled. "Keep walking. Back behind those pines over there we'll come to two horses."

Again, Nosey was tempted to speak, but the man's threat clanged in his head like a brass bell. And then he got an idea. "Why are you doing this? Rollie doesn't even like me."

Again the man chuckled. "I doubt that. He trusts you enough to run his bar while he's away. If I'm wrong, I'll shoot you and find someone else. If I'm right, Stoneface will turn up sooner than later. If there's one thing I have some of, it's time. And don't think I didn't notice you spoke before I said you could. Don't make that mistake again."

Nosey coughed and clipped it short, worried that a cough might be mistaken for a word. No bullet ripped through him. He walked closer to the trees, aware like no other time in his life of the sounds about him. There was a breeze, high up, moving the tall, needled branches of the ponderosas. By his feet, scattering as they walked, bugs chirped—were they crickets? He'd spent nine months out here in the wilderness of the world but knew precious little about it. He really should pay more attention to such things.

Like the way the air felt cool against his stubbled cheeks. He'd meant to shave this morning, he really had.

He hoped the man wasn't going to kill him, not the way he looked. Not with everything he had planned to do out West.

If he lived through this, he was going to get the hell out of Boar Gulch and track down those men he'd only dreamed of tracking down. Earp, Cody, that Black Bart character, all of them. He would write those books, make the money he needed to clear his name, maybe make a small fortune in the process . . . and then what?

Settle on the Barbary Coast in Frisco, that's what. *Think of it, Nosey, my boy,* he told himself, *writing up a storm all day, tall tales about tall men doing mighty deeds!* Little if any of it true, but who would know or care? That's what readers of the dime novels wanted. And then he'd spend his evenings gambling among the velvet-lined splendors of that fair city's finest gaming halls. He smiled.

Something rammed hard into Nosey's back.

"Ow! Hey!"

"Get moving."

He remembered he was back in Boar Gulch with a madman, close to the brink of death itself.

"We only stop when I tell you to stop. Understand me? Now, over behind those trees to my horses."

True to the man's word stood two horses, one a pack-horse wearing a pannier laden with gear. Nosey saw the black handle of a fry pan, the top of a gray enamel coffee-pot, two long items wrapped in canvas that could well be long guns, and other bulging bags and bits of gear.

"You'll be riding on Tommy, the mule. Plenty of room if you arrange your legs right. Don't try to do anything I wouldn't want you to, because I'll be riding behind you, and my gun will core your guts clean out. Tommy won't flinch. He's stalwart."

"That's not a word I have heard much out this way." Nosey had intended to say more but realized he'd spoken and shut up tight. His shoulders hunched and he edged around the mule, hoping the man might not shoot him yet.

"Aw, you can talk now. But not a lot. I didn't want you to go blathering while we were in earshot of the town."

"Fine. How did you come to know a word such as stalwart?"

"You cut right to it, don't you?" The man wagged the gun. "Lead him to that stump and use it to climb aboard." He waited until Nosey did as he'd instructed, then said, "As to your question, I'm not as simple as you might think. I have had a solid education, and I held a good job, as well. No, I see a question forming on your face. Never you mind what my job was. But my point is, don't judge a man by what you see. You will often miss the mark."

Nosey nodded. "That's fair. When you see me, for instance, what do you suppose I am?"

The man sighed and mounted his own horse. "I don't know, and I don't much care right now. We'll be riding that way." He pointed. "Southwest."

"For how long? The nights grow cold hereabouts."

"Not where we're going. And don't you worry about it none."

"I am going to worry about it because my life is at stake. The least you can do is engage me in conversation. There are many things people derive enjoyment from in life. Some like to gamble, some like to drink, some like to dally with women, some like to ride horses fast and

hard. I enjoy conversation. Of all sorts and with all sorts.
I meet interesting people that way."

Nosey heard nothing from the man, but noticed the
mule's hoofbeats were the only ones he heard. He turned
to see his captor had slumped in the saddle, pistol aimed
at Nosey, but his eyes looked to be closed, or nearly so,
and his lined cheeks lighter in color. Then he scrunched
his features as if deciding a difficult purchase.

Presently, the man sighed and heeled the horse into a
walk, drawing closer. "Why do you like to talk so much?
I am regretting this course of action. Bear right down there
at the bottom of the hill."

"I can no more answer your question than I can tell you
why I am the height I am or why my feet reach the ground.
Or why I am being kidnapped by a mysterious madman."

That set his captor to chuckling. "You remind me of my
little cousin, Vincent."

"Why?"

"Because he was annoying as all get-out. I vow you top
him in that, though. We'll ride on this course, better part
of a mile."

"What's there? And I have been called annoying before,
you know. I take it as a compliment." Nosey straightened
his shoulders and raised his head high.

"Wasn't intended as such."

They rode the rest of the way in anything but silence.
Nosey asked questions and his captor sighed and told him
to shut up, which did no good.

Finally, the man said, "See that clearing up to your left?
That's where we'll camp."

"Camp? Why? We're not all that far from town."

"Because I said so. Now climb down and build a fire up there where the rock wall angles. You'll see the spot. Others have made camp there. And do me a favor, don't talk while you're doing it."

"Why a fire?"

"Good lord, man, shut up and do as you are told." The man groaned. "I fancy a cup of coffee is why." But his words came out high, as if forced between his teeth.

Nosey nodded and gathered sticks, dry needles, and larger jags of dried branches that were close by. He assembled them in a rough jumble beneath the scorch marks on the rock where previous travelers had made their fires.

"You'll find matches in that saddlebag. Make them count. They come dear."

"If you don't mind me saying so, you don't look well. Can I fix you a spot to sit?"

"No. I'll lean here a moment. I—" He broke off and Nosey looked over at him. It appeared as though the man had fallen asleep or passed out while leaning on the rock face. It seemed as if the color of the man's cheeks above his beard changed from ruddy to gray as he watched. His lips blued and his breathing came hard, his chest working as if by weak strokes on a bellows.

Nosey walked closer, an arm out. "Are you . . ."

The man's eyes flicked open and he focused on Nosey. He thumbed the hammer back once more. "Get to that fire, boy."

Nosey nodded and set to the task. He'd filled the coffeepot and was about to place it on rocks beside his modest blaze when a voice from below shouted, "Tate McCallum!"

Nosey spun to see Rollie standing below with Cap a

few yards behind. Rollie had his rifle aimed up at the mysterious man.

"Stoneface Finnegan, as I live and breathe," said Nosey's captor, pushing off the rock face, and swinging a rifle to bear on Rollie while keeping his shiny pistol aimed at Nosey. "I did not expect to see you so soon."

"Here I am. Let my man go."

"I think not. I have things to say first."

"Let my man go and then talk all you want to."

Tate McCallum sighed and closed his eyes. "You are as tiresome as ever. All right, then. I was wearying of his constant chatter anyway." He raised the pistol and wagged it. "Go on, son. I won't shoot you. Though any more annoying questions and I feared I may have had to."

Nosey descended the rock face, sliding the last five feet until he landed in a squat a few feet from Rollie. Rollie did not look at him. "Why are you here?" he shouted up at McCallum.

"Why?" McCallum chuckled. "With all your questions, you are beginning to sound like your man there." His face grayed once more and he closed his eyes a moment and leaned against the rock face. He seemed to catch his breath. "Okay then, I'll scratch that itch for you. Because you are the only man in my whole grown life who has ever bested me at anything. And it doesn't sit right with me. I will not go to my Maker without having gained that upper hand. It might mean little to you, but it means everything to me."

"Enough to die for it?" said Rollie.

"Yep." McCallum sighed and leaned back once more. "Going to anyway."

"What's that mean?" Rollie kept the Winchester raised and aimed at the man.

"Means I have a cancerous growth somewhere in me. That's what the doc in Putney, Nevada, tells me, anyway. 'Big as a baby's head,' he said. Why, you should have seen him say that. Eyes wide and bright like a child at the candy counter. I wanted to reach right down his throat and pull up a hunk of him about the size of a baby's head just for good measure."

"Why didn't you? The old Tate McCallum would have."

McCallum smiled, nodded. "Yeah, I reckon." He lost the smile and stiffened. "Don't sugar-talk me, Finnegan. I came here to kill you. Don't deprive me."

Rollie never flinched. He kept his gaze sighted along the barrel of his rifle. "I could walk away, Tate. I doubt you'd shoot a man in the back."

Once more the man sagged and then dropped his rifle. It slid, clattering to the rock by his feet.

"Tate?"

"Yeah." The man's face was gray, and he seemed to collapse further in on himself.

"Do for yourself . . . and you'll have beaten me to it."

At that, the man's eyes opened, his bushy brows rising. "You think?"

"Yep." Rollie lowered his rifle and turned his back on the man. "So long, Tate McCallum. Good luck . . . wherever you end up." He walked down the trail, scooped up Cap's reins. "Come if you're coming," he said as he passed Nosey.

For once, Nosey didn't say anything.

The two men and one horse were a quarter-mile away

when they heard a quick, lone pistol shot that broke apart on the breeze.

After a few moments, they heard only breeze.

Nosey said, "I'll send Bone and his boy to fetch him and the horses."

Rollie nodded and kept walking.

Later in the bar, Nosey faced Rollie. "I think I deserve to know what that was all about, don't you?"

Rollie looked at him. "No." He walked past him.

"Well, say what you will about Tate McCallum, he was an engaging, if reluctant, conversationalist. That's more than I can say for you, Rollie."

Wolfbait nodded and Nosey walked over. "You said the man's name was Tate McCallum?"

"That's what Rollie called him, yeah."

"I think I know who he was." Wolfbait looked down at his empty glass, then back at Nosey.

"Oh, for heaven's sake, all right. But it better be good or I'm charging you."

Once the fresh beer was set before the old man, he took a sip, said "Aah," and set it down.

"Well?" said Nosey, leaning on the bar and staring at him.

"Tate McCallum was what was called an enforcer for a railroad tycoon. I forget his name, but Tate's I remember because I ran across him once."

"You did?"

"Sure did. It was his job to stop railroad laborers from unionizing. By any means necessary."

"So how did you know him?"

"I was working from the inside, trying to get the union up for the workers. McCallum was a bigger man then. And meaner. He swung a mighty club, a table leg, I think it was. Famous for it. Bloodied it up in good shape, too. Heads, arms, legs, men, women. Didn't matter to him. I don't recall hearing he ever killed anybody, not that I'd know, of course, but—"

"He only killed one person, as far as I am aware." Rollie appeared beside them, arms folded, but he looked above them at the far wall. "A young man named Vincent something or other. Hit him in the head and dropped him. Tate claimed self-defense, of course, but nobody who was there agreed with that. He ended up in prison. Took the fall for his boss, the owner of the Anderson and Whitney-Pike Railroad. He was the one I really wanted. Almost lost my job over it."

"Why?" said Nosey.

Rollie sighed. "Because we were hired by that railroad man as special operatives during a strike, guarding his strikebreakers. But that boss had his own men, men who got unruly. McCallum was one of several who carried it too far."

Wolfbait sipped his beer. "Following his employer's orders."

"Yep," said Rollie. "Same as me."

Wolfbait slid off his stool and ambled to the door. "Good night, gentlemen. See you tomorrow."

"I always wondered how Wolfbait got that horrible limp," said Nosey.

"Now you know." Rollie scooped up the empty glass and walked behind the bar.

CHAPTER TWENTY-SIX

"Something's off." Rollie lifted his head and stared into the dark.

"Like a smell? Bad meat?" said Pops.

"No." Rollie's voice was little more than a whisper.

"What do you think?" said Pops in the same quiet tone. He was tired and wanted nothing more than to snore for a few hours, but if Rollie's sniffer picked up on an oddness, there was something to it.

Then Pops heard it, too. A faint gurgling sound. "Hmm," he said, not moving. But Rollie was moving, sliding from his bunk with a few creaks and pops that didn't come from the bed's wooden frame.

Pops couldn't help wincing. Rollie wasn't an old man, but he'd been through enough injury that his body sounded like dry wood crackling in a fire when he first got up of a morning.

The gurgling sound seemed to have drifted from one side of the building to the other. Pops thought he could smell something, and he didn't like what it was. He, too, slid from his bed, hand already reaching for Miss Mess Maker and a bandolier of shells. He tugged on his boots and hat and walked on his knees to the back door.

Rollie was doing the same toward the front, both men decked out in their longhandles, guns, hats, and boots. *All a man really needs,* anyway, thought Rollie fleetingly. "You smell it, too?" he whispered.

"Yep. Coal oil. Gonna burn us out."

"Yeah, but who?"

"You tell me." Rollie knew Pops didn't expect an answer. "See you outside."

"Yep," said Pops.

"And don't shoot me," said Rollie.

"Nope."

Each man made for their doors and opened them. Pops peeked out into the night left then right, but saw nothing moving. The pungent stink of greasy lamp oil filled his nose and watered his eyes. Whoever did it had soaked a whole lot of it all over the place. Hoping to burn them alive, he bet, and all it would take was a quick flared match. *Time to move,* he thought.

Pushing to his feet, he bolted down the ramp, and bending low, darted to the left, eyeing the side of the saloon as he ran. He tried to recall what was back there invisible in the night, so he didn't bark a knee on something, trip himself up, touch off a trigger, and give himself away.

Convinced he hadn't been seen, but likely had been heard, Pops kept low and hoped whatever passed for scant moonlight that night wouldn't light up his faded longhandles.

He thought he could see a dark shape along the side of the bar. He listened for a moment and swore he heard the glugging sounds once more. Time to move again. Maybe brace the culprit before he struck a match. The only tricky bit would be not shooting Rollie in the process.

He catfooted along the length of the bar, about ten feet away from the side of the building. Even at that distance, he smelled the oil. It wasn't good. Life was the most important thing, sure, Pops knew. But saving his entire wad of cash as well as the only things he owned, the bar included, was pretty damn important, too.

"Hold it there!" Rollie's voice bit through the chill night air, followed by the hard steel-ratcheting sound of him cocking the lever of his Winchester.

That emboldened Pops and he ran harder, his boots grinding gravel. Maybe they could get the rascal in a crossfire position.

The next thing he heard was a solid thump, as if someone had been punched. Another and another, each followed by groans and grunts. Was it Rollie doing the doling of blows or the receiving?

Then he saw Rollie, kneeling on something and raising his rifle butt up high, ramming it down hard.

"Rollie!" Pops shouted. "He alone?"

"Don't know. Check behind me—the other side!" Then he brought his rifle butt down hard once more. Whoever he was beating ceased to flail.

Pops got his answer as a match flared bright and quick about thirty feet ahead of him, far along the long left side of The Last Drop.

"No!" he shouted and received a blast from a revolver in reply.

Pops dove to his right, heard a tight, whistling sound overhead, and rolled back to face the shooter once more. Too far to trigger a shotgun blast and have it count. He ran forward, low, once more, the Greener gripped tight, her deadly end facing smack where the blast came from.

He knew Rollie would have shot by now, but Pops wanted to make certain he was close to what he was aiming at. He'd seen plenty of times when a shot from too great a distance strayed and winged or killed a bystander. He didn't like that. He was fairly certain nobody up to good things would be skulking around the bar at this late hour, pouring coal oil on its pilings, but it paid to be damn sure.

"Pops?"

It was Rollie, from far behind him. He couldn't reply and risk giving away his location to the shooter. Didn't bother him much. Rollie would do the same thing. Pops ran forward, cutting back and forth, covering the distance. The shooter was there, fumbling in the dark.

Before Pops could get another step closer, the night lit bright as a match tasted its nectar—the drizzled fuel caught and bloomed bright, a racing line of jumping flames. It was a sickening sight, and the smell was nearly as grotesque.

The only good thing about it was that Pops could see who was shooting at him, the same man who wielded the matches. The swarthy whip of a man bent low and backed away from the heat. His face turned from Pops, but not before Pops saw the wide grin and the tip of a pink tongue gripped between teeth as if the man were giggling and choking back a laugh.

Gripped in the man's left hand was a revolver aimed in Pops' direction. Pops was a dozen feet away. He triggered Lil' Miss Mess Maker and flame barked. The shot caught the swarthy grinner in the side of his gut and whipped him around in a dervish dance. His arms flailed as a burst of blood ribboned high as if he were painting the night with his own blood.

"Dance, Fire Boy."

The man's hurtling body spun its last and flopped to the ground, faceup, his legs kicking in jerks, one, then the other, as if he were learning to walk while lying on his back. The arm that had gripped the gun was a shredded mess, pocked with shot and blood and bone and shreds of cloth.

Of the gun there was no sign. In the dirt somewhere. Pops didn't care. This jackass was his least concern now. He bolted for the far end of the saloon, eyeing it quickly, and deciding no one else who intended him harm was lurking in the flickering night. Pops laid the Greener to the side against a stack of lumber he'd been stockpiling to build a storage shed, and scrambled up the back ramp.

As he kicked in the door, smoke washed over him like a foul, humid summer breeze. He heard shouts then, no doubt of their neighbors. They were good people, even the ones he didn't particularly care for—those who called him names to his face—and yet he knew they would hustle to fill buckets from the stream that flowed along the far side of the main street. A bucket brigade it was called.

That would be a good and welcome thing. Yet the timber-and-tent structure that formed The Last Drop was likely doomed. Didn't mean he couldn't rescue what he might.

The fire was a ripper and gaining fast, particularly once its greedy tongues licked the canvas siding and roof. He didn't have much time, had to throw out back whatever he could and hope his luck would hold and he wouldn't burn to death. What good would it do to risk his neck if the fire claimed his goods once they landed out there in the night?

A figure appeared in the doorway. "Pops? You okay?" It was Rollie, coughing and lit from all sides and looking like a frenzied, haggard devil from beyond the grave. The man's silver-black hair was wild, his long, usually curled and waxed mustache drooped, framing his long O of a mouth like demon whiskers.

"Yeah! Help me. We'll lose it all if we don't get busy!" The effort of shouting those few words caused Pops to double up in a cough.

With no more words said, the two men began to grab and throw anything they could.

Most of their bar stock was stacked in that room, the storeroom, which also doubled as their sleeping quarters, but it was their personal gear they grabbed hold of first. Each man had nested deep in his own war bags and separate wooden locker his own personal items—scant mementos, letters, carvings, books, tintypes, and most important to each, buckskin sacks of money they had earned.

It was all they had to protect them from the vile shadows of the world and keep their own future safe. They hoisted the wooden lockers, helping each other lug them to the back door and toss out into the night when Geoff the Scot, the Pulaskis, and Bone and his boy appeared, backed with a handful of others, all in their nightclothes, and all with their arms held out, ready to grab whatever was passed their way, to haul it to safety.

And that's how it happened. For the next few, frenzied minutes, the townies of Boar Gulch, the mayor included, helped their own.

Case after case of rye whiskey, bourbon, and wine were passed out the back door as the night sky filled with bright daggers of flame. Howls of pain rose from people whose hair and clothes were set upon by falling embers.

"We have to get out of here!" shouted Rollie, grabbing Pops' arm.

"One more case!" shouted Pops as he snatched blindly in the smoke-filled hell that had been their home and business.

"No! Now!" Rollie grabbed his pard about the shoulders and pitched and dragged him toward the back door.

All told, the rescue of their possessions and stock lasted but a few minutes. And The Last Drop succumbed to flames in little more than that amount of time.

The people outside kept up a constant line of work, passing goods from one person to the next to get everything well away from the flames. The building was situated far enough from others on each side that the only danger was of falling sparks that spiraled into the night on columns of heat-driven smoke.

The night sky was bright and filled with the winking embers and the shouts of people as they looked on and wondered if their own lives would ever be affected in such a manner.

More miners ran to town, having heard the commotion and seen the bright flames in the sky, ran to the aid of those ferrying buckets sloshing and slopping, from one person to the next, to douse the flames. They knew they could not save The Last Drop, but maybe they could prevent the fire from spreading. Others ran circles around the building, stomping racers of flames that found whatever dry materials they could to trace their consuming power to other structures, other lives.

Rollie and Pops joined the bucket brigade and coughed and spat and hoped no one beyond the vile two who did this would be hurt. Among the townsfolk that night, there was an odd but good affinity for their fellow Gulchers in the choking smoke and blackened, spark-filled air. As quickly as the flames began, the collective efforts of the residents tamped down the beastly brute of a fire to a mewling, simpering beast.

Dawn was slow to show itself, as the fire had been defeated hours before its first gray shades appeared.

"There's only one thing I want to do right about now and it's not see what has become of The Last Drop in the full light of morning." Pops sighed and rubbed a sore shoulder.

"I tell you what," said Rollie. "If ever I am tempted to complain about my lot in life, I will shut my mouth. Tonight reminded me that come what may, people who have it a lot worse off than me have something I tend to forget about. Their lives." *And I'm endangering them,* he thought.

Rollie knew the fire was started with intention, and he knew he was the target. Long before he paused to lean on his shovel, he had decided that his presence in town was causing a whole lot of people a whole lot of grief, and worse. If anyone came to harm because of him, he'd never forgive himself. He'd realized it before. The risk had been as vivid and real, but somehow the fire this night was a kick to the face. It was time for action. Even if that meant calling an end to his time in Boar Gulch.

He didn't want to leave Pops with the headache of cleaning the mess and rebuilding the bar, but. . . .

"Hold right there," said Pops, coming up alongside him. "You're thinking something foolish, I can tell. You got that look."

"What look?"

"The one that tells me you're about to do something foolish."

"Talking with you is like herding snakes sometimes, you know that?"

"Don't get testy with me. I can't rebuild this place by myself."

"I been thinking about that."

"Yeah, I know you have. See?"

"Before I decide to do much of anything, I have to tend to the one man alive—here, at least—who can answer questions about this mess," Rollie nodded toward the smoldering pile that had been their saloon.

"I thought you killed him?"

"Not yet. I left him trussed up across the street by the big rock."

Pops knew the spot. The long shelf of stone was a favorite location to swap lies and windies with other folks. He'd done that very thing the morning before, enjoying a pipe and a cup of coffee, talking with Bone and Nosey when the latter should have been working in the bar.

"You want a hand with him?"

"Sure. Maybe I can find out something useful before I hang him. I doubt it, but you never know."

"That's you," said Pops. "Always hopeful."

They walked across the road, but even in the dim light of a half-dozen lanterns and the pulsing glow from the embers of the charred ribs of their saloon, they saw no one tied up at the rock shelf. But they did see Nosey Parker seated on the stone and holding his head.

"What happened?" said Rollie.

Nosey looked up and they saw blood on the side of his face beneath his hand. "I was struck by an ungrateful rascal, that's what's happened!"

"No, not to you. Where's my prisoner?" Rollie stalked up and down before them, hoisting his lantern head height as if he might see beyond its meager light into the dark of the early morning.

"That's what I'm trying to tell you—and thank you for your concern."

Rollie leaned in and snatched a wad of Nosey's shirt-front, pulling the journalist close. "You want concern from me, tell me where he got to."

His menacing growl caused several people nearby to pause and look their way. He didn't care. "Now, which way?"

"I . . . I don't know. He said he wanted to help with the fire. That he'd been tied up by mistake."

"And you believed him?" said Pops, shaking his head.

"Why wouldn't I? There have been so many newcomers lately I thought in the confusion someone had mistaken him for a miscreant."

"Nosey," said Pops, "you ever seen someone tied up accidentally? Did it ever occur to you that the fire was set by somebody? Nothing that went on here tonight was an accident."

"Oh, but. . . . Oh." Nosey rubbed his tender head and looked at his feet.

"I have to go find him, Pops," said Rollie.

"Not alone you don't. Could be he's watching us right now, you know."

"They why isn't he shooting?" growled Rollie, sneering into the dark.

"'Cause he'd get himself caught. I reckon he and his partner figured they'd be in and gone by the time the fire was roaring good."

Rollie nodded. "I understand, but I'll take that chance. He likely would have gone to wherever they kept their horses." He turned to Nosey. "Make yourself useful and go find the horse of the dead man. Me and Pops will get our own mounts ready." He turned to Pops. "You armed enough?"

"Yep. Could use some trousers, but I'll get along. Let's go."

They made their way to where they corralled their horses out back behind the bar and found them, spooked and crowding the back rail.

While they saddled up, Pops said, "You think you were too harsh on Nosey back there?"

Rollie said nothing for a moment while he adjusted his saddle on the blanket. "Nope. He's a good kid, but he's an idiot sometimes. No practical sense about him."

"He thought he was doing the right thing."

"Yep, and innocent people might be in danger now because of him. I should have shot the man when I had the chance."

"Who? Nosey?" Pops paused in tightening his cinch.

"No, the—" Rollie looked up at his partner, saw that smile, and chuckled despite the situation. Leave it to Pops to crack wise at a dark moment.

Rollie led Cap to the rail, tied him, and slipped through

to rummage in their big, sloppy pile of gear rescued from the fire. He found his war bag and tugged out more ammunition and a pair of trousers.

Pops was doing the same, and yanked on a canteen strap, toppling the side of the pile. "I'll go fill this, then where to? You figure the man hit the trail or is sticking close, hoping to get at you again?"

Rollie shrugged. "I was that desperate, I'd ride. But he came here with murder in mind, and he failed. My guess is he'll hole up, maybe try again."

"Then we best get him first."

"Where are you men going?" said a voice behind them. It was the mayor. "You have work to do here. We can't tend to your mess all night."

"Fine, Chauncey." Rollie handed the little portly man his reins. "Then you find the escaped prisoner and I'll sit here and stare at the embers."

"Oh, well, no, I won't prevent you from doing your job."

Rollie and Pops saddled and rode away from the mayor.

"But I expect no less than a successful hunt, gentlemen!" Chauncey's words rose in pitch the farther they rode from him.

"Man works up more hot air than the fire did," said Pops, reining up in front of Nosey in the street.

"I haven't found a horse at all over that way." The journalist jerked a thumb southward. "But it's dark." He shrugged and rubbed his head. "I make no promises."

"Okay. Now search every tent, every home, every building in town. You don't find him there, try the miners' camps." That was all Rollie offered before he rode off.

Pops gave Nosey a quick smile and a one-finger salute off the brim of his hat, then caught up with Rollie. The two men rode in silence, angling in a switchback pattern up the east-flanking hill behind the main street.

At the top Rollie reined up. "We get into the trees, I'll take the south road, you double back and take the north end. If you see him, shoot first, even in the back if you have to. He's ruthless, Pops. No need to play nice with him."

"Don't worry about me. You best have eyes in back and on both sides, too."

Rollie nodded and chewed the inside of his cheek. Early gray light had begun. As soon as they disappeared into the trees, Rollie and Pops offered each other a quick nod. They split up without a glance back.

Each knew that one or both of them might well end up dead.

CHAPTER TWENTY-SEVEN

Rollie knew they had a thin chance at best of cutting the man's sign, but they had to do something. He almost cursed Nosey aloud once more, but decided to keep his mouth shut. The horse's steady footfalls clunking rock while he stepped with caution weren't muffled enough on the needle-padded ground. The last thing he needed to do was invite a bullet by being loud and foolish.

Rollie kept his Schofield drawn, and bending low, used the weak early light to help scour the ground and above at horse height for rubs, scrapes, bent branches, breaks. He saw no sign and realized how absurd this chase was. The man could have chosen any direction at all.

North of him, riding low in his own saddle, and doing much the same as Rollie, Pops kept his unlit corncob pipe clamped in his teeth and his eyes on the ground, flicking up every few yards to scan branches, looking for sign. He hated this time of day for such work. Made him feel too exposed. If he could begin to see shapes at this gloomy hour, then the man he was hunting could, too.

A soft, quick sound like a fist hitting an open palm was all the warning Pops received before a hard weight dropped on him. As he piled out of the saddle, he knew what had happened—either a mountain lion had peeled him off his horse or the man they were hunting had done it.

In the next moment, his nose told him the answer. The attacker smelled of the harsh, ghosted remains of raw fire, even to a man who had spent the previous few hours breathing in nothing but smoke. He rolled with the attack, landed smack on his shoulder, then lost his grip and dropped his Greener.

Pops winced inside at the raw sound his beloved shotgun made as it clunked and clattered against unforgiving rock. *Worry about that later,* he told himself. *Right now, fight for your life. And pray the man doesn't have a knife on him. Or at least not drawn.*

That could be one advantage Pops would have on the man.

He grunted, heard his foe do the same, heard the raspy, seething breaths of a tensed-up man unwilling to fight with anything less than full strength. *That makes two of us,* thought Pops, as he closed the fingers of his right hand around the thick handle of his sheath knife.

"No!" barked the attacker, shoving and punching at Pops' knife hand. He'd seen the knife and didn't like the idea of having that blade slide into his guts.

"Yes!" said Pops, finding it difficult to resist mixing a little discouragement into the scuffle. His horse sidestepped and thrashed, stomping in place before bolting southward.

His attacker fought like an angry Apache, and Pops felt his own strength begin to falter. The man chopped down with a vicious swing and knocked the knife from Pops' hand. The hilt clunked his boot, and Pops hoped it would stay there within reach while they grappled.

Both men, faces inches apart, growled and huffed at each other. Pops could see him, and something about the man's nose and eyes was familiar. He'd seen enough of the man's face earlier at the fire to know he was a thin, angry soul with more muscle and bone than anything else.

They gripped each other's wrists and shoulders. The man bent his face low, his teeth coming together hard and fast, trying to bite Pops' right ear. The idea of such brute fighting made Pops angrier and he bucked and kicked like a cornered mustang.

Something solid connected with Pops' left temple. Felt like a boot. He barked a quick oath and shook his head as if to dispel an irksome bee. "Play nice, you . . ." he muttered and ducked his head low, expecting a second hit.

A second hit did swing down at him and he felt the breeze of it. He rammed forward as if he were a human sledge. The top of his head connected with the man's side. The man stopped short, prevented by something, likely a big ol' ponderosa. Pops kept ramming his head into the man's lower chest like a battering ram and felt something crack and pop within the man.

Air whooshed out of the man's mouth in a gasping wheeze. Sounded to Pops as if he'd busted some of the man's ribs. But the belligerent burner kept clawing and snapping his teeth as if he were trying to bite at Pops' hair. At the same time, Pops dragged a hand along the ground beneath him, felt no knife. Stepping forward from the momentum, a hard knob wedged beneath his boot sole. His knife. Had to be. He would not consider otherwise.

One more bend down low and he'd have it in his hand.

But it was not to be at that moment, for despite the man's cracked ribs and wheezing, short breaths, he shoved himself at Pops in a desperate, growling frenzy, like a skinny, cornered bear whipsawing at the presence of a mightier enemy.

"Give . . . I give!" grunted the man.

But Pops had heard such lies before, and was proved right as he saw the man's outstretched arm clawing for the knife. One quick jerk downward and Pops rolled, snatched up the blade a breath before his foe, and in the same motion, rammed it upward, his fingers closing around the comfortable bone handle, as if shaking hands with an old friend. As if he'd planned out the most perfect way for the situation to unfold, his strike met soft flesh, slashing through stringy muscle as it drove in, caroming off bone.

"Aah!" the man screamed and thrashed away from him. "You stabbed me in the . . . leg!"

The leg? thought Pops. *I meant to gut the fiend.* He pushed away from his writhing foe and struggled to his feet.

Pops looked down at his attacker. The morning sun had risen enough that, even under the dense canopy of trees, he saw the man clearly. He was lean, on the young side, with short dark hair, and high, sharp cheekbones.

He looked none too tall, but it was difficult to determine as the man was sprawled on his back, his hands opening and closing, trying and failing to grasp his half-drawn leg, his head whipping side to side against the tree trunk. His eyes fluttered, and his chest rose and fell with speed. His breathing sounded rough.

If he hadn't been trying to kill Pops, he might feel bad for him.

"You going to stare him to death?" said a voice from behind Pops.

Even before he glanced over his shoulder, Pops knew it was Rollie. "Yeah, that's how I usually work it."

"God, help me . . ." burbled the man on the ground.

"I expect he's the only one who can now," said Pops to the man. To Rollie, he said, "You have questions, you might want to ask now, as I stoved him up in good shape. And while his injuries won't kill him, the pain is going to get worse before it gets better."

Rollie didn't need reminding. He was already at the man's side and toed him in the ribs. The man howled and his eyes flickered open.

"Who sent you?"

"Huh?"

Rollie kicked him again.

Again, the man groaned and sucked in a hard breath through clenched teeth.

"Who sent you?"

"Have . . ."

Another kick. "Who?"

"Aaah! Haverty! Haverty's idea. Said . . . said we'd collect the bounty."

Rollie looked over at Pops, who pulled his pipe from his mouth.

"Bounty? On who?"

The man on the ground opened his eyes and stared up at Rollie. A thin smile pulled his sweaty lips tight. "On . . . Stoneface Finnegan. On . . . you!" A wheeze burbled up from his mouth. It became a dry chuckle before collapsing into a rattling cough.

"Whose bounty?"

The man kept laughing and coughing. Rollie kicked him again, harder this time.

"Gaaah!"

"Who set the bounty?"

"Okay, okay . . ." The man licked his lips and forced his eyes open again. "Don't know. Have to ask Haverty."

"Can't," said Rollie. "He's dead. I'm asking you."

That opened the man's eyes wide. "Hav's dead?" He slumped back against the tree with a wheeze. "Aw, no, no. He's too smart for that." He began laughing again. "I told him he wasn't no smarter than me. Guess I was right."

"Don't count on it." Rollie walked to his horse and returned with a coil of rope. At the sight of it, the man on the ground tried to scrabble backward, his game leg seized stiff and blood pumped from the knife wound. He fought the pain with gritted teeth and hard, quick breaths, but never took his wide eyes from Rollie's busy hands. "What you gonna do, man?"

"What's it look like, son?" said Pops, drawing on his lit pipe. "You got something you think we might want to hear, you best say it."

"Oh no, no! I can't be held to blame for Haverty's ideas! He's the one, not me."

"You had a torch in your hand when I found you. Did Haverty put it there?"

"No, I mean yes, I . . . oh hell, mister. I don't know nothing. I swear it."

"That much I guessed." Rollie whipped the freshly tied noose up over a stout branch. "On your feet . . . whatever your name is."

"No!" The man's eyes widened until they seemed to Pops to be all white. "I won't! No, I won't!"

Rollie sighed. "All right." He bent to the man with the mouth of the noose looped wide. "I'll jerk you up. Won't be as quick or as clean, but the day's young. I'm up to the task."

"Oh God, oh no . . ."

"There you go again. You have something to say to your Maker, you best get at it," said Pops. "We're busy men."

The man regarded each of them and shook his head. Rollie sighed once more and shucked his Schofield. "Get up or get shot."

The man reached behind him and used the rough trunk of the pine to squirm and wheeze his way upright.

"That's better," said Pops. "Now you sure you don't know who set the bounty on Mr. Finnegan's head?"

The man's face worked back and forth in a quick shake as if palsied. "No! I'd tell you if I did. I—" He licked his lips. "Don't that prove I'm telling the truth? I could as easy lie to you, but I ain't, am I?"

"That's true," said Pops, rubbing his chin. "But it wouldn't matter none. You see, you and your chum, Haverty was it? You both tried to burn me and Mr. Finnegan to death in our sleep, no less. That's not right. No, no sir, not right at all." Pops shook his head and made a clucking sound. "Shame on you. What's your name, anyway, son?"

"Why?"

"Have to know where to send notice of your demise, don't we? We're not animals, after all."

A quick yelp jumped out of the man's mouth and he lunged to his left as if to run. He piled up on the needles and jags of granite with an "oomph!" and moaned, scrabbling as if trying to stand.

"You ought not to do that," said Pops, pointing with his pipe. "That leg of yours won't take much more abuse."

"Enough, damn your murderous hide," growled Rollie. "Short of convincing me you weren't the man holding the torch and giggling as you lit our saloon on fire, and with us in it, you'll be swinging in a minute or so. Now take it like a man. I'm offering to end your life with a whole lot more dignity than you were fixing to end ours."

"But it ain't right! It ain't right!"

"Maybe not, but it's justice, son. Now stop pretending you're a man and die like one."

The man on the ground seemed to cave in on himself. The only movement he made came from his torso heaving and jumping in time with his choking sobs. Long drips of snot trailed down his face and to the ground.

Rollie traded a glance with Pops, eyebrows raised. When he looked back he was surprised to see the tiny snout of a two-shot derringer shaking slightly, staring straight up at him. And behind it . . . yellow teeth bared behind tight-stretched lips ribboned with snot.

"What you gonna do now, huh?" The man snickered like a drunk coyote, rolled his head back a moment, glancing up at the branches.

That was all Rollie needed. The ex-Pink stepped forward fast and raised one leg. He stomped down hard as the man looked back toward Rollie. The shriek almost, but not quite, drowned out the sound of the man's leg bone snapping at the knee.

The man filled the ridgetop forest with agony howls.

The derringer spun by the ringlike trigger guard on his right hand's pointer finger and then slipped to the packed forest floor. It clunked against a jag of stone and triggered, sending a bullet into the thigh of his stabbed leg.

For a long moment, there was near silence, skinned over only by the echoes of his previous cries. The man resumed his screams again, keeping it up for a full half minute. His eyes bulged outward and his mouth was wide enough that Rollie wanted to jam a fist straight into it. But he held back out of deference to the fact that the man was about to die anyway.

Pops puffed his pipe, cradled one arm in another, and shook his head as if he'd heard something down at the general store that sounded too odd to be true. They waited the man out. It worked, always did in such situations. The man worked his howls and screeches until they trailed out to a dribble of cries, then simpers, then sobs. His shoulders convulsed, sending tremors down the length of his body.

"Okay then." Rollie stepped forward once more.

Despite the doomed man's obvious agonies, he flinched, and offered a weak thrashing response when Rollie slipped the noose over his head and tightened it.

Pops stepped over and the men nodded to each other. Each grasping the rope, they hoisted the energized man to his feet and let him totter there a moment.

"Last words?" said Rollie, reaching to loosen the noose for a moment.

The man spit a clot of snot and blood straight into Pops' face.

Pops' jaw muscles clenched and he dragged a shirt cuff over his cheek and closed eye, wiping away the offense. Then he joined Rollie in sending the degenerate skyward, arm over arm, one heaving rope pull at a time.

The man's legs pedaled and whipped, his hands clawing in desperate drags at the tight rope. Scratching his own flesh as it bulged out over the rope left bloody runnels as his flesh purpled and veins grew, pushing outward. They looked like the rivers on maps come suddenly alive with color, with life, even as the man's own life was pinching out.

The two men watched from a safe distance as the whipping and bucking continued. One of the man's legs looked to be lengthening, until they saw it was his left boot sliding off. A quick, snapping kick sent the boot pinwheeling in an arc right between the two spectators' heads.

"He's a fighter," said Rollie. "Didn't expect him to be much. At least not until he pulled that derringer on me."

"Speaking of that little gun, if you don't have designs on it, I think that would make a nice pistol for Nosey."

"Yeah, fine with me."

"You still angry with him, huh?" said Pops as he bent to retrieve Little Miss Mess Maker. He was pleased to find she was not badly damaged. Not that she wasn't damaged—there was a knick in the smooth fore stock, a dent in the polished rear stock, and a couple of fresh scratches on her black barrels. He cracked her open, thumbed out the shells, and inspected the barrels skyward, eyeballing the twin discs of gray morning light. No visible dents in or out. Satisfied for the time being, he reloaded the shells, closed her with that satisfying *punk* sound, and cradled her once more in the crook of his arm.

"Wouldn't you be?"

Pops shrugged, then said, "Look out." He nodded toward the swinging man.

His trembling legs were leaking out urine and worse. His left unbooted foot hung limp, the hole-filled sock begrimed, wet, and dripping. Finally, the man ceased his struggles.

"Wish he would have taken it better. I hate to see a man meet his Maker with spite on his lips, anger in his eyes, and mean on his mind."

"We gave him the chance."

"That we did." Pops walked around the slowly spinning dead man and nudged in the pine duff for the derringer.

"More to your right," said Rollie. "See it by that stone?"

"Ah, good. Thanks."

"I was afraid of this."

"What? The derringer?"

"The bounty. That fool girl's newspaper notices are drawing flies and one of them got the wise idea to put a price on my head."

"Wasn't her, though," said Pops, drawing in his pipe. "I expect she spent her wad on the notices."

"Right. But she was the catalyst."

"You and your dollar words again." Pops shook his head, smiling.

Neither man spoke for long moments, then Rollie said, "Well, we better find his horse and yours. I expect yours will have nosed back to the Gulch, but his might be wandering or snagged or worse. Which way did he come from?"

Pops let out a brief, low chuckle. "Came from out of the sky."

"What?"

"Jumped on me like a wildcat. That tree there, I think. Or maybe off of that big ol' rock."

"Likely heard you, or expected someone might come along trailing him. I'll look over that way."

"You want me to cut him down?"

"Not yet. We're not all that far from town. Let's leave him be for a day. He won't get any straighter. Make it easier to bury him."

Pops didn't argue with Rollie. After fighting the fire and eating smoke and ash for hours, then wrassling with the spitfire would-be killer, he was well and truly exhausted. Let Rollie find the horse. He'd rest up and contemplate the insides of his eyelids for a spell. Seemed he'd no sooner decided that when he was poked in the back.

"Hey."

Pops shot forward, keeping low, and spun, Lil' Miss Mess Maker leveled on Rollie's trim gut. He saw a Schofield staring him down from Rollie's left hand, the reins from a bay in the other.

"Easy, Pops."

"You too, Finnegan."

Both men relaxed.

"Shouldn't have spooked you. I thought you heard me."

"Should have," said Pops, blowing out a big breath. "More tired than I thought."

"Me too." Rollie sighed. "I hate getting old."

"Getting? Man, you already are old. I'd say somebody forgot to tell you." Pops chuckled and took the offered reins in hand. "I'll see if I can hoist my old body up onto this steed and track down my own horse."

"Seems gentle enough. We're building up a right fine herd lately."

"Yeah," said Pops. "Wish we didn't have to."

"I don't see any way around it. But it's my fight, Pops.

I never expected you or anybody to be caught up in this thing. Now more than ever, considering there's a price on my head by somebody for some amount."

"Nothing like being sure of a thing, is there?" Pops mounted up and the horse barely twitched. "Hmm. Less jumpy than that roan I've been riding."

"Sound looking, too."

"Now, as to that woe-is-me bit you were yammering on about before," said Pops. "You know, how this is your fight and all? I hear that foolishness from you again and I'm liable to give you something to really cry about, little boy."

Rollie paused in climbing aboard his horse and stared at Pops over his saddle, eyebrows raised. "First you insult me by calling me old, then you berate me and call me a little boy." Rollie hoisted himself up into the saddle, smoothed the reins between his fingers. "Guess it's true what they say about folks getting confused when they reach a certain age."

"Ha!" said Pops and heeled the bay into a gallop past Rollie. "Old folks can't do this!"

Rollie smiled for the first time in long hours and followed suit. Both men felt oddly good considering what they'd been through.

After all, reasoned Rollie as they thundered down the trail toward Boar Gulch, they'd cheated death at least a couple of times since waking. Surely their week could only get better. What else could go wrong?

The next day, out behind the smoking ruins of the bar, Rollie and Pops, with the help of Wolfbait, Nosey, and

Bone and his son, stomped the earth around the perimeter of the used but mended canvas campaign tent they'd purchased from Horkins' Hardware.

"It ain't a palace." Wolfbait turned and glanced down the street at the rising structure at the far end. "Nor a grand hotel such as our esteemed mayor is cobbling together"—he shook his head at what he considered a folly"—but it is a place for The Last Drop to keep up with the competition."

Pops bent low behind a sloppy stack of crates and planks topped with dirty shirts and came up holding a bottle of whiskey in each hand. "I'd say we all earned a dollop or two, right, Rollie?"

Rollie looked up from untangling a clot of rope. "Huh?"

"I see you haven't had enough of playing with rope lately."

"Mmm," he scowled and bent back to his task.

Pops shook his head and poured out a healthy dose of whiskey for all involved in helping them set up the tent. He held out a glass to Rollie, who looked at the drink, dropped the wad of rope, and took the glass. "You're right."

"'Course I'm right," said Pops and made to sip.

"Uh-uh," Rollie shook his head. "First, a toast." He raised his glass. "To friends. Much appreciated, and thank you."

Nosey Parker walked around the tent, mud smudging his face and hair, his knees, and arms.

"Come on over here, Nosey. Wrap a hand around this glass." Pops held out a tumbler of whiskey. "Me and Rollie appreciate what you did earlier. Helping to track down that man's horse and all. Ain't that right, Rollie?"

The ex-Pinkerton operative grunted, sipped his whiskey, and looked down at the snarled rope at his boots.

"I said, 'Ain't that right,' Mr. Stoneface Finnegan?"

That brought him around. He shot Pops a flinty glare.

Pops laughed long and loud, his deep, chesty chuckles eventually cracking everybody's face into smiles, including Rollie's.

CHAPTER TWENTY-EIGHT

"I caught this runt with a ham in his coat and holding a dollar's worth of boiled sweets!" Geoff the Scot had a balled-up handful of the collar of a filthy, skinny kid with mangy hair so thick with lice Rollie could see them crawling.

The kid's stance and eyes told Rollie a lot in a short bit of time. He wasn't big, but he was feisty, judging by the way he thrashed. Not a simple task as Geoff was a large man with shoulders wider than most doorframes. The kid was also angry, and probably afraid, but he hid that well behind narrowed eyes and browning teeth clenched in a mouth that seethed hard breaths and spittle.

Rollie looked at the eatery owner. "Far as I can recall, having a ham in one's coat is not an unlawful offense."

"It was my ham, man!" bellowed the big Scot. "And my sweets!"

"Oh, I see," said Rollie, glancing at Pops.

"Okay, laddie, have your fun at my expense. That's fine, but I want justice. This one's been lurking for a couple of days and food has gone missing. I want restitution."

"And you came to me?" said Rollie.

"You're the law, so says that fool mayor, anyway." The Scot jerked the kid closer to Rollie so he could lean in. "And besides, he says you owe the town because of all the rough play that's been going on here lately. Says you're the cause."

"He said that, did he?" Rollie stood and eyed the kid. "Pops? You have a hank of rawhide handy?"

"Coming right up," said Pops as he disappeared inside the tent. He emerged a few moments later with a couple of tough leather thongs and handed them to Rollie.

"Turn around," said Rollie.

The kid sneered and stayed put.

"The man said turn," said Geoff, spinning the kid.

Rollie lashed the boy's wrists together. "I expect we can take it from here."

"What about my stolen goods?"

"You got your ham and sweets back, didn't you?"

"Yes, but before that!"

"Proof?"

Geoff eyed Rollie, then shook his head quickly.

"Okay, then."

The big Scot turned away, then Rollie said, "Geoff, you getting enough to eat nowadays?"

"Yes, why—" he turned, mumbling and shaking his head as he stalked back to his establishment, which had become a combination open-air food hall and butchery, offering a limited selection of tasty treats such as boiled sweets.

Pops steered the kid back to a chair outside the saloon tent and forced him to sit. Nosey and Wolfbait's heated conversation dried up.

"Who's he?" said Nosey. "Why is he bound at the wrist? What did he do?" A glance from Rollie shut him up.

Rollie and Pops pulled chairs over to the kid, sat with their fronts to the chair backs, and stared at him until he squirmed and sneered even more, if that was possible.

"Heard tell in some foreign lands they chop off a man's hand if he steals."

Rollie nodded at Pops. "Now that's not a bad idea. Certainly prevent a body from grabbing anything else that didn't belong to them."

"It would sure work on me," said Wolfbait. "I need my hands. How else would I hoist my glass?"

"You could get yourself married," said Pops. "A doting wife would help you with your beer."

"Oh no, I've been down that road. Happiest day of my life was when she told me she was taking up with a traveling preacher who sold tinctures on the side. Or maybe it was the other way around. I don't recall. Anyways, she said I was an immature oaf and that her mother had been right all along." Wolfbait giggled. "Last thing I said to her before I shut the door of our love nest was that she should have listened to her mother. Would have saved us all a three-year headache. I shut that door and heard a china teacup smack it right where my face had been." He sipped his beer and shook his head. "Yes sir, waste of a good cup."

"As amusing as that story was, Wolfbait, we were trying to figure out the best way to discipline thieves in Boar Gulch." Rollie turned a blank face on the young man in their midst.

Up until that moment he'd been quiet, even through the chatter about the lopping off of hands. But something about Rollie's gaze directed at him broke the last of the kid's gritted-teeth resolve. A thin, quick whimper escaped his lips and he looked away. Rollie noted, too, that the kid tried to jam his tied hands down behind his thigh.

"Boy," said Pops, "you do understand that life is all about chance and opportunity. You don't take advantage of the right opportunities, and you end up making the wrong choices. Why, you can ruin your whole cake. You understand?"

From the look on his face, the kid had not understood Pops' speech.

Truth be told, Rollie didn't, either. "What my partner's trying to tell you is you made a poor choice and will have to be punished for it. As it's early days here in Boar Gulch, we have to make an example out of somebody. And that somebody is you. Can't have people stealing from one another."

The kid gulped, then he licked his lips. "Ain't there nothing I can do?"

"Not if you want to stay in Boar Gulch. Wouldn't do to have a criminal walking around with both his hands. Now would it?"

The kid's eyes widened. Rollie could tell he was thinking hard. He swore he could almost hear the kid's painful thought process, as if the boy's head was filled with wooden clockwork gears.

"I . . . I could leave. You'd never hear from me no more. I'd be gone like . . . like something that goes away and never comes back!"

"A fleeting thought, perhaps the kiss of a long-ago love . . ." Wolfbait's eyes were closed and he smiled. Everyone else stared at him.

"Methinks Wolfbait has unplumbed depths," said Nosey.

"Bah," said the old man, and sipped his beer. "Don't insult me, you whelp."

"I don't know," said Rollie. "Goes against my grain to turn a criminal loose on the world without him doing hard time."

"Maybe one finger," said Pops, tugging out his sheath knife and rotating it in his hand. He kept the steel blade polished and honed keen. Sunlight glinted off its menacing length.

"Ohhh . . ." said the kid, eyeing the blade, his hands balling into tighter fists behind him.

"Tell you what," said Rollie. "The kid's first idea wasn't so bad. I'd only consider it if you were to promise me we'd not see your face around these parts again."

It took less time for the kid to understand that. He nodded. "Uh-huh, you bet."

Rollie regarded him a moment more. "I'm going to need time to think on this. In the meantime, we have a few chores that need doing."

"I can work." The kid puffed up. "I can do most anything I turn my hand to."

"Good, that's good. First, we were all about to have a bite of food. Bread and cheese. You want some?"

"I . . . I can't pay," said the kid, looking at his lap. Rollie noticed for the first time how young the boy actually was. Maybe not yet fourteen.

"That's no worry. I wouldn't charge a man if he was going to do chores for me." Rollie pulled out cash from his pocket. "Nosey, you do me a favor. Go to Geoff's, buy a nice ham."

Nosey took the money and nodded. At the doorway he

stopped. "Boss, would you mind if I bought some candy for dessert? I have a powerful sweet tooth."

"Say, that's a good idea. I could do with such myself." He turned back to the kid. "Now, after we eat, we'll talk about the best way for you to clean the outhouse out back."

The kid gulped, but nodded.

They kept the youth, Terry Beedle, hopping for three days, chopping wood, scrubbing the outhouse, clearing the last of the charred debris, and helping to set posts for the new bar. They also learned the kid had an aunt in Missouri he was trying to get back to. He'd been living rough for two months since his father had died, stomped in the gut by a rogue stallion while helping out at a railway landing yard in Nevada.

By the morning of the third day, he had even begun to lose the squint of mistrust and the smirk, replaced instead with an occasional smile, and once or twice a quick laugh.

On the evening of the third day, Rollie leaned on his shovel handle and looked at the kid. "Pops will be heading down the mountain tomorrow morning with Wolfbait on their weekly supply run. There's a stage that will take you to the train in Bentonville. Make sure you're on it. Your passage will be paid up, straight through to your aunt's place."

The next morning, after Pops had instructed the kid on the fine art of scrubbing himself with soap and sand down at the creek, Terry presented himself back at the saloon, his ears and face and hands glowing red and no longer speckled with dirt.

Rollie looked him up and down, then nodded. "I have operatives along the route who'll report back to me, so don't think of doing anything stupid like stealing. Your aunt will be expecting you. And we'll be expecting a letter letting us know how you're getting along living with her, okay?"

The kid had tried to look Rollie in the eye while the gruff man spoke. The best he could manage was to stare at the man's waxed, curled mustache. He was thinking maybe he'd grow that sort of thing one day himself. "Yes sir," he said, tugging at the collar of the new gray-and-red plaid wool shirt Rollie, Pops, Nosey, and Wolfbait had bought him.

Rollie stuck out his hand and they shook. "Okay then, lug your bag to the wagon out front and stow it so it doesn't rattle on out the back."

"Thanks, Mr. Finnegan. I—" Terry turned away, then spun back and gripped Rollie about the middle hard for a moment. He ran out the door, struggling with the weight of the satchel, the bag clunking against his hip.

"What did you put in that bag, Rollie?"

The barkeep turned away. "Food."

"Maybe a ham and boiled sweets?" said Pops.

His partner shrugged and busied himself wiping already clean glasses.

CHAPTER TWENTY-NINE

Chauncey Wheeler shook the grains of fresh-ground beans into his coffeepot. The fire that morning hadn't taken well for some reason and he'd had to cuff the slow-burning sticks with his steel poker, then go at it again with another kitchen match.

He'd often wondered how much simpler his mornings would be if he didn't have to brew hot coffee or hot tea, for that matter. Why couldn't he be satisfied with a drink of cool water and then scrub himself, tug off any garments that may be growing ripe, and pull on a cleaner replacement?

"Life," he sighed, "is a whole lot of work." And that thought led him to dwell once more on the wonders of owning a fine, stately home in a city somewhere. *Anywhere,* he thought. *And stocked with servants.* While he was dreaming about it, why not one servant for each little thing he might require in a day's time. *Or a night's time,* he thought, chuckling.

"Well, what have we here?"

Chauncey looked up quick. The lid of the coffeepot

rattled down into place. Standing inside by the front door of the store, a tall, solid-looking fellow stared at him.

"Who are you? And how did you get in here?"

"Me?" said the man, jerking a thumb at his chest as if he was surprised at having been asked. "I'm nobody you need to be fearful of. Or at least not yet. Concerned with, sure. Seeing as how I am in your mercantile, after all."

"Yes, well, it is before hours. How did you get in, anyway? I double-check my locking each night. I . . . I don't like this."

"Are you Chauncey Wheeler""

"Well yes, I am the mayor of Boar Gulch . . ."

The stranger laughed. "And also Chauncey Wheeler?"

"Yes." Chauncey stood straighter, held a hand over his belly as if to hide it.

"Then you're the man I want to see. All you need to worry about is answering my questions and making me happy. If I end up smiling after my time in Boar Gulch, that means I got what I came here for."

"And . . . what did you come here for?" Chauncey felt something hot near his leg, through the striped flannel sleeping gown he was wearing. He always kept it on until he got at least one cup of coffee inside him. The heat came from the open door on the potbelly stove in the middle of the room, one of the drawbacks of having your home sharing space with a mercantile. Chauncey closed the little door. It squeaked and clunked shut.

The man laughed again and stepped forward. Chauncey could see he wore a long canvas coat, leather gloves, black or dark brown—hard to tell which in the one lamp's low light—and held a mammoth rifle, thick in every way from the barrel through the stock. If he was right, and Chauncey fancied he knew more than most about guns, even if he didn't like the crass things, the man held a buffalo gun. And he carried it cradled in one arm, the barrel angled down by his knee-high leather boots.

His head looked large, but Chauncey figured that had more to do with the hat the man wore, a tall-crown affair with a wide brim that barely curled at the lip. Beneath the hat, long hair flowed outward and looked almost arranged on his shoulders, as if the man had fluffed it before he began his day. Though his eyes were in part shadow, owing to the hat brim, the earliness of the morning, and the low light, the lower half of the stranger's face was lit enough that Chauncey saw a trim, blond beard speckled with gray and a long nose bent at the bridge.

"I hear you are harboring a killer and a thief in Boar Gulch."

"Oh, well I think you are mistaken, sir. We have a whole lot of miners, some with their faults to be sure." He chuckled, but left off when he saw his words meant nothing to the man, who was moving closer. Chauncey saw his eyes, cold-looking marbles that didn't seem to blink.

"No. This man is a killer and a thief, plain and simple. Hard to miss once you know who you're looking for. Has a fancy waxed mustache and a lack of chattiness. You might know him as Rollie Finnegan."

Chauncey nodded and gulped. "I know Finnegan. He's one of our town's leading merchants." Wheeler stood as tall as he was able and refused to look the man in the eye any longer. Also, it was easier that way. The man's glare and smile were unnerving.

"Why do you call him a killer and a thief? To my

knowledge he was an upstanding man with a past as a decorated Pinkerton operative."

"Ha! That's what he wants you to think. In truth, he abused his power, led people to their deaths, and what others didn't die he robbed of their lives by forcing them into prison. Not someone I'd call an upstanding member of a community. 'Course, I have certain standards likely of a higher order than yourself. I wouldn't, for instance, live in a town such as this. Oh, don't get me wrong, I'm certain this is fine for some folks, those among us whose intellect rivals that of a goat."

"Insults are a fool's refuge." As soon as he said it, Chauncey gulped back a hard knot of regret. Though he was afraid, Chauncey had also grown more annoyed with this blustering character with each passing moment. He was good and fearful, especially when the man swept back his coat and rested a hand on the ivory butt of a revolver.

The man sighed and whatever forced lilt had previously been in his voice sloughed away. "You, Mr. Wheeler, may be more than happy to fritter away this precious early morning with foolish chatter that circles around on itself and gets us nowhere. But not me. Today, I have things to do, people to see, one man in particular, and you, Mister Mayor of Boar Gulch, will lead me to him. Right now." He let out a breath. "Or at least as soon as you pull on some presentable duds, that is. Good God, but for a little fat man, you sure have bony legs. Remind me of a chicken."

"I'll thank you kindly for not mocking me, sir."

"Duly noted. And yes, I will take a cup of that coffee, thanks."

"I didn't offer you any."

"I ain't asking."

"Ah, yes. As soon as it boils."

"Good. Now fetch yourself some trousers and a shirt." The man raised the buffalo gun's barrel so that it pointed at Chauncey. "And don't do anything dumb. I would like your help, but I suspect I can find Finnegan without it. And you can likely do without a head-size hole in your gut."

Chauncey's mouth sagged open. He looked down at his protruding belly, then nodded and made for his quarters to get himself dressed. He wasn't certain what the day was going to bring, but he suspected it would be one he'd long remember.

When he walked back into the mercantile, clothed for the day and buttoning his shirt, he stopped short and stared in silence at what faced him. A half-dozen men stood about the room, prodding his meager products with grimy fingers, helping themselves to sweets, pawing through the tobacco, and one man, Mexican by the looks of him, leered at him while he sawed at a cured sausage with a beastly knife.

For the first time that day, Chauncey Wheeler cursed Rollie Finnegan. And suspected it would not be the last.

CHAPTER THIRTY

"Boy. Hey, Nosey . . ." Wolfbait did his best to hustle his hop-along step on up the trail toward town. He was on his way in, as each morning's dawn found him of late. He'd taken to greeting the day with Pops and Rollie, pitching in here and there to earn the coffee he sipped. Mostly he was lonely, and too sore and old and lazy, if he had to admit it, but only to himself, to work too hard at scratching in the dirt for sign.

Between his meager savings from past ventures and what promising ore he could find on his claim, which included placer pickings from the stream that bordered the northeastern edge of his claim, he was able to keep himself in food, beer, and bullets. Once in a while he was able to replace a shirt or socks that had grown too weary of being tended and mended.

An unexpected bonus in walking in to Main Street early each day had been in finding Nosey Parker making the same trek several days a week. Sometimes Wolfbait would walk along beside the younger man for several minutes before Nosey appeared to notice him.

Sometimes that kid was numb as a thumb struck by a hammer, but for all that he was a good lad. Heart was in the right spot, and that's more than Wolfbait felt he could say about a number of folks he'd met in his life. Rollie and Pops, too, were good men. Would have to be, he told himself, elsewise he wouldn't bother with them. But he craved conversation nearly as much as he did coffee, and he could get a solid cuppa from Rollie and engaging chatter from Pops.

On this day, Wolfbait had been pleased as always to see the young man sharing the trail.

"Ease up there, son. I ain't but half the man I used to be. 'Course, that's about twice what most men amount to these days." He chuckled and walked up alongside Nosey Parker, who was busy reading what looked to be a dime novel.

It was so early that the lavender glow that usually washed over their valley, so called the gulch, had barely begun its show.

"How can you see a blamed word in that little book you're reading?"

"Huh?" Nosey turned. "Oh, Wolfbait, good morning to you. I didn't hear you sneak up on me."

"Sneak up? Boy, any louder and I'd be a cannon. I was saying you're gonna go blind if you keep up that reading in the dark."

Nosey closed his novel and pushed his spectacles back up the bridge of his nose. "I don't buy into that line of thought. In fact"—he raised a finger and paused in the graveled lane—"I read a treatise some months ago on this very topic. It was fascinating—"

"Hold it, kid." Wolfbait held up a hand. "I ain't got time in my days nor breath enough in my body to listen to treatises. Don't be offended, but I haven't had a sip of coffee since I woke about an hour ago. Now, I make no promises, but you find me a cup of hot coffee and I suspect I'll be more open to listening to this treatise you're so excited about."

Nosey's frown had barely begun before it was interrupted by a gunshot, then another and another, all from the direction of Main Street, not far ahead in the dim morning light.

The two men ducked down, and looked at each other. "What do you reckon?" said Wolfbait, whose right hand had slipped down over his service revolver, ancient but in solid working order.

Nosey was about to speak when Wolfbait slipped a gnarled hand over the younger man's mouth and jerked his chin toward the trailside where boulders clustered along most of the route. The sound of hooves ahead on the trail's hard-packed surface told Nosey what Wolfbait had already heard. Someone was coming.

Not unusual, save for two things. In the course of their morning perambulations, the men had rarely if ever heard or seen a horse and rider out and about that early. And the shots they had heard moments before, coupled with the fact that these were especially tense times to be a Gulcher, given Rollie's presence, made life in Boar Gulch an increasing worry.

Trouble was, so much promising sign had been found of late that Boar Gulch was on the cusp of being considered and reported by every chinwagger as the next boomtown in Idaho Territory. With that slowly leaking news came a steady drip of newcomers. Because of Delia Holsapple's notices in big-city papers about Rollie Finnegan's whereabouts, the steady drip of newcomers to the gulch was polluted with folks seeking vengeance on the man who'd wronged them somehow in the past. At least that's the way they saw it.

The two men could hardly be blamed for rabbiting at the first sign of early-morning trouble. Within moments they would be glad they did.

Wolfbait and Nosey had scrambled up over one jag of granite and tucked themselves behind its neighbor, a bigger jut half the size of a miner's one-room cabin. They crouched behind it, peering around the near edge toward the trail. Wolfbait had his revolver out and cranked back. He reached over and patted Nosey's brown wool coat with his left hand until his fingertips felt something hard by the young man's chest. He patted it twice and nodded at Nosey, who nodded back.

Nosey knew what Wolfbait meant. From within the coat he retrieved the two-shot derringer Pops had given him and held it in his right hand, though he was a left-handed writer. In truth, he had no idea which hand to hold the gun in. He'd never been much for the things, but since Rollie Finnegan had come to the Gulch, Nosey had had more than his share of guns and rough play. He had to admit he didn't hate it.

The sound of pounding hooves drew closer and then, with no warning, from around the corner ahead a striking Appaloosa galloped into view. Riding it was a swarthy-looking fellow with dark eyes, a dragoon mustache of flowing black, and a sugarloaf crown hat. The impressive man and beast thundered by, then reined to a stop a half-dozen yards back up the trail.

While the horse blew, the rider muttered something in a thick voice, the words Spanish but too muted for the hidden men to decipher. The man appeared to be looking for something. He kept glancing down the trail toward where it forked, leading up over rock piles, down through ravines, and spidering off to various claims. He craned his neck, peering into the dim morning light, but appeared unsatisfied.

"Bah!" he finally said, and with twin heel jabs, sunk vicious-looking rowels hard into the heaving horse's barrel, forcing a grunted snort from the big beast even as it leapt forward, carrying the rider back toward town.

As the sound of the drumming hooves faded, Nosey said in a whisper, "What do you reckon?" echoing Wolf-bait's question of moments before. Neither man looked at each other but continued to stare at the trail yards before them.

Wolfbait finally shrugged. "Don't know, but I bet you a beer it ain't good."

"We have to get to town," said Nosey, slipping the der-ringer back into his coat picket.

"You didn't cock that thing, did you boy?"

Nosey patted himself. "No, that is to say I don't think so." He pulled it back out and held it, barrel pointed at Wolfbait's face.

"Good Lord, son, careful with that thing! I don't have much but what I do have is among the living. I'd like to keep it that way a while longer." He peered close at the little gun. "No, you're good. Put that away. And remind me, when whatever this is is over with, that you need lessons in gun handling."

"And shooting," said Nosey, looking up the trail, suddenly convinced that he was long overdue for what Pops had been trying to talk him into for weeks. Shooting lessons.

"Yeah, that, too."

Nosey began walking, but Wolfbait clamped a horned old hand on his upper arm. "Hold on a minute, son. We best get a plan together before we wander into something we can't wander out of."

Nosey nodded. "You're right. I was thinking of Rollie and Pops and the others. Something's going on, and it can't be good. That fellow looked mean. Like he rode out of the pages of a dime novel and couldn't wait to kill something."

"Or someone," said Wolfbait, scratching his chin. "Okay, first things first. We're closer to town than we are to either of our cabins. Like a fool, I left my scattergun at home. And from the looks of you, you don't have one on you, either."

"No." Nosey shook his head. "Pops told me I should take the one from the bar with me at night, but I forgot. As to strengths, I can run but I can't shoot all that well. Whereas you, if you'll permit me saying so, can shoot at marksman caliber. However, your running days, I'm sorry to say, are behind you."

A smile cracked Wolfbait's bearded face. "Boy, if this writing thing doesn't work out for you, you might want to try your hand at politicking. You got the slick palaver down fine."

"What do you mean?"

"You delivered the kindest, most roundabout insult I

have ever received. I plumb enjoyed it. Yes sir, I did."
Wolfbait nodded his head. "Now, about our predicament.
I concur with your assessment of my infirmities."

Nosey looked at the old man as if he hadn't heard him
right.

"Don't give me that look, kid. You ain't the only one
who can talk fancy. I don't trot out the dollar words all
that often 'cause it ends up costing me money and it makes
me tired."

"Oh, well, yes, that is to say I . . ." Nosey turned a
deeper shade of crimson and rubbed the back of his neck.

"What I think you're getting at is that together we make
one useful fella. I'll take that. I expect if we can figure out
how to get you to run for us, and me to shoot for us, we'll
come out with a winning hand."

"Any thoughts as to how to accomplish this?" Nosey
looked at Wolfbait.

"No, but let's stick close to the side of the trail as we
walk, in case that dime-novel bandit decides to return."

The trail they were on branched left, connecting with
the north road out of town that in turn became Main
Street. The closer they walked, the slower they walked,
instinct goading them into caution. They'd heard one more
far-off gunshot since resuming their trek, and that had put
a lid on their nervous chatter. Wolfbait told Nosey to put
his derringer and spare bullets in whichever of his large
side coat pockets was best for whichever hand he would
consider his gun hand.

This puzzled Nosey, but he settled on his left, as that
was his writing hand. As to spare bullets, he hadn't
thought to bring the box of them that Pops had given him

along with the gun. He knew there were two in the gun itself, because he'd watched Pops load them in.

He did, however, have his used but stalwart two-blade Barlow folder that he had learned as a boy to keep as sharp as he was able. "A sharp knife will never cut you, boy," his grandfather had told him.

The notion had puzzled him until the old man had explained that a dull knife will not sink into the matter at hand, but will slide off and into soft flesh of a man's fingers. But a sharp knife will find purchase in wood or meat or bone and do the job it was invented for, leaving a man's fingers uncut and fit to flex another day.

In addition to his service revolver, Wolfbait wore his Green River knife, a midsize, utilitarian skinning and all-around knife that he'd acquired off the atrophied body of a dead man on his journey west forty years before. He'd found the man more by stink than sight, having been curious and as yet unfamiliar with the smell of a greening carcass.

As soon as he saw the man, he knew two things. Someone had been there before him—the dead man's person had been rummaged; and he wished he hadn't been curious. But now that he'd seen the man he felt an obligation to bury him.

Whoever had gotten there before him had taken the man's clothes, left him wearing naught but a death's-head grimace—all sunken eyes, bared teeth and drawn lips—a pinked and critter-chewed set of longhandles, and no boots. Wolfbait, who at that time was going by his original given name of Reginald, wrapped a bandana twice about his mouth and nose and commenced to digging the man a grave right beside the laid-out corpse.

Since Reginald was on his way west to make his fortune digging for gold, he had a decent shovel strapped to his pack. It came in useful that day. When he'd tipped the dead man up with his gloved hands to flop him into the shallow grave, he noticed a badly puckered leather belt wadded beneath his back.

He finished laying the man out in the grave and before he covered him over, nudged the knot of belt with a boot toe. The handle of a sheathed knife appeared, partially covered in the gravel beneath the belt. Reg tugged the affair free of the earth, pulled the blade from the sheath, and was pleased to see it was a good, stout, carbon steel blade.

Payment for my efforts, he thought piously as he set it to the side along with the stiff, puckered leather belt, which he thought might be saved with diligent effort and enough bear grease.

From that day forward, he'd rarely seen the sun set on a day when he'd not called on the fine blade's service in its original sheath which hung on its original belt. All this ancient history flitted through his mind as his hand rested on the butt of the knife's walnut handle.

However, that was all the inventory of weapons the two men could rely on, at least until they could make it to The Last Drop and the relative security of Rollie and Pops' arsenal.

It took them another twenty minutes to get to the end of town behind Chauncey's mercantile. They hid once more behind boulders and eyed the back of the building, which prevented them from seeing down the length of Main Street.

"If it weren't for these things," said Wolfbait, patting a

big hunk of rock with a gnarled old hand, "we'd be dead right now."

If Nosey agreed or if he even heard him, he never said. They hunkered there for a few quiet moments, hearing shouts from seemingly all directions throughout the little downtown, random gunshots punctuating them.

"We can't hide here!" whispered Nosey without looking at his companion.

"I agree. I don't want to sit here doing nothing, either, but until we know what's waiting for us on the other side of that building, I don't think it'd be too wise of us to go rampaging in there until we know what's what."

Nosey's face grew tight and he ground his teeth together. "Fine. In the meantime, our friends could be in danger. You heard those shouts, didn't you? Those are the shouts of frightened people, not from whoever it is perpetrating the crimes going on here!"

"While I tend to agree with you, Nosey, we don't have any proof that crimes are taking place up there."

"You have to be joking, Wolfbait. Did you hear those shots? That shouting? Did you see that rogue on the pretty speckled horse?"

"Appaloosa."

"Huh?"

"The horse," said Wolfbait. "He was riding an Appaloosa."

"Oh, okay. I don't care. I need to get to the tent, see what Pops and Rollie make of all this."

"I think it's more likely that Rollie's the reason for whatever this is, don't you?"

"All the more reason to get over there. We might be of use to them."

Wolfbait sighed and said, "Okay, Nosey. You win. I

don't have strength enough to keep you from running out
there and getting yourself shot full of holes. At least wait
for me. I think if we cut to the right, kept to the trees, we
can get close enough to throw something at the tent,
maybe get their attention. But if I know those boys, they
won't stay put. They'll be more curious than we are to
figure out what's going on."

They made it to the corner of Chauncey's mercantile
and peered up the street.

The first flaw in Wolfbait's plan happened when they
darted across the mouth of the roadway to the right of the
mercantile. They made it across the lane and made use of
six stacked barrels in differing degrees of rupture, and
were about to peer down the long main street when shooting opened up from the slope flanking the east side of the
street.

Smoke clouds drifted up into the morning air from
at least four different spots. Their shots seemed to be
directed at . . . The Last Drop, from which a number of
shots were being lobbed back.

The boys were pinned down.

Nosey said, "Oh no."

Just then a voice behind them said, "Hey, you!"

Wolfbait and Nosey turned to see the very man they'd
seen earlier, the swarthy Mexican with the impressive
mustache and sugarloaf hat. He stood on the bottom step
of the three steps that led to the small loading dock out
the back door of the mercantile's storeroom.

In one hand he held a long-barrel revolver that gleamed
along its length, even that early in the day before the sun
committed to shining full down on Boar Gulch. In the
other hand he held a healthy nub of cured sausage, the

muslin wrap hanging down in shreds. His mouth was full, and he was chewing with it open. Even from across the lane, the men could see the masticated mess in his mouth.

Wolfbait had his own pistol drawn, but because he was angled, it hung, hammer back, at his side, blocked from the Mexican's view.

Nosey stood to his side, trying to use the old man's body to shield his left hand from slipping into his coat pocket to retrieve his derringer.

"Don't do it, boy," whispered Wolfbait out the side of his mouth. "Get ready to dive behind that last barrel, then run hell for leather for that pile of wood the mayor says will be a hotel."

"I'm not leaving you."

"You got to. Only way to go get more guns from the boys."

"I said, 'Hey, you!'" The Mexican sneered at them through a mouthful of half-chewed meat. He tossed the hunk of uneaten sausage to the dirt, stepped down, and advanced, his gun held up, the snout aimed in their direction.

"We heard you, you oaf!" Wolfbait bared his teeth as if he were an old, bearded dog.

"What are you doing?" whispered Nosey, trying to figure out how to loop an arm around the old man's neck without breaking it, then dragging him backward behind the barrels. He guessed the Mexican would likely get off three or four shots in the time it would take him to do that.

"Trust me," said Wolfbait. "I'm calling him out. He'll respond. Because he's an oaf."

"I think you made that fact plain," said Nosey.

"What did you call me, mister?" As the Mexican said

it, he stepped closer, his large yellow horse teeth showing beneath his big mustache. "I think you are going to die, old man."

"When I say so, you tuck low and scamper!" whispered Wolfbait to Nosey. To the Mexican he said, "Would you like me to tell you how many men have told me that?"

The swarthy man advanced another three feet and stood in the middle of the lane, about twenty feet from Nosey and Wolfbait. He thumbed back the hammer of his gun and kept walking toward them, slow and steady.

"Yeah, go ahead, old man. Tell me."

Wolfbait pooched out his lower lip, barely visible buried beneath the curly hairs of the wiry beard growing around his mouth. "Oh . . . let's see. What day is it today?"

That did what Wolfbait had hoped it would.

The Mexican's eyebrows rose. "Huh?" he said, unnerved for the brief moment the old man needed.

Wolfbait barked, "Now, Nosey!" In the same moment, he spun as if he were twenty and not well-north of sixty, dropped to his left knee, raised his right arm steady with the gun, and sent a pair of slugs into the man's chest a finger snap's worth of time before the Mexican did the same to him. "You're the ninth."

The Mexican's eyes explained everything he was going through. From wide surprise that broadened into realization, then squinting as the pain of the bullets clanged gongs of doom in his meager brain, rallying the man's death knell. Or at least that's what went through Nosey's mind as he watched in the span of two, perhaps three seconds, as the swarthy would-be killer's face transformed from the living to the standing dead.

The Mexican's arm that held the long pistol aloft,

dropped as if he were wielding an axe poorly. The hand twitched and the revolver slipped from his grasp and lay at his feet. His knees buckled, first the left then the right, and he seemed to collapse on himself like a stack of playing cards someone had pulled out starting from the bottom.

The last thing he did was flop backward in the dirt, one leg tucked beneath him in a most uncomfortable-looking manner, his spur's rowel spinning one last time.

Wolfbait looked from the dead man to his left, to the slack-jawed Nosey Parker standing beside him. "I see you didn't do as I told you, you whelp!"

"I'm not a child, Wolfbait. And I didn't want to leave you in the clutches of that madman." He folded his arms and looked back toward the forest.

"Good way to get yourself dead. Now get down." With that, Wolfbait tugged the younger man down to a crouching position. "Gunfire usually draws the curious, and some of them might not be happy to see what I did."

"Ah, I see."

"Good. Now, I didn't say I don't appreciate your willingness to die on my behalf, boy. But can we agree that I have a few years on you?" He looked at Nosey, who finally looked at him.

"Yes," said Nosey, sighing.

"Fine. Then can we also agree that because of those years, I might have some hunk of brains about me that you haven't yet figured out how to accumulate?"

Nosey's brows drew in tight. "I'm not sure what that means, but I'm tired of crouching down here and talking in whispers, so I will agree with you. From here on out, and forever, if that will appease you, Wolfbait."

The old man smiled. "I'm not saying you're smart, or even clever, but I will allow that you might have promise. Might be we'll all be glad one day that you weren't eaten as a baby . . . while your bones were soft."

"My God, Wolfbait, I—" Nosey looked at his companion, saw the smirk there, and smiled himself. "You are a man of many surprises."

"Yep," said Wolfbait, glancing up and down the street. "And I'm also tired of talking about nothing. Now, when I say it's safe, you dart out there and grab that revolver. And strip off his gun belt, too. We'll have need of the ammunition." Wolfbait looked toward the main street, then at the mercantile. "Okay, do it now, boy—I got you covered!"

Nosey pulled in a deep breath, then bent even lower and, glancing both ways as if he were crossing a street in Boston busy with carriage traffic, he low-walked out to the sprawled Mexican. Despite the fact that he knew the man had to be dead, Nosey wasn't fully committed to the notion. He dropped to his knees at the man's side, but felt drawn up inside, tight like a coil of rope. What if the Mexican was playing a game with them? What if it was some sort of pistolero's ruse?

"Hurry up, dammit!"

Nosey glanced back at Wolfbait, licked his lips, and snatched up the gun. He noticed it was on full cock. He swung it toward Wolfbait. "Do I—"

For the second time in the past few minutes his companion belied his age by dropping flat to the ground. "Aim that at the sky, boy! Now!"

Nosey shook his head at the old man's nervous ways. The gun bucked in his hand and sent a bullet somewhat skyward. "Oh!" he said when he regained control of the heavy, lurching thing. "Where will that land?" He raised his free hand and clapped it on his head.

"Stupid boy! Get over here and stop being stupid!"

Nosey did as Wolfbait had ordered and joined the man crouching behind the barrels. On seeing Wolfbait's gritted teeth nested in that full, straggly beard, he chose to keep mum about the man calling him stupid twice in one breath. Even if it was redundant.

It seemed to them that the shouting up the lane had ceased a moment, but only for a moment. It resumed louder and bolder. Shouts volleyed back and forth across the street, and though he couldn't make out the words, he did think that one of the voices sounded like Rollie's.

Both men knew the big flaw in their plan would be when they became exposed as they emerged from out behind the stacks of logs and rough lumber Chauncey had been amassing close to the site of his hotel that was slow in progress. But there was no choice. They had to get to the saloon. Gut instinct told them their friends needed help.

The future hotel lay north of The Last Drop by a half-dozen lots. Between Chauncey's Folly, as some folks in town had begun calling the hotel, and the saloon sat two cabins. One was storage for spare drilling and blasting equipment, the other was the village stable with a corral out back. Only two horses currently resided in the little corral. They belonged to Chauncey, a sturdy team that pulled his freight wagon for stock runs.

As the two men catfooted forward, Nosey did his best to not let Wolfbait straggle behind, in part because the older man cursed him with each wheezing, crouched step forward they took. But also because Wolfbait had a six-gun and had proven he most definitely bore the skill to use it.

Ahead, they spied the tent set up behind the slowly emerging new version of The Last Drop saloon, but near the temporary residence of Rollie and Pops, they saw no sign of activity.

Wolfbait squinted his eyes, said, "There!" and pointed a gnarled old finger toward the half-built saloon.

Nosey nodded. He saw it, too. A slight movement of someone inside.

Wolfbait spoke again, whispered the same word, and pointed. "There."

Nosey followed the old man's sightline and saw Rollie shimmying out the back, from under the floor of the saloon.

"Smart," said Wolfbait. "Else they'd be pinned down in there."

"But that means Pops is in the bar."

Wolfbait nodded. "Got to see if we can help somehow."

"I don't think so, boys."

Neither man had to turn to know the voice behind them wasn't that of someone they knew. And then they heard the throaty, metal clicks of a hammer pulling back.

CHAPTER THIRTY-ONE

The shooting began at cock's crow. Rollie had been tugging up his braces on his return from the privy to the rear of the tent that had for the previous weeks doubled as their temporary saloon and living quarters. He'd glanced southward along Main Street toward the hardware shop and the eatery and saw two men rein up and dismount in a hurry between those businesses.

He'd seen another riding in from the southwest trail, and saw higher up, southeastward along the thinly treed ridgetop skirting the downtown, the flickering passage of at least a half-dozen riders moving steady. He thought, too, he saw long guns balanced upright on riders' thighs. This was no early-morning arrival of hopeful newcomers seeking diggings.

Rollie spun, tugging up his second brace. "Pops! Hell with the coffee—we have company. A lot of it." He didn't stop to explain further. He knew Pops would understand the meaning of his barked words and do what he needed to.

In two steps, Rollie was at his cot. He flipped it up and did the same with the lid of his battered wooden chest. He snatched out two boxes of shells, and, though he knew it was there, he slid his hand down to brush the Schofield at his side. As he strode from the partitioned room at the back of the tent that served as his and Pops' living quarters, he snatched up his Winchester rifle.

By then, Pops had his prize Greener cradled in his arms, his pipe puffing up a chimneylike cloud—Rollie noticed Pops always puffed harder when something exciting was about to happen—and had his Colt revolver on his waist.

He followed Rollie out the front of the tent toward the raw wood skeleton of the emerging saloon between the tent and the street. They were rounding the front corner, and Rollie was about to speak as he motioned toward the ridge and the south end of Main Street, when a gunshot cracked the silent morning air. It came from their left, across the street and up on the tumbledown hillside flanking the town proper. That meant they were exposed.

As they flattened against the new saloon's gappy north wall, a second shot ripped into boards above their heads. They didn't need more convincing. They catfooted low back the way they'd come and made it around the back corner of the structure as another bullet chewed a furrow in the stout corner timber.

"Dammit!" growled Rollie. "Putting holes in our new building."

"That all we have to worry about?" said Pops, eyeing the street through the length of the unfinished structure.

Rollie ignored the crack and told Pops what he had seen moments before. He was almost done when a deep, shouting voice from up on the opposite hillside shouted, "Hello the bar! We have your town all but surrounded.

Everybody here has either been run off or taken prisoner. If you don't do as we say, we will commence shooting each and every one of these fine folks in the head. Between the eyes, I do believe."

"Gee," said Pops, "I wonder who he's after?"

Rollie growled and squinted around the corner of the building toward the hillside. This was not how he had expected to begin his day.

"Before you shout your own challenge back, I suggest we put something between them and us, like a half-built building. I feel naked out here." Pops cut to his right and laid Lil' Miss Mess Maker on the floor before him. He hoisted himself trough the gap that would become a double back door for the saloon. They'd designed it like that to make it easier to move stock in and out.

Rollie grumbled, then said, "Better than the tent, I guess."

"Oh, feel free to hole up in the tent. I aim to take cover behind as much thick wood as I can." Pops glanced up the hill behind the saloon while he said it.

Rollie did, too, while he climbed in after Pops. "I don't think they'd have time to get up there yet. But then again, what do I know? I didn't even know they were in town."

"Heck, we don't even know who they are."

"The only thing we do know is that they want my hide," said Rollie, sneering. He bent low and hustled to the front of the building, then crouched beneath a window hole in the nearly complete front wall. Gaps showed between the vertical planks because they'd not yet nailed up battens on the outside.

"You out there!" he shouted. He'd never liked the sound

of his voice while shouting and had rarely raised his voice in a shout throughout his life.

"Good start," said Pops, eyebrows raised. He nodded once, urging Rollie on.

Rollie sighed.

The big booming voice from before said, "Yeah?"

"Who do you want?"

"Don't be stupid, old man! We want Stoneface Finnegan. Might be you. Come on out!"

"And if he doesn't?" Rollie already knew the answer, they'd said as much a few minutes before. He was stalling, buying time, but he doubted it was going to work.

"Then we'll commence the killing!"

Rollie waited, leaning against the wall, aware that a bullet could gnaw its way through and into him any second.

"Well?" came the voice from across the road.

That gave Rollie hope. They might be a little desperate after all, or maybe a little hesitant to shoot innocents. It wasn't much of a hope, but a sliver was better than nothing.

"How do I know you have anybody hostage?"

There was a long moment's pause, during which neither Pops nor Rollie breathed. If they heard a scream or shout followed by a gunshot, the invaders had called Rollie's bluff and shot an innocent townsperson.

The man's voice boomed out once more. "Ha! You best believe it, mister. Before we shoot somebody, maybe that big goober at the restaurant—good pie, by the way—I think we'll open this ball with a little fun! Boys? Let 'em fly!"

No sooner had he said that than shots from what sounded like all directions filled the air of Boar Gulch. And from the sound of where they were landing, every bullet in the world was directed at the half-clothed skeleton of The Last Drop. Wood splintered and cracked and chips flew. Shouts that sounded a whole lot like the cackles of laughter punched through the air when there were pauses between gunshots.

CHAPTER THIRTY-TWO

"You still think this was a good idea, Pops?" Rollie forced the grim words through gritted teeth as he peered around a stack of planking waiting to be nailed in place on the improved saloon. He wasn't so certain that would happen now. At the very least, if they lived through this fusillade, they'd have to replace half the lumber already nailed up.

"Now," Pops ducked low, whacking his chin on the floor of the half-built saloon as a bullet zipped through where his forehead had been. "Which of my excellent ideas are you referring to?"

Another bullet chewed a furrow in the honeyed wood of the pine plank beside Rollie's head. He smelled the tang of pitch and wished he was out riding Cap in some far-off forest, with no two-legged predators dogging his trail. "The notion that I should stay in Boar Gulch . . ." He snaked the Schofield around the base of the stack and cranked off two shots in the general direction of the diseased devils who had them—and the entire town—pinned down.

"And?" Pops glanced at his partner a dozen feet to his left.

"Instead of pulling up stakes and leading these—whoever they are—away from innocent folk!"

"Innocent? In the Gulch?" Pops laughed and refilled the wheel on his Colt. "We need a plan, Rollie. Can't sit here all day and wait to get picked off. One of them's bound to be cutting a wide loop around town right now."

"I know. I figured as much—they'll be coming in on us from behind. Trouble is," he gritted his teeth and scooched lower as another bullet shattered a pitchy knot a foot to his left. "I don't see a way to get out of here that doesn't involve stomping fast across the wide open all around us."

Rollie considered the situation. By now the miners in the outlying cabins would be curious and ambling their way to town on all the little feeder trials and lanes that leached outward from the beating heart that was Boar Gulch's Main Street.

"Nosey got anything more on him than that two-shot you gave him?"

Pops nodded. "Supposed to. I told him to take the scattergun from the tent."

"Good."

"Unless he didn't remember to take it with him."

"Oh. Well, if he has it, he can't miss with that thing."

"Don't be so certain. That kid can write up a storm and ask more questions than the good Lord has answers for, but I never saw anybody as poor a shot as Nosey Parker."

Rollie nodded. "Hopefully he's with Wolfbait. He might be old and cranky, but he's a solid shot."

"Yep, can't run worth a bean, but he's a decent shot."

The men sat quiet for a moment longer, each considering a course of action—any would do now that they were pinned down. It was embarrassing enough without being able to help another blessed soul in town.

"Maybe the mayor has a plan!" Pops didn't laugh after he said it.

Rollie looked over at him and that's when Pops laughed. Rollie couldn't help himself. He shook his head and smiled. "How many do you think are out there waiting on us?"

"Hard to tell," said Pops. "But from the angle and direction of the shots so far, I'd say three, maybe four. Spread out, likely from behind the big rock, then from the slope north of it."

Rollie nodded in agreement. "And south?" He squinted southward through a gap in the plank.

"Could be holed up in Geoff the Scot's fine dining establishment."

"That means they're eating all the pie. Dammit. Not much I like about that surly Geoff, but he can make a mean pie."

"That's a fact. Be a shame to lose a man with such a talent."

"That's it. I'm done with this foolishness. If I'm what they want, there's no need for the town to suffer for it." He shoved up onto his left knee, wincing at the pain from crouching for the past hour.

"Rollie, no! That's what they want!" Pops was too far away to wrestle his bullheaded pard to a standstill, so he threw a scrap of wood at him. The ragged nub end of plank caught Rollie in the leg.

"Hey!"

"Stay put. Has to be a smarter way out of this than getting shot!"

Another bullet whistled in and chewed a furrow in the floor behind them. Rollie glanced at it. "Hey."

Pops looked at him. "You said that already."

"I don't see nail heads on that flooring back there where the bar's going to go."

"If we ever get this thing built! But yeah, now you mention it, that doesn't surprise me. I believe Nosey was responsible for that task yesterday. You thinking what I'm thinking you're thinking?"

Rollie shrugged. "You're starting to sound like Wolfbait. I'm going to scoot back there, pry up a couple of those boards, and squirm my way down through. Should be far enough back that they can't see under from the front."

"Then what?"

"Then I'll crawl underneath and head for the outhouse."

Pops laughed. "You have to go that bad?"

"Yeah, and when I'm done I'll try to make it up the hill and—"

"And?"

Rollie shoved himself backward, lugging a wide plank before him as a scant shield. "And I'll figure it out once I get up there!"

"No offense, Rollie, but you aren't as fast or as flexible as a man thinking of doing that ought to be. Let me do it."

"No offense taken. And no way. This is my fight, Pops. Besides, I need you to send out cover shots while I go. I make it up there, you use the same route before they catch on. I'll cover you from you there."

"Okay, but I say I should go first."

Rollie looked him in the eye and shook his head. "See you soon, pard."

"Oh, Rollie?"

Finnegan sighed. "What?"

"Take a leak for me while you're in there, okay? All that coffee's working on me."

Rollie smiled and shook his head once more, then shoved himself backward. In a few moments he'd managed to make it to the blunt end of a wide plank, another staggered joint to its neighboring plank not far away. Perfect. He pried open the short blade of his folding Barlow, and managed to pry up the near plank enough to wedge his fingers beneath.

I will never again complain about Nosey not seeing a task through, he thought. He quickly decided that was a promise he couldn't keep. Parker was a good kid but he wasn't deserving of that much slack.

Rollie worked up the plank high enough to slide it onto and past the next. With that next plank, he did the same, creating a gap wide enough that he slipped into it with little sound, save for soft scraping and grunting. His gun belt fetched up a moment, then he was freed and dropping down below the floor.

His knees hit the hard ground sooner than he'd hoped, which meant he wouldn't have much space to crawl on his belly toward the back of the building. Good thing he didn't have much of a slop gut.

Pops saw the top of Rollie's head sink below the floor and turned back to face the street once more. "Okay then, let's get to it." He thumbed back the hammer on the Colt and, eyeing down the barrel, saw something across the street from the bar shift slowly, no more than a shadow. It was right where he thought one of the shooters might hunker behind the north end of the big rock they all used as a morning meeting spot. "Far, but worth"—Pops raised the barrel a hair and squeezed the trigger—"a shot."

A puff of powder rose up and Pops knew, despite his effort, that he'd nicked the big rock. But the reaction from the shadowed spot was immediate and brought a smile to Pops' gray-stubbled face. "Damn," he said as whoever he'd shot howled and brayed and carried on from behind the rock.

"Shut up!" a hard voice shouted from southward and uphill, in roughly another of Pops' guessed spots. And definitely too far for him to waste a lucky shot. But then again, what did he have to lose? He had to keep up the firing to distract the would-be killers from paying attention to Rollie's progress.

Whoever he'd hit didn't take the advice of his fellow gunman. His howling grew louder. Pops got an even bigger surprise. The yowling man behind the rock stood up and staggered forward, around the end of the rock and into the street.

"I'll be . . ." said Pops, aiming once more with the convenience of seeing his target.

The man held his hands to his head, and Pops saw blood leaching out between his fingers, on the right side of his face. He figured he'd grazed the man's scalp deep, maybe even to the skull bone, which would darn sure account for the blood and the frenzy the man was in.

"Gaaah!" The man shouted over and over, "Help—oh,

oh, aaah!" as he lurched in no particular direction. He
wagged his elbows like a flustered chicken and lost his
balance once, dropped to a knee, then popped up again.

He bent at the waist and shouted something that sounded
to Pops like, "My head!" but could also have been, "I'm
dead!" as blood flecked from his bleeding pate.

"So now the man's a fortune-teller," said Pops.

"Shut the hell up!" shouted the voice from the hill once
more, but louder. The big, full, deep voice ragged its rage
at the wounded man.

"Stop that dancing, you fool," muttered Pops, sighting
along the Colt's barrel once more. He had Lil' Miss Mess
Maker with him, but she was for close-in work, not distance shots. Not that a revolver was any better, but he got
lucky once. Why not again? He tracked the man and was
a breath from triggering a fresh shot at him when a rifle
thundered from the hillside.

Pops saw the bleeding man jerk into his final dance.
The rifle shot—a big caliber, judging from the sound and
the force it delivered—caught the bleeder high in the chest
as if he'd been punched by some mighty cosmic fist.

The man's arms flew outward from where they'd
gripped his head, jerking like tree branches caught in a
sudden, hard wind. His body snapped upward, his boots
whipped higher than his head and kept right on going,
arcing in a backward somersault, the boot toes catching
up with the shower of blood and bone that pinwheeled
high, spraying the sky, then the street.

The moment looked to Pops as if it had been slowed
by time. The blood splashes drizzled outward into spatters,
then droplets, then spray, skylining against a backdrop of
sparse, broad Ponderosas reaching high into the blue of

a day the dancing man would never again enjoy. The moment sped up and *Whap!* the man slammed hard on his chest into the graveled and dung-riddled street, his head bent forward.

Even from his distance, Pops heard the carrot-snap sound of the man's neck breaking. The man was still. His head bent beneath his chest, raising his body up slightly, looking as if he was fixed on gnawing at his own chest.

It was a chest that was all but missing, judging from the hole in the man's back where the mighty bullet had clawed its way out. Maybe the dead man was trying to see that pretty blue sky, one last time, through his own back.

Pops whistled low, forgetting for the moment to shoot at the cloud of smoke rising up off the hillside, the spot where the shot had come from. "Must have been a Sharps." He turned and did his best to send a bullet back where the killer had been.

He was not rewarded with a shriek and felt like a fool for giving himself away. An answering shot came from the same spot, but it sounded like a carbine. Pops returned fire, but it did occur to him that it was likely the same man who'd sent his own compadre to hell using a buffalo gun, notorious as a long-range weapon which, if handled by someone who knew the worth of a dead buffalo for eating, was likely good with the sights.

If that was the case, Pops was a sitting dead man. "Hope you're ready, Rollie," he muttered, "because it's time I vacated these premises." He dropped low once more and glanced back to see where Rollie had built his impromptu trapdoor. Pops began shoving himself backward across the floor on his belly toward the hole.

With the Colt in his right hand and Lil' Miss Mess Maker in his left, he'd gone a couple of feet when the world exploded around him. Jags of pine showered the air above him, right where his head had been moments before.

Splinters of the raw wood drove into Pops' forehead, his scalp, his cheeks and ears, and through his shirt into the meat of his shoulders and neck. He let out a low, quick moan, then shut himself up. *No worse than the lash,* he told himself. He'd tasted its sting plenty in the past.

He kept shoving backward until his toes slipped into the gap. He felt the warmth of blood trickling through his hair, down his cheeks, in his eyelashes, and on his shoulders, but he shoved harder and dropped his knees into the hole in the floor. Only then did he look up and see the fist-size pucker hole in what had that morning been nothing more than part of the front wall of The Last Drop.

It was a bullet-hole-riddled mess, bright morning light piercing the pine planking. Pops blinked back blood, licked his lips, then hawked a mouthful of blood and spit. "Clean that up later," he said, and triggered a shot with the Colt back through the ragged hole and in toward that devil-pocked hillside. Then he dropped down into the meager crawlspace, spun around, and dragged himself toward the rear of the new building, hoping like hell Rollie was safe.

And if he was, then he'd best commence with some cover fire of his own, "Because," Pops muttered, "I'm coming on through, like it or not."

CHAPTER THIRTY-THREE

The dirt beneath the raised platform they'd built for the new version of The Last Drop was as dusty as the rest of the dirt in Boar Gulch, but at least it was somewhat smoothed out and even between the pilings they'd sunk. Rollie had Nosey to thank for insisting they cuff the dirt flat before building on it.

Rollie dragged himself forward, expecting any second to feel the drilling, exploding heat of a choice shot sent his way. Surely somebody had seen him inching backward and then dropping from sight. The walls of the half-built saloon were full of gaps at best, and mostly missing.

He heard a gunshot from Pops. A loud shot. Somehow the wood transferred the sound down through the thick floor planking and made him grit his teeth tighter. He heard Pops mumble something and he swore he could hear screaming. Too far off to be Pops. Could his partner have hit someone? With a revolver? Maybe whoever it was had ventured closer.

Rollie rammed his elbows in harder and clunked his head for the second time on a log stringer. The bark was sharp, raw, and made him growl. "Ow!" He looked ahead.

For the first time he saw how little daylight was between the very back end of the timber platform and the ground. Enough gap there to jam an arm through, but definitely not enough to crawl through.

The screams and shouts from the direction of the street got louder and odder as he glanced to his left and right. He was nearly in the center of the floor. Choose a side and hope like you've never hoped before that no one who knows there's a price on your head is looking that way. He spat grit and gravel, glanced left once more, then crawled hard and fast to his right.

He reached the edge of the space and heard a thunderous boom from across the street, far to his right. It was sudden and sounded to him like the singular pounding of a buffalo rifle. He didn't hear anything scuffle and groan and thrash from above, so Pops hadn't been the target. Yet. But thankfully the infernal screaming and yowling and moaning from the direction of the street had ceased. *Interesting.*

Rollie knew that as soon as he snaked his head out from under The Last Drop, he could be sniped. But it was too late to turn back. Not for the first nor would it be the last time that day, Rollie Stoneface Finnegan growled low and deep in his chest, pulled in a deep breath, and checked his weapons. Time to fight back.

He shoved himself out through the gap between the earth and the log forming the side floor joist. He shot a quick look to his right at what he could see of the hillside, but didn't slow his pace. He had to make it around the back of the saloon, behind the outhouse, and then up the hillside before the attackers circled back there. It wouldn't be long until they did. They were on horseback.

The good news was that in order to stay out of gun range of whoever might shoot at them from town—Rollie and Pops—they would have to cut a wide trail to get in a position of surrounding the small cluster of buildings that formed Boar Gulch.

It was that slim chance that Rollie hoped hadn't passed him by. That he hadn't been shot at from the hillside behind the bar gave him hope. He lurched and heard a gunshot at the same time he shoved off with his boots and tucked and rolled onto his right shoulder, ending in a heap behind the near angled corner of the tent. Scant cover, but he was closer to the outhouse. He rolled up onto his al- ready-aching knees and shoved off once more, running low and tight for the backside of the outhouse. No shots followed him.

He straightened to full height behind the narrow struc- ture and wrinkled his nose. Even early like this the thing was a ripe spot. He'd have to do something about that. Glancing uphill he decided to head slightly to his left, toward a jut of gray ledge that would provide decent cover. From there it would be a wide-open run of at least two hundred feet when he'd be exposed for the world to shoot at. Then he'd be up on the top berm and close to the trees. *Then what?* he asked himself as he dug in his boot soles, zigzagging upward toward the boulder.

He heard a cracking sound at the same time his left foot whipped outward, driving his knee into the slope. He pushed of to his feet again, the thought that he'd been shot flitting behind him. He didn't feel any pain from it, but that could come any second. He was capable of continuing on upslope, and that's all he cared about. He reached the boulder and dove behind it. He had to start firing back, sending out cover fire so Pops could get out through the back of the building.

He also had to confirm that the invaders hadn't reached the hilltop above him yet, and had to somehow tell Pops the way was clear. But first he had to check his left foot. Sure felt to him as if he'd been shot, the way his boot kicked out to the side like that.

Turned out the stacked leather heel of his boot became a victim of a bullet. It was half-gone, blown off, and the bit that was left flapped like a chewed tongue, cobbler's nails poking from the wagging bit. Rollie gritted his teeth and bit back a curse. He liked those boots, dammit.

"Hey!"

Rollie looked up. Who was that?

"Hey . . . it's Pops! I'm comin' up!"

"No—too dangerous!"

"Too dangerous? Too bad! Cover me, man!"

Rollie cursed and peered low around the edge of the boulder in time to see Pops' bowler bob into view.

He shook his head once quickly, then said, "Okay," and began sending rounds high across the road into the far hillside, all the while keeping an eye on the terrain to either side. He could do little about whoever might be behind him. *A man can only do so much,* he reminded himself.

He felt something hit him in the back. Before he could turn, it happened again right away. He bent low and spun, sneering and leveling his revolver, expecting to see a stranger bent on killing him.

Instead he saw Pieder Tomsen, the blacksmith, who'd been tossing rocks at him. The man's black curly hair and thick, beard topping his daily garb—a scorched, stained, thick leather apron from chest nearly to his boots. He was bent low and cradled a single-barrel shotgun.

He eyed Rollie and pointed over his own left shoulder, then held up two fingers. He pointed over his right shoulder and did the same—two invaders. Four in all.

Rollie knew Pieder was somewhat safe where he was. Atop the hill was a depression a couple of feet deep. But he wouldn't be able to fend off four men for long. Likely he'd been driven from his blacksmith shop or had seen the invaders coming and knew they were up to little good.

Shots rained across the street and chewed their way into the gravel beside Pops. It didn't go unnoticed by Rollie that whoever fired them could likely have made them more effective, not that he wanted them to. What was their game if not to kill them off?

Bounty, of course. Might be they wanted him alive. But for who? Rollie shook his head. No need to worry about that yet. The day was young, and he and Pops were alive—so far—and they had ammo. And a quiet but tough-as-an-anvil blacksmith backing them. Literally.

"Get up here, old man!" growled Rollie. That's all it took for Pops to grind harder and faster up the last twenty feet. Another bullet zinged in, nicking the boulder. Rollie ducked out of instinct as Pops piled in beside him behind the boulder.

"Who are you calling old . . . old man?"

Pops was about to speak again when Rollie jerked his head behind them. "Tomsen's above us in that gulley. Two men to either side back there. I'd say beyond his shop but converging fast. They'd have to be blind to not know where we are by now."

"Then we traded one fire for another," said Pops. "At

least from here we can see them coming. And Pieder will work on them, too. I assume he has that single-barrel of his?"

Rollie nodded. "But I don't want to sit here pinned."

"No other place to go. I say we lay low, cover each other, try to inch up to Pieder in the gulley. We could cover the top and this downslope from there."

"Yep," said Rollie. "Thing is, I bet Cap's first-born that they want me alive. You, too, for some reason."

"Cap's a gelding, Rollie."

"I know." He grinned and dropped to his belly. "I'll go, and I'll keep an eye to the left as I crawl. You try to look to the right."

"Try? You know I will."

As he wriggled forward, hampered by the awkward firearms, Rollie spoke low but clearly to the blacksmith. "Pieder, we're coming up to you. Me first, then Pops."

He was about six feet from the rock when the bullets began again. They drilled closer, and when he felt one stab through the floppy cloth of his upper right sleeve, Rollie doubted his theory that they wanted him alive. He crawled faster.

As he crested the slight hump at the edge of the gulley, he saw Pieder Tomsen grinning at him—first time he'd seen the sooty-faced, bearded man smile—and his thick arm swung over and grabbed Rollie by the collar and dragged him forward toward him as another bullet sizzled in, popping up a cloud of dust from the dry slope.

Rollie rolled into the ditch and caught his breath. "Obliged," he said. He was pleased to see that in addition to his shotgun, Pieder wore a revolver tucked into the thick leather belt around his apron.

The quiet blacksmith nodded once, then resumed scanning the terrain behind them. In the distance his shop and small attached home sat empty, a thinner trail of black smoke than usual rising from the central chimney in the midst of the open-sided shop.

Two work wagons stood before the shop, creating another layer of shadow, deeper in shade the farther Rollie's eyes had to travel, until the recesses of the shop sat in near-blackness.

Pops searched the same view. "Pieder, either you have a helpmate back there or somebody's lurking deep in."

The blacksmith grunted and squinted at his shadowed shop.

"I take it you are as alone there this morning as you were yesterday when you fixed that ladle for me." Rollie didn't have to hear the taciturn man speak to know the answer. Somebody was in there. Pops' eyes wouldn't lie. Rollie looked to the right and left. No telling how many or what they were up to.

The three men, in silent consensus, kept watch out of the gully in each direction. Nothing moved save for the infrequent swish of a horse's tail down by Horkins' Hardware.

"The mayor's mercantile looked to be closed up tighter than a bull's backside. You know he can't be happy about that."

"I wish I cared," said Rollie. "Hey, that tree look thicker than you remember it being?" Pieder and Pops looked southward toward the edge of the stump field to where the pines hadn't yet been felled.

"By that pile of slash?"

"Yep, to the right."

Pops nodded. "Good eye you have there."

Rollie knew coming from Pops that was a compliment. Pops didn't brag on his own ability, but as Wolfbait had put it not long ago, "He could see the pecker on a blue-bottle at a hundred paces."

"Okay, they're getting in position. I expect they will try to wait us out."

"It might work," said Pops. "I don't get my afternoon coffee, I will be surly and apt to leave this hole in search of a hot cup."

"You there!" came a voice from the shade of the same tree line. "We know you're there in the trench. Come on out or we will kill the locals off one at a time."

Pops and Pieder looked at Rollie.

He sneered and shouted, "I've heard that before. Get on with it!"

"You think that was wise?" said Pops.

"No, but—" Rollie didn't have time for more because they heard hooves thundering. Two men on horseback appeared to rise up out of the earth fifty yards to the north. The visual trick could be blamed on the lumpy hill leading up to where they lay protected at the top.

"Pops, watch the woods. They're trying to distract us. Pieder, you take behind us. I'll get these two and watch the downslope below us."

The riders dipped down almost disappearing, then reemerged before slowly coming into full view, silent and bent low in the saddle. As they crested the plateau, they broke apart, the one on the left veering wide. He held his reins in his teeth and levered a round into a carbine. His black hat's brim flattened against the crown as they ran, his horse wild-eyed and huffing hard at the sudden pain the man's ramming rowels caused.

Pops left the blacksmith to keep an eye on the downslope and the tree line to their left that held the shadowed form by the tree. He laid the Greener gently by his left knee and pulled the Colt free. He'd checked moments before that it was loaded, and thumbed back on the hammer, aiming at the rider. "Come on then. I'll give you something to chew on, jackass."

As if the rider heard him, he cut wider and raised his rifle, propping the fore stock on his left arm. Pops fired at the same time the rider did. He didn't like to shoot at a man on horseback, especially at a dicey range and with a pistol. No call to be hurting a horse with a bad shot.

He heard the blacksmith shout a quick, clipped word that sounded like German. Pops spun to his left and saw the leather-clad man bent low, his pistol at his knees, the fingers of his big left hand clamped over his right shoulder. Blood sluiced between the fingers. The man caught Pops' eye and shook his head, his teeth gritted.

Pops wasn't certain if the man was about to bite him or if he was ticked off that he'd been hit. He chose to think the latter. But that was all the time he could give the man. Pops had an invader to deal with.

By the time he turned back around, he saw that the rider had used the moment to thunder closer, that rifle's snout pointed right at him. Pops heard a shot from Rollie's rifle but had no time to see if his pard had dealt a useful blow. He ducked low, snatched up Lil' Miss Mess Maker, and cocked both barrels as he raised her and triggered them, all in one slick move. He had to because the rider was about to squeeze a rifle round in his face.

CHAPTER THIRTY-FOUR

Rollie ignored the other rider making for Pops and concentrated on the fat man bearing down on him. The man's ample paunch slopped up and down in time with the pouches of his thinly whiskered cheeks. A fawn hat lifted free of his fleshy topknot and whipped away, revealing a jouncing, wide head, mostly bald and pink, and trailing long, wispy strands of ginger hair above two egg-shaped eyes staring right at Rollie with undisguised bile.

Rollie's shot caught the man in the throat and he jerked upright, gazing at the sky as his blood spattered outward to both sides. His arms flipped upward as if he were tossing the rifle into the air in celebration and then he flopped to his left and his left boot spun down, caught in the stirrup. His fat body slammed the sparse grass hard before he reached the gulley.

The horse veered right. Rollie saw its eyes wide and white and bugging, its teeth showing in a foam-flecked mouth as it struggled with the sudden, flopping dead-weight. The cinch snapped, and the fat man's weight pulled the saddle free of the horse. The entire affair slopped to a rolling stop a foot from the gulley, pushing a dust cloud over the three crouching men.

The retreating horse cut a wide loop and galloped toward the meadow beyond the blacksmith shop, puffs of dust rising from its hoofbeats. Rollie watched it go with regret. One of them might have been able to use it to make it to the tree line.

Right beside Rollie, Pops heard a slicing zing and felt his hat whip from his head. His world bloomed in an explosion of shotgun blast, of screams and bellows, of vivid colors of blood and hair and bone, of grit and dust. And the stink of hot horse breath and smoke and gunpowder.

A whoosh of hot air and dust and dirt boiled over the gulley. Something hard pounded into Pops' chest, caromed off, then followed with something larger. It shoved him backward, and any air in his lungs pushed out.

I'm done, thought Pops. I'm done and I haven't even taken care of what I promised my wife I would do. Dammit.

But he wasn't knocked unconscious. He was slammed backward into the far slope of the gulley, felt the vague softness of another body beside him, thought maybe it was Rollie or the blacksmith.

He heard only a steady, dull pounding, not with his ears but with his entire body—*boom boom boom*—sounded like his blood pumping hard to do its job in his body. Then the world opened up a little bit more, and he heard a horse in howling agony, and the disaster of previous seconds came clear. Pops knew right away what had pounded into him. He thanked whatever god was responsible for such things that the horse hadn't—as yet—collapsed on him.

Had he hit the horse? He thought he'd aimed high enough. And then he felt another hard thing hit him twice quick in the chest and the side, a horse's hoof? And it kept on doing it. Finally when he had decided it was either a steady volley of bullets or a horse's hoof rapping away as if knocking on a front door, he heard a voice close by his face.

"Pops!"

Something slapped his face.

"Pops, come around!"

"Rollie?" It felt to Pops as if he was trying to talk through mud. And he'd barely heard his own voice. He felt something pulling him upright to a sitting position, arms tugging under his. "Huh?" he tried to shake his head to stop the buzzing. It didn't work.

"Getting you out from under that horse, Pops. Don't fight me."

The pain in his thigh bloomed deeper, hotter. He gritted his teeth and used the pain to help rouse himself from feeling fuzzy-headed.

"No use, you're pinned. You with me?" It was Rollie.

"Yeah, just a minute." Pops breathed deep. His chest was sore but nothing felt mortally wrong yet. "How's Pieder?"

The blacksmith leaned over, and despite his bullet-chewed shoulder, he gave Pops a toothy smile and a nod. "Good."

"Okay, I think I'll join you, then." Pops tried to push himself up to a higher sitting position but Rollie was right, the horse had him pinned. He heard a sound and looked to his right.

The bloody stump of a man mewled and shivered on

the gravel before them. One wide, white eye was visible. It looked to Pops as if the man's eyelids had been peeled off and tossed aside, the ripped flesh at their base burned with a match. Other than that, there was little recognizable to the man's face.

The lips and nose were gone. The teeth, much like the lone eyeball, glared white and quivery and snapping. A tongue stump slowly flicked like the tail of a stomped snake. The wreck of a man shuddered and was dead.

"What in the hell . . ." said Rollie.

"Had to," said Pops.

"I know!" Rollie's response came out as a quick shout, because he'd lunged at the thrashing horse with his hip knife.

"Did I hit it?"

"I don't think so—but this dead man's weighing it down!" Rollie kicked and stomped on the man's shoulder. It helped stretch the cinch, make it taut enough for him to slice through. But the horse wanted none of it and thrashed harder.

"Settle down!" shouted Rollie, to no avail. The beast was lusted with frenzy and thrashed all the more, eyes rolling white and mouth champing and foaming. The stink of fear rising off the beast clouded the men's faces. Pops shook his head to dispel the clinging vestiges of dizzying sound and bent to settle the beast.

He received a knock to the head by the horse's own thrashing head, and it dizzied him further, but he maintained his grip on the slick-hided beast. He spread his arms wide, hoping to buy Rollie the quick moment he needed to slice though the cinch without cutting the horse.

It worked. As soon as the knife freed the saddle, the

horse seemed to know it and shoved hard upward with all four hooves. One of the hooves was braced against Pops' right thigh, and he howled as the huge, desperate beast regained its legs. The horse whipped its head to the left, then it made to lunge upward.

"Grab those reins!" shouted Rollie, even as he dove over Pops for the trailing lines.

The blacksmith was quicker and snatched them with a bloodied hand, gripping them tight. He thrust them at Rollie with a tight nod, then clamped the hand back over his shot-up shoulder, glaring down at the dead invaders littering the ground at their feet. He spat on the bloodied, pulped mess that had once been the man's face, and growled a word they couldn't make out.

"Get on!" shouted Rollie to Pops. "Get on the high side of the ditch and climb on! We'll use it as a shield and fire to cover us! To the trees!"

"Not me! I can't make it!"

Rollie looked quickly down at Pops' leg. Where the horse had stepped, his trousers were torn and the muscle and meat of his thigh were visible. "No!"

The blacksmith grabbed a thrashing, cursing Pops and shoved him upward, onto the quivering horse's back. Resigned to his status of momentary invalid, Pops bent low and snatched for the reins. "My Greener!" he shouted, and Rollie slapped the bulky brute of a shotgun into Pops' waiting hand. He ejected the spent shells and thumbed in two fresh shells.

There was no time to consider the finer points of what struck them all as a fool's game, but they had little choice. They were sitting ducks in the gulley. With Pops in the saddle, Pieder and Rollie crowded the horse's left side.

Pops kept low, hugging the horse's neck, the Greener cocked and balanced behind the saddle horn.

Pieder walked first, bent low and threatening to outdistance the horse with each angry stride. Rollie crouched behind him, trying to keep his steps measured enough so as to not stomp the back of the blacksmith's boots. It wasn't easy walking for Rollie, as his boot heel had been all but removed by that bullet, but he compensated, altering his usual limping gait.

The awkward caravan angled toward the tree line to the south at the fastest pace it could manage, Pops keeping an eye on the blacksmith's shop, Pieder watching the tree line toward which they were running and where they hoped to find cover, and Rollie watching the slope toward town. As soon as they began their odd little trek he knew they'd be visible from Main Street.

Couldn't be helped. They had to make it to the trees. What was waiting for them they didn't know. Pops had spied one shady shape moving in there, and with vermin, Rollie knew if you could see one, a dozen others might be lurking behind.

CHAPTER THIRTY-FIVE

Rollie had been gnawing over in his mind who might be the attackers. It seemed like a well-organized band, and a lot more of them than he'd experienced thus far. The whole damned mess could have been avoided had he trusted his gut and left Boar Gulch behind. As he hobbled forward, scanning the downslope terrain, he cursed himself for listening to Pops.

The fusillade began again.

The horse was the first to get hit. Rollie heard the hard, tight smack as the bullet slammed into its flank behind his own shoulders. Instinct pushed him down farther in his crouch and with his inner hand he grabbed the front of the saddle and shouted, urging the horse to move faster. "Work her, Pops! We're in trouble!"

They were five yards from the trees when Pieder shouted a word Rollie had never heard, hoisted his shotgun, and running, launched himself at a dark shape in the trees. The leather-clad man's gun barked flame and smoke and then he was on whoever was in there.

Good luck, thought Rollie. He had all he could do to

return fire in the direction he guessed the shots were raining from—his side. Someone was below the top of the slope that led down to Main Street, hiding like a coward and peppering them as they ran.

They reached the trees, and the horse kept going, neighing from down deep in its chest. Rollie saw a bleeding wound midflank ooze a thick rope of crimson blood. Already the beast's leg was drawing up, but it barreled gamely into the trees.

He heard Pops doling out shots from his Colt as they ran. At least they had given themselves an option. In Rollie's long experience, as long as you had an option, you didn't have to resort to the final possibility, which was to put a bullet in your own head. Or do it Alamo style and go down, overrun, howling for blood, and blazing away.

Rollie peeled off away from the retreating horse with Pops jostling atop, doing his best to stay in the saddle and not get scraped off by a pine.

Rollie darted low, angled around a clot of logging slash, brambly branches, and sags of crumbling bark jutting in every direction. It had been piled there some time ago by whoever had cut the trees to build a cabin. Might even have been Pieder, seeing as how they weren't all that far from his shop.

Shots volleyed, but the cover of the woods likely confounded the shooters. A branch cracked behind him and Rollie spun, the Schofield a breath away from speaking the only way it knew how.

Pieder's grim face peeked around a pine. "Okay?"

Rollie nodded, motioned for him to come ahead, join

him behind the slash mound. Once the man made it beside him, Rollie nodded toward his shoulder. "Bad?"

"No, okay." The blacksmith flexed his fingers and offered a quick smile. "Good."

Rollie spied through gaps in the branches. "Wish I knew how many there are."

Pieder nudged him with an elbow. "Come." He jerked his head toward the direction he'd come from. "Come," he said again.

Rollie shrugged. *Why not?* He trusted the man, though he had no idea what Pieder was talking about. Rollie found out the moment they rounded a cluster of boulders a few paces behind a big pine. Sprawled against the rocks leaned a young stranger with a bloodied gut. Had to be one of the invaders. He'd been shot, but his chest rose and fell. The young man's eyelids fluttered, fought to open.

"You do this?" Rollie said to the blacksmith.

Pieder nodded.

"Thanks. Keep an eye. I'll try to get him to chat."

The blacksmith nodded and crouched down. Eyeing the dappled woods about them, he poised his gun for action.

"Hey!" Rollie grabbed the wounded man's boot and jiggled it. "Hey!" He jerked it back and forth.

The young man groaned and his eyes fluttered open, lazed back and forth. As Rollie kept jerking the foot, the eyes focused on his face.

"No . . . stop it!"

"Sure." Rollie crouched low and leaned closer to the man's face, his pistol ready to bark if the man made an unexpected move. "Glad to, once you answer a few questions."

"No, no way. The boss, he'd kill me."

"Guess what? My friend here beat him to it."

"Huh?"

"Look, son, you're gut shot. About to meet your Maker. Or not."

"What do you mean?" the man's eyes widened.

"I mean, you shuffle off as you are now, you'll be going down, not up." Rollie hoped the fool was at least raised by Christians who'd laced his youth with the fears of sizzling brimstone, of the might and mayhem of heaven and hell.

"Why?" The young man swallowed, fought to keep his eyes open. His left cheek twitched and he groaned as pain surged his insides.

"Hey, stick with me, kid." Rollie snapped his fingers and lightly slapped the man's face. "Tell me something I can use. Something that will help me save all those innocent people in town might earn your place way upstairs. You follow me?"

The young man tried to nod, grimaced, then said, "Boss was hired—"

"By who? Come on, who?" Rollie smacked the kid's face again, harder this time. He knew he was losing him.

"Kid! Who's your boss?"

The young man's eyes opened again. "Cleve . . . Cleve! Oh, I don't wanna go to hell . . ."

And that was it. The kid sagged into himself. Rollie was tempted to shake the damn fool by the shirtfront but it would be fruitless.

That odd name the kid said, *Cleve,* told Rollie more than he could have imagined. If it was who he suspected, that explained a whole lot about how the day was going.

Cleve Danziger was a hired gun, perhaps the most

famous of all alive or dead that Rollie was acquainted with. He sold his services to anybody who met his high-end rates. He was employed by wealthy absentee ranchers, railroad owners, and lumber, gold, and silver tycoons. Eastern banker types.

Danziger had been pointed out to him perhaps six years before, in Sheridan, Wyoming. Rollie had been at a cattlemens' luncheon as an unofficial keeper of the peace between the ranchers and the farmers whose land the ranchers wanted. Try as Pinkerton and the law might, nothing stuck to the oily Danziger.

In hiring Danziger, an employer would also get a gang of killers, rapists, and thieves Cleve hired to help him enforce his employers' wills. And they would help him track down the gimped-up old former Pinkerton detective who caused the employer grief years before. But to risk bracing an entire town in pursuit of one man? Surely he wasn't that ruthless.

"Great," said Rollie, squinting into the trees and seeing nothing resembling Cleve Danziger. "Good luck, kid." He looked down once more at the dead man, pushed off of the rock, keeping low, and glanced again for weapons he might have missed. The young man's holster was empty.

"Rollie." The blacksmith pronounced Rollie's name awkwardly, and held up a revolver.

"Keep it. You'll need it. I have to get down there." Rollie nodded toward Main Street, unseen downslope beyond the trees. "You're welcome to come along, but I—" He needn't have wasted the breath.

The taciturn blacksmith nodded once and cut wide into the forest, the arm below his shot-up shoulder swinging slightly less than the other.

Good man, thought Rollie. *And a town full of folks who are the same.*

He ducked low, hobbled his way through the trees, paralleling the blacksmith. Both men moved in near silence as they wove a route that would take them downslope toward the south end of town. Toward what, they knew not.

But both knew it was not going to be pretty.

CHAPTER THIRTY-SIX

Pops rode that beast as hard as he could, knowing the horse was flagging. It pained his wounded leg with each jostling step the horse took, but it pained him more to know he was pushing the creature far beyond the kindness he'd always felt toward beasts of burden.

"I am sorry, horse. But the lives of all those folks in town, innocent as yourself, need whatever we can give them. We make it through this mess and I will do what I can for you. You have my word."

If the horse understood him, it gave Pops no indication. If anything, it seemed the man's brief speech slowed the horse. He reined up and slid from the saddle, wincing as the foot on his bum leg hit the ground. "Okay, okay then." He patted the trembling horse's neck. "Let's look at that wound you got yourself."

Pops hopped to the horse's flank, steadying himself with one hand on the horse. With the other he kept the Greener balanced atop the saddle. It was an awkward pose, but they both needed to stop. The bullet had punched into the horse's left rear thigh, leaving a puckered, bleeding wound.

He saw pink flesh beneath the hide in a hole big enough

to stick his thumb in. The horse had drawn its leg up and stood breathing hard, lathered, and quivering. Its eyes were wide, showing raw fear that Pops could only imagine, though he felt as though he'd experienced something of the same in his past. It was the gnaw of cold uncertainty, of confusion, of not knowing what might happen to you in the next second, the next minute.

"Well now, what we got here? An uppity slave boy making off with one of our horses?" The man speaking emerged from behind a jumble of gray boulders about twenty feet downslope of Pops. To the man's right, another leaned into view. He was a bald, squat man with a mustache. His quirley smoke reached Pops' nostrils, and he cursed himself for not paying more attention. He should have picked up on that pungent smell.

"Now, now," said the first man, a tall, stubble-faced fellow with dark, long hair that looked as if it needed a washing. His revolver was drawn and leveled in Pops' direction. And Pops wasn't behind the horse, but standing with his back half-turned toward the newcomers.

"Correct me if I'm wrong, Clem," said the first one to his smoking chum. "But I do believe that man has shot himself a white man's horse. And none other than Petey's horse, too, from the looks of it."

"Yep," said the bald, smoking man.

"Shot it and stole it and likely did for Petey, too. Now that can't stand."

"Nope."

"See," the man advanced to within ten feet of Pops, who had his hand on the Greener, balanced atop the saddle. It was in plain view, so they knew he was armed.

"Where we come from, a black man who kills and steals is worth nothing but to decorate the end of a rope with."

Pops continued to eye them in a sideways fashion over his left shoulder. His shotgun gripped in his left hand, his right stroked the horse slowly. He knew he needed a plan, one that made more sense than to try to spin and shoot all at once. He'd been fast in his life, but with a ripped, bleeding leg that pained him something fierce, he knew he was, at best, on the wishful side of this fight.

So he did the only thing he could think of. He screamed quick and fast and loud, smacked the poor horse hard on the rump, and spun, dropping low. He kept on screaming because he'd collapsed and was facing his two foes down on his wounded leg. It was all by design, but that didn't make the pain any less severe. The horse did as Pops hoped it would—it bolted, despite its own wound.

As if by instinct, Pops' big thumb rammed down hard on Lil' Miss Mess Maker's twin steel hammers, all the way back. The momentum he'd conjured swept the heavy, blunt gun from right to left, and as it passed the tall, dark-haired talker, Pops triggered a barrel. The clot of shot caught the man between the crotch and knees, shoving him backward as if he'd been tripped up by a yanked rope. He slammed facedown on the rocky slope, his chin gouging into the thin soil.

Pops' spin kept on whipping left to meet up with the advancing bald, smoking man. As Pops touched off the Greener's second trigger, the man did the same with his drawn Colt. Pops' bowler, jammed down hard and clamped above his ears, whipped off his head and he felt a distinct feeling as if his close-cropped hair had a new part.

No time to worry about that. He kept low and continued

his roll. Down onto his shoulder, then up again, his momentum slammed him into an upthrust of granite. It knocked the wind from him. Dizzy, he clawed for a new set of shells. He had none in his usual trouser pocket. Must have lost the extras some time in the big dust-up on the hill behind town.

He patted for his revolver. That, too, was gone, as was his hideout gun, which he recalled he hadn't snatched up that morning. All this took a second or two, as he regained his buzzing senses. Pops liked his gun fine, but she had a throaty roar of a voice that he figured he'd never quite get used to.

The shotgun blast had caught the bald man right in the midsection, and he, unlike his chatty cohort, lay faceup. But he was unmoving. The first man, however, was mewling and scratching at the ground with long, clawing fingers. From the blood on and near each man, Pops doubted life was long for either. He didn't much care.

Even with the boom of the shotgun's twin roars filling his head so that it felt like he was on the battlefield once more back in the war, he shoved up on a knee and hopped over to the nearest of the two. The bald man was a bloodied mess, but Pops kept away from striking range should the man be playacting he was dead and lash out with a hand.

Pops reached with the shotgun and prodded the man. Nothing. He shoved the barrels' snouts hard into the freckled skin on the side of the man's head and shoved. That would make a faker take notice. Nothing. Pops saw the man's revolver ahead of him. Must have lost it when he pitched backward.

Without a working gun, Pops was in no condition to

turn down such an offer. He retrieved it, checked the wheel, and decided he'd need the man's ammunition belt as well. Stripping it off the dead man took some doing, until Pops realized he had to set down the Greener. He laid her beneath the sloped edge of a boulder and covered her with pine duff. "Be back for you, Miss Messy. You sleep it off." He winced his way back to the bald man, peeled off the gun belt, and buckled it on. It fit as if custom made for him.

The entire time he kept glancing at the first man, who by then had stopped scratching and whining. Pops assumed the man was dead, but knew enough to not trust such a judgment. He proceeded with the same caution he'd given the first. Remembering his sheath knife, his fingertips confirmed it was with him. He skinned it out and prodded the long-haired man in the shoulder with the blade's deadly tip. Again, the action would make a faking man howl. This one, not even a flinch.

Pops toed away the dead man's revolver within reach of the clawed right hand, and picked it up. He looked at the prone man and decided he needed that gun belt, too. "Why not?" he said and with much grunting, managed to strip off the man's belt. It was a bit bloody, but Pops figured he was beyond caring.

As to blood, he thought, looking down at his left leg. He was pleased to see the bleeding had slowed. It throbbed, but it was with him. He'd hold off wrapping a tourniquet above the gash until he needed to. With that in mind, he bent back to the nearest dead man and untied the man's bandana, then draped it around his own neck and retied it.

Pops stood upright and breathed deeper. As his hearing

was dulled, he kept up a steady flickering of sight all around him, up-, down-, and sideslope, but saw no one else.

He spied the wounded horse a good thirty yards away, partially upslope, standing as it had before, belly heaving with the effort Pops had regretfully forced upon it.

"Beats another bullet, horse," he said. "I'll be back for you. Right now, I have to get on down the hill to the Gulch. See if I can't dish out some more of Pops' special recipe before this day gets any more out of hand."

With that, he limped crisscross fashion on down the hill, pausing at trees, taking in the terrain about him. One revolver nestled in his right hand, one in a holster, ready for the left.

CHAPTER THIRTY-SEVEN

Nosey glanced to his side, caught Wolfbait's gaze.

The voice behind them wasn't one they recognized.

Something in the old man's eyes told him not to turn and not to open his mouth. But that had never stopped Nosey before. He slowly turned his head. "Boy, are we ever glad you showed up."

"I doubt it," said the man who'd come up behind them. He was a large fellow, broad of shoulder, and with a tidy, yellow bristly mustache. He wore a short-brim straw hat pushed back on his broad forehead.

"No," said Nosey, turning more toward the man. "We've been trying to get a bead on those two over there in the bar, but no luck as yet."

The man looked toward the bar, then back at his captives. "I don't think so. You aren't with us. I should know. I help the boss with the payroll." He smiled, show-ing a wide mouth filled with large, white teeth. "Give you credit for trying, though. Now," he wagged his revolver. "Toss those away."

"Toss what where?" Wolfbait's tone may have been soft and confused sounding, but his eyes bristled with hate.

"I think we should," whispered Nosey out the corner of his mouth as he tossed aside the gun he'd appropriated from the Mexican.

"Listen to your wise partner there, old-timer."

Wolfbait growled and pushed up off his knees to stand. "Now you listen. I've had about enough of you interlopers coming in here and calling me old!"

"Would you rather I call you dead?" said the man, taking a step forward.

Nosey grabbed Wolfbait's forearm.

"What is it you heathens want from us, anyway?" said the old man.

The big stranger shrugged. "Nothing from you, I reckon, except that man name of Stone-something or other." He shrugged again as if it were an affliction.

"Well you can't have him. He ain't here. He's gone. Never was here. Never will be. You're off your trail, blood-hound. Tell that fool boss of yours you're all loco!"

"Wolfbait, stop antagonizing him," hissed Nosey.

What he didn't see was Wolfbait's right hand inching down toward his holster. He'd angled himself enough, he hoped, when he stood that he could disguise his intentions until it was too late for the big man.

That's not how it worked. Wolfbait hadn't considered the big man's height, which gave him the advantage of sight over the scene. And the big man didn't like what Wolfbait was up to. And he didn't waste time.

As a volley of steady, if random, shots echoed from all quarters of town, and some from off in the hills ringing the Gulch, the straw-hatted man stepped in fast and close toward Wolfbait. At the same time, with his left hand he shoved Nosey in the chest, sending the demure journalist stumbling and landing on his backside. With his long-barrel Colt in the right hand the big man reached out and slammed the length of the barrel in a clean, quick blow above Wolfbait's left ear. It dropped the old buck in a sudden heap at the big man's feet.

"I do hate the mouthy sort. Only thing worse is one who thinks he's smarter than me."

"Should be *I*," said Nosey. "I think. Though perhaps not."

"What?" The big man turned toward Nosey and was rewarded with a view of the trim man crouched low and hopping first to one side, then the other, back and forth, his hands held out before him like hatchets, as if he were about to tuck into a pile of firewood.

Nosey Parker hopped to his right, but kept glancing at Wolfbait, who lay immobile and in a position he was sure to regret, if he were alive. The sight of his troublesome friend, helpless and suddenly so old, heaped on the ground at the feet of this town-wrecking buffoon was too much for him. What if the old fool was dead?

From down deep in his throat, Nosey conjured up a rumbling, gargling sound that rose in pitch and in volume until it issued forth from between his lips in a mixture of sounds resembling a Lakota war cry and a cat fighting with another cat.

"Stop that," said the big man. He made to step in close to Nosey.

Nosey jumped backward, flailing his arms before him and howling louder.

"I mean it. I will lay you low and not care about it afterward!"

But Nosey had angled closer to Wolfbait and turned his body so that his left hand slid into his coat pocket, where he'd stuffed his two-shot derringer. He palmed it and pulled it out, hidden.

If it worked for Wolfbait with the Mexican, he thought, *then why not me?* He refused to give thought to the fact that the same feeble maneuver had failed his old friend.

The big man stepped within two feet of the still-moving Nosey, and raised his big pistol to bring it down on Nosey's head. The smaller man cocked the derringer and shouted louder, ducking to his right as the long-barrel Colt arced down fast toward him. He'd had no intention of actually shooting the man, but with Wolfbait laid low and his own lurching dance—he reasoned he was nervous— and the big intruder lunging at him, Nosey's finger must have twitched.

The little gun barked, and the big man screamed and dropped his Colt. He spun around in a circle, clutching his left wrist with his right hand. "What did you do?" He righted himself and turned on Nosey, his eyes like chunks of granite, his mustache bristling like a porcupine's tail, and Nosey stepped backward and tripped over Wolfbait.

The derringer snapped once more. The big man screamed once more and fell to his side in the dirt, howling louder than ever and holding his right boot, which sported a neat hole right in the middle above the toes, a hole that welled and bubbled blood.

Any words the big man could form were mashed together in his mouth with the shrieks of pain he pushed out. Tears drizzled from his eyes and he swung his head as if in strong disagreement with an unseen presence. He rolled on the ground and Nosey scrambled backward over the unmoving Wolfbait.

The big man regained some sense of himself and began crawling toward them. Between the flopped Wolfbait and the big man lay the long-barrel Colt. Nosey was closer and not afflicted by fresh bullet wounds. He dove for it and managed to close his hand around the surprisingly heavy gun moments before the big man's working right hand snatched at it.

The big man growled and said something that sounded to Nosey like, "Give it here!"

Nosey shook his head and backed up, regaining his feet. The big man crabbed forward, groaning, dripping snot on himself, and slammed his palm against Wolfbait's face. It looked to Nosey as if he were about to crush his old friend's head in a frenzy of rage, so Nosey did to the big man what he'd done to Wolfbait and had tried to do to Nosey.

Without much thought about it, he drove the butt of the gun straight down on the big man's bare head. It connected with a dull thud, as if he'd hit a fence post square on top with a maul. The big man wheezed, his eyes rolled upward, he turned white as goose eggs, and with a last, "Gaaah!" he collapsed, half on Wolfbait's torso.

The bulk of the brute seemed to have a reviving effect on the old man, and he sputtered and coughed like a long-dormant steam engine being coaxed to life.

"Wolfbait!" With much effort, Nosey shoved the big man aside, then knelt beside his friend. "You're alive!"

"'Course I'm alive." He tried to sit up but his head kept dipping down to the ground, as if weighted. "Help me up."

Nosey complied and Wolfbait sat up for a moment, steadying himself with his hands on the ground. He tenderly touched the side of his head. His fingertips came away sticky. "Benjamin Franklin was never treated like this."

"You know Franklin?"

"How old do you think I am, you whelp?"

"I meant his writing. Look, Wolfbait, can you walk? We have to get out of here. They're bound to come this way looking for him. Or else he'll revive, and I don't think he'll be happy to see me staring down at him. I can't imagine hitting him again."

"What did you do to him, boy?"

"Too much, I'm afraid. Come on. We have to get out of here." He helped Wolfbait to his feet, but the man wobbled and slumped against Nosey.

"No good, boy. Can't see straight. It's like I'm on a ship in a storm."

"Okay, I'll carry you."

"What? Well, wait. Get the guns first. All of them. And that beast's gun belt, too. We'll need them and he won't."

Nosey protested but saw the logic. He loaded his pockets and his waistband, and prayed nothing went off. He had no desire to go through life with unnatural holes in his body. By the time he was ready, Wolfbait had leaned against a rock and closed his eyes.

Nosey bent low before the old man and said, "Okay, move forward. That's it. Okay, now you're on my back. Drape your arms about my neck. Too tight!"

In that manner, they made their way toward the one spot Nosey knew he could get something for Wolfbait to help his head and where they might be able to hole up until he could figure out what to do next.

Wolfbait raised his head and saw the mercantile bump into view. "But boy, that's the lion's den . . ."

"Yes, well, that's appropriate, as I'm feeling particularly ferocious. Now hush," said Nosey as he readjusted Wolfbait's surprisingly solid form atop his shoulders.

They crossed the street at the far end, half-shaded by trees, and entered the back door, the same one the Mexican had exited sometime before.

Nosey hoped that the men he'd heard talking and retreating earlier had been leaving the mercantile behind. If he found any of the vermin inside, he resolved to do the only thing that could be done to them in such a situation. He would shoot them. Unless he could think of an alternative.

He'd set a foot on the bottom step when he heard a shout for help.

"Who's that?" said Wolfbait in his ear.

"I don't know. Could be a ploy."

"Bah, you think those crazy killer men would shout for help? At this point, I'd say they'll shoot us and be done with it."

"Oh."

Then they heard it again.

"Sounds like it's coming from the outhouse," said Nosey.

"Set me down, I'm all right, boy." Wolfbait struggled, and Nosey lost his feeble grasp of the old man. Wolfbait slid to the ground and managed to stay upright. "Go peek in there and see what's what. I'll wait here and keep an eye out. Take a gun. But don't shoot yourself!"

"Thanks for your support, Wolfbait."

"Don't mention it."

Nosey approached the outhouse with a revolver held high. He figured it would be safer for all involved if he used it as a club. He stood to one side of the door and knocked. "Hello? Anybody in there?"

"Help! Get me out of here!"

Nosey opened the outhouse door and couldn't quite figure out what he was seeing. The two-holer bench had been ripped apart and scraps of wood now hung. Some of the lumber leaned against the wall. But the most curious sight was the top of a man's head peering up at him from down in the muck hole.

"Mayor? Is that you?"

"Yes! Nosey Parker? For heaven's sake, get me out of here!"

"What are you doing down there?"

"I'm enjoying bonbons and a bath, you idiot! This is no time for your questions!"

"Why don't you climb out?"

"My hands and feet are tied! Now get me out of here!"

By then Wolfbait had ambled over, wobbly but carrying a gun and keeping a lookout lest all the shouting draw unwanted attention. "Mayor, somehow I'm not surprised to see you down there."

"Gaaah!" shouted the mayor. "Get me out of here!"

CHAPTER THIRTY-EIGHT

"Pieder!" Rollie waited for the blacksmith to look at him. He held a hand out to halt the swarthy man and cut upslope to him.

Visible below them were the roofs of the businesses and a scattering of homes lining the south end of Main Street.

"I'm going to angle higher and come down the east side slope, see if I can cut the head off this snake." Rollie gathered from the blacksmith's squint and cocked head that the phrase was lost on him. "The leader is Cleve Danziger. I have to find him. I'd also like to find out how Pops is doing. He should be up there somewhere. I heard that shotgun of his, but the townsfolk . . ." He looked downslope.

Pieder nodded and rapped a fist on his chest. "Pops, then I go"—he nodded downslope—"to town. You"—he smiled—"kill the snake."

"Thank you, Pieder." Rollie touched the man's forearm, then they split up.

Pieder continued in the same direction they'd been headed, but climbed upslope. Rollie glanced back at him for a brief moment, then nodded and set off at a hobbling run in a near-opposite route. The speed he gained was impressive, considering his game leg and the boot heel he'd lost to a bullet that had come too close.

Anger and desperation churned in his gullet, rising up his gorge and tasting like bile with each lunge he took downslope. He had to get to Danziger before any innocents were killed on his behalf. The foolishness has gone on long enough. If he couldn't kill Danziger, and hopefully end the mess that way, he'd give himself up and hope whoever hired Cleve wanted Rollie brought back alive.

The thought spurred him into an even faster gait, and soon his bum lung whistled in counterpoint to his punching steps. He forced thoughts of Pops and Nosey and Wolfbait and Pieder out of his mind. No room or time for sentiment. He had to be on the scout for Danziger's men. If the attack on the hill was an indication, they could be anywhere.

As if to prove the point, a man upslope of Rollie shouted, "Hey! Hey, it's him!"

Rollie cleared leather, giving the shouter a quick glance before shooting upslope. It wouldn't do much but show them he wasn't an easy pick.

The man returned fire and bark sprayed off a big pine ten feet to Rollie's left. He might not be so lucky with the next shot. But he was close to a rocky ravine that carried storm runoff. If he could make it to that, he could travel within the deep gully for quite a distance, getting him almost directly above the spot where he thought Cleve Danziger might be located.

Rollie was going on guesswork, but he suspected the

earlier shouting match he'd engaged in with the bossy man on the slope across from the saloon had been Cleve.

Whoever had spotted him wasn't alone. Rollie heard two men huffing far behind. He sent another bullet up at them, and their pounding steps ceased. He reached the edge of the ravine, slid on his backside a few feet, and dropped the rest of the way, a good five feet. It wasn't a spot the men could see easily.

He pivoted and aimed up. The first man made it to the top of the ravine before he windmilled his arms and shouted curses. Too late. He was in sight, and Rollie let him have it.

The angle was awkward, and his bullet drilled into the invader's shoulder, but it was enough to knock the man backward as he screamed a quick, gurgled cry of agony. The second man must have seen what happened to his compadre. Though Rollie heard him, he saw nothing of him. The man might crawl close and peer in from another angle, but Rollie would be long gone.

He heard the shot man wailing and cursing as he scrambled as best he could through the spiny wreck of boulders lining the bottom of the ravine. At its base it narrowed to shoulder width, while at the top it was twenty feet across in places.

He risked that someone might see him from above and take a shot down at him, but it concealed him well enough. He moved as fast as his leg and busted boot heel allowed, but kept noise to a minimum. Good thing, too, as he heard voices up ahead to his left and right. Another few feet, another dogleg to the right, and he saw men on either side of the ravine, yammering low back and forth to each other.

"Great," muttered Rollie, trying to figure out how to

get rid of them without shooting. Not that he had a problem with dispensing of the invading trash, but he was close to his destination and didn't want to risk killing anybody of importance before he had a chance to deal with them.

He retreated, made it back around the dogleg. At the top of the near edge, the boulders stuck out of the earth enough that he might be able to climb up. From the topmost rock, it was three, four feet to the top of the ravine. He holstered the Schofield, hating to do so, but he needed both hands for climbing.

Rollie poked his head up prairie dog style and peered left toward where he'd come from. The slope was dippy and full of trees and boulders, any one of which might harbor an invader. He had to risk it. Random shots cracked the air from down in town. He heaved himself up onto his belly, scraping skin where his shirt had dragged out of his trousers.

Even before he rose up off his knees, he tugged the revolver free. This would be tricky but it had to be done, no other way would get him where he needed to be quickly and without bullet holes in his hide. He low-walked forward, angling downslope, and heard a grunting sound behind him.

He looked and saw, behind one of the boulders, a man squatting, his back to the rock face. He was a jowl-faced beast with a black beard. His black hat was pushed back high on his forehead, his eyes were closed, and he appeared to be gritting his teeth as he struggled with his task.

Glad I'm not downwind of him, thought Rollie. The discovery made his plan easier. He hoped. He strode toward the man quickly. "Hey!" he growled low, aiming the gun at the squatting man's bulk.

The man spun his head. "What are you doing?"

"A question I don't have to ask you." Rollie wagged the revolver. "Stay right like that and toss your gun over here."

"This ain't right! At least let me stand up."

"Nope. Don't want to see any more than I have already."

The man made a growling sound and, with much effort and more grunting, unfastened the gun belt and tossed it toward Rollie. He picked it up, buckled it, and since it belonged to a fat man, he draped it over his head and across his chest, bandolier style.

"Now stand, pull up those trousers slowly, and keep your hands up by that big head of yours."

The man stared at him as if he didn't understand the directive.

"Now! Do it!"

"No need to be insulting," said the man as he rose and grunted to do as Rollie ordered.

"Now, walk." He jerked his pistol downslope. "And if you speak, I'll shoot you."

"You'd shoot a man in the back?"

"Yep."

"You must be him."

"Must be."

It didn't take long to walk to where he'd seen the two men on opposite sides of the ravine, conversing. Of them, he saw but one on his side of the ditch.

The man heard movement behind him and turned. At first he only saw the fat man. "Cuthbert, what are you doing?" And then he saw Rollie.

"Same thing you'll be doing in about ten seconds. Raise those hands."

"Like hell I will."

Rollie sighed and shot the man in the thigh. He screamed and spun and flopped to the ground, writhing and bleeding.

"That was cold, man!" said Cuthbert.

"Yep. Go get his gun off him, and do it slow, or I'll shoot you, too."

The fat man gulped and waddled down to his wounded fellow.

Rollie walked closer. "Easy now, Cuthbert. Easy."

Successful in pulling the gun belt off his friend, Cuthbert was holding it out in one hand like a rancid fish when the shot invader pulled out a second, short-barrel revolver from a shoulder holster. Rollie ducked low and fired before the man could cock his gun. Rollie's bullet dug a tunnel straight into the man's forehead, giving his sneering face a third eye, one that pumped a thick stream of hot, red-black blood down his face.

Cuthbert screamed, dropped the gun belt, and ran off to his left. He covered ten feet or so, tripped, went down on one knee, and tried to rise.

By then Rollie had snatched up the second gun belt and almost made it to the struggling Cuthbert. "Get up or I'll give you something to grunt about."

"Don't kill me!"

"Don't give me any more of a reason to. Now get up."

The fat man complied and Rollie said, "Now walk. No, that way."

"Where we going?"

"To see your boss."

Cuthbert stopped. "Oh no, I can't do that. If he sees me like this he'll shoot me."

"And if you don't do as I say, I'll shoot you where you stand. Your choice. You have two seconds to decide. Time's up."

"Okay, okay. But he isn't going to like this."

"I'm not here to please Cleve Danziger."

They walked a few yards and Cuthbert said, "How'd you know it was him who's here?"

"I'm special like that. Now shut up and walk."

CHAPTER THIRTY-NINE

"Psst! Pieder!"

The blacksmith had been crouched behind the rear wall of Horkins the Younger's assay office. Knowing who it was, he turned to face the man who'd addressed him. He nodded at Pops, a little shocked to see the state of the man.

Bent at the waist, Pops sported lacerations from saloon splinters. He dragged his left leg and carried a couple of revolvers, one in each hand. Despite all that, Pieder Tomsen had to smile when he saw the man making his way down the slope toward him. Pops wore a grin on his mouth and mischief in his narrowed eyes.

He assumed that because Pieder was exposed, this end of the woods around town was clear of invaders, at least for the time being. He crouched beside the blacksmith. "You okay?" he whispered. Pieder nodded. "Rollie?" Again the man nodded, pointing along the east slope.

Pops considered. That meant Rollie was going to make a play for whoever that shouting boss man had been from earlier. Nothing he could do but wish Rollie luck and try to increase the odds in his favor. He nodded toward the building. "Anybody here?"

Pieder understood. "Yes. Others . . . there." He jerked his chin toward Geoff the Scot's eatery.

Pops strained to hear and thought he could make out low voices, men talking. "How many?"

Pieder shrugged and held up five fingers "Bad, maybe more. Others"—he shrugged again—"more."

"Okay, they're likely prisoners. We have to free them. Need a distraction." Pops looked around. "Out back, over that-a-way."

He'd barely finished speaking before Pieder nodded and thumbed his chest. "I"—he rubbed his chin, then looked at Pops once more—"make noises."

"Good, yes, and I'll go on in. See what I can do from the inside once you make your noises."

"Okay." Pieder made for the slope, giving himself enough distance from the buildings that he could get a shot at whoever was coming out.

That left Pops with the task of getting in there and dropping what invaders he could without jeopardizing the innocent folks. "Easy enough," he whispered, waiting for Pieder to kick off the ball.

The blacksmith didn't waste any time. He glanced down at Pops, saw he was ready, and shouted, "Hellooo! Hey . . . hey! Bad men! Hey hey! Hello!"

He kept this up for half a minute, and began throwing rocks down at the building. A couple of them connected, banging and clunking off the log and plank wall. Pops heard a woman shriek within the building, then grumbling and shouts.

As the first of the men peered around the back edge of the shack, Pops backed around the other side, keeping an eye behind him. He saw three armed men emerge from around the far side of the shack, shouting and looking. Then they saw Pieder, who wasted no time in shooting at them.

Pops hobbled around the front of the building, saw no one there or down the length of the street, and hoped there weren't too many more of the invaders left inside with whoever was holed up in there.

He grasped the steel-loop door handle, thumbed the latch, and shoved the door inward.

He took in the room quickly, seeing a number of folks he knew and one he didn't. A short, homely man held a revolver out before him. With his other hand he was running a grimy finger up and down Mrs. Pulaski's cheek. She winced and looked at her husband, who had a bloody head and was seated on a bench along the back wall seething at what he was seeing.

Pops said, "You could at least wash your hands, mister."

The stranger said, "Huh?" and faced Pops, who didn't want to risk a shot so close to the others.

Geoff the Scot helped decide the matter for him. Pops' entrance had proved distraction enough, and the big cook used the moment to knock the man on the head with a piece of assay equipment that looked to be heavy and made of metal. It dropped the gunman in a heap.

Pops felt a tap on his shoulder. He spun, gun cocked, but it was Pieder. "How'd you make it down here?"

The blacksmith shrugged. "They are . . . done."

"You got all three of them?"

"Yah. Now . . ." He looked past Pops at the room, assessing the situation.

"All set in here. We got him, too." Pops nodded toward the dropped gunman lying on the floor, his head bleeding.

Already Geoff the Scot, Horkins the older, and Horkins the younger were lashing his wrists and ankles with rope.

"Good," said Pieder.

"Now we'll see if we can't help Rollie and the others." He turned to the rest of the townsfolk. "Anybody wants to lay low, I understand. This ain't your fight."

"Nonsense," said Geoff the Scot. "They ate me out of a week's supplies and clubbed me in the head. It's my fight as much as anyone else's." He stood and grabbed a shovel leaning in the corner.

"Same goes for me," said Mr. Pulaski of the Lucky Strike saloon.

His wife beside him said, "And me."

"And us," said the Horkins brothers.

Soon, the entire group of ten was on its feet, looking to Pops and Pieder for orders.

"Okay, then, here's what we're going to do." Pops rubbed his chin and laid out a basic plan.

CHAPTER FORTY

Rollie had draped the second confiscated gun belt about his chest, crisscrossing the first. He shoved Cuthbert between the shoulder blades when the man's pace flagged.

They topped a short rise and his fat captive seemed to drop from sight right in front of him. He'd flopped to the ground and tucked himself into a large ball and tried to roll downslope, shouting and cursing as he rolled, slower than if he had decided to run.

Even then Rollie had no intention of shooting the idiot, but the shouting had done what the fat man intended. Three men whose backs had been to them spun around. Luckily all were within Rollie's view, two to his right, one to his left. If he shot at the barking Cuthbert, one of the others would shoot hm. He waited, three men pointing their guns at him.

He could get the two to his right, but the man to his left would lace him with a bullet before he could swing on him.

For two, three tense seconds there was no sound, then one of the men to his right raised his rifle to his shoulder and Rollie dropped down on his racked knee, shot twice, and kept rolling onto his shoulder. If he lived through the day, he would pay hell in the morning for all the tumbling about those spiny hills.

His first shot punched into the gut of the rifle toter and he doubled over. The second shot tore a furrow into the meat of the second man's left arm. He howled, dropped his gun, and clutched at his bloody wing.

The shooter to his left, the one Rollie was most concerned with, had fired at Rollie but missed. Before Rollie could finish his return swing, the man shot again, and Rollie felt a hard punch up high on his left arm and knew he'd been shot. How badly, he would soon learn. But first he had to finish the job he'd begun.

He shot once, twice, a third time. He managed to use his torso to give him quick momentum, enough to get his feet under him once more. Had he hit the man?

Maybe it would all end with somebody he'd never before seen laying him low. The relief of not caring emboldened him and he heard a loud, growling shout as he bolted forward, his left arm numb and wet but useful.

The growl came from his own mouth and he realized he was on the man who'd shot him before he expected. The stranger was unarmed and sagged against a tree. His revolver lay at his feet, his eyes shut tight against the pain given him by two smoking, bloodied holes in his blue shirtfront.

Rollie stood before the man, breathing hard, his growl tapering to a grumble. What a waste it all was. The shot man's eyes flickered open. He tried to speak, but couldn't. Rollie shoved him to the ground where he piled up and groaned his last. He glanced around but saw neither the man he'd winged nor fat Cuthbert.

As he checked his gun, a voice from downslope shouted up at him. "Got you dead to rights, Stoneface Finnegan! Give up your foolishness and raise 'em high."

"Cleve Danziger." Rollie barked the name without turning.

"Now, how did you know that? Oh, let me guess—one of my men. Yes, near useless they are."

As the man spoke, Rollie looked around. One long step would get him behind the tree the shot man had been leaning against. His own revolver was empty, but he had the other two riding across his chest, the barrels nesting awkwardly under his armpits. That left arm had begun to throb, each pulse like a smithy's hammer blow. Risk the lunge to the tree?

"Come on, now, Stoneface. I have other business to attend to, and you have already wasted enough of my precious time."

"Who hired you?"

"Wouldn't you like to know!"

"Yep. That's why I asked."

"Well, I am not going to tell you. But I will say this individual has more money than sense. Good taste in who he hires, but no brains otherwise."

"Have you hurt anyone in town?"

"None that didn't require it."

"What's that mean?"

"Find out for yourself. Raise those hands . . . Stoneface."

Rollie ducked low and leapt to his left, collapsing behind the wide pine, hoping he was worth more alive to

Cleve than dead. He was rewarded with a distinct lack of gunfire. Instead he heard Danziger laughing.

Rollie struggled to stand, his left arm aching. He inspected the wound for the first time and saw a bloody, blackened tear. A deep graze. He'd had worse.

He used the tree to slide upright, pulled Cuthbert's revolver free and checked it, then stuffed in two shells. "How do I know I can trust you? You are a hired killer, after all."

"All those years as a Pink made you loopy in the head!"

Rollie sighed then shouted, "Insulting me won't bend matters in your favor."

"You are a bold one. But I tell you plain: You can trust me. I give you my word, or I am not Cleve Danziger."

"Coming from you, that means less than nothing."

Again, his response was met with a guffaw.

Rollie chewed the inside of his cheek. It had come down to this—either give up or expose himself and shoot it out with the man. No other choices. He was pinned and tired of this foolishness. End it now and a lot of innocents could go about their lives.

He raised the pistol, cocked it, and was about to step out from behind the tree, ready for come what may, when movement to his right caught his eye. He saw an arm waving at him from behind another sizable pine upslope and ten yards away. He saw Pops' smiling face.

Pops raised his thumb, nodded, and kept on smiling.

Rollie hoped what his partner meant was that the town was secure, but he had no way of asking it. Pops kept up the goofy grin and wagging of his big thumb. Rollie nodded and smiled back. He knew what he was going to do.

"You want me so bad, Cleve, come and get me!"

"I thought you might be belligerent about it," shouted Cleve. "I held off all day in doing this, as it means more explaining on my end, but you've given me no choice. If you don't come peaceable, I am going to kill off one fresh-faced member of this dandy little community for every minute that passes. I'll give you . . . two minutes to decide. Your choice, Finnegan!"

Rollie didn't need two minutes. He didn't need one minute. He barked his reply. "Go to hell, Danziger!"

"Fine, then."

Rollie heard boots on rocks, and he assumed the man was turning, looking for one of his men. Then Danziger shouted and confirmed it.

"Wesson! Pigg! Doyle?"

The shouts were met with silence.

"Cuthbert! Where in the hell are you?" Danziger's voice had grown louder and more bellowing, his obvious rage pushing out the words, words that were greeted with silence.

"Give it up, Danziger! They're all dead and done!"

That was met with a long pause.

"I don't buy it, Finnegan. You are bluffing me!"

"Suit yourself. I have all day."

From the hill above, Rollie heard voices to his left. He pulled the second pistol, checked it, and hoisted it in his weakened hand. If the rest of Danziger's men were on their way for him, he was going to make it uncomfortable for them. But what he saw confused him.

Topping the far rise, he saw not the swagger of seasoned gunmen descending on him, but a handful of men in worn clothes and slouch hats, proceeding forward with caution.

They carried long guns and revolvers and what looked like shovels and picks, and all walked forward in a ragged line.

Rollie looked about him and saw dozens of strange men in all directions, close by, down along the main street, and on the slope across, as if the town were being invaded anew. How big was Danziger's army?

He was ready to groan in ultimate frustration then recognized one face as the man drew closer. Then another and another. They were the miners who lived outside of town, the men who showed up at his saloon on a regular basis.

One man offered a quick wave and a nod, then gripped his rifle once more.

Far below, through tree trunks and boulders and branches, what patches of Main Street he saw were pocked with similar advancing shapes. Then shouts, low and hoarse, came from some of them, followed by gunshots. The ragtag brigade advanced on what Rollie saw was a handful of retreating forms. Cleve's men? But which ones?

Rollie heard boots on rocks behind him and stepped out from behind the tree at the same time a large man in a tall hat and long hair stepped forward from behind a jumble of large boulders where he'd been completely hidden. He held a thick rifle that looked to be a Sharps.

"Danziger," Rollie said, nodding.

The man returned the slight nod. "Finnegan." He breathed deep through his long, bent nose. "Looks to me like you have hoodwinked a pile of folks hereabouts. From the sounds of it, my men have the town locked up tighter than a bull's backside. They'll gladly corral this ragged lot and make a massacre of it should I pass the word."

"I think not, you heathen!"

Rollie looked quickly to the right and saw Chauncey Wheeler among a cluster of the newcomers. His clothes and face were filthy and his hair stood up straight. The men flanking him were Nosey Parker and Wolfbait. They, too, were begrimed, though to a lesser degree. And they appeared to want to step away from the Chauncey.

"Well, Mister Mayor, I see you clawed your way out of the outhouse!"

That made little sense to Rollie but he didn't dare look away from Danziger again. Both men faced each other, Rollie with two revolvers leveled on Cleve and the mercenary with his Sharps held belly height, leveled on Rollie.

"If you're waiting for your men, you might want to make yourself cozy. Gonna be there a while!"

Rollie didn't have to look to know it was his pard, Pops.

The wide, disgusted smile on Danziger's face twitched, nearly faltered. "I think not!"

"Then tell me why you're standing here alone on a hill surrounded by the good people of Boar Gulch." Rollie could see his words were like a slap to Cleve's big face.

"Cuthbert! Where'd you go?"

No response.

"Doyle! Wesson! Damn you, Pigg, where you at?"

Nothing.

"I'd say they're either smarter than I'd give anyone who'd work for you credit for, and have cut bait and run, or they've been cheered by my townsmen. And by townsmen, I mean all these folks surrounding you with guns."

The last of the mercenary's sneer slipped away, replaced with bared teeth and flexed nostrils. Heavy-lidded eyes directed a withering gaze at Rollie.

"Who hired you?"

"Go to hell." Danziger's forearms flexed and his big hands tightened their grip on the rifle, the finger on the trigger bunching as it squeezed back.

"You shuffle the cards." Rollie squeezed both revolvers' triggers a blink before the Sharps boomed. "And I'll be there."

Rollie's twin shots drove straight and hard into the middle of Cleve Danziger's broad chest, forcing the Sharps's load to scream above Rollie's head and shatter branches a few yards beyond.

It seemed to take a full minute for the man to fall. It didn't happen all at once, but began with a tremor in the arms. They finally dropped and unhanded the Sharps, which clattered on the rocks and roots.

One eyelid twitched, and his eyes widened as if he were witnessing a monumental surprise. His lips parted, and he made as if to utter a word of wonder. But all that leaked out was a long, slow, wheezing breath.

Finally his right leg bent, followed by his left and he collapsed, dropping hard on the knees, one with a solid smack on a rock. He wavered like that, his large hands looking soft, the fingers curling in on themselves. His eyes closed and he flopped forward, his face smacking the ground flat on.

His hat brim hit at the same time, and his hat popped off his head and rolled to one side. The man's long combed hair hung about his neck and shoulders like a fan of grasses. The entire top of the man's head was a pink shiny surface, bereft of hair.

"I had no idea the boss was bald-headed," said Cuthbert.

Rollie looked up. He'd not heard the fat man approach. "Shut up, Cuthbert."

The fat man complied.

As he looked down at the dead, infamous mercenary, Rollie suspected that if there was such a spot as the innermost bubbling heart of hell, ol' Cleve was there, holding down the position of chief tine sharpener at the pitchfork foundry.

CHAPTER FORTY-ONE

In the hours after Cleve Danziger yipped his last, some of the good people of Boar Gulch tended to their own. Others rounded up the living—Cuthbert and two more—and the many dead of Cleve's crew. While the riled Gulchers argued out in the middle of Main Street over boots and horses and firearms, Pops and Rollie watched them from the front of the tent that served as The Last Drop saloon.

Rollie saw Camp Sal fluttering about Pieder Tomsen. She'd ripped off the sleeve of his shirt, exposing his injured shoulder, and was bathing the wound with gentle pats of a wet cloth. Though Rollie didn't know the man well, he though the burly blacksmith looked quite pleased with the situation.

Pops shook his head and limped over to the woodstove for more coffee, his leg thick with bandages. He sat down on a keg and hefted Lil' Miss Mess Maker. It had been retrieved by Nosey, along with the wounded horse, which had been tended to and was now resting in a corral out back.

"You honestly believe if you leave all this trouble will

magically follow you and not land here like stink on dung? Think, man. The next batch of crazies is coming and you know they will ride into little ol' Boar Gulch and they won't hear a thing these good folks say. They will tear this place apart, plank by plank, person by person. Only thing to do is—"

"Give myself up," said Rollie.

"No, that's foolishness, too."

Rollie sighed. "What do you suggest I do, then, Pops?"

Pops lit his pipe, billowed up big, blue clouds.

Those are his thinking puffs, thought Rollie.

A smile split Pops' face, and he pulled the pipe from his mouth. "It's simple, Rollie. I don't say it's something you want to hear, not if I know you as I think I do, and I do."

"You're sounding like Wolfbait again," said Rollie.

"That's 'cause we spend so much time palaverin' on our weekly supply runs down the mountain."

The familiar voice caused Rollie to turn. Here came Wolfbait, limping worse than ever and with his arm in a sling, and a thick dollop of gauze wrapped on his head. Nosey was right behind him, not looking wounded so much as begrimed and giving off a ripe odor.

He hadn't opened his mouth yet so Rollie wondered if Nosey wasn't able to speak. A treat for the rest of them, but a likely brutal punishment for Nosey. It might be funny if Nosey didn't look so mired in despondency.

Wolfbait winked at Rollie. "Get on with it, Pops. We're all dying to know this great plan of yours."

Pops nodded and then looked past Wolfbait toward the doorway. Yet another figure stood there.

It was the mayor. "Gentlemen. I come here as repre-sentative of the city council of Boar Gulch."

"Since when did we have a city council?" said Rollie.

"Since now. And stop interrupting me. That's likely an offense. I haven't finished writing down the bylaws and codes and whatnots, but I will. Now . . ." He thumbed the lapels of his filthy black frock coat, spatters stained his once-white dress shirt. He also exuded a pungency that was beginning to water the eyes of everyone in the room.

"I'll need you all to accompany me out to the main street. We have an official town-wide meeting called to order and your presence is demanded." He stopped and stared at them. Nobody moved.

"Now!" barked the pudgy little mayor.

They all flinched and followed him out the door like ducklings after their mama.

Sure enough, gathered outside in a ragged half circle facing the bar, stood much of the populace of Boar Gulch, looking haggard. Some were wearing bandages, most stood with arms folded, staring at them without smiles. Rollie wasn't much for feeling self conscious, but he felt it now and wished he could walk back inside.

"As you are all well aware," began the mayor, "we are in need of law. Not merely justice, as you both have so doggedly put it. And so, the town council, which means everybody you see assembled here, has taken a vote. You, Mr. Rollie Stoneface Finnegan and you Mr., um, Pops, have been chosen to be our law. Divide up the duties as you see fit, but let it be known that you are hereby appointed as Boar Gulch's first town marshal and deputy." He gave his lapels an extra tug and rocked back on his heels, a smug smile on his fleshy face.

"Nope," said Rollie.

Pops said nothing, but smiled and stared at the ground, his hands in his pockets, light smoke rising from his pipe.

"I don't think you understand me"—the mayor looked about him and spread his arms wide—"us, I mean. This is not a job offer, sir. Oh no, this is not even an ultimatum. No, this, Mr. Rollie 'Stoneface' Finnegan, former Pinkerton Detective, is your only option. You will serve as a lawman for Boar Gulch or . . . well, that is it."

Rollie felt his face heat up, saw red clouding the horizon. "How dare you tell me what I can and can't do with my life?"

He was used to seeing people back up when he barked. But his fellow Gulchers barely flinched.

"Mr. Finnegan," said the mayor, "only a heartless cretin in your position would move on and leave us to that fate, a fate none of us asked for."

Rollie folded his arms and sighed. "I'm not wearing a badge."

"Why not?" said the mayor.

"Because," said Pops, stepping forward, "a man doesn't need to call attention to the fact that he's the law in a place. Besides, it's not law that Boar Gulch needs. We have enough laws already. The mayor sees to that." He winked at the pudgy, scowling man. "What the Gulch needs is justice. I say we take care of things right here in Boar Gulch as we have been doing."

"This is too complicated," said Geoff, holding a bloody bandage to the side of his head. "Wear a badge or not. I don't care, but if somebody comes to town and hurts someone, they get treated in kind by you and Pops. And if you need help, you know you'll get it." He received nods. "Especially after today's raid. That nearly broke us, Rollie."

Rollie regarded them all a moment, then nodded. "We may need to hire on a couple of deputies now and again." He cast his gaze to Nosey and Wolfbait.

The old man winked and Nosey nodded, then pulled out his notebook and began writing.

Murmured assent rippled through the crowd.

Yep, thought Rollie, as he looked around at his neighbors and friends. *Right back where I began—a lawman who isn't one.* He smiled. It felt right.

"Come on everybody!" He turned and headed for the door of the tent that was The Last Drop. "Drinks are on the house!"

In a low voice, Pops said to him, "Enjoy it now, because I have a feeling deep in my bones those men today were the tip of a mountain about to come down on us."

"Then we best get busy," said Rollie. "Tomorrow."

He walked behind the makeshift bar, tossed a towel over his good shoulder, and lined up the glasses.

WILLIAM W. JOHNSTONE *and* J. A. JOHNSTONE
A QUIET LITTLE TOWN
A Red Ryan Western

JOHNSTONE COUNTRY. ONE WILD RIDE.
*Stagecoach guard Red Ryan has managed to survive
every dirty, danger-filled trail in Texas.
But this time, the journey is hell on four wheels.
And the next stop could be his last . . .*

BIG TROUBLE IN A SMALL TOWN
It starts with an unusual request: "On this trip there will
be no cussing, no drinking, no gambling, and no loose
women." No problem. Or so Red Ryder thinks—until he
meets the passengers. They include four holy and silent
monks, one beautiful lady tutor, and a drunken washed-up
gunfighter. Even worse, they're crossing the wild
Texas hill country, where bloodthirsty Apaches are on
the loose and a mad-dog killer is on the prowl.
But that can't compare to what's waiting for them at
Fredericksburg. In this quiet little town, every man,
woman, and monk will reveal their true colors.
Green for greed. Yellow for cowardice.
Black for pure unadulterated evil.
Which leaves *Red* gunning for his life . . .

CHAPTER ONE

The moment tall Texan Burke Forester stepped off the steam packet *Manxman*'s gangway onto a London Harbor dock he became the most dangerous man in England . . . if not the entire British Empire.

Forester's welcoming committee was sleet driven by an icy wind that cut to the bone and, a cable length away, swept the deserted decks of three great ironclads anchored in a dredged deepwater channel awaiting their turn in dry-dock. A few tattered gulls braved the elements, flapped above the tall masts of the warships, and stridently yodeled their hunger.

Wearing a black, caped greatcoat and red woolen muffler against the cold, Forester made his way toward a labyrinth of warehouses, a sugar refinery, and a paper mill that marked the limit of the dock area and began the adjoining industrial district. He'd been the *Manxman*'s only passenger, and there was no one else around. He carried a large carpetbag that contained a change of clothing and a Colt revolver, and in his gloved left hand he held a sword cane with an elaborately carved ivory handle in the shape of a Chinese dragon with emerald eyes. The sword had a twenty-three-inch steel blade, razor-sharp, a gentleman's weapon and a deadly one.

Forester's thoughts were on the cab that presumably awaited him and thereafter a blazing fire and perhaps a glass of hot rum punch. On that particular Sunday morning in civilized London town, he gave little thought to the cane as a weapon, considering it more of a fashion accessory. In that, he was mistaken. The blade would very soon be called into use . . . with horrifyingly fatal results.

Forester wore the high-heeled boots and wide-brimmed Stetson of a Western man, and, head bent against the slashing sleet, he didn't see the dockworker stride toward him until the man was almost past, his eyes fixed steadily on a point ahead of him.

Out of the corner of his mouth, the worker said, "Be careful, guv."

And then he was gone, and Forester briefly wondered at his warning and then dismissed it. After all, the English were a polite breed, much given to strange greetings.

This was a little-used, hundred-year-old dock once trodden by Admiral Lord Nelson that was scheduled to be closed. After a couple of minutes of walking, Forester found himself on a deserted concrete pathway between the paper mill and a rust-colored, corrugated iron warehouse. The mill was silent, its pious owner observing the Sabbath, but a massive ship's boiler awaiting the scrap heap took up much of the space on the path, and a pile of empty tea chests had fallen over in the wind and were scattered everywhere. Huge Norwegian rats, afraid of nothing, ignored the approaching human and scuttled and scurried among the debris of ten thousand spilled cargoes.

Forester saw the cab ahead of him, waiting for his

arrival as it had for the past six days, be his ship early or late. The top-hatted driver muffled in a greatcoat, a woolen scarf covering his face to the eyes, sat in a spring seat at the rear of the vehicle. Despite the biting, cartwheeling sleet, he seemed to be dozing, and the Texan was close enough that he heard the clang of the impatient horse's hoof as it pawed the wet cobbles.

Forester quickened his pace, desirous of the cab's meager shelter, but he stopped in his tracks as three men, tough-looking brutes wearing flat caps and rough, workmen's clothing, stepped into his path.

The biggest of the three was a ruffian with simian features and massive, stooped shoulders. His hands hung at his sides like ham hocks, the knuckles scarred from many a fistfight, and his thick lips were peeled back from decayed teeth in a snarl that passed for a grin. "'Ere, matey, I be Bill Hobson, a well-known name in old London Town, and what's a toff like you doing, a-walking around my turf like you owned it?" he said.

"He's a toff right enough, Bill," another man said. "Looks to me that he can pay his way . . . for a safe passage, like."

The human gorilla named Bill widened his grin. "Truer words was never spoke, Johnny," he said. "Money for a safe passage it is, so give us your wallet and watch, your bag, and whatever other valuables you own." He bowed and waved in the direction of the street. "And then you can go in peace."

"And we'll be a-taking of your fancy cane," Johnny said.

Burke Forester was irritated at being forced to stop in the middle of a sleet storm, but since his mind was on other, more pressing business, he was willing to let this matter go. After all, three impudent toughs were just a temporary inconvenience.

"You boys step aside," he said. "This is a public thorough-fare, and I have no money for you." He motioned with the cane. "Now, be on your way and give me the road."

Bill Hobson's gaze became more calculating, mea-suring the Yankee's height and the width of his shoulders. The man seemed capable, and that gave Bill pause, but more disturbing was the fact that he wasn't in the least bit scared . . . and he sure as heck should be. Did the dandy know that he was facing three of the toughest men from the violent, disease-ridden cesspit that was the East End of London? Did he realize he faced men who could kick him to death if the need arose? Bill smiled to himself. Maybe the fool needed a harsh lesson . . .

For clarity's sake, it must be noted here that Burke Forester was a professional assassin and a noted *pistolero* who'd put the crawl on half a dozen named men, including Wes Hardin and the notoriously fast King Fisher. Histori-ans disagree on the number of men Forester killed, and a man in his line of business didn't boast of it. For him, it sufficed that his reputation was known to the rich and powerful businessmen, industrialists, and cattle ranchers who mattered and who considered him an efficient, and above all, discreet, executioner. Let Forester's lowest es-timated number of kills stand at sixty-three, fifty-eight by the Winchester rifle and Colt's gun, three by the bowie knife, and two by his ever-present sword cane. Those numbers are probably near to the truth.

In sum, Burke Forester was a sudden and dangerous killer and a man best left the hell alone . . . something that

Bill Hobson and his two companions soon would learn the hard way.

Forester realized that the Englishman's talking was done when the man reached into the pocket of his ragged jacket and produced a lead-filled leather sap, a vicious, bone-breaking weapon ideal for a close-range fight against a large opponent. Hobson grinned and tapped his open palm with the sap. "Come and get it, fancy man," he said. Then he swung the blackjack at Forester's left temple, trying for a killing blow.

But the Texan had already moved.

He leaped to his right, dodged the sap, and with incredible speed and dexterity, drew his blade from the sheath. Off balance, Hobson stumbled and desperately tried to regain his footing, his face panicked. But not for long. An accomplished swordsman, Forester flung his left arm wide and at the same time turned from the waist and elegantly thrust with his blade, running Hobson through. Three feet of steel rammed into his guts will shock a man dreadfully, and Bill Hobson's scream was a shrieking mix of pain, fear, and despair. As the Englishman slowly sank to the sleet-soaked ground groaning, holding his belly with glistening, scarlet hands, one of his cohorts turned and scampered, but the third, the man Hobson had called Johnny, slipped a set of brass knuckles onto his right fist and came charging. Forester was surprised by this aggression and reluctantly recognized the ruffian as a fighting man. It took sand to take on a sword with nothing but a knuckle-duster. As a mark of respect, the Texan decided there and then to spare Johnny the pain he'd inflicted on his gutted companion. He backed off a step, away from the man's clumsy swing, and his blade flickered like the tongue of an angry serpent, and the point sank into Johnny's throat just under his larynx. A quick thrust and the steel projected four inches from the back of the man's neck and then was withdrawn. Dying on his feet, Johnny stared at Forester in bewilderment for long seconds and then sank to the ground, his face in the black, liquid mud.

Savvy swordsmen never sheathe a bloody blade since it can corrode the steel. Forester ripped the cloth cap from Hobson's head and wiped the sword as clean as he could. He then took a silk handkerchief from his greatcoat pocket and finished the job. He slid the sword back into the cane as Hobson whispered, scarlet blood in his mouth, "You've killed me."

Forester nodded. "Seems like. You won't survive that wound, my man."

"Damn you. Damn you to Hades."

"Better men than you have told me that."

"I need a doctor," Hobson said. "Get me a doctor."

Foster smiled and shook his head. "No, my friend, you don't need a doctor, you need an undertaker."

"I've got a wife . . . four . . . four kids still alive," Hobson said.

"That's sad. So very tragic," Foster said. He glanced at the leaden sky. "Well, I can't tarry here talking any longer. *Tempus fugit,* as they say."

"Don't go, mister. Help me."

"You're beyond help, pardner," Forester said. "All you can do now is die. A *balestra* followed by a thrust to the belly is always fatal." The Texan nodded, as though agreeing with himself. "Ah yes," he said. Then, "Well, I'll be on my way."

Hobson, his throat thick with blood, called out something, but Forester wasn't listening. He made his way to the waiting cab, walking head bent through driving, icy sleet made even colder by a savage north wind.

Only the driver's pale blue eyes were visible under the brim of his top hat as he looked down at Forester, sizing him up as the American gent he was there to meet.

"Been waiting long?" Forester said.

"Six days long, yer worship," the driver said, by his accent a cockney from the London East End. "From dawn to dusk, me an' his 'ere 'orse."

"The ship was caught by a winter storm in the mid-Atlantic," Forester said. "We were driven back by the gale. That's why I'm late."

The driver's shaggy eyebrows were frosted with rime. He nodded and said, "I got no time for ships and oceans. I'm a landlubber, meself."

"Well, I hope they're paying you enough," Forester said. "It's no fun sitting out for hours in this vile weather."

"That they are," the cabbie said. "They're paying me handsomely." Then, to Forester's surprise, he added, "The one who ran away is Charlie Tompkins. He lives with a loose woman in the East End and hangs around the docks, thieving whatever he can. He won't snitch to the law, never fear. They'd love to get their 'ands on old Charlie, the coppers would."

Sleet gathered on the shoulders of Forester's greatcoat, and he was anxious to get inside. "Maybe he'll talk, maybe he won't, but he should be taken care of," he said.

"He will be, and the two dead men back there," the driver said. "Mr. Walzer don't leave no loose ends."

"Ernest Walzer is a careful man," Forester said.

"That he is," the driver said. "There's a flask of brandy

and a box of cigars inside, 'elp yourself. It's an hour and a half's drive to Mr. Walzer's house and most of it over cobbles."

Forester settled in the cab's leather seat, glad to be out of the storm, though the air inside was still bitterly cold. His breath steamed as he poured a brandy from the flask into its silver cup and then lit a cigar. Back in Texas, his rancher client had paid him well for acting as a go-between, making sure that Ernest Walzer held up his end of the contract, and Forester decided that he deserved every cent . . . nobody had warned him about the lousy British weather.

CHAPTER TWO

"Did you have a pleasant crossing, Mr. Forester?" said Ernest Walzer, a round-shouldered man of medium height, his intense black eyes dominating a sensitive, fine-boned Semitic face. He wore a ruby red smoking jacket and a round black hat with a tassel. He had Persian slippers on his feet, and Forester guessed him to be somewhere in his mid-sixties. But he could have been any age.

"Pleasant enough until halfway across the Atlantic, when we ran into a storm," Forester said. "Pushed us back toward New York for four days."

Walzer smiled. "I hope you're a good sailor."

"I'm not. I was as sick as a poisoned pup the whole time."

"Ah, well, you're on dry land now," Walzer said. "The sherry is to your taste?"

"It's just fine," Forester said.

"I'm distressed about your unfortunate encounter with low-class scoundrels," Walzer said. "On behalf of my country, I offer you an apology."

"A minor incident of no great account," Forester said.

He waved a careless hand, and the blue smoke from his cigar made curling patterns in the air.

"Nevertheless, the one called Tompkins will not live out the day," Walzer said. "You can be assured of that."

He and Walzer sat on each side of a blazing log fire in the mansion's study that was furnished very much in the current, upper-class style, crowded and ornate with well-polished wood, stuffed animals and birds under glass domes, and thick Persian rugs. A portrait of grim old Queen Victoria hung above the fireplace. The room was warm, cozy, hazy from cigar smoke, and spoke of great wealth.

Walzer studied the Texan for a few moments and then said, "It was Tom Watkins who told me about the difficulty you had at the St. Katherine Dock."

"The cabdriver?"

"Yes. I have a dozen cabbies on my payroll. They are my eyes and ears and keep me informed. Rich people are such fools, Mr. Forester. They pay the driver no heed and indulge in the most intimate conversations. Little do they know that the cabbie up there on his high seat sees and hears everything, and in turn, so do I."

"And what do you do with the information?" Forester asked.

Walzer shrugged. "Besides my other businesses, I dabble in blackmail and extortion. It's a profitable venture that requires little capital investment."

"There were three of them at the dock," Forester said.

"Yes. Dock rats, louts, ruffians, the poorest of the poor and of no account," Walzer said. "As I said, the one who ran away will be dead by nightfall and the two you . . . ah . . . terminated have already been dumped in an East End alley. The authorities won't even investigate. Violent death in all its forms is a daily occurrence in the slums, and seldom do the police get involved. More sherry?"

Forester extended his glass. "Please."

Walzer refilled from the decanter and said, "You have questions?" An Eastern European accent shaded the man's English, but Forester didn't notice. To him, all limeys sounded alike.

"Tell me this," the Texan said. "How did my client know you were in this line of work?"

"What line of work?" Walzer said.

"Hiring assassins."

"Well, he didn't know, because hiring assassins is not part of my usual business." Then, frowning, Walzer said, "How much of this affair are you entitled to know?"

Forester said, "All of it." The frown didn't leave the older man's face, and the Texan added, "My client trusts me."

Walzer nodded. "I'm aware of your reputation and your client's faith in you. He made that clear in his letters. I must confess, I wonder why he didn't hire you for this undertaking. You seem the ideal man to get the job done."

Forester shook his head. "No. I'm too close. I've done gun work for my client in the past, and a clever lawman might draw the right conclusions. My client must have no direct connection whatever to the assassins, and I hope you didn't disclose his identity to the men you hired."

Walzer said, "Of course, I did not. They were told the mark, his location, and nothing else. Professionals need no further information than that. By this time, they're already in Texas, and when the undertaking is finished, they will scatter and make their separate ways back to London and then to . . . well, wherever they hail from."

Forester said, "Tell me this, how did my client . . ."

"Between ourselves, let us drop the pretense, Mr. Forester," Walzer said. "Your client's name is Gideon Stark, and he's a big rancher who wants to be bigger, an empire builder who dreams of founding a dynasty. You know this and I know this, and it's all that I know. But at least now our masks have been removed."

A few moments of silence stretched between the men. A log fell in the fire and sent up a cascade of scarlet sparks. Sleet battered at the parlor window, and the frost-rimed wind raged around the mansion like a ravenous gray wolf.

"All right, then, as you say, our masks are removed," Forester said. "How did Gideon Stark choose you to take care of this matter?"

"He didn't, at least not directly."

Forester made no answer.

"This is very much between us," Walzer said. "Due to the sensitive nature of what I'm about to tell you, we will deal only in suppositions, Mr. Forester, not in facts. Do you understand?"

The Texan drew on his cigar before he spoke. "I catch your drift."

Walzer nodded and said, "Good. Then let us suppose that there is a certain English gentleman rancher in West Texas, the youngest son of a belted earl, who is prospering mightily in the cattle business. His fond papa is a nobleman who quickly ran through his wife's inheritance and now the meager rents from the kilted tenants of his Scottish estates do not support his extravagances, namely gambling and expensive mistresses. The earl is always, as the sporting crowd says, down to his last chip and in the dumps. Let me refill your glass."

Walzer poured more sherry and then said, "Now, shall we surmise, and this is all supposition, mind, that the earl is a member of the British Foreign Office and desperate for money. Could it be that happenstance threw the wretched blue blood in my direction, and we at once entered into a business arrangement?"

"What kind of business arrangement?" Forester said.

"If such were the case, one must imagine that money lending would be the likely arrangement," Walzer said. "But then we must answer the question: Would a savvy businessman lend money to, as you Americans say, a deadbeat . . . a worthless, sponging, idler like the exalted earl?"

"I guess not," Forester said. "Sure doesn't sound like a sound investment."

"And you guess correctly," Walzer said. "But what if the nobleman had valuable information to sell because at one time or another his position in the Foreign Office put him in the front parlor of a score of tin-pot dictators and warlords in India, the Orient, and South and Central America? What do such despots need to stay in business, Mr. Forester?"

"Money?" the Texan said.

"High taxes usually provide more than enough of that. No, tyrants need arms, cannon, rifles, carbines, and sabers for their cavalry and a plentiful supply of ammunition," Walzer said.

"And you supply them," Forester said. He smiled. "Hey, here's a battery of cannon, no questions asked."

"I will not say yes, and I will not say no, but it is always possible that I deal in arms of all kinds, and that I use the earl as my go-between in those transactions. If that were the case, and I don't say that it is, I would pay him handsomely and keep him in line with five-pound notes, threats of blackmail . . . and worse."

Forester smiled. "In other words, Mr. Walzer, you're a world-class gunrunner?"

"Gunrunner. Yes, that's another of those new crude and hurtful American terms and one I would never use," Walzer said, frowning. "If I engaged in such a business, I'd call myself a contraband weapons dealer."

Forester made no comment on that. He said, "Gideon Stark has all the weapons he needs. What he does need are men who can use them."

"And he has them, four of the best I could find," Walzer said.

Forester shook his head. "How did one of the biggest ranchers in Texas ever shove his branding iron into your fire, Walzer?"

The older man smiled. "His branding iron into my fire? Hah, that's a colorful way of putting it. But here's how it might have happened, the very nub of the matter you might say."

Walzer took time to pour more sherry, and Forester said, "You'll make me drunk."

"I doubt it," Walzer said. He sipped from his own glass, the crystal engraved with an elaborate coat of arms. Forester guessed it was Russian, judging by the double-headed eagle.

Walzer said, "Gideon Stark and the earl's son, the young rancher I told you about earlier, share a fence and are neighbors and close friends. Or do you already know that?"

"Stark told me only what I needed to know for this job," Forester said. "He's a tight, closemouthed man. He didn't mention an Englishman, neighbor or no."

"Ah, leaving no loose ends also applies to the hired help, huh?"

"I guess it's something like that," Forester said.

Walzer fell silent as a tall, thin, melancholy man dressed in butler black stepped into the room and added a log to the fire. He bowed slightly from the waist and said, "Will there be anything else, sir?"

Walzer shook his head. "No, Mr. Lewis, nothing more for today."

"Very well, sir," the butler said. "Mr. Forester's room has been prepared, and the fire is lit."

Walzer nodded and said, "I took the liberty of assuming you'd sleep here tonight, Mr. Forester. I told the cabbie to pick you up in the morning after breakfast. As you know, I'm very isolated here. One can't just step out of the front door and hail a passing cab."

"Suits me just fine," Forester said. He glanced out the window. "Is that sleet, snow, or rain?"

"All three," Walzer said. "And there might soon be thunder. British weather, you know." He turned his attention to Lewis. "You may take the rest of the day off to visit your ailing . . . sister . . . isn't it?"

"Yes, my sister Ethel, sir," the butler said. "She's down with female hysteria and a wandering womb, and her husband's at his wit's end."

"So sorry to hear that," Walzer said. "Your brother-in-law is in service?"

"Yes, sir, he's third footman to Lord Rancemere."

"Then take the pony trap, Mr. Lewis, and I'll see you tomorrow morning."

Lewis bowed. "Yes, sir. Thank you, sir."

The butler glided silently to the door, and Walzer called out after him. "And Mr. Lewis, for goodness sake wear your oilskins and stay dry."

The butler turned and managed a ghost of a smile. "Certainly, sir. It's very kind of you to be so concerned."

Walzer waved a dismissive hand. "Think nothing of it, Mr. Lewis."

The door closed noiselessly behind the butler, and Walzer said, as though the interruption had not occurred, "I wasn't there, of course, and this is all supposition, but I imagine Mr. Stark conversed with the earl's son and happened to mention that he was looking for some skilled men to carry out an enterprise for him."

Forester smiled, "Murder for him, you mean?"

"Yes, just that. But Mr. Stark likely stipulated that the assassins must be unknown to the American and Mexican authorities and that after hitting their target they'd disappear back into their holes. Of course, the earl's son would recommend me as a discreet man who can get things done."

"How would he know that?" Forester said.

Walzer shrugged. "I suspect the young man is privy to all his father's secret dealings. I gather from the earl's letters that his son is not a stickler for the law and has hanged or shot many a man without trial."

"Rustlers and nesters, probably," Forester said. "Plenty of those in West Texas."

"Just so," Walzer said. "Now let's be frank. It's time for some plain talk. Several months ago, Mr. Stark and myself entered into a correspondence during the course of which

I agreed to help him by providing assassins. For a fee of course." Walzer spread his thin-fingered hands and smiled. "And now here you are, Mr. Forester."

"The money is in my bag," the Texan said. "Five thousand in gold."

"And . . ." Walzer prompted.

"You'll get the other five thousand when the job is done and an additional sum to pay the returning killers."

"Quite acceptable," Walzer said. "Judging by his correspondence, Gideon Stark is a hard, unbending man, but I judge him to be honest in his dealings. Is that not so. Mr. Forester?"

"He's hung and shot more than his share his ownself, but I'd say he's honest enough," Forester said.

The day was shading darker, and the light from the fire cast a crimson glow on the high bones of Walzer's cheeks and deepened the shadows in his eye sockets and temples. Momentarily, as he leaned over to poker a burning log, his face looked like a painted skull.

"Since we're plain talking," Forester said. "Who is the mark?"

"Yes, a plainly asked question that deserves a plain-spoken answer," Walzer said. "The man's name is Ben Bradford . . . *Doctor* Ben Bradford."

Forester was surprised. "A doctor? All this secrecy and fuss over a pill-roller? Heck, if Stark had asked me, I'd have put a bullet in him as a favor."

Ernest Walzer shook his head. "My dear Forester, in this affair there are wheels within wheels that you know nothing about. Stark wants the man dead, yes, but nothing, and I mean nothing, about the killing must be linked to him. He's got to come out of this . . ."

"As clean as a whistle," Forester said.

"Cleaner. Smelling of roses. No loose ends, Mr. Forester. Above all, no loose ends."

Burke Forester sat back in his chair. "Well, I did what Stark paid me to do, and now I'm out of it." His gaze moved to the darkening window where lightning glimmered on the wet panes, the flashy herald of the coming thunder, and then he said, "As a matter of interest . . ."

"Ah, another question," Walzer said. "I was always told that Americans question everything."

"Just as a matter of interest," Forester said. At Walzer's nod, he added, "Who are the assassins?"

"No one you would know. The names are obscure."

"Try me."

"Ah . . . this is so tedious," Walzer said. "I grow weary."

"Let me decide what's tedious," Forester said. "After all, I'm in the same profession. It's always wise to be aware of the competition."

"Yes, there's always that, I suppose," Walzer said. "Then let me see . . . Ah yes, the most dangerous of the four is the Russian, Kirill Kuznetsov. He is very much in demand in Eastern Europe, and his fee for a kill is around five thousand of your US dollars. He's said to be very strong and can kill with his hands, but he's also expert with a pistol, as they all are. Salman el-Salim is an Arab, and he boasted to me that he's carried out two hundred assassinations with the jambiya fighting knife. Sean O'Rourke is an Irishman, a disgraced British army officer, and a hired killer. He's said to be very efficient. And finally, the German Helmut Klemm, a crack shot with a rifle who often kills at a distance. He never leaves Europe but made an exception for Stark since it's such a big-money contract. He talked about retiring to his estate in Bavaria after this task is done."

Forester sighed, less than impressed. "Heck, Stark could've hired four guns in Texas to do the job, men who work cheap and know how to keep their traps shut."

Walzer shook his head. "Not, not that, never that. Mr. Stark has too much at stake, too much to lose, and I mean losing something . . . very precious to him. The assassins he's hired will return to Europe after they honor the contract and will never be heard from again. Your Texas gunmen may know how to keep quiet . . . until they get drunk and boast to a gossipy whore about all the men they've killed or suddenly get a taste for a little blackmail. No, the risk is too great to use homegrown gunmen." Walzer shook his head. "It's out of the question."

He clapped his hands and said, smiling, "Now, enough of business for tonight. Are you sharp set?"

"I had breakfast on the ship and nothing since," Forester said.

"Then, as an honored guest I must feed you," Walzer said. "Unfortunately, I gave cook and the maids the day off, idle tongues you know, but the scullery maid is here. She's a stupid, doltish girl, but she cooks plain fare quite well. I ordered a meal of roast beef, gravy, and potatoes if you'd care to make a trial of it."

"Suits me," Forester said. "I got my belt cinched to the last notch."

"On the bright side, I have a very fine Napoleon brandy you can have with your coffee."

"Does the scullery maid make good coffee?"

"No."

"Then thank God for Napoleon," Forester said.

Connect with

Visit us online at
KensingtonBooks.com
to read more from your favorite authors, see books
by series, view reading group guides, and more.

Join us on social media

for sneak peeks, chances to win books and prize packs,
and to share your thoughts with other readers.

facebook.com/kensingtonpublishing
twitter.com/kensingtonbooks

Tell us what you think!

To share your thoughts, submit a review,
or sign up for our eNewsletters, please visit:
KensingtonBooks.com/TellUs.